Selected Praise for Caitlin
White Magic series

"Definitely a don't-put-this-down page-turner!"
—*New York Times* bestselling author Mercedes Lackey
on *The Mountain's Call*

"Animal lovers and romantic fantasy aficionados alike
will appreciate this…coming-of-age story and an
exhilarating romantic adventure."
—*Romantic Times BOOKclub* on *The Mountain's Call*

"A riveting plot, complex characters, beautiful
descriptions, and heaps of magic."
—*Romance Reviews Today* on *The Mountain's Call*

"Caitlin Brennan has created a masterpiece of legend and
lore with her first novel. Hauntingly beautiful and extremely
powerful…. Take Tolkien and Lackey and mix them together
and you get this new magic that is Caitlin's own. You will
stay enthralled with each page turned."
—*The Best Reviews* on *The Mountain's Call*

"This is the second book in this magnificent romantic fantasy
series…is full of more action, romance and drama than its
prequel…. The battle scenes are magnificent, the characters
are realistic and the storyline is pure magic; readers will
eagerly await the next book in this tantalizing series."
—*The Best Reviews* on *Song of Unmaking*

CAITLIN BRENNAN

SHATTERED DANCE

LUNA™
www.LUNA-Books.com

LUNA™

First trade printing: October 2006

SHATTERED DANCE

ISBN-13: 978-0-373-80248-7
ISBN-10:   0-373-80248-X

Copyright © 2006 Judith Tarr

Author Photo by: Lynn Glazer

www.LUNA-Books.com

Printed in U.S.A.

For Moon, Mickey and the rest of
the inmates of Riders' Hall—
with laughter, song and the Great Debate:
Euan or Kerrec? Should a woman have to choose?

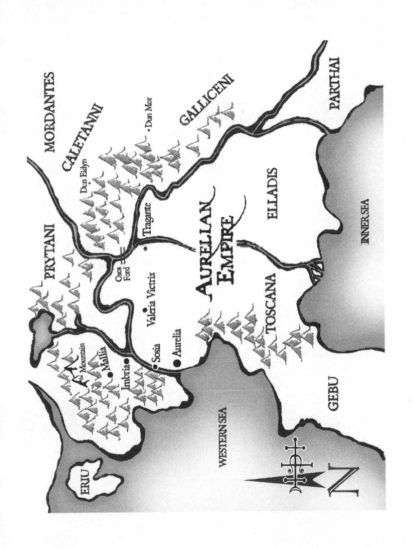

Chapter One

The ninth challenger was the strongest. He came out of the setting sun, bulking as broad as the flank of Dun Mor that loomed behind the killing ground. The potent animal reek of him washed over Euan Rohe, sharp as a bear's den in the spring.

Euan swallowed bile. For three long days he had been fighting, at sunrise, noon and sunset. Eight warrior princes of the people lay dead at his hand.

Now this ninth and last came to contest Euan's claim to the high kingship. He was the champion of the Mordantes, blessed by the One God with a madness of battle. Fear never touched him. Pain never slowed him.

Euan's many bruises and countless small wounds ached and stung. His arm was bound and throbbing where the third challenger's blade had slashed it open. He looked into those too-wide, too-eager eyes and saw death.

His lips drew back from his teeth. He laughed, though his throat was raw. The seventh challenger had come close to throttling him.

One more battle and he was high king—or dead. He shifted his feet, gliding out of the direct glare of the sun. The Mordante hunched his heavy shoulders and rocked from foot to foot. His hands clenched and unclenched.

One of those hands could have torn Euan's head from his shoulders. Euan was not a small man, but he was built long and rangy, like a wolf of the steppe. This challenger was a bear with a man's eyes.

There were stories, tales told on dark nights of men who walked in beast form and supped on human blood. Time was when Euan would have called them children's tales. Then he had walked on the other side of the river and seen what imperial mages could do.

His mind was wandering dangerously close to the edge. He wrenched it back into focus.

The Mordante was still rocking, growling softly. The crowd of tribesmen blurred behind him, a wide circle of faces, winter-gaunt and hungry, thirsting for blood.

Euan's adversary had no weapon but his massive body. Euan had a knife and a hunting spear and his roving wits. He lifted the spear in his hand, weighing it, aiming for the heart beneath the bearskin.

The Mordante lunged, blindingly fast. Euan's spearpoint glanced off the heavy pelt. The haft twisted out of his hand.

A grip like a vise closed on his wrist, pulling him up against that hot and reeking body. He groped for his knife, but it was caught between them. The hilt dug into his belly, a small but vivid pain.

He went limp as if in surrender. The Mordante grunted laughter and locked arms around him, crushing the breath out of him.

Euan let his knees buckle and his body go boneless. He began to slide down. The Mordante clutched at him. His free hand snapped upward.

Blood sprayed from the broken nose—but Euan had not struck high or fast enough. It had not pierced through to the brain.

Still, it was a bitter blow. The Mordante dropped, blind and choking.

Euan was nearly as far gone, his ribs creaking and his sight going dark and then light. He staggered and almost went down.

Already the Mordante was stirring, drawing his legs under him, struggling to rise. His heavy hands clenched and unclenched. Euan's death was in them, blood-red like the last light of the sun.

Euan's knife was in his hand. He had one chance—one stroke. He was dizzy and reeling and his body was close to failing.

The Mordante lurched up. Euan dived toward him.

All his focus had narrowed to one spot on that wide and bristling chest. The bearskin had fallen away from it. He could hear the heart beating, hammering within its cage of blood and bone.

The whole world throbbed to that relentless rhythm. Euan's blade thrust up through the wide-sprung ribs, twisting as the Mordante tried to fling himself away from it. But it was already lodged inside him.

Again it was not enough. The man was too big, his body too heavily padded with muscle. His long arms dragged Euan in once more, his hands groping for Euan's throat, to crush the windpipe and break the neck.

Euan had no defenses left. All he could do was keep his waning grip on the knife's hilt and let the Mordante's own weight thrust it deeper.

The pounding went on and on. It was coming from outside now. The tribes were stamping their feet, beating on drums and shields, roaring the death chant.

It was very dim and far away. With the last of his consciousness, Euan felt the knife's blade pass through something that resisted, then gave way. The hilt throbbed in his hand, leaped out of it and then went still.

Euan spun down through endless space. Pain was a distant memory. Fear, desperation—only words. Sweet darkness surrounded him. Lovely death embraced him.

It was warm. He had not expected that. He could almost believe it had a face—a woman's face, a smooth oval carved in ivory, with eyes neither brown nor green, flecked with gold.

He knew that face, those eyes, as if they had been his own. He reached for them, but they slipped away.

The thunder of his pulse had shaped itself into human sense. Voices were chanting over and over.

Ard Ri! Ard Ri Mor! Ard Ri! Ard Ri Mor!

They were acclaiming the high king.

The Mordante was dead. Euan had felt his heart stop. He was dead, too. Then how—or who—

A sharp and all too familiar voice filled the world. "Up now. Wake. I'm done carrying you."

Purest white-hot hatred flung Euan back into the light. More hands than he could count lifted him up. He rode on the shoulders of his warband, his most loyal companions.

The sun had died in blood, pouring its death across the sky. The royal fires sprang up around the killing ground and along the hilltops. They would be lit from end to end of the people's lands, leaping across the high places, declaring to all the tribes that there was a king again in Dun Mor.

Euan looked for the man who had dragged him back from the edge of death. All the faces around him were familiar and beloved, his blood brothers and his kin. He had to look far into the shadows to find the slight dark figure with its terrible weight of magic.

By the One God, he hated the man—but there was no denying that Euan owed him a debt. He had brought Euan out of the dark. Euan was awake again, alive and aware.

Euan straightened painfully. The strongest men of his warband lifted a shield and held it high. The rest reached to lift him up, but he had a little strength left.

He snatched a spear from the hand of a man who was shouting and brandishing it. All his aches and wounds cried protest. He ignored them.

A path opened before him. He sprinted along it, grounded the spear and launched himself toward the shield.

He hung in air, briefly certain that he had failed. He would fall. If he was lucky he would break his neck rather than suffer such an omen against his kingship.

His feet struck the shield with blessed solidity. It rocked under his weight but steadied. He stood high above the people, dizzy and breathless, grinning like a mad thing.

He spread his arms wide as if to embrace the world. He had done it. He had won. He was the Ard Ri, high king of all the tribes.

"Now you have what you wanted," Gothard said. "Only remember. Glory always has a price."

"I could not possibly forget," Euan said.

He had danced and drunk and feasted from night into morning, then slept a little and woke to Gothard's face staring down at him. It was not the sight he would have liked to see on his first day as Ard Ri. He would have given much never to see it at all.

But there the man was, squatting in this still unfamiliar tent. Neither the warband nor the royal guard had managed to keep him out.

Nothing in this world could, maybe. Gothard was a dead man, a sorcerer who had been destroyed and his body unmade—but he had come back through the power of his magic to walk among the living. The peculiar horror of his existence was not that he was terrible to look at or speak to, but that he seemed so mortally ordinary.

Euan sat up carefully. While he slept, he had been bathed and salved and his arm newly bandaged.

Except for Gothard's presence, Euan felt remarkably well. His head barely ached and his wounds were no trouble.

Even his badly abused throat was less raw than he might have expected.

He would have been smiling if anyone but Gothard had been watching. As it was, his frown was not quite as black as it could have been. "What do you want?" he demanded—rude, yes, but the two of them were long past any pretense of civility.

"It's tradition, you know," Gothard said. "When the new king first wakes, his most loyal servant admonishes him against excessive pride and bids him remember the price of glory. It's usually a priest who does it. Aren't you glad I came instead?"

"No," Euan said. It was hard not to growl, the state his voice was in, but this was intentional.

"I do smell better," Gothard pointed out. For him, that was rollicking humor. "You're given three days to enjoy your elevation. Then the reality of it comes crashing in. I'm to remind you that these aren't the tribes your predecessor ruled. They've suffered a monstrous defeat and great loss of life and strength. The winter has been brutal and the weak or wounded who did not die in battle are dead of starvation and sickness. It's a raw, bleak spring with a grim summer ahead, while the empire strips us of what little we have left and crushes us under the heels of its legions.

"You are high king of the people, and that's a great thing—but it's also a heavy burden. Even if they were victorious, you would still bear all their ills as well as their triumphs. Now in defeat, it's all on your shoulders. You bear the brunt and you carry the blame."

Euan's shoulders sagged as if they were indeed loaded down with all the horrors of a disastrous war and its even grimmer aftermath. But he was no mage's toy, whatever Gothard might hope to make of him. He shook off the spell with a snap of contempt. "You don't think I know all that? This is mine and always has been. I was meant for it."

"Surely," said Gothard, "but are you prepared for the bad as well as the good?"

"I've ridden out two great defeats," Euan said. "There will be no third. You are going to help me make sure of that."

Gothard's brows arched. "A new plan, my lord?"

"Maybe." Euan rose carefully from his blankets. "Maybe the same one, with refinements. We don't need to destroy the imperial armies if we destroy its leaders. We've known that from the beginning."

"But war is so much more glorious than conspiracy and assassination." Gothard's tone was mocking but his eyes were deadly earnest. "Will the tribes understand, do you think?"

"The people won't be going to war again for a long time," Euan said. "It's not a choice between glory and practicality. There's no glory left."

"You want revenge."

"Don't you?"

Gothard's smile showed an edge of fang. "What do you have in mind?"

"Come to me after the kingmaking is over," Euan said. "It's time to strike the deathblow against the empire. We've failed twice. Third time will end it—one way or the other."

The gleam of Gothard's eyes told Euan his words had struck home. Gothard was half an imperial. The late emperor had sired him on a concubine, and by that accident of birth denied him the right to claim the throne—a fact for which Gothard hated his father with intensity that had nothing sane about it.

Gothard had raised the powers that destroyed the emperor and almost taken the rest of the world with him. If he had his way, his sister who was soon to be crowned empress and his brother who was something else altogether would be worse than dead—Unmade, so that nothing was left of them, not even a memory.

Gothard said no word of that, nor had Euan expected him to. He turned on Euan instead and said, "You'd die and abandon the people?"

"I'll go down with them," Euan said, "if that's how it has to be."

"Maybe you are meant to be king," Gothard said.

"If I had been king sooner, we would not have lost the war." Euan could feel the anger rising, old now and deep but as strong as ever. He throttled it down. There was no profit in wasting it on Gothard, who was his ally—however unwelcome.

He forced a smile. It was more of a rictus grin, but it would have to do. "Still. Now I am the Ard Ri. Maybe I'll do better than the one who went before me. Maybe I'll do worse. But I'll do the best I can for my people. That, I'm sworn to."

It was not so far off from the oath he had taken while the last challenger's body was still warm, when he was lifted up in front of the people and invested with the mantle and the spear and the heavy golden torque. But now, in front of his most hated ally, he spoke from the heart. He felt the earth shift under his feet, rocking and then going still, as it was said to do when a man of power swore a great oath.

Caitlin Brennan

He meant every word. He would live and die by it. Life and soul were bound to it.

That was as it should be. He left the tent that he had won and the ally the One God had imposed upon him, and stepped out into the cold bright morning, the first morning of his high kingship.

Chapter Two

The Mountain slept, locked deep in winter's snow. Far beneath the ice and cold and the cracking of frozen stone, the fire of its magic burned low.

It would wake soon and send forth the Call, and young men—and maybe women—would come from the whole of Aurelia to answer it. But tonight it was asleep. One might almost imagine that it was a mortal place and its powers mortal powers, and gods who wore the shape of white horses did not graze its high pastures.

Valeria leaned on the window frame. The moon was high, casting cold light on the Mountain's summit. It glowed blue-white against the luminous sky.

"Has anyone ever been up there?" she asked. "All the way past the Ladies' pastures to the top?"

Kerrec wrapped her in a warm blanket, with his arms

around that, cradling the expanding curve of her belly. He kissed the place where her neck and shoulder joined and rested his chin lightly on her shoulder. His voice was soft and deep in her ear. "There's a legend of a rider who tried it, but he either came back mad or never came back at all."

"Why? What's up there?"

"Ice and snow and pitiless stone, and air too thin to breathe," he said, "and, they say, a gate of time and the gods. The Great Ones come through it into this world, and the Ladies come and go, or so it's said. It's beyond human understanding."

"You believe that?"

"I can't disprove it," he said.

"Someday maybe someone will."

"Not you," he said firmly, "and not now."

She turned in his arms. He looked like an emperor on an old coin, with his clean-carved face and narrow arched nose—not at all surprising, since those bygone emperors had been his ancestors—but lately he had learned to unbend a little. In spite of his stern words, he was almost smiling.

"Not before spring," she conceded. She kissed him, taking her time about it.

The baby stirred between them, kicking so hard she gasped. He clutched at her. She pushed him away, half laughing and half glaring. "Stop that! I'm not dying. Neither is she."

"Are you sure?" he said. "You looked so—"

"Shocked? She kicks like a mule." Valeria rubbed her side where the pain was slowly fading. "Go on, go to sleep. I'll be there in a while."

He eyed her narrowly. "You promise? No wandering out to the stable again?"

"Not tonight," she said. "It's too cold."

He snorted softly, sounding exactly like one of the stallions. Then he yawned. It was late and dawn came early, even at the end of winter. He stole one last kiss before he retreated to the warmth of their bed.

After a few moments she heard his breathing slow and deepen. She wrapped the blanket tighter.

Inside her where the stallions always were, standing in a ring of long white faces and quiet eyes, the moon was shining even more brightly than on the Mountain. Power was waking, subtle but clear, welling up like a spring from the deep heart of the earth. The world was changing again—for good or ill. She was not prophet enough to know which.

She turned away quickly from the window and the moon and dived into bed. Kerrec's warmth was a blessing. His voice murmured sleepily and his arms closed around her, warding her against the cold.

Kerrec was gone when she woke. Breakfast waited on the table by the fire, with a Word on it to keep the porridge hot and the cream cold. Valeria would rather have gone to the dining hall, but she had to smile at the gift.

She was ravenously hungry—no more sickness in the mornings, thank the gods. She scraped the bowl clean and drank all of the tea. Then she dressed, scowling as she struggled to fasten the breeches. She was fast growing out of them.

Her stallions were waiting for her in their stable. She was not to clean stalls now by the Healer's order—fool of a man, he persisted in thinking she was delicate. But she was still riding, and be damned to anyone who tried to stop her.

Sabata pawed the door of his stall as she walked down the aisle. The noise was deafening. Oda, ancient and wise, nibbled the remains of his breakfast. The third, Marina, whickered beneath Sabata's thunderous pounding.

She paused to stroke Marina's soft nose and murmur in his ear. He was older than Sabata though still rather young, taller and lighter-boned, with a quiet disposition and a gentle eye. He had been the last stallion that old Rugier trained, a Third Rider who never rose higher or wanted to—but he had had the best hands in the school.

Rugier had died after Midwinter Dance, peacefully in his sleep. The next morning Marina moved himself into the stall next to Oda's and made it clear that Valeria was to continue his training.

That was also the morning when Valeria confessed to Master Nikos that she was expecting a child. She had planned it carefully, rehearsing the words over and over until she could recite them in her sleep. But when she went to say them, there was a great to-do over Rugier's passing, and then there was Marina declaring his choice of a rider-candidate over all the riders in the school.

"I suppose," Master Nikos said after they had retreated from the stable to his study, "we should be thinking of testing you for Fourth Rider. You're young for it, but we've had others as young. That's less of a scandal than a rider-candidate with three Great Ones to train and be trained by."

"Are you sure I'm ready?" Valeria asked. "I don't want to—"

"The stallions say you are," Nikos said. "I would prefer to wait until after Midsummer—if you can be so patient."

"Patience is a rider's discipline," Valeria said. "Besides, I suppose it's better to wait until after the baby is born."

For a long moment she was sure he had not heard her. His mind was ranging far ahead, planning the testing and no doubt passing on to other matters of more immediate consequence.

Then he said, "That's what I've been thinking."

Valeria had been standing at attention. Her knees almost gave way. "You—how—"

"We're not always blind," Nikos said.

She scraped her wits together. "How long have you known?"

"Long enough to see past scandal to the inevitability of it all," he said. "The stallions are fierce in your defense."

"They're stallions," she said. "That's what they're for."

Master Nikos sighed gustily. "You, madam, are more trouble than this school has seen in all its years. You are also more beloved of the stallions than any rider in memory. Sooner or later, even the most recalcitrant of us has to face the truth. You are not ours to judge. You belong to the gods."

Valeria's mouth was hanging open. She shut it carefully. "Do the other riders agree with you?"

"Probably not," he said, "but sooner or later they'll have to. We all profess to serve the gods. That service is not always as easy or simple as we might like."

"I'm going to keep and raise this child," she said. She made no effort to keep the defiance out of her voice. "I won't give her up or send her out for fostering."

Master Nikos neither laughed nor scowled. He simply said, "I would expect no less."

He had caught Valeria completely off balance. It was a lesson, like everything else in this place. People could change.

Minds could shift if they had to. Even a senior rider could accept the unacceptable, because there was no other choice.

In this early morning at the end of winter, three months after Master Nikos had proved that not everything a rider did was predictable, the stallions were fresh and eager. So were the riders who came to join Valeria in the riding hall. The patterns they transcribed in the raked sand were both deliberate and random—deliberate in that they were training exercises, random in that they were not meant to open the doors of time or fate.

Valeria could see those patterns more clearly the longer she studied in the school. She had to be careful not to lose herself in them. The baby changed her body's balance, but it was doing something to her mind as well. Some things she could see more clearly. Others barely made sense at all.

Today she rode Sabata, then Marina, then Oda—each set of figures more complex than the last. Her knees were weak when she finished with Oda, but she made sure no one saw. The last thing she needed was a flock of clucking riders. They fussed enough as it was, as if no other woman in the history of the world had ever been in her condition.

It was only a moment's weakness. By the time she had run up the stirrups and taken the reins, she was steady again. She could even smile at the riders who were coming in, and face the rest of the morning's duties without thinking longingly of her bed.

This would end soon enough—though she suspected the last of it would seem interminable. She unsaddled Oda and

rubbed him down, then turned him out in one of the paddocks. He broke away from her like a young thing, bucking
and snorting, dancing his delight in the bright spring sun.

Chapter Three

Morag left the caravan in one of the wide stone courts of the citadel. "Be sure you take your medicine for three more days," she warned the caravan master by way of farewell, "or the fever will be back, no better than before."

"Yes, my lady," the man said. "I won't miss a dose, my lady."

"See that you don't," she said. She considered reminding him that she was not a noblewoman and had no slightest desire to be one, but that battle was long lost. She fixed him with a last stern glare, at which he duly and properly flinched, then judged it best to let him be.

She found a groom to look after her mule and cart and paid him a silver penny to guard the belongings in the cart. Not that that was strictly necessary—there was a Word of guard and binding on them—but the boy had the lean and hungry look of a young thing growing too fast for himself.

He seemed glad enough to take the penny. He told her in careful detail where to find the one she was looking for, although he said, "You won't get that far. They keep to themselves, that kind do."

"I'm sure they do," Morag said and thanked him. He seemed a little startled by that. Manners here on the Mountain were not what they might be.

Too many nobles, not enough common sense. She shook her head as she made her way through this unexpected place.

She had expected a castle with a village of farmers nearby to keep it fed. This had the fields and farms all around it, but it was much more than a fortress. It was a city of no mean size, built on the knees of the Mountain.

Ordinary people lived in it, servants and artisans and tradesmen. There were markets and shops, taverns and inns, and once she passed a theatre hung with banners proclaiming some grand entertainment direct from the empire's capital.

The groom had warned her not to wander to the west side—that, he said, was the School of War. The greater school lay to the north and east, toward the towering, snow-crowned bulk of the Mountain. She could see it everywhere she walked, down alleys and over the roofs of houses.

The power of its presence made her head ache. It must be sending out the Call. She was not meant to hear it, but her magic was strong. She could feel it thrumming in her bones.

She refused to let it cow her. Magic was magic, whatever form it took. She advanced with a firm stride toward the gate with its carven arch.

There were no guards standing there. She had seen riders walking in the city, men and boys—never women or girls—dressed like servants in brown or grey. But no servant ever walked as they walked, with a casual arrogance that put princes to shame.

None of them guarded the gate to their school. There was no magic, either, no wards as Morag would have known them. And yet she paused.

The carving of the arch was worn with age and almost indistinguishable, but she could make out the shapes of men on horseback. The men rode light and erect. The horses were blocky, cobby things, thickset and sturdy—there was nothing delicate or ethereal about them. They were born of earth and stone, though their hearts might be celestial fire.

Morag shook her head to clear it. The gate blurred in front of her. It was trying to disappear.

"Clever," she said. It was a subtle spell, masterfully cast. She might not have detected it at all if she had not been looking for it.

Once she recognized it, she saw the way through it. She only had to walk straight under the arch and refuse to see any illusion that the gate might weave for her.

It did its best. The wall was thick, but it tried to convince her that the passage through the gate was a furlong and more. Then it tried to twist and fling visions at her, armed guards and galloping horsemen.

The visions melted as she walked into them. The turns grew suddenly straight. She stood in the sunlight of a sandy courtyard surrounded by tall grey walls.

Windows were open above, catching the warmth of the day. She heard voices reciting and a lone sweet tenor singing, and at greater distance, the high fierce call of a stallion.

Beneath it all ran a steady pulse. It had the rhythm of a slow heartbeat, but there was a ringing depth to it that marked it as something else.

Hoofbeats. The gods were dancing in their courts and halls.

She followed the beats that seemed most in tune with her own heart. They led her down passages and along the edges of courtyards. Some had riders in them, mounted on white stallions, or men on foot plying long lines while the stallions danced in circles or twining patterns around and across the sandy spaces.

None of the riders took any notice of her. They were in a trance of sorts, intensely focused on their work. The horses flicked an ear now and then, and once or twice a big dark eye rolled in her direction, but they made no move to stop her.

They knew her. She could not say they offered her welcome, but the air seemed a little less thin and the place a little less strange.

She granted them a flicker of respect. Their awareness guided her to the northern wall of the citadel, a long expanse of grassy paddocks in clear view of the Mountain. Blocky white shapes grazed and gamboled there, and at the western end was another court where yet more riders danced.

She turned away from the court toward the colonnade that ran along its edge, ascending a stone stair into a tower that, as she went up, overlooked the citadel and the fields and forest that surrounded it and the Mountain that reared above them all.

Just short of the top was a room surrounded by windows, a place of light. It was empty but for a man who sat on one of the window ledges. He was an old man, his faced lined and his hair gone grey, but he was still supple enough to fold himself into the embrasure with a book on his knees.

Morag waited for him to finish reading his page. She made no effort to intrude on his awareness, but he was a mage. He could sense the shift of patterns in the room. After a while the awareness grew strong enough that he looked up.

His expression was bland and his tone was mild, but annoyance was sharp beneath. "Madam. All the servants should know I'm not to be disturbed."

Morag folded her arms and tilted her head. "That's refreshing. Everyone else persists in taking me for a noblewoman."

His brow arched. "Should I recognize you?"

"Not at all," she said. "My daughter takes after her father's side of the family. How is she? Still here, I hope. I'd be a bit put out if she turned out to be in Aurelia after all."

He blinked, clearly considered several responses, then stopped as the patterns fell into place around her. It was fascinating to watch. Morag had a bit of that kind of magic—it was useful for a wisewoman to be able to see where everything fit together, the better to repair what was broken—but this was a master of the art. *The* Master, to be exact.

At length he said, "Ah. Madam. My apologies." He unfolded himself from the window ledge and bowed with courtly grace. "Not a noblewoman, no, but a great lady. I see it's no accident your daughter is what she is."

Morag studied both the face he showed her and the one, much younger and brighter, that she could see behind it. "You respect her," she said. "Good. Even after…?"

"The white gods and the Ladies have made it clear," the Master of the riders said, "that she is their beloved. What-

ever she does, whatever becomes of her, she has their blessing. Riders are stubborn and mired in tradition, but even we
can learn to accept what we can't change."

"I'm not sure I believe you," said Morag.

His smile was wry. "Do you know, she said the same. It's
no less true for that."

"I hope so," Morag said, "for your sake. So she's well? Not
locked in a dungeon?"

"Well, loved, pampered—the child when it comes will
have a hundred uncles."

Morag allowed herself to soften just a fraction. "Good,
then. I'm spared the trouble of setting this place to rights.
Now if you'll excuse me, you have an hour left of your escape from duty and tedium, and I have a daughter to find."

"She's down below," the Master said.

"I know," said Morag, gently enough when all was considered. She nodded briskly. He nodded back with more than
the hint of a bow.

Good man, she thought, and no more of a fool than any
man was inclined to be. He had reassured her more than he
knew. Her opinion of the riders and their school had risen
somewhat, though she was still reserving judgment.

Chapter Four

"Straighten your shoulders," Valeria said. "Good. Now lift him with your tailbone—yes, so."

The stallion who circled Valeria sat for an instant, then floated from a cadenced trot into a slow and rhythmic canter. The young rider on his back flashed a grin before he remembered to be properly serious.

She bit her lip to keep from grinning back. She had to be proper, too, if she was going to pass muster to become a Fourth Rider. Riders might have changed enough to accept a woman among them, but they still had certain expectations as to manners and deportment.

She shifted on the stool the Healers had insisted she resort to when she instructed her handful of rider-candidates, and rubbed her back where the baby's weight was taking its toll. She had had to stop riding a few days ago, out of pity for her poor stallions who had to carry her burgeoning bulk. She missed it less than she had expected. Now all she wanted was to be done with this labor of growing a child.

Rider-candidate Lucius was losing that lovely canter. "Hold and release," she said quickly. "Shoulders straight, remember. Now, sit back and hold."

Lucius held just a fraction too long. Sabata's ear flicked. With no more warning than that, he stopped short. Lucius lurched onto his neck.

Valeria held her breath. But Sabata had decided to be merciful. He let Lucius recover his balance and his breath, and did not tip him unceremoniously into the sand.

For that the stallion had earned an extra lump of sugar and a pat on the neck. Even a season ago, he would have yielded to temptation. He was growing up.

The baby woke abruptly and kicked so hard Valeria wheezed. Fortunately Lucius was too busy dismounting to notice. She eased from the stool and eyed the distance from it to the colonnade, then from there to the schoolroom where she was to assist First Rider Gunnar with a particularly obstreperous roomful of second-year rider-candidates.

The day's lesson was clear in her head. History and philosophy, dry but essential for understanding the patterns that made the empire what it was. But first she had to get there.

Sabata's whiskers tickled her ear. She ducked before he snorted wetly in it. He presented his shoulder.

"You don't want to carry me," she said. "I'm like a sack of barley."

His ears flattened. She was being ridiculous and they both

knew it. He folded his forelegs and lay down, saddle and all—to Lucius' vocal dismay.

She sighed, but she yielded to superior logic. She stepped astride.

He rose as carefully as he could. She could not deny that his back was a warm and welcoming place, even as badly balanced as she was. He professed not to mind.

He carried her all the way to the outer court, attracting glances and occasional expostulations, but no one was fool enough to risk Sabata's teeth and heels. At the door to the schoolrooms, he deposited her with exquisite care.

She had a fair escort by then, rider-candidates of various years and a rider or two. Not all of them were on their way to the afternoon's lesson.

They would have carried her up the stair if she had let them, but she was humiliated enough as it was. "Damn it!" she snapped at the lot of them. "I'm not a cripple. I can walk."

"So you can," said a voice she had not expected to hear at all—not for another month.

She whirled and nearly fell over. Her mother measured her with a hard, clear eye. "Walking's good for you. Riding, not so much."

"He insisted," Valeria said, jabbing her chin at Sabata. The stallion stared blandly back, as if anyone here could believe that he was an ordinary animal.

"He must have had his reasons," Morag said. "Whatever you were planning to do up there, unplan it. You're coming with me."

"I am not—" Valeria began.

"Go on," said Gunnar, looming above the pack of boys. He was half again as big as the biggest of them, a golden giant of a man. "I'll manage with this lot."

"But—" said Valeria.

"Go," the First Rider said.

That was an order. Valeria snarled at it, but there was no good reason to disobey it. She was tired—she had to admit that. She wanted to lie down.

That made her angry, but she had enough discipline, just, not to lash out. She caught Sabata's eye. There was an ironic glint in it. She was growing up, too.

Morag's examination was swift, deft and completely without sentiment. When she was done, she washed her hands in the basin that she had ordered one of the servants to have ready, then sat beside the bed in which Valeria was lying. "You're certain when you conceived?" she asked.

"Why?" Valeria demanded. She tried to throttle down the leap of alarm, but it was hard. "Is the baby too small? Is there something wrong?"

"Nothing wrong at all," said Morag, "but she's nearer being born than I'd expect. Are you sure you're not a month off in your calculations?"

"Positive," Valeria said. "She's really all right? She's not—"

"All's well as far as I can see," Morag said, "but you'll be pampering yourself a bit more after this. If you're tired, you rest. And no more riding—no matter how much the horse may insist."

"I was tired," Valeria said. "That was why—"

"It was considerate of him," her mother said, "but you

won't be doing it again until this baby is born. Which may be sooner than any of us expects. Have you had any cramping?"

"Nothing to fret over," Valeria said.

"Ah," said her mother as if she had confessed to a great deal more than she intended. "You rest. I'll let you be. Are you hungry?"

"Not really," said Valeria. "Where are you going? What—"

"I'll fetch you a posset," Morag said. "Rest. Sleep if you can. You'll be getting little enough of that soon enough."

Valeria let the storm of protest rise up in her and die unspoken. Morag was already gone. She was almost sinfully glad to be lying in her bed, bolstered with pillows, with the curtains drawn and the room dim and cool.

It was decadent. She should not allow it. But she had no will to get up. The baby stopped battering her with fists and heels and drifted back into a dream. She was as comfortable as she could be, this late in pregnancy.

She let herself give way to the inevitable. Sleep when it came was deep and sweet, with an air about it of her mother's magic.

Kerrec was putting a stallion through his paces in yet another of the many riding courts that made up the school. Morag watched him with an eye that was, if not expert, then at least interested.

He had changed since she last saw him, back in the autumn. The gaunt and haunted look was gone. He was as relaxed as she suspected he could be. He would always have a hint of the ramrod about him, but he looked elegant and disciplined rather than stiffly haughty.

He was a beautiful rider. He flowed with his horse's movements. There was no jerkiness, no disruption in the harmony.

His face was naturally stern, with its long arched nose and somber mouth, but there was a hint of lightness in it. He was smiling ever so slightly, and his odd light eyes were remarkably warm.

This was a happy man—in spite of everything he had suffered, or maybe because of it. Morag did not like to cloud that happiness, but there were things she had to say.

He was aware of her—she felt the brush of his thoughts—but he did not alter the rhythm of his horse's dance. Morag waited patiently. This was a subtle working but a great one, a minor Dance of time and the world's patterns. The sun was a little warmer for it, and the day a little brighter.

The Dance ended with a flourish that might be for the watcher, a dance in place that stilled into a deep gathering of the hindquarters and a raising of the forehand. The white stallion poised for a long moment like a statue in an imperial square. Then, with strength that made Morag's breath catch, he lowered himself to stand immobile.

She remembered to breathe again. Kerrec sprang lightly from the saddle and bowed to the stallion. The beast bent his head as if he had been an emperor granting the gift of his favor, then lipped a bit of sugar from his rider's palm.

A boy led the stallion away. Kerrec turned to Morag at last. "Madam! Welcome. I've been waiting for you."

"Have you?" said Morag.

He stripped off gloves and leather coat and began to walk toward the edge of the courtyard. She fell in beside him. He

was only a little taller than she—not a tall man, but graceful and compact and very strong.

He did not respond until they had entered the shade of
the colonnade. There was a bench there, though he did not
sit on it. He stopped and faced her. "You've seen her. What
do you think?"

"I think the baby will come within the week, if not sooner,"
Morag answered. "She seems to be in a hurry to be born."

"It's not terribly early," he said. "Is it? She'll be safe. They
both will."

"Gods willing," Morag said. "Why? Is something troubling you?"

He shrugged. He looked very young then, almost painfully uncomfortable with the emotions that tangled in him.
"It's just fretting, I'm sure. The Healers say all is going as it
should. She's managing well. There's nothing to fear."

"Healers aren't midwives," Morag said, "or wisewomen,
either. Yes, you're fretting, but sometimes there's a reason for
it. I don't suppose you've taken any time to find a wetnurse?"

He frowned. "A nurse? Are you afraid she won't be able
to—" He stopped. His whole body went still. "You think
she's going to die."

Morag glared. "I do not. I'm being practical, that's all.
How long do you think she'll let herself be tied down to a
baby? She'll be wanting to ride and teach and work magic
as soon as she can get up."

"Yes, but—"

She cut him off. Men were all fools, even men who were
mages and imperial princes. "Never mind. I'll see if there's
someone suitable here. If not, we'll send to the nearest city."

"I'm sure there's someone here," he said a little stiffly. "I'll see to it today."

"I'll do it for you," Morag said. "You go, do what First Riders do on spring afternoons. Valeria isn't going to die, and she's not likely to drop the baby tonight. We'll both watch her. Then when it happens, we'll be ready."

He nodded. Some of the tension left him, but his shoulders were tight. She had alarmed him more than she meant.

Maybe it was to the good. Kerrec had certain gifts that made him a remarkable assistant during a birthing. If he was on guard, those gifts would be all the stronger.

She patted his arm, putting a flicker of magic into it. He relaxed in spite of himself. "Stop fussing," she said. "I'm here. If I have to go to the gates of death and pull her back with my own hands, I will keep my daughter safe. You have my word on it."

"And your granddaughter?"

She almost laughed. Trust that quick mind to miss nothing. "Safer still. She'll have a long and prosperous life, if I have any say in it."

"And I," he said with an undertone that made her hackles rise. She should not forget that he was a mage and a powerful one. Even the gods would yield to his will if he saw fit to command them. In this, for the woman he loved and the child of his body, he most certainly would.

Chapter Five

Valeria woke to morning light, a noble hunger, and a plump and placid girl sitting by the window, nursing an equally plump child.

She scowled. It was her window, she was sure of that, in the room she shared with Kerrec. And here was this stranger, who might be a servant, but what was she doing with a suckling child?

Morag's tall and robust figure interposed itself between Valeria and the girl. "Good morning," she said. "Breakfast is coming. Come and have a bath."

Valeria sat up. She had been dreaming that the baby was born and she was her slender self again, riding Sabata through a fragment of the Dance. The dream had been sweet, but her mood was strange.

She felt heavier and more ungainly than ever. The bath

soothed a little of that. Breakfast was more than welcome, but her appetite faded as fast as it had risen. She ate a few mouthfuls and pushed the rest away.

In all that time, Morag had not explained the girl by the window. The child finished nursing, clambered down from the girl's lap and came to stand with his thumb in his mouth, staring at Valeria with wide brown eyes.

"This is a rider's son," Valeria said. "Is that his mother?"

"That is Portia," Morag said. "Portia is deaf and mute, but she's quite intelligent. She'll nurse your daughter when you go back to being a rider."

"She will not!" Valeria said fiercely. "I'll raise my child myself. I don't need—"

"Of course you do," said Morag. She dipped a spoonful of lukewarm porridge and cream. "Here, eat. You're feeding the baby, too, don't forget."

"Are you trying to make me sorry you ever came?"

"You'll be glad enough of me before the day is out," Morag said. "Finish this and then we'll walk. You want to visit your horses, don't you?"

Valeria glowered, but there was no resisting her mother. "This argument isn't over," she said. "When I come back, I want that girl gone."

"I'm sure you do," Morag said, unperturbed. "Eat. Then walk."

Morag was relentless. Valeria did not like to admit it, but she was glad to be up and out. She was not so glad to be marched through the whole school and half the city, then back again. She was a rider, not a foot soldier.

At least the long march included the stable and her stallions. Sabata and Oda were in the paddocks behind the stallions' stable. Marina was instructing a rider-candidate under Kerrec's stern eye.

Orontius was a competent rider, but he was profoundly in awe of Kerrec. That awe distracted him and made him clumsy. He almost wept at the sight of Valeria.

She forgot her strange mood and her body's sluggishness. "There now," she said. "Remember what we practiced yesterday? Show us how it went."

Orontius breathed so deep his body shuddered. Then, to Valeria's relief, he remembered how to focus.

Marina's own relief was palpable. A stiff and distracted rider was no pleasure for any horse to carry, even one as patient as the stallion. As Orontius relaxed, his balance grew steadier and his body softer. He began to flow with the movement as a rider should.

Kerrec would hardly unbend so far as to laugh in front of a student, but his glance at Valeria had a flicker of mirth in it. He knew how he seemed to these raw boys. Sometimes it distressed him, but mostly he was indulgent.

Valeria could remember when he had been truly terrifying. He was merely alarming now. He was even known, on rare occasions, to smile.

She slipped her hand into his. His fingers laced with hers, enfolding her in warmth. She knew better than to lean on him in front of half a dozen rider-candidates and their instructors, but his presence bolstered her wonderfully.

Orontius finished his lesson without falling into further

disgrace. Lucius was waiting his turn, holding the rein of Kerrec's stallion Petra. Valeria caught his eye and smiled.

"I'll teach this one," she said.

"Are you sure?" Kerrec asked.

He was not asking her. His eyes were on Morag.

Valeria's temper flared. She opened her mouth to upbraid them both, but the words never came. She felt...strange. Very. Something had let go. Something warm and wet. Something...

Kerrec swept her off her feet. She struggled purely instinctively, but his single sharp word put an end to that. She clutched at his neck as he began to run—biting back the question that logic bade her ask. "Why carry me? Can't I ride?"

She knew what his answer would be. *Not now.*

The baby was coming. Not this instant—Valeria was not a mare, to race from water breaking to foal on the ground in half a turn of the glass. Human women were notably less blessed. But the birth had begun. There was no stopping it.

She had thought she would be afraid. Fear was there, but it was distant, like a voice yammering almost out of earshot. The pains were much more immediate.

They were sharper than she had expected, and cut deeper. They wrenched her from the inside out.

Kerrec was with her. He would not let her go.

A very remote part of her was comforted. The rest was in stark terror.

The pains were too strong. They should not be like this. They set hooks in the deepest part of her, the part that she had buried and bound and prayed never to see again.

The Unmaking had roused. Absolute nothingness opened at the core of everything she was.

All because she had read a spell in an old and justly forgotten book, not so long ago. It had been quiescent since she came back to the Mountain from the war and the great victory. She thought she had overcome it.

She had been an idiot. It had been waiting, that was all, biding its time until she was as vulnerable as a human creature could be.

She should be riding out the pains, guiding her child into the light. Instead, all the power she had went into holding back the Unmaking.

She did not have to panic. Her mother was there. So was Kerrec. They would keep the baby safe. She had to believe that.

She could feel Kerrec around her, holding her. His quiet strength brought comfort even through the terror that was trying to swallow her. It was always there, always with her, no matter where she was or what she did. It was as much a part of them both as the color of their eyes or the shape of their hands.

She leaned back against him. It was a strange sensation, as if she moved her body from without with a third hand while the rest kept a death grip on the Unmaking. His lips brushed her hair, a gesture so casual and yet so tender that she nearly wept.

She had no choice but to hold on and be strong. No one could help her with this. No one here even knew.

They could not know. If they did, they would try to help— and the Unmaking would lair in them, too. She would rather give herself up to it than destroy them.

That hardened her heart. Her grip had been slipping, but

now it firmed. She walled the Unmaking in magic, calling on the strength of the Mountain and the stallions who were always within her.

She would never have dared to do that if it had not been for the three whom she protected—not only her lover and her mother but the child who struggled to be born. The Unmaking must never touch them. That was a great vow, as deep as the Unmaking itself.

Valeria lay barely conscious against Kerrec's body. Pains racked her, but her spirit was elsewhere. She had gone far inside herself behind walls and wards so strong he dared not break them for fear of breaking her.

"Is it always this way with mages?" he asked her mother.

Morag's frown was etched deep between her brows. "I've never midwived a horse mage before. No one has. Her body is doing well enough. The baby is coming as it should. But—"

"But?"

"I don't know," Morag said, and that clearly angered her. "Is there something about horse magic that makes this unduly difficult?"

"Not unless the old riders are right and it matters that she's a woman." Kerrec shook his head as soon as he said it. "No. That's not what it is. It's not our magic at all."

"Then what—"

"I can't tell," Kerrec said with tight-strained patience. "She won't let me in. And no, I can't force it. She's woven the wards too well."

"We'll do our best without her, then," Morag said. "Damn the girl! She's never in her life made anything simple."

Kerrec bit his lip. He would be the first to admit that the two of them were all too well matched.

The body in his arms went stiff with a new and stronger contraction. The life inside sparked with fear. He smoothed the world's patterns around it—not so much that the birthing stopped, but enough to take away the worst of the pain.

He walled his own fears inside. That much of Valeria's example he could follow. He had to be steady and strong to bring his daughter into the world.

There was a deep rightness in that. The patterns opened to accept her. She was a strong spirit, brimming with magic. She yearned toward the light.

He showed her the way. It seemed terribly long and slow, but as human births went, it was remarkably fast.

Valeria woke in the middle of it. Her consciousness flared like a beacon. The child veered away from Kerrec and toward that much brighter light.

He caught them both. Valeria was reeling with pain and confusion. All her patterns were scattered, her magic trying to shake itself to pieces.

The child's own confusion and the shock of birthing drove her toward her mother—like calling to like. Kerrec throttled down panic. Now of all times, he must be what he was bred and trained to be.

He breathed deep and slow, as he willed Valeria to do, and quieted his mind and heart and the rushing of blood through his veins. As he grew calmer, the patterns around them lost their jagged edges and smoothed into the curves and planes of a world restored to order. For strength he drew from the earth, from the Mountain itself that was the source of every rider's magic.

The stallions were there, and their great Ladies behind them, watching and waiting. Kerrec was bound in body and soul to the stallion Petra, whose awareness was always with him. But this was a greater thing.

He had never sensed them all before. Sometimes he had seen them through Valeria's eyes and known for an instant how powerful her magic was. She could see and feel them all, always.

This was not a shadow seen through another's eyes. It was stronger, deeper.

The white gods had drawn aside the veil that divided them from mortal minds and magic. None of them moved, and yet this was a Dance—a Dance of new life and new magic coming into the world.

Kerrec dared not pause for awe. The gods might be present and they might be watching, but they laid on him the burden of keeping his lover and his child alive. They would do nothing to help him.

It did no good to be bitter. The gods were the gods. They did as they saw fit.

Under that incalculable scrutiny, he held the patterns steady. The pains were close together now. Valeria gasped in rhythm with them. She spoke no word, nor did she scream. She took the pain inside herself.

Morag moved into Kerrec's vision. He had all but forgotten her, lost in a mist of magic and fear.

"I need you to hold her tightly," Morag said, "but don't choke the breath out of her." She placed his hands as she would have them, palms flat below the breasts, pressed to the first curve of the swollen belly. "When I give the word, push."

Kerrec drew a breath and nodded. His legs were stiff and his back ached with sitting immobile, cradling Valeria. He let the discomfort sharpen his focus.

Morag's voice brought him to attention. "Now," she said. "Push."

Valeria began to struggle. She was naked and slicked with sweat, impossibly slippery in Kerrec's hands. He locked his arms around her and prayed they would hold.

Morag slapped Valeria, hard. The struggling stopped. Valeria was conscious, if confused.

"Now push," Morag said to them both.

Valeria braced against Kerrec's hands. He held on for all their lives and pushed as Morag had instructed.

For the first time in the whole of that ordeal, Valeria let out a sound, a long, breathless cry. Kerrec felt the pain rising to a crescendo, then the sudden, powerful release. Valeria's cry faded into another altogether, a full-throated wail.

"Her name is Grania," Valeria said.

She was exhausted almost beyond sense, but she was alive, conscious and far from unmade. The Unmaking had subsided once more, sinking out of sight but not ever again out of mind.

Morag and two servants of the school had bathed Valeria and dressed her in a soft, light robe. Two more servants had spread clean bedding, cool and sweet-scented. Valeria lay almost in comfort and held out her hands.

Kerrec cradled their daughter, looking down into that tiny, red, pinched face, as rapt as if there had never been anything more beautiful in the world. He gave her up with visible reluctance.

"Grania," Valeria said as the swaddled bundle settled into her arms. Maybe the child would be beautiful someday, but it was a singularly unprepossessing thing just now. She folded back the blankets, freeing arms that moved aimlessly and legs that kicked without purpose except to learn the ways of this new and enormous world.

Valeria brushed her lips across the damp black curls, breathing the warm and strange-familiar scent. "Grania," she said again. And a third time, to complete the binding. "Grania."

She looked up. Morag was smiling—so rare as to be unheard of. Grania had been her mother's name. It was an honor and a tribute.

Valeria was too tired to smile back. Kerrec sat on the bed beside her. She leaned against him as she had for so many long hours. As he had then, he bolstered her with his warm strength.

She sighed and closed her eyes. Sleep eluded her, but it was good to rest in her lover's arms with their child safe and alive and replete with the first milk.

Her body felt as if it had been in a battle. Everything from breasts to belly ached. That would pass. The Unmaking...

Despair tried to rise and swallow her. She refused to let it. She should be happy. She *would* be happy. That old mistake would not crush her—not now and not, gods willing, ever after.

Chapter Six

The room was full of shadows and whispers. All the windows were shrouded and the walls closed in with heavy dark hangings. But the floor was bare stone, and a stone altar stood in the center, its grey bulk stained with glistening darkness.

Maurus struggled not to sneeze. He was crowded into a niche with his cousin Vincentius. They each had a slit to peer through, which so far had shown them nothing but the altar and the lamp that flickered above it.

Nothing was going to happen tonight. Vincentius had heard wrong—there was no gathering. They had come here for nothing.

Just as Maurus opened his mouth to say so, he heard what he had been waiting for.

Footsteps, advancing deliberately, like the march of a processional. Maurus' heart pounded in his throat.

The door opened behind the heavy sway of curtains. Maurus stopped breathing. Vincentius's face was just visible beside him, pale and stiff. His eyes were open as wide as they would go.

This was the gathering they had come to see. When the full number had come through the door and drawn up in a circle around the altar, there were nineteen of them.

They were wrapped in dark mantles. Some hunched over as if trying to be furtive. Others stood straight but kept their cloaks wound tight.

Vincentius thrust an elbow into Maurus' ribs. Maurus had already seen what his chin was pointing at. One of the figures nearest them had a familiar hitch in his gait.

Maurus' brother Bellinus had been born with one leg shorter than the other. It made no apparent difference on a horse and he had not been judged unfit to inherit their father's dukedom, but lately he had been acting odd—bitter, angry, as if he had a grievance against the world.

Maurus bit his lip to keep from making a sound and tried to breathe silently. Vincentius' breath was loud in his ears. Any moment he expected one of the people in the circle to come looking for either or both of them.

The circle turned inward on itself. The air began to feel inexplicably heavy. Maurus' head ached and his ears felt ready to burst.

Out of that heaviness grew a deep sound, deeper than the lowest note of an organ, like the grinding of vast stones under the earth. The floor was steady underfoot, but far down below it, Maurus thought something was stirring, something he never wanted to see in the daylight.

The circle moved, drawing together. Blades flashed in unison. Each shrouded figure bared an arm and cut swiftly across it. Blood flowed onto the already glistening stone.

Those arms were scarred with knife cuts healed and half-healed and barely scabbed over. It was true, then, what Maurus had heard. These worshippers of the unspeakable had been meeting nearly every night to make sacrifice in blood.

No one had been able to say what that sacrifice was for. Something dark was all Maurus could be sure of.

He had imagined that he could do something to save his brother from whatever it was. But hiding behind the curtain, huddled with his friend whose elder brother was also somewhere in the circle, Maurus felt the weight of despair. He was a half-grown boy with a small gift of magic. He should never have come to this place or seen what he was seeing.

The sound from within the earth grew deeper still, setting in his bones. Blood congealed on the altar. The circle began to chant.

It was all men's voices, but they sang a descant to the earth's rumbling. The words were not in a language Maurus knew. They sounded very old and very dark and very powerful.

They tried to creep into his mind. He pressed his hands to his ears. That barely muffled the sound, but the words blurred just enough that he could, more or less, block them out.

His skin crawled. His head felt as if he had been breathing poison. He was dizzy and sick, trying desperately not to gag or choke.

It all burst at once with a soundless roar. The earth stopped throbbing. The chant fell silent.

Above the altar with its thick shell of clotted blood, the

air turned itself inside out. Maurus' eyes tried to do the same. He squeezed them shut.

He could still see the flash of everything that was the opposite of light, of nothingness opening on oblivion. As terrified as he was, he needed to see it clearly—to know what it was. He opened his eyes, shuddering so hard he could barely stand up.

Oblivion spawned a shape. Arms and legs, broad shoulders, a head—it was a man, naked and blue as if with cold. He fell to hands and knees on the altar.

Lank fair hair straggled over his shoulders and down his back. He was so gaunt Maurus could see every bone, but there was a terrible strength in him. He raised his head.

His eyes were like a blind man's, so pale they were nearly white. But as he turned his head, thin nostrils flaring, he made it clear that he could see. He took in the circle and the room and, oh gods, the curtains that shrouded the walls.

He must be able to see the boys hiding there. Maurus tried to melt into the wall. If there had been a way to become nonexistent, he would have done it.

The strange eyes passed on by. The pale man stepped down from the altar. He was tall, and seemed taller because he was so thin. One of the men who had summoned him held out a dark bundle that unfolded into a hooded robe.

That face and that lank hair were all the paler once the body was wrapped in black wool. The voice was surprisingly light, as if the edges had been smoothed from it. "Where is it?" he asked. "It's in none of you here. Where are you hiding it?"

"Hiding what, my lord?" asked one of the men from the circle.

The pale man turned slowly. "Don't play the fool. Your little ritual didn't bring me here. Where is the maw of the One?"

The man who had spoken spread his hands. "My lord, all we are is what you see. We summoned you by the rites that were given us by—"

"Empty flummery," the pale man said. "Great power called me. Your blood showed me the way. Now feed me, because I hunger. Then tell me what you think you can do to bring the One into this place of gods and magic."

"We trust in you, my lord," said the other. "The message said—"

"I was promised allies with intelligence and influence," the pale man said. "I see a pack of trembling fools. That's comforting in its way, I do grant you. If you're such idiots, those we want to destroy might even be worse."

"My lord—" said the spokesman.

The pale man bared long pale-yellow teeth. "This game we play to the end—ours or theirs. We've failed in the Dance and we've lost in battle. This time we strike for the heart."

A growl ran around the circle, a low rumble of affirmation. Obviously they took no offense at anything this creature might say.

The creature swayed. "I must eat," he said. "Then rest. Then plan."

"Of course, my lord," the spokesman said hastily. He beckoned. The circle closed around the pale man. It lifted him and carried him away.

Maurus swallowed bile. The stink of blood and twisted magic made him ill. He was afraid he knew what they had been talking about—and it brought him close to panic when he thought of his brother caught up in such a thing.

There had been other plots against the empire. The emperor had been poisoned and the Dance of his jubilee broken, with riders killed and the school on the Mountain irreparably damaged. Then in the next year the emperor had gone to war against the barbarian tribes whose princes had conspired to break his Dance. With help from two of the riders and the gods they served, he had destroyed them—but their magic had destroyed him.

Now his daughter was shortly to take the throne as empress. There would be a coronation Dance. Surely the riders who came for that, along with every mage and loyal noble in the city of Aurelia, would be on guard against attack.

Which meant—

Maurus did not know what it meant. Not really. He did know that his brother was caught up in it, and that was terrible enough.

Vincentius slid down the wall beside him. His face was the color of cheese.

He always had been a sensitive soul. Maurus pulled him upright and shook him until he stood on his own feet again.

The worshippers of the One had gone. The corridor was silent. The lamp guttered over the altar.

Maurus dragged Vincentius with him around the edge of the room—as if it made any difference now how furtive they were—and peered around the door. The passage was deserted as he had thought.

It was almost pitch-black. The lamps that had been lit along it had all gone out. Only the one at the farthest end still burned, shedding just enough light to catch anything that might have stirred in the darkness.

Maurus eyed the light over the altar, which was burning dangerously low. He was not about to climb on that blood-slicked stone to retrieve the lamp. He would have to brave the dark, and hope no one came back while he did it.

Vincentius had his feet under him now. He could walk, though he had to stop once and then again to empty his stomach.

That might betray them, but there was nothing Maurus could do about it. He dragged his cousin forward with as much speed as he could. His mind was a babble of prayer to any god that would hear.

Halfway down the corridor, something scraped at the door. Maurus froze. Vincentius dropped to his knees, heaving yet again, but this time nothing came up.

There was nowhere to hide. Maurus pressed against the wall—as if that would help—and bit his lip to keep from making a sound.

The scraping stopped. Maurus waited for what seemed an age, but the door stayed shut.

There was no one on the other side. The stairway leading steeply upward was better lit but equally deserted.

Maurus stopped at the bottom and took a breath. There was no escape on that ascent. If he was caught, he could be killed.

The men who kept this secret would not care that he was noble born, only that he had spied on their hidden rite. He set his foot on the first step and began the ascent. Vincentius was already on the stair.

Maurus followed as quickly as he could. His heart was beating so hard he could not hear anything else.

He had not been nearly as afraid in the dungeon below. That had been plain insanity. This was the edge of escape. If he failed, the disappointment would be deadly.

Vincentius reached the door first. His hands tugged at the bolt. The door stayed firmly shut.

Maurus' terror came out in a rush of breath. He pushed Vincentius aside and heaved as hard as he could.

The door flew open. Maurus nearly fell backward down the stair.

Vincentius caught him. The eyes that stared into his were blessedly aware. They dragged one another through the doorway and into a perfectly ordinary alleyway in the city of Aurelia.

The sun was up. They had been all night in the dark below. People would be looking for them.

"Let's go to Riders' Hall," Vincentius said, putting in words what Maurus was thinking. "We'll say we thought one of the mares was foaling. Maybe she did. If we're lucky."

Maurus nodded. "I wish Valeria was there. Or even—you know—him. They'd know what to do."

"Riders will be there soon—a whole pack of them. Coronation's in less than a month. They must be on their way from the Mountain by now."

"But," said Maurus, "what if that's the plot—to stop the Dance again? Or if it's supposed to come off before they get here? Or—"

Vincentius looked as desperate as Maurus felt. "I don't know. This wasn't even my idea. Didn't you make any plans for after?"

"I just wanted to see what Bellinus was doing," Maurus said. "I thought I'd corner him later and make him stop. Even though I knew, from what I'd heard, that nobody can do that. The only way out is to die."

"What about us, then? Do we even dare to tell? We don't know what they'll try to do. Mages must be spying, too. Someone must know—someone who can do something about it. They'll stop it before it goes any further."

"Are you sure of that?" Maurus said. "Maybe we should go to the empress."

"Nobody gets near her," Vincentius said. "Even if we could, what would we say? I thought I recognized some of the voices. That's all well and good, but if I give any of them up, how do we know they won't lead the hunters to your brother?"

Maurus' head hurt. The only clear path he could see still led toward Valeria. She had taught him to ride last year before she ran off to save the world, she and the First Rider who had been born an imperial prince.

Valeria was the strongest mage he knew, and one of the few he trusted. She would know what to do.

What if she did not come with the riders to the Dance? Would they even let her off the Mountain after all she had done?

He would have to reach her somehow. A letter would be too slow. He did not have the rank or station, let alone the coin, to send a courier all the way to the Mountain.

He would find a way. Then she would tell him what to do. Valeria always knew what to do—or else her stallion did. He was a god, after all.

Maurus set off down the street as if he had every right to

be there. Vincentius, who was much taller, still had to stretch to keep up. By the time they reached the turning onto the wider street, where people were up and about in the bright summer morning, Maurus felt almost like himself again.

Chapter Seven

The school on the Mountain was in a flurry. For the second time since Valeria came to it, the best of its riders and the most powerful of its stallions were leaving its sanctuary and riding to the imperial city.

That was a rare occurrence. Considering how badly the last such riding had ended, it was no wonder the mood in the school was complicated to say the least. Nor did it help that by ancient tradition the coronation must take place on the day of Midsummer—and therefore the strongest riders and the most powerful stallions would not be on the Mountain when this year's Called were gathered and tested.

They had to go. One of their most sacred duties was to Dance the fate of a new emperor or empress. They could no more refuse than they could abandon the stallions on whom their magic depended.

And yet what passed for wisdom would have kept them walled up on the Mountain, protected against any assault. Nothing could touch them here. The gods themselves would see to that.

The Master had settled on a compromise. Half of the First Riders and most of the Second and all of the Third and Fourth Riders would stay in the school. Sixteen First and Second Riders and sixteen stallions would go to Aurelia.

Valeria went as servant and student for the journey. Then in Aurelia she would stay after the Dance was done, under Kerrec's command.

They were going to try something new and possibly dangerous. But Kerrec had convinced the Master that it might save them all.

He was going to extend the school to Aurelia and bring a part of it away from the fabled isolation of the Mountain into the heart of the empire. If their magic could stand the glare of day and the tumult of crowds, it might have a chance to continue, maybe even to grow.

It needed to do that. It was stiffening into immobility where it was.

In the world outside its sanctuary, all too many people had decided the horse magic had no purpose. Augurs could read omens without the need to study the patterns of a troupe of horsemen riding on sand. Soothsayers could foretell the future, and who knew? Maybe one or more orders of mages could try to shape that future, once the riders let go their stranglehold on that branch of magic.

Valeria happened to be studying the patterns of sun and shadow on the floor of her room as she reflected on time, fate and the future of the school she had fought so hard to join. The only sound was the baby's sucking and an occasional soft gurgle.

The nurse sat by the window. Her smooth dark head bent over the small black-curled one. Her expression was soft, her eyelids lowered.

Valeria's own breasts had finally stopped aching. After the first day there had never been enough milk for the baby, but what feeble trickle there was had persistently refused to dry up.

However much she loathed to do it, she had had to admit that her mother was right. She needed the nurse.

The woman was quiet at least. She never hinted with face or movement that she thought Valeria was a failure. She did not offer sympathy, either, or any sign of pity.

"It's nature's way," Morag had said by the third day after Grania was born. The baby would not stop crying. When she tried to suck, she only screamed the louder. Yet again, the nurse had had to take her and feed her, because Valeria's milk was not enough.

"Sometimes it happens," Morag said. "You see it with mares, too, in the first foaling, and heifers and young ewes. They deliver the young well enough, but their bodies don't stretch to feeding it. You'd put a foal or a calf with a nurse. What's so terrible about doing it with a baby?"

"I should be able to," Valeria said, all but spitting the words. "There's nothing wrong with me. You said. The Healers said. I shouldn't be this way!"

"But you are," her mother said bluntly. "Stop fighting it, girl, and live with it. There's plenty of mothering to do outside of keeping her belly filled."

"Not at the moment there isn't," Valeria said through clenched teeth.

"Certainly there is," said Morag. "Now give yourself a rest while she eats. You're still weak, though you think you can hide it."

Valeria had snarled at her, but there was never any use in resisting Morag. The one time she had succeeded, she had had the Mountain's Call to strengthen her.

The call of mother to child was not as strong as that—however hard it was to accept. She had bound her aching breasts and taken the medicines her mother fed her, and day by day she had got her strength back.

Now, almost a month after Grania was born, Valeria was nearly herself again. She had even been allowed to ride, though Morag had ordered her to keep it slow and not try any leaps. She might have done it regardless, just to spite her mother, but none of the stallions would hear of it.

They were worse than Morag. They carried her as if she were made of glass, and smoothed their paces so flawlessly that she was ready to scream.

"I *like* the big, booming gaits!" she had shouted at Sabata one thoroughly exasperating morning. "Stop creeping about. It's making me crazy. I keep wanting to get behind you and push."

Time was when Sabata would have bucked her off for saying such things. But he barely hunched his back. He did, mercifully, stretch his stride a little.

It was better than nothing. After a while even he grew tired of that and relaxed into something much closer to his normal paces. Valeria was distressed by how hard she had to work to manage those. Childbearing wrought havoc with a woman's riding muscles.

On this clear summer morning, several days after her outburst to Sabata, she was done picking at her breakfast. Grania was still engrossed in hers.

It was hard to rouse herself to leave them, but each day it grew a little easier. The stallions were waiting. There were belongings to pack and affairs to settle. Tomorrow they would leave for Aurelia.

Today Valeria had morning exercises to get through, classes to learn and teach and the latest arrival of the Called to greet. Last year's flood of candidates had not repeated itself. So far this year, the numbers were much more ordinary and the candidates likewise. None of them was already a mage of another order, and they were all boys, with no grown men taken unawares by the Call.

She was glad. This was not the year to tax the riders with more of the Called than they had ever seen before.

She should get up and go. But the sun was warm and its patterns on the floor were strangely fascinating. She had been studying the art of patterns, learning to see both meaning and randomness in the veining of a leaf, and significance in sunlight.

Riders were mages of patterns more than anything, even more than they were both masters and servants of the gods who wore the forms of white horses. The pattern she saw here was exquisitely random. Shadows from the leading of the window divided squares and diamonds of sudden light.

The different shapes blurred. Valeria blinked to clear her sight. The oddness grew even worse.

It did not look like sunlight on a wooden floor any longer but like mist on water with sunlight behind it. As she peered, a figure took shape.

She had played at scrying when she was younger, before she came to the Mountain. A mage filled a cup of polished metal—silver if she could find it, tin or bronze if not—and turned it so that the light fell on but not in it. Then if one had the gift, visions came.

Valeria had never seen anything she could use. She was not a seer. That magic had passed her by.

And yet this pattern on the floor made her think quite clearly of scrying in a bowl. There was a face staring at her out of the mist, young and worried and startlingly familiar. It brought the memory of last summer in Aurelia before Kerrec ran away to the war, when six young nobles had come to Rider's Hall to learn to ride like horse mages.

Maurus was the first who had come, along with his cousin Vincentius. He had been one of the better pupils, too. In time he might make a rider, though he had no call to the school on the Mountain.

He was staring at her with such a combination of recognition and relief that she wondered what had made him so desperate.

If she had fallen into a dream, it felt amazingly real. She heard Maurus' voice at a slight distance, as if he were calling to her down the length of a noble's hall, but the words were clear. "Valeria! Thank the gods. I didn't know if this would work. Pelagius promised it would, but he's only a seer-candidate, and I wasn't sure—"

His head jerked. It looked as if someone had shaken him. When he stopped shaking, his words came slower and stopped sooner. "I'm sorry. I didn't mean to babble. I couldn't think who else to talk to, and I was afraid you weren't coming to the coronation Dance. You are coming, aren't you?"

"I do intend to," Valeria said.

"Good," he said. "That's good. I hope you get here in time."

"Why?" said Valeria. Her stomach knotted. It was not surprise, she noticed. It felt like something she had not even known she was expecting. "What's wrong?"

"Pelagius says I can show you," Maurus said, "but you have to help. It's pattern magic, he says. You have to bind it to my face and voice, then you'll see it."

Maurus did not sound as if he knew what he was saying. Somehow that convinced Valeria that she was not dreaming. This really was the boy from Aurelia, and he really had reached her through a scrying spell.

However fond Maurus might be of his own voice, he was not a frivolous person. If he had gone to such lengths to convey this message to her, it must be urgent.

It could be a trap. Both the empire and the Mountain had powerful enemies, and Valeria had attracted her fair share of those. She would not put it past one of them to bait her with this child and then use the spell to destroy her.

She could smell no stink of betrayal in either Maurus or the working that had brought his consciousness here. What he asked of her, she could do. It was a simple magic, taking the patterns of the message and opening them into a whole world of awareness.

There were rough edges in this working, raw spots that told her the mage who wrought it was no master. She had to be careful or her own patterns would fall apart, trapping her inside the spell.

It had been easier when she did it in the schoolroom with First Rider Gunnar steadying her. She had to be the steady one here.

She bound her consciousness to each thread of the pattern that Maurus had brought with him. When she had every one in her control, she turned her focus on the center and willed it to open.

It burst upon her in a rush of sensation. She saw and heard and felt and even smelled the dark room, the altar, the circle, the creature they conjured out of nothingness. The words they spoke buried themselves in her consciousness.

As abruptly as the vision had come, it vanished. Maurus stared at her from his puddle of sunlight. He was dimming around the edges and his voice was faint. "Valeria? Did you get it?"

"I have it," Valeria said.

"What should we do? Do you know what it is? Do you think you can stop it?"

"I don't know yet," Valeria said, trying not to be sharp. "I have to think about it. I'll do what I can—that much I promise."

Maurus sighed. She barely heard the sound. "I trust you," he said, "but whatever you do, I hope you can do it quickly. I don't think there's much time."

"I'll try," she said. "We'll be in Aurelia in a fortnight. If something threatens to happen before then, go to the empress and show her what you showed me. Don't be afraid— and don't hesitate. Tell her I sent you."

Maurus' mouth moved, but Valeria could not hear what he said. The light was fading. The working was losing strength.

Before she could ask him to speak louder, he was gone. An empty pattern of sun and shadow dappled the floor. Grania was asleep in her nurse's arms, and Valeria was unconscionably late for morning exercises.

Chapter Eight

Valeria went through the morning in a daze. It seemed no one noticed but the stallions—and they did not remark on it. Their mortal servants were distracted by the preparations for the riders' departure.

She did not remember what she taught the rider-candidates in her charge, except that none of them suffered loss of life or limb. Her own lessons passed in a blur.

For those who were traveling to Aurelia in the morning, there were no afternoon lessons or exercises. They were to spend the time packing their belongings and seeing to it that the stallions were ready for the journey.

Maurus' message changed nothing. She was still leaving tomorrow. That battle was long since fought and won, and she had no intention of surrendering after all.

The baby was old enough to travel. The nurse would help

to look after her, and Morag was riding with them as far as the village of Imbria. Grania would be nearly as safe on the road as she was on the Mountain.

It was by no means a surprise that a faction of nobles was plotting against the empire. That was all too commonplace. But that Maurus should have come to Valeria in such desperation and nearly inarticulate fear, made her deeply uneasy.

It was not like Maurus to be so afraid. He was a light-hearted sort, though not particularly light-minded. Very little truly disturbed him.

This had shaken him profoundly. It was dark magic beyond a doubt, and what it had conjured up was dangerous.

The barbarian tribes were Aurelia's most bitter enemies. They lived to kill and conquer, and they had waged long war against the empire's borders. Their warriors worshipped blood and torment. Their priests were masters of pain.

If a conspiracy of nobles had summoned one of those priests to the imperial city, that could only mean that they meant to disrupt the coronation. They would strike at the empress, and they well might try to break the Dance again.

Valeria could not believe that the empress was unaware of the threat. Neither Briana nor her counselors were fools. Both coronation and Dance would be heavily warded, with every step watched and every moment guarded. What could a single priest of the One do against that, even with a cabal of nobles behind him?

Valeria had been walking to the dining hall for the noon meal, but when she looked up, she had gone on past it down the passage to the stallions' stable. She started to turn but decided to go on. She was not hungry, not really. Maurus' message and the vision he had sent had taken her appetite away.

She rounded a corner just as Kerrec strode around it from the opposite direction. She had an instant to realize that he was there. The next, she ran headlong into him.

He caught her before she sent them both sprawling, swung her up and set her briskly on her feet. She stood breathing hard, staring at him. She felt as if she had not seen him in years—though they had shared a bed last night and got up together this morning.

They had not done more than lie in one another's arms since Grania was born. That was all Valeria had wanted, and Kerrec never importuned. He was not that kind of man.

Just now she wished he were. It was a sharp sensation, half like a knife in the gut, half like a melting inside. When winter broke on the Mountain and the first streams of snow-cold water ran down the rocks, it must feel the same.

She reached for him and found him reaching in turn, with hunger that was the match of hers exactly.

How could she have forgotten this? Having a baby turned a woman's wits to fog, but Valeria had thought better of herself than that.

It seemed she was mortal after all. She closed her eyes and let the kiss warm her down to her center. The taste, the smell of him made her dizzy.

They fit so well into each other's empty places. She arched against him, but even as he drew back slightly, she came somewhat to her senses. This was hardly the place to throw him down flat and have her will of him.

She opened her eyes. His were as dark as they ever were,

more grey than silver. He was smiling with a touch of rue-
fulness. "It's been a little while," he said.

"Too long," said Valeria.

"We can wait a few hours longer," he said.

She trailed her fingers across his lips. That almost broke
her resolve even as it swayed his, but she brought herself to
order. So, with visible effort, did he. "What is it? Is there
trouble? Is it Grania?"

That brought her firmly back to her senses. "Not Grania,"
she said, "or anyone else here."

His brows lifted at the way she had phrased that. He
reached for her hand as she reached for his. By common and
unspoken consent, they turned back the way he had come.

The stalls were empty. All the stallions were in the paddocks or at exercises. The stable was dim and quiet.

The stallions' gear was packed and ready to travel. The
boxes of trappings for the Dance stood by the door, locked
and bound, and the traveling saddles were cleaned and polished on their racks. She blew a fleck of dust from Sabata's
saddle and ran a finger over one of the rings of his bit. It
gleamed at her, scrupulously bright.

Kerrec did not press her. That was one of the things she loved
most about him. He could wait until she was ready to speak.

He would not force her, either, if she decided not to say
anything. But this was too enormous to keep inside. She
gave it to him as Maurus had given it to her, without word
or warning.

It said a great deal for his strength that he barely swayed
under the onslaught. After the first shock, he stood steady

and took it in. He did not stop or interrupt it until it was done. Then he stood silent, letting it unwind again behind the silver stillness of his eyes.

Valeria waited as he had, though with less monumental patience. He was a master. She was not even a journeyman. She was still inclined to fidget.

After a long while he said, "The boy would have been wiser to go to my sister."

"He didn't think it worthwhile to try," Valeria said. "She's the empress, after all. He'll never get through all her guards and mages."

"Someone should," Kerrec said. "They've conjured a priest of the barbarians' god—and from what the boy saw of him, he's even worse than the usual run of them. We're weaker than we were when his kind broke the Dance. My sister's hold on court and council is still tenuous. Even fore-warned and forearmed, she's more vulnerable than my father was. She's all too clear a target."

"I'm sure she knows that," Valeria said. "Can you relay this message to her?"

"I can try," he said, "but she's warded by mages of every order in Aurelia. I'm strong, but I'm not that strong."

"You are if you ask the stallions to help."

He arched a brow at her. "I? Why not you?"

"You're her brother," Valeria said, "and much more skilled in this kind of magic than I am. I'm just learning it. It's not so hard face to face, but across so much distance…what if I fail?"

"I doubt you would," Kerrec said, "with the stallions behind you."

"You're still better at it," she said.

He pondered that for a moment before he said, "I'll do it."

"Here? Now?"

"When I'm ready."

The urgency in her wanted to protest, but she had laid this on him. She could hardly object to the way he chose to do it.

He smiled, all too well aware of her thoughts. His finger brushed her cheek. "It won't be more than a few hours," he said.

"That's what you said about us."

He had the grace not to laugh at her. "Before that, then."

That did not satisfy her. "What if those few hours make the difference?"

"They won't," he said. "I can feel the patterns beginning to shift, but they won't break tonight. It takes time to do what I think they're going to try. They'll need more than a day or two to set it in motion."

"What—how can you know—"

"If you know where to look, you can see."

She scowled at him. Sometimes he forced her to remember that he was more than a horse mage. He had been born to rule this empire, but the Call had come instead and taken him away.

Kerrec had died to that part of himself—with precious little regret. Then his father had died in truth and given him the gift that each emperor gave his successor. All the magic of Aurelia had come to fill him.

It had healed Kerrec's wounds and restored the full measure of his magic. It had also made him intensely aware of the land and its people.

His sister Briana had it, too. For her it was the inevitable consequence of the emperor's death. She was the heir. The land and its magic belonged to her.

It was not something that needed to be divided or diminished in order to be shared. The emperor had meant it for both reconciliation and healing, but maybe it was more than that. Maybe Artorius had foreseen that the empire would need both his children.

Kerrec seemed wrapped in a deep calm. His kiss was light but potent, like the passage of a flame. "Soon," he said.

Voices erupted outside. Hooves thudded on the sand of the stableyard. Riders were bringing stallions in to be groomed and saddled for afternoon exercises.

Valeria stepped back quickly. There was no need for guilt—if everyone had not already known what was happening, Grania would have been fairly strong proof. But it had been too long. She was out of practice.

Kerrec laughed at her, but he did not try to stop her. She was halfway down the aisle by the time the foremost rider slid back the door and let the sun into the stable.

Kerrec was more troubled than he wanted Valeria to know. He would have liked to shake the boy who, instead of taking what he knew to the empress like a sensible citizen, reached all the way to the Mountain and inflicted his anxieties on Valeria. Was there no one closer at hand to vex with them?

That could be a trap in itself. Valeria was notorious among mages. She was the first woman ever to be Called to the Mountain and a bitter enemy of Aurelia's enemies. She had twice thwarted assaults on the empire and its rulers. In certain quarters she was well hated.

Kerrec was even less beloved, though the brother who had hated him beyond reason or sanity was dead, destroyed by his own magic. There were still men enough, both imperial and barbarian, who would gladly have seen Kerrec dead or worse.

This kind of thinking was best done in the back of the mind, from the back of a horse. He saddled one of the young stallions, a spirited but gentle soul named Alea.

The horse was more than pleased to be led into one of the lesser courts, where no one else happened to be riding at that hour. Kerrec had been of two minds as to whether to bring the stallion with him to Aurelia, but as he smoothed the mane on the heavy arched neck, he caught a distinct air of wistfulness. Alea wanted to see the world beyond the Mountain.

"So you shall," Kerrec said with sudden decision. He gathered the reins and sprang into the saddle, settling lightly on the broad back.

Alea was young—he had come down off the Mountain two years before, in the same herd that had bred Valeria's fiery Sabata—and although he was talented, he had much to learn before he mastered his art. Kerrec took a deep and simple pleasure in these uncomplicated exercises. They soothed his spirit and concentrated his mind.

As he rode each precise circle and undulating curve, shifting pace from walk to trot to canter and back again, he began to perceive another riding court in a different city. The horse under him was a little shorter and notably broader. The neck that arched in front of him was narrower and lighter, and the mane was not smoky grey but jet-black. The little ears that curved at the end of it were red brown, the color called bay.

Kerrec kept his grip on the unexpected working. He bent his will until his awareness separated from that other rider, so that he seemed to ride side by side with his sister. Alea bowed to Kerrec's sister's mount, the bay Lady who alone of all the mothers of gods had chosen a mortal rider and left the Mountain.

They were riding the same patterns. That was not a coincidence. Each bend and turn brought them into harmony.

Briana smiled at her brother. "Good afternoon," she said as serenely as if they had not been riding this paired dance across eighty leagues of mountain and plain.

Kerrec acknowledged her with an inclination of the head. With the Lady leading, the pattern was growing more complex, though still simple enough for Kerrec's young stallion. In its curves and figures was the vision Maurus had given Valeria.

Briana's expression did not change. She had taken it in, Kerrec did not doubt that, but she showed no sign of what she was thinking.

He would not ask, either. He had done what was necessary. The empress knew what Maurus had seen. It was for her to decide what to do about it.

The ride went on, which somewhat surprised him. It was a Dance, a doorway through fate and time, though there was no ritual and no formal occasion and no flock of Augurs to interpret it. To a Lady, all those things were inconsequential.

She had chosen to Dance now for reasons that might have little to do with Kerrec's message. The only wise course was to ride the Dance and ask no questions. Answers would come when, or if, the Lady pleased.

These patterns seemed harmless and sunlit, but Maurus' vision underlay all of them. A priest of the One God, a cabal of idle and disaffected nobles, an altar of sacrifice that had seen long and bloody use—all that was clear enough, one would think. Yet another conspiracy raised itself against the empire, or more likely this was an offshoot of older and failed conspiracies.

But the priest had said something that would not let Kerrec go. The creature had mocked the circle that summoned him. Something beyond them had brought him there—some great power in Aurelia, strong enough to conjure evil out of air.

That made Kerrec's back tighten. He caught himself before he passed that stiffness to Alea. The stallion did not deserve it, and the Dance assuredly did not need it.

Tomorrow Kerrec would ride to Aurelia. Whatever was going to happen there, he would do his best to be ready for it. So would his sister. So would everyone else whom either of them was able to warn.

Meanwhile he rode the Dance, taking its patterns inside him, committing them to memory. They might be useful or they might not. The gods knew. It was not for a mortal, even a master mage, to judge—though he might come to conclusions of his own, given time and space to think about it.

Chapter Nine

"You're sure of this?"

Valeria paused in tightening Sabata's girth. The rest of the caravan was still forming in the pale dawn light. The question did not surprise her, but the one who asked it did.

Master Nikos held the rein of a stallion nearly as majestically ancient as Valeria's Oda, who waited patiently in the line of stallions who would go riderless on this first day of the journey. Valeria acknowledged Master and stallion with a nod of respect. "I am sure," she said.

The Master glanced at the cluster of people beyond Valeria. Morag was already in her cart with the nurse beside her. Grania, having eaten a hearty breakfast, was peacefully asleep.

"They'll be safe," Valeria said. "My mother may be only a village wisewoman, but she's a strong mage."

"Your mother is not 'only' anything," the Master said. "I don't fear for her or even the child. It's you I'm thinking of."

"I'm not weak," Valeria said. "If I'm even slightly tired, I'll ride in the wagon. My mother has already delivered the lecture, sir."

Master Nikos' lips quirked. "Of course she has. My apologies. We're overly protective of you, I know. For all the grief we've laid on you, you are precious to us."

Valeria almost smiled. Her eyes were trying to go misty—a last remnant of the easy tears of pregnancy. "I know that, sir," she said. "I won't do anything foolish. I promise."

He patted her hand a little awkwardly—such gestures were foreign to him—and led his stallion on past toward the head of the caravan.

Valeria finished tightening the girth with a little too much help from Sabata. He was losing patience. He could never understand why caravans took so long to move. If he had had any say in it, they would have been gone an hour ago.

Valeria slapped his questing nose aside and swung into the saddle. He nipped at her foot, but he did not swing his hindquarters or try to buck. He knew better.

His flash of temper made her laugh. She was still grinning when Kerrec rode up beside her. He grinned back and stole a kiss.

"You're in a fine mood this morning," she said.

"So are you." He let the reins fall on Petra's neck and turned to scan the faces of the riders who had come out to see them off. Everyone was there, from the youngest rider-candidate to the First Riders who would stay behind to welcome the Called and dance the Midsummer Dance.

Valeria's eyes lingered on each face. All of her yearmates were staying behind to continue their studies, along with the rest of the recently Called. She caught herself committing them to memory, as if she never expected to see them again.

She shook herself before she fell any deeper into foolishness. She was only going away for a season or two. The Mountain was still home and always would be, however far she traveled.

Still, this was a new thing she and Kerrec were doing. No one could be sure what would come of it. Then there was Maurus' message. She was not fool enough to think that because armies had been defeated and mages destroyed, others would not spring up to take their place.

For today she would focus on her increasingly fractious stallion and her still recovering body and try not to wallow too much in the last sight of the school that she would enjoy until at least the coming of winter. The caravan was beginning to move. The sun was up and the night's mist was blowing away. It was a glorious morning, a fine day to be riding to the imperial city.

Morag kept a careful eye on her daughter. Valeria, like most young things, suffered from delusions of invincibility. She was still recovering from a hard birth—harder than she or her otherwise perceptive lover seemed to understand.

If Morag had had any hope of being listened to, she would have kept Valeria in the wagon from the start. But Valeria was a rider. She had to ride—it was as vital to her as breathing. So, it seemed, was her insistence on riding the wildest of her three mounts.

God or no, the beast was being an idiot. Morag let him know it in no uncertain terms.

She was somewhat gratified that he deigned to notice. He still jigged and danced, but he stopped plunging and flinging himself about. After a while he settled even more, until he was walking more or less quietly, with only an occasional toss of the head or lash of the tail.

Valeria was still riding with that upright and beautiful carriage which distinguished the riders of the school, but Morag could see the subtle stiffness in her shoulders. Just as Morag decided to comment on it, Valeria swung her mount in toward the wagon and stepped from his back to the wagon's bed.

It was prettily done. Morag acknowledged it with a sniff. Valeria was a little pale but otherwise well enough.

The tension left Morag's own shoulders as Valeria made herself comfortable amid the bags and bundles that Morag had agreed to carry for the riders. The nurse, who was no fool, handed the baby over to her mother.

Valeria did not melt as some women did in the presence of their offspring. Her affection was a fiercer thing. She cradled the small blanket-wrapped body in her lap, head tilted slightly, and watched the child sleep.

Morag was growing drowsy herself. The wagon's rocking and the clopping of hooves and the slowly rising warmth of the mountain summer were incitement to sleep.

She had little need to guide the mule. The caravan surrounded her with protections as strong as she could manage herself. It was full of mages, after all.

They were quiet about it, but they were on guard. Very

little would get past them unless they let it. They had learned that lesson all too well.

Morag slid into a doze. She kept her awareness of the road and the caravan and the magic that surrounded it, but her consciousness slipped free.

It wandered for a while, drifting into Imbria and passing by her husband and children who were there. That was a pleasant dream, and it made her smile.

Gradually the dream darkened. It came on like a summer storm, a wall of cloud rolling in from the east. There was no clear vision in it, only formless darkness and the howl of wind.

A tower rose on a bleak hilltop like one of the old forgotten fortresses in her native Eriu. Wind and rain battered it. Lightning struck it and cast it down.

In the ruins where it had been, the earth opened like a mouth. The heart of it was nothingness.

That nothingness swallowed everything. Earth and sky vanished. There was nothing left but oblivion.

Valeria gulped air. In her dream there had been nothing to breathe, nothing to see, nothing at all except the Unmaking.

She lay in her nest of bundles and bags. Dappled sunlight shifted over her. Her daughter stirred in her arms.

She welcomed every bit of it—even the knot in her back and the whimper that turned to a wail as Grania woke to pangs of hunger. In Valeria's dream, it had all gone. The Unmaking had taken everything.

She surrendered Grania to the nurse and sat up in the wagon bed, rocking with it as it descended a long slope.

From the driver's seat, her mother looked over her shoulder. Morag's green eyes were unusually dark.

"You saw, too," Valeria said. The words slipped out of her, too quick to catch.

Morag's nod was hardly more than a flicker of the eyelids.

"That's not good," Valeria said. "If it's as strong as this, this close to the Mountain..."

"Maybe you should turn back," said Morag.

"We can't do that."

"But if the Mountain can protect you—"

"Who will protect the empress?"

"Doesn't she have every order of mages at her command?"

"Not against this."

Morag turned on the bench, leaving the mule to find its own way. "What about the baby, then?"

Valeria's glance leaped to the bundle in the nurse's arms. Her face flushed. She had not thought that far at all.

"I'm not a good mother, am I?" she said. "I love her. I'd kill anyone who laid a hand on her. But there's so much more to the world than that one thing."

"There is," Morag said in a tone that gave nothing away.

"She doesn't come first," Valeria said. "You knew it before I did."

"I know you," Morag said. "You're not meant for the small and homely things."

That was the truth. Valeria had not expected it to hurt quite so much. All the dreams she had had while she carried Grania, the things she had imagined that she would do, beginning with the simple human task of feeding her, had melted as soon as Grania saw the daylight. The agony of bearing her and the torment of the Unmaking had come too thoroughly between them.

Valeria shook her head, sharp and short. She was making excuses.

The truth was much simpler. Valeria was born this way. No amount of wishing could change her.

Grania had finished nursing. Portia's eyes asked and her arms stretched out, offering her to Valeria.

Valeria shook her head again, just as sharp as before. She turned back to her mother. "Will you take her? Just until we see what's happening in Aurelia?"

"That would be sensible," Morag said. "Unless her father objects."

"He won't," said Valeria. At least, she thought, not to that. He would agree that Grania was safer in Imbria than at the heart of whatever was coming. What he would say to Valeria's making the decision without him...

She would face that when it came. They had the journey. She could still see him happy, delighting in his child. Before the clouds rolled in. Before the world's weight was on them again, as sooner or later it always seemed to be.

Chapter Ten

Kerrec found his daughter fascinating and somewhat terrifying. She was so small and so utterly dependent on her elders, and yet the patterns that took shape around her promised to be as wide as the world.

Even more terrifying was what happened to his heart when he held her in his lap. He was a cold creature—all his passion was given to his art and to Valeria. Even his father's magic had not been enough to give him a warm heart.

When he looked at his daughter, he burned so hot he did not recognize himself. He had heard of people who would die for their children—women usually, mothers possessed of a love so fierce there was no end to it. He had thought those claims exaggerated until he held this mite of a thing in his hands, wet and squalling from her mother's womb, and knew they were a dim shadow of the truth.

Time's passage did not lessen this feeling at all, but it did teach him to contain it. From being so full he could hardly think, he advanced to merely being besotted. Eventually he supposed he would simply be madly in love, and that would be the way of it for as long as he was alive.

Madly in love, he could understand. He had that for Valeria. He did his best to see this in a similar light, if only to make the rest of life easier.

He had traveled the road from the Mountain so often that it was nearly as familiar as the way from his rooms in the school to the stallions' stable. But Grania's presence in her grandmother's wagon made it all seem new. He was more alert than he had ever been, more watchful for any sign of danger.

He could laugh at himself, recognizing the stallion's instinct to protect his offspring, but his wariness was no less for that. He had been ambushed on this road before and carried off to torments he would never forget, no matter how old the scars were or how thoroughly they had healed.

Nothing like that would happen now. Those enemies were dead, and their plot in the end had failed. Whatever new evil was brewing, the riders were no longer cursed with naiveté. They would never be caught off guard again.

As a First Rider, Kerrec lent his magic to the working of wards and his strength to sustaining them. By the third day out from the Mountain, the spells were strong enough to stand on their own. No one rider needed to watch over them.

All the while he focused on protecting the caravan, he was aware under his skin of his lover and her mother and his daughter whom they guarded. A riders' caravan had never brought women who were not Valeria with it before, let alone a baby. Kerrec had thought that some of the riders would grumble, but they were almost as besotted with Grania as he was.

There was always someone riding beside the wagon or even sitting in it, hovering over the baby and, when she was not riding among them, Valeria. Grania was never alone and never unprotected. Her mother and grandmother slept with her at night and guarded her by day with an intensity that began to make Kerrec uneasy.

Between those two and himself, Kerrec would give little for the chances of anyone who presumed to lay a hand on Grania. But there was more to it than that.

They knew something. He wanted to believe they were not hiding it from him deliberately, but at camp in the evenings, Valeria had little to say though she was perfectly willing to join with him in other ways than words. Her mother was preoccupied with the nurse and the baby. No one else knew there was anything to notice.

He resolved to wait them out. Whatever it was, it would not strike the caravan without raising the alarm.

To be sure of that, Kerrec heightened the defenses with a portion of the magic he had from his father. Now the earth was on the alert and the land was armed. Whatever came would have to contend with the deep magic of the empire as well as the stallions and their riders.

The working came wonderfully easily. Horse magic and imperial magic flowed together. They were all one. There was no division within them.

Kerrec had not expected that. As always, the Mountain strengthened some powers and suppressed others. He had been growing unawares, becoming something quite other than he had been before.

It was not a frightening prospect, though it fluttered his heart somewhat. There was a profound rightness in it. As he rode out of the mountains, he basked in magic that was whole and more than whole.

He would never take it for granted again. Nor would he forget that the higher his fortunes rose, the lower they could fall.

Valeria could feel Kerrec watching her. She had not wanted to worry him unnecessarily, but he was too perceptive. He knew she was keeping something from him.

He would not ask. When they lay together, he said nothing but a murmur of endearments. Time and again, she meant to say something, but she let each moment pass. She was a coward and she knew it, but she could not seem to help herself.

The longer she waited, the harder it was to break the silence. She had to do it soon. The days were passing and the road was growing shorter. The time would come when Morag left the caravan and turned toward Imbria. Grania would go with her—but Grania's father would quite naturally want a say in it.

The night before Morag was to go, Valeria sat up late with her. The nurse snored softly in the tent.

It was a clear night, starlit and warm. Valeria rocked Grania in her lap. "I swear," she said, "she smiled at me today. It wasn't gas pains, either."

"No doubt," said Morag. "She's waking to the world as they all do. She knows her mother, too."

Valeria's mood was as changeable as summer weather. It

clouded swiftly and completely. "Does she? How long will that last?"

"I'll make sure she doesn't forget."

"Maybe it will be only a few days," Valeria said. "Maybe a week. Or two. Just a little while."

"Maybe," Morag said.

Valeria resisted the urge to clutch Grania to her breast. That would only alarm her and set her crying. "Gods. What are we doing?"

"Keeping her safe," said Morag. "One thing we can say for all those royal and noble conspirators. Unless they need fodder for their wars, they seldom trouble to notice the lower classes. As long as we keep our taxes paid and our heads down, they stay out of our way."

Valeria nodded reluctantly. "What's another peasant's brat? Even if they knew to look for her, they wouldn't know where to begin."

"Wouldn't they?"

Valeria started violently. Grania woke and opened her mouth to wail. Kerrec gathered her up and crooned at her. She subsided, staring rapt at his firelit face. After a moment she crooned back.

Valeria was not breathing. Kerrec knelt and then sat beside her, careful not to jostle the baby. Grania gurgled at him.

That *was* a smile. Even Morag could not fail to see it.

It gave Valeria little joy. Her heart stabbed with guilt.

Kerrec looked up from his daughter's face to her mother's. His gaze was level. "I think you have something to tell me," he said.

Valeria swallowed. Her throat was dry. "I'm sorry," she said. "I should have—I have this terrible habit of—"

"Yes," he said. "What is it? What do you see?"

"Unmaking," she said baldly.

There was a brief, perfect silence. Then he said, "Ah." Only that.

"We didn't destroy it," she said, "or the people who worship it. It's still there. It still wants us. We're everything it isn't, you see."

"I see," he said. "The coronation?"

"Or the Dance. Probably both. Briana is wound up in it so tightly I can't see where she begins and the rest ends. It's Maurus' vision and more. They—whoever they are—have opened doors that should have been forever shut."

He nodded slowly. His eyes were dark in the firelight. "So you'll send Grania out of the way."

"I hope so," said Valeria. "Are you angry?"

"No," he said. "If this storm swallows everything, she'll be no safer in Imbria than in Aurelia. But she might last a little longer."

"She's going to last a lifetime," Valeria said fiercely. "I'll stop it. I don't care what I have to do, but I will do it."

"So shall we all," he said. He held his finger for Grania to clasp. She reached for it with clear intent and caught hold, gripping as if she would never let go.

They parted with Morag at the crossroads, half a day's wagon ride from Imbria. Grania was asleep in the nurse's arms. Valeria should not have been disappointed—this was a six-weeks-old child, too young to know anything about grief or farewells—but the heart was not prone to reason.

She kissed the small warm forehead. For an instant she paused. Was it too warm? Was Grania brewing up a fever?

If she was, all the better that she was going to Morag's house instead of traveling on to Aurelia. The wisewoman would look after her.

It hurt to pull away. Valeria embraced her mother quickly and tightly, then half strode, half ran toward Sabata. If Morag said anything, Valeria never heard it through the roaring in her ears.

Kerrec took longer to say goodbye, but even that was only a few moments. When Valeria looked back, he was riding toward her with a perfectly still face and the wagon was rattling away over the hill to Imbria.

Valeria stiffened her spine. She had done the best she knew how. Grania was as safe as anyone could be.

The rest of them were riding into the whirlwind. She reached for Kerrec's hand.

It was already reaching for hers. With hands clasped, riding knee to knee, they turned their faces toward Aurelia.

Chapter Eleven

Briana was playing truant. There was a hall full of nobles waiting for her to open their council and another hall full of servants intent on making this coronation more splendid than any that had gone before, and a temple full of priests awaiting a rite that she could not put off. And here she was, dressed in worn leather breeches, creeping off to Riders' Hall to see if Corcyra had foaled yet.

Her heart was remarkably light. Too light, she might have thought. It was a kind of madness, as if after a long and arduous struggle she had come to the summit of a mountain—and leaped.

The earth lay far below, just visible through a scud of cloud. Her body would break upon it, she knew with perfect surety. But while she rode so high, all that mattered was the joy of soaring through infinite space.

It was still early morning. The air was cool and sea-scented. The night's fog had burned off already, promising a warm day later.

As she walked down the passage between the palace and Riders' Hall, her back straightened and her shoulders came back. The weight of her office was no more than she could bear—she was born and bred for it and trained from childhood to carry it. But even she needed to escape now and then.

The passage had numerous turnings and branches. The one she chose ended in the stable, which at the moment was empty except for a stocky bay mare and the young black, Corcyra. All of her sisters had foaled days ago. They were in pastures outside of Aurelia now, running with their offspring and getting fat on the rich green grass.

With just the two of them in residence, the stalls were open for the mares to come and go. They could go out into the riding court if they liked, which at the moment they did not choose to do. The bay Lady was nose-down in a manger full of sweet hay. Corcyra dozed in a stall.

Briana's eyes narrowed. The mare seemed placid. Her belly drooped and her sides seemed oddly flat. Her rump was sunken, her tail limp. She looked just as she should at the very end of her pregnancy.

"She'll go tonight," Quintus the stableman said as he came up beside Briana. "She's crossing her legs and holding her breath as it is."

Briana shook her head and sighed. "Mares," she said.

Corcyra barely acknowledged her as she came into the

stall. Briana stroked the sleek neck and rubbed the little lean ears. "Only a little while longer," she said.

The bay Lady snorted derisively. She was a horse by courtesy and physical semblance, but in the world of the spirit she was greater than gods. It was her choice to live here in Aurelia, pretend to be the empress's favorite mount and bide her time for some purpose known only to herself.

Briana would never presume to ask what it was. The Lady had chosen Briana for her rider—a thing no Lady had done in a thousand years. Ladies lived on the Mountain. They showed themselves to no mortals except those select few riders who attended them in their high pastures.

This Lady came and went as she would and did as she pleased. Briana existed to serve her, no more and no less.

Maybe that was why she had chosen Briana. An empress more than any needed to be reminded that there were powers higher than she. In front of this blocky, cobby, yet rather pretty little horse, Briana understood the meaning of humility.

This morning the Lady was even more inscrutable than usual. Some of the reason for that came clear in Quintus' words. "I had a message last night, lady. The riders will be here by tonight, or tomorrow morning at latest."

No doubt a similar message was waiting among the hundreds that Briana had eluded in coming here. She nodded and sighed a little. "Good," she said. "I'm glad. They're all safe? No one's missing?"

"Everyone's well," Quintus said. "The road was clear and nothing got in their way."

"Send word when they come," Briana said. "Will you do that for me?"

"Of course, lady," said Quintus.

Briana withdrew regretfully from the stall. Duty was calling more loudly with every hour that passed.

She paused to stroke the Lady's neck and head and feed her a bit of sugar. The Lady ate every scrap and demanded more. Briana laughed, spreading her hands. "Look, see. You ate it all."

The Lady snorted wetly over her hand. Briana grimaced and wiped it on her breeches.

She opened her mouth to say something appropriately cutting. The words never came. The Lady's head had turned, her ears pricked.

Quintus was still outside Corcyra's stall. Corcyra had roused abruptly and was circling in a way Briana had long since learned to recognize. Her body was tense and her mind focused inward. Her tail flicked restlessly. She pawed, paced then pawed again.

She went down abruptly. As she dropped, water gushed. Briana started forward but forced herself to be still.

The mare stiffened in spasm. The silver bubble of the caul appeared under her tail, with the foal dark inside. Briana saw the sharp curve of hooves—one behind the other—and the blunter shape of the nose.

It was all as it should be. Every one of this season's foals had been, as if their ancestry protected them from the dangers of mortal birth. They were a white god's get, sired by the stallion Sabata over the course of long summer nights.

The foal seemed to take a very long time to be born. It

could not even be half a turn of the glass, or Quintus would have been in the stall, doing what needed to be done. Instead he stood with arms folded, watching calmly.

When half the foal was out, it broke the caul, scrambling with its front feet, digging into the straw of the stall. Its head was already up and seeking, its lips working. It butted its mother's side imperiously, demanding the teat, though she was still racked with the pains of birth.

It was dark as all these god-begotten foals had been. There was a thumbprint of white on its forehead. When it dried, no doubt it would be black as Corcyra. Maybe it would stay black, or more likely it would turn grey as it grew, like its father.

Almost before the rest of it emerged from the mare, Briana knew it was a filly like all of its siblings. Even so new, it was a solidly built young thing, with a big square head and broad haunches.

That was its father's legacy. So were the eyes that turned to her. They were preternaturally bright and focused.

One last, powerful spasm cast the whole of it in the straw. The mare lay for a moment, breathing hard. Then she raised her head, peering along her body at the wet and glistening thing that had come out of her.

Her nostrils fluttered. The filly stretched out her nose. They touched.

Briana's throat closed. Maybe it was foolish, but that first touch, that moment of tender recognition, never failed to melt her heart.

The Lady's breath tickled her ear. She pressed her cheek to the broad, flat red-brown one and trailed fingers down the soft muzzle.

The Lady had foaled in her time, Briana knew without words. It was a great thing, a blessed thing. The gods were glad because of it.

But now Briana had to be empress. Her hour's escape had stretched too long. The empire would hardly fall about her ears, but it did need her hand to steady it—especially now that she was about to be crowned.

The Lady offered her shoulder, then her back. It would be ungracious to refuse the gift. Briana caught a handful of mane and swung astride.

Bareback and bridleless, she rode out of the stable into the sudden glare of daylight.

The outer court was full of people and horses. Most of the horses were stocky and grey or white, and most of the riders were dressed in grey or brown. They rode with a particular grace and quiet elegance that persisted even after they had dismounted.

Briana laughed for joy. Two of the riders turned together. They were shoulder to shoulder, and they were almost exactly of a height. One smiled, warmth flooding into silver eyes. The other grinned as wide and white as a boy, but there was nothing male about her.

"Kerrec!" cried Briana. "Valeria!" She hardly remembered leaving the Lady's back or leaping toward them until she found herself with arms wrapped around both of them, hugging them tight.

Her brother let her go first and held her at arm's length, searching her face keenly.

She had last seen him broken and half mad, all but destroyed by hatred and pain. Now he was whole again. He was beautiful.

Not that she would say such a thing—he was vain enough already. She settled for a grin and a deceptively ordinary word. "You're looking well," she said.

"And you," said Kerrec. "The burden of empire agrees with you."

"Not always," she said wryly. "I'm running away this morning."

"It looks as if you were running back when we came in," Valeria said.

As Briana nodded, Kerrec caught her glance and held it. "Have you found anything?"

"Nothing out of the ordinary," Briana answered. "And you?"

"All's quiet," said Kerrec.

"They're biding their time," Valeria said.

"I'm sure they are," said Briana. In due time she would find that troubling, but for the moment she let the joy of their coming overwhelm everything else.

The rest of the riders had hung back, but as she turned to face them, she met a circle of smiles and the occasional grin, with here and there an inclination of the head. Since riders never bowed to any mortal, that was as royal an obeisance as she was likely to get.

She bowed to them all as was proper and greeted the Master with deep respect. "Sir. You've come in good time."

"So I gather," Master Nikos said. "We go into seclusion in the morning, but tonight we're still in the world. Perhaps, after all our day's duties are done, we may dine together?"

"I'll be honored," Briana said.

"Tonight, then," he said.

No other words were said, but as he withdrew to duties that she had no doubt were pressing, the rest of the riders scattered as well. Kerrec and Valeria stayed, but Briana could tell they were a little torn.

"Go on," she said. "I'll come back tonight."

Valeria nodded and smiled, and embraced her quickly. Kerrec took more time about it, kissing her forehead before he let her go. "It's good to be back," he said.

Brianna's eyes widened slightly. After all he had been through in or for Aurelia, that was remarkable.

It was wonderful. She kissed him back and sent him on his way.

The Lady was waiting, and so were her duties. This time Briana was glad to face them. The sooner she did that, the sooner she could come back to Riders' Hall.

Chapter Twelve

Valeria should have been reassured. The city of Aurelia was warded with such strong magics that her head buzzed. Nothing short of a god could get through such protections—and whatever the barbarian priests were, gods they were not.

Now the white gods had brought the Mountain's power to the city. The bay Lady had been there to welcome them, and she was stronger than all of them put together.

Everything that anyone could do had been done. The Dance would be safe. So would the empress.

And yet even in Riders' Hall, with the stallions safe in the stable and the riders settled into their rooms, Valeria could not help feeling that they had all missed something. She could not begin to say what it was, but her mind kept reaching for some scrap of knowledge it could not quite find. Something, somewhere, was not as it should be.

She would mention it tonight when they were all together. Surely others had felt it, too. They were all mages of patterns here. If a pattern was out of place, one of them should be able to detect it.

In the meantime she had horses to help settle and Quintus to meet again and a new foal to marvel at. By the time that was done, her room was ready in the hall and she was ready to rest.

She was not sharing the room with Kerrec. Beginning in the morning, all the riders would go into seclusion to prepare for the Dance. Since she was not riding in it, like the rest of the lesser riders, she would sleep and eat and perform her duties outside the wards.

She took great pains to face the separation with disciplined calm. It was not even worth acknowledging the part of her that wanted to know why she could not ride the Dance, too. Could she not master all the stallions? Was she not a stronger mage than any of them?

She was all of that. She was also a rider-candidate who had not yet been tested for Fourth Rider's rank. Last year the stallions had insisted that she ride in the Midsummer Dance, and Oda had come down off the Mountain to carry her. This year they were silent.

The Dance would proceed according to tradition—to the riders' manifest relief. Likewise according to tradition, Valeria would care for the stallions, wait on the riders until they went into seclusion and, when the day of the Dance came, serve as groom and servant.

There was a kind of guilty contentment in it. For once she was an honest rider-candidate. After the Dance, before the

Master went back to the Mountain, she would be tested. Then if she passed, there would be a new Fourth Rider in the world.

She went about her duties with as light a heart as she had had since she received Maurus' message. She saw that all three of her stallions were comfortable in their stalls, looked in on Kerrec's Petra and young Alea and paused by the mare's stall to assure herself yet again that, yes, Sabata's daughter looked exactly like him.

The sense of unease tried to come back when she left the stable and turned toward her room. She pushed it down. She needed to rest now—her whole body ached.

Her room was one of several along a nondescript corridor. It was tiny and ascetic, but it had a window that opened on one of the riding courts. The ranking riders had the floor above. This floor belonged to the lesser riders, most of whom, like Valeria, were taking advantage of the chance to rest after the long journey.

She lay on the bed, which was not as uncomfortable as it looked. Her insides felt strangely empty.

Grania was safe. No one not of the Mountain except Valeria's family even knew she had a child.

That was the way she wanted to keep it. If Kerrec was a rare target and Valeria rarer still, she hated to think of what their enemies might do to their daughter.

She had been going to tell Briana. Now she wondered if she should. Briana would be furious if that of all secrets was kept from her, but if it kept Grania out of danger, maybe it was worth it.

As if her thoughts had drawn him in, Kerrec squeezed

himself onto the narrow bed beside her. Guilt made her voice sharp. "Don't you have a bed of your own to lie in?"

"Yes, and it's wider than this one, too," he said. He made no move to go. "What are you angry at? Grania's better off where she is. Her grandmother loves her. I'm sure her grandfather adores her."

"And my brothers and sisters are spoiling her rotten." Valeria scowled at the ceiling. There was a crack in the beam just where the light struck it. "I'm not sorry she's there. She's well out of the way of whatever's coming. But I'm thinking maybe your sister shouldn't know about her. No one should outside of the Mountain or Imbria."

"No one but Briana," he said.

"But what if she—"

"What? You think she could betray us? She's the last person who would ever do such a thing."

Valeria could feel the heat of his temper though his voice was calm. No wonder, too. He was right. He usually was.

She did not have too much pride to admit it. "I know that. But if something happens to Briana and it's forced out of her, you know where they'll go. Grania is the last of your blood. Until Briana gets herself a consort, she's the only heir the empire has."

"She is not," Kerrec said—a little quickly, maybe. "I'm no longer in the line of succession, therefore neither is she. She's a rider's child. Blood binds her to no one but us. The riders are all the family she has."

"Maybe so," Valeria said, "but will that matter if the throne is empty and there's no one else to take it? Can you think of a more valuable pawn than a baby with that breeding?"

"All the more reason for my sister to know," he said. "She's entitled. She's mage enough not to let it slip."

Valeria barely heard him. She was just now realizing what she had said. She clutched at him until he grunted in protest. "Is that it? Is that what they're plotting? Did they find out somehow, and they're looking to get rid of Briana and put Grania in her place? That must mean—if it goes all the way to the council—if they're plotting to seize the empire through a regency—"

"Stop," he said quietly but so firmly that her mouth snapped shut. "If that is what's happening, Briana needs to know more than ever. She's in the best position to find and stamp out the treachery in her council."

Valeria could not reasonably argue with that. It did not keep her from trying. "I still think—"

"I know what you think," he said. "You never have trusted the highborn. Even me."

"That's not true," Valeria said.

"You know it is." He did not sound as if the knowledge caused him much pain. "Can you trust us just this once? Let my sister know."

"She's your daughter, too," Valeria said.

His brow arched. "You admit it?"

She hit him—not nearly hard enough in such close quarters, but it got his attention. "You know what I mean."

"Then I'll tell her," he said.

The knot inside Valeria, with the Unmaking inside of that, swelled so large she could hardly breathe. If she had had any breath left, she might have kept on arguing. As it was, she wrapped herself around him and pressed her head to his chest and let his heartbeat bring what calm it could.

His lips brushed her hair. "She's a rider, too, remember. Or did you forget?"

Valeria had forgotten. She flushed so hot he must have felt it through his shirt. "I'm sorry," she said. "I haven't been thinking."

"Not about that," he said. "You've been overly focused. It's a weakness we all have. All we can see is the Mountain. We forget there's anything beyond it."

"I more than anyone should know better," she said.

He did not deny it. But he did say, "That's why we've come here—to teach ourselves to look beyond the Mountain. I need you for that, and I need my sister. The three of us are notably stronger together than apart."

Valeria nodded. The Mountain was the empire's heart—that was the ancient tradition. Its magic and the emperor's were two halves of a whole.

It was significant that in this generation, both an emperor's firstborn and his heir had been Called by the gods. That had never happened before. What it meant, even Augurs and Seers did not know.

Valeria thought she could guess. The empire's heart and its head had been divided for a thousand years. Now they were to come together.

Grania might be the key. Or she might not.

Valeria could not see her daughter on the throne. None of the patterns around her pointed toward the empire. She was meant for the Mountain. Briana's heir must be the one who would do it—or maybe Briana herself.

First they all had to survive the coronation. Then Briana had to live long enough to take a husband and bear a child. Any plot against her would do its best to prevent that. It did not even have to kill her—simply keep her from doing her duty.

Or better yet, it could corrupt her. If she turned against the Mountain—

That would never happen. The Lady would not let it.

She might if it suited her divine and inscrutable purpose.

Valeria's head had begun to pound. All these gods and emperors and plots and counterplots were more than her poor peasant brain could stand. Life should be simple. Death should be clean, not tainted with Unmaking.

It was her fault for stumbling into this world of power and princes. If she had stayed in Imbria as her mother wanted her to, none of it would be any concern of hers—at least until the darkness came and everything vanished into it.

That was the trouble with destiny. Sooner or later it swallowed everyone. Valeria could be simple mindless prey, or she could fight back. She had that choice.

She held on to Kerrec as if he had been a rock in a storm. His arms were secure around her and his magic blessedly safe around that. For this little while, nothing could touch or trouble her.

She was not a woman to submit blindly to any man's protection. But she was also a mage, and she was learning to accept that the occasional power might be stronger than hers.

Kerrec's certainly was. Someday she might be his equal in skill—as in raw strength she was his superior—but for now she was an apprentice and he was a master.

It was unusually humbling to contemplate that. Humility was a rider's virtue. It was good for her to cultivate it.

Sleep was closing in on her. She fought it by reflex, then sighed and let it have its way.

Chapter Thirteen

After her morning's fit of truancy, Briana found the weight of the day a little lighter. She had eluded a council and a session of the court, but one duty she was pleased to perform. It was the first rite of her coronation, the first step that would seal her to the empire.

It was also the oldest of the rites and the most nearly solitary, with no one to share in it but the gods' servants who celebrated it with her. Part of its lesson was humility and part was remembrance—of who she was, what she was and where she had come from. Before every court and every gathering of the people, she was to remember that in her essence she was alone. No one else could be what she was or share what she had, either the good or the ill.

The rite began shortly after noon, as the long summer day began its slow descent into evening. Priests and priestesses

of Sun and Moon met her in the palace, blessed and conse-
crated her and led her outside the city by a way that was only
taken when the imperial heir was about to be crowned.

She found herself in an ancient and overgrown garden,
where a long-forgotten door led to a passage that might be
older than the palace itself. The scent of magic was strong in
it. Parts of it might not be properly in the world—Briana felt
strange as her guides led her through them, as if her substance
had shifted and subtly changed, then been restored to itself.

*There are more magics in the world than your orders may
know of.*

At first she did not know where the words had come
from. They were in her head, clear and faintly luminous.
Then she recognized the Lady's presence.

It was vanishingly rare for the Lady to resort to words. Because of that, they burned themselves in Briana's mind. Someday maybe she would understand why they were so important.

Today she descended deeper into the earth and farther into
the heart of her empire's magic. She was long out of her reck-
oning. If her guides were not to be trusted, she could vanish and no one would ever know what had become of her.

They were properly inscrutable, four shaven-headed men
in saffron robes and four women with plaits of hair to their
heels and gowns of stark and pristine whiteness. Two of each
paced ahead of her and two of each behind.

When she had lost all sense of time, they began to chant
in the most ancient of the hieratic languages. The men's deep
voices boomed beneath the women's sweet descant. Briana
was no scholar, but she caught enough to recognize a hymn
to the setting Sun and an invocation of the rising Moon.

The land of Aurelia had been alive inside her since her father left for his war. He had given her that most imperial of gifts to hold and protect until he came back, and to keep if he died in battle. After he was killed, she had thought the full power was hers.

She had been a child, with a child's understanding. This took her breath away—and it was only the first of eight days of ritual and preparation before the throne was hers by the full rite.

Today she was to dedicate herself at the shrine of the first emperor, to recall his life and sufferings and remember from what he had come and to what he had risen. Tomorrow would be another rite in the city, in the Temple of Divine Compassion. Then each day thereafter she would dedicate herself in a different temple, until she came to the Temple of Sun and Moon and the crowning that made her surely and forever empress.

As Briana's mind ran ahead from temple to temple, the tunnel turned a corner and opened into a cavern. The walls were dim and far away, and the air was full of the sigh of the sea.

They emerged from the cave's mouth into pellucid light. The long summer twilight had begun. The sun rode low over the sea, and the waxing moon hovered almost at the zenith. Both their faces were stained as if with blood.

Briana stood on a rocky escarpment that rose sheer out of the waves. The city was hidden behind the jut of cliff. She could feel it inside her in all its manifold beauty and ugliness, but it seemed faint and far away, as if she had only known it in a dream.

Here the first Aurelius had come after his whole clan and

tribe had been slaughtered by a bandit king. There had been no city here then, only a village of fishermen who eked out their meager living with petty piracy. He was wounded, grieving and in despair. The gods had turned against him, and mortals were only too happy to oblige them.

He had lain down on this cliff to die. But as he offered himself to the powers that so clearly loathed him, one had come to him with a glimmer of hope.

In that vision it wore no body. It spoke to him out of a white light, filling him with knowledge beyond words. It showed him the shape of a Mountain and a steep and stony track, and then a high pasture full of horses. There were mares and foals and a band of stallions roving the edges, while the king stallion paid homage to the ancient and snow-white mare who ruled them all.

Briana saw the vision as he had seen it. Standing where he had fallen, she knew the intensity of his despair and the shock of his incomprehension. What in the gods' name did a herd of masterless horses have to do with his life or imminent death?

One of her guides touched her hand. She turned where the priestess directed her. A narrow track ran along the edge of the crag, ending at the gate of a tiny and visibly ancient temple.

The gate was open. Light shone from within. It was as simple and homely as candlelight, but it was born of magic.

"Come and pray," the priestess said—the first words any of them had spoken since they came to her in the palace.

Briana inclined her head. When she paced toward the shrine, her guides stayed behind. This was hers to do alone, as Aurelius had been when he followed his vision.

She was serene inside herself, basking in the long light and the stark beauty of the place. Aurelius's bafflement and slowly dawning hope shimmered around her, set deep in the memory of these stones. Each heir of his line had remembered as she was doing, and each memory had made the magic stronger. After a thousand years, this was a place of power like few others in the world.

The Mountain was stronger by far, and yet it drew its magic from the same source. That source was inside her, growing and blooming, until in eight days she became indelibly a part of it.

She paused just inside the gate. It was a very small temple indeed, hardly larger than a stall in the palace stable. Pillars of dove-grey stone held up a dome that had once been painted to imitate the sky. Faint suggestions of blue paint lingered along the edges, and she could see where a sun had been—with flakes of gold still clinging to the plastered stone—and a silver moon.

If the walls had ever been painted, none of that was left. They were starkly plain and simply beautiful. She stood in the center under the opening of the dome and looked up. Directly overhead, still wan with daylight, shone a single star.

Briana reached as if to touch it, then smiled at herself. She was at peace here as she had not been since last she went to the Mountain. All of her troubles and confusion had faded away. This was her place and this was her world. She was born to rule it.

It seemed appropriate that she should kneel in the light of that star. She offered no formal prayer. As with the Lady, words were superfluous. She gave her heart and spirit and offered her magic to the empire that had begun in this place.

Night was falling. So was Briana. Darkness came not from the sky but up from below, rising out of the earth that a moment before had been so perfectly hers.

This was nothing that she or any mortal could ever own. It was absolute darkness, night everlasting, oblivion incarnate.

The trap had been waiting, baited with serenity and poisoned with complacence. The Unmaking opened under her feet. The star above the dome shifted and changed. It was a spear of diamond, a weapon forged of living malice.

Behind it she saw a man's face. He seemed to be standing in a tower window, spear poised in his hand. She might have taken him for a priest, with his gaunt cheeks and black-robed body, but there was nothing holy about him.

His eyes were so pale they seemed blind, but they all too obviously were not. He balanced the spear easily, lightly, as a warrior might. His lips curved in a faint, mocking smile.

Briana was not a hot-tempered person, but that smile woke in her such rage that she reached down into the earth, even against the Unmaking, and drew from the well of the empire's magic. The tides of oblivion did their utmost to overwhelm it, but it held its ground. It roared up in her.

Far from flinching, the man in black laughed. She snatched at the thing she had unleashed—but it was too late. The trap was sprung.

The mage-bolt flew unerring toward its target. He flicked the spear sidewise. The bolt struck it amidships—and rebounded.

She was a poor strategist and a worse ruler, and there was nothing whatsoever she could do about it. The blast of power that should have smitten the black priest turned back on her with redoubled force.

She had no time to raise a shield. She had all the time in the world to see it coming and know that when it struck, it would destroy her.

She wrenched herself aside. The bolt missed the heart—but only just. The lash of it cracked through her body.

The Unmaking receded. The sky was clean again. Both the priest and the false star had vanished. Briana could not feel anything at all.

She floated above the temple, as remote as a god. If she deigned to look down, she could see the tiny charred thing that had belonged to her.

Others were scattered not far from it, broken figures in fire-darkened saffron and singed and blackened white. They were all dead, her priests and priestesses. The flames had devoured them.

A shadow of the rage that had brought all this on was still in her. She should never have let it overwhelm her. But this was a welcome warmth, a focus in the vagueness that had become the world.

She would not surrender. Oblivion beckoned, but she refused the temptation. Sorrow and pain lay below in the flesh she had escaped.

She was not afraid of pain. Sorrow was harder. She steeled herself to face it.

Chapter Fourteen

Briana was a long time coming. Valeria slipped into the kitchen for a loaf of bread and a nub of sausage. She got her hands slapped for the theft, but her belly was glad of it.

Kerrec and the Master were made of sterner stuff. They spent the time in meditation, preparing for the gathering of magic that would begin in the morning.

When she had eaten enough to hold her, she took the most leisurely way back to the room where they were sitting. The kitchen had a garden with a wall that, if one climbed to the top and perched on one corner, allowed one to look down across the city to the harbor. It was a pleasant place to watch the sun set.

Valeria should have been in a bright mood. She was safe in Aurelia, no one had been hurt or captured on the way from the Mountain and she was about to dine with a dear friend. But her mind had darkened as the day waned.

As she drew near the wall, an odd sound made her shoulders tighten. It was like the growl of the sea when a storm was coming in, but the sky was clear and the air serene.

The small hairs rose on her arms. That was no human or mortal sound. Somewhere close by, a mage was fighting for her life—and her enemy wielded the Unmaking.

The seed of it within Valeria called to that other power. It took every scrap of will she had to keep it warded and apart.

The cooks—even those who had a smattering of magic—had sensed nothing. No use to alarm them. Valeria made her way through them as quickly but as casually as she could, then once she was out of sight, bolted toward the riders' tower.

The Master and the First Rider were just as she had left them. Clear evening light fell across their faces. They looked remarkably alike, the old and the young, both with the sharp-cut features of old emperors.

A rider had no family but the school and no past but the Call. That was tradition. Kerrec and Valeria had not been able or willing to observe it.

Master Nikos came from an older time. Valeria had never paused to reflect on who he might have been or what town or lineage he had left behind. It had never mattered.

Still, in this pellucid and deceptively peaceful evening, she could not help but notice the resemblance between the late imperial prince and the Master of the riders. Probably they were kin. Gods knew, enough nobles had been Called from this city, though before Kerrec, the Mountain had never gone so far as to Call the emperor's firstborn son.

It mattered no more now than it ever had. Her mind was avoiding the thing that had brought it here. Something had roused the Unmaking, and something else had fought it and lost.

Valeria gathered herself to break into the riders' trance. Master Nikos was closer to full awareness than Kerrec. His eyes moved under the lids, flicking as if they scanned swiftly down a written page.

She drew breath to speak.

Kerrec's eyes snapped open. They were the color of molten silver.

A bolt of pure white agony lanced through Valeria. The pains of birth had been nothing to this. They, for all their deadliness, had ended in joy.

There was no joy in this. Somehow she kept her feet. She saw the same terrible pain in Kerrec's eyes.

"Briana," she said. "Oh, dear gods."

Kerrec was on his feet. Valeria was already running. She was dimly aware of Master Nikos following with remarkable speed.

He kept his wits enough to summon the rest of the riders as he ran. Valeria's summons aimed higher.

Their stallions were waiting in the outer court. They were saddled and bridled and ready to go.

Valeria caught Quintus' eye in the shadow of a corner and nodded slightly. Maybe he had failed the testing after the Call, but he was a horse mage. He had known.

She sprang astride Sabata and aimed him toward the gate. It opened just before he burst through it.

The rest of the stallions followed. None of the riders carried a weapon, but they needed none. They had their magic and the white gods.

They roared through the city like a wave of the sea. Valeria made no effort to direct Sabata. He was following paths that had little to do with mortal roads.

The gate he chose was not one she had seen before. It was small and hidden in a corner of the wall. It was barely wide enough for one rider and just tall enough for Gunnar to pass.

They rode out onto a long pale-grey strand. Breakers rolled in and sighed out again. There had been a road once, but wind and waves had battered it and sand had drifted over it.

The stallions ran light-footed where it had been. Up above them rose a promontory. It seemed hardly taller than one of the city's towers, but as they drew nearer, Valeria could see that it was both steep and high.

A track wound up it. Like the gate, it was barely wider than a single horse. Sabata ascended as if it had been a level street. The rest of the stallions clattered and scrambled behind.

Valeria would have given a year of her life for a gull's wings. Then she could have flown up over the crag toward the thing that waited on the summit. What had risen there should never have touched that high and holy place. It should never have been at all, not in this world or any other.

Valeria was tainted with it. It hounded the empire and its rulers. Enemies wielded it, but it was older by far than they.

It had killed the Emperor Artorius on the battlefield. Now it had struck Briana.

Valeria was deeply and viscerally angry. That anger carried her almost as strongly as Sabata did. He sprang up over the summit onto a brief level.

There on the windy height in the last of the daylight, she saw the temple in smoldering ruin and eight priests and priestesses lying where the fire had flung them. She did not remember leaving the saddle. As she sprinted toward the fallen columns and the melted and broken gate, someone else passed her.

Kerrec's feet barely touched the ground. He darted through the wreckage toward a crumpled shape that lay in the center. Valeria followed only a little more slowly.

Briana was neither a tiny nor a childlike woman. She was as tall as Valeria and somewhat more strongly built. For all the hours she spent sitting in court or council, she devoted nearly as many to riding and dancing and practicing with weapons.

This shrunken thing could not be Briana. It lay on its back, its eyes open and blank, staring sightlessly at the sky.

She looked as if she had been washed in fire. Her face and hands were blistered and her clothes were charred. In places they still smoldered.

Valeria knew too well the mark of a mage-bolt. This had not killed—not quite. Briana clung to life by a thread.

Kerrec knelt by his sister's side. With exquisite and painful care, he gathered her in his arms.

Petra picked his way through the rubble and lowered himself to his knees. Kerrec mounted, cradling Briana. The stallion rose as smoothly as he could.

The rest of the riders moved among the dead, gathering them together and laying them reverently in the broken temple. None but Briana had survived. Whatever defenses they had had, those had not saved them.

Sabata pawed imperiously. They were done here. It was time to go.

His impatience shook Valeria out of the trance of shock. She mounted with much less than her usual grace and let him carry her where he would.

Petra led the line on the descent. Sabata brought up the rear. As he bore Valeria away from the temple and its burden of dead, the anger rose so high and strong that she could not contain it. She loosed it in fire—striking with the knowledge even as she did it that Briana had done exactly the same thing. It was written in the patterns that coiled all around this place.

Valeria was fortunate that whatever enemy Briana had been trying to destroy was gone. There was nothing to fight, and no trap left. Her bolt, unlike Briana's, flew true.

The temple collapsed in a cloud of ash and acrid smoke. Valeria shuddered. Almost inadvertently, she had unmade it.

Gods forbid it be an omen.

It was dark when the riders returned to the city. All the gates were shut and the walls warded against the night, but the stallions had no concern for such things. They passed through as if there had been no barrier at all, either mortal or magical.

The city appeared to know nothing of what the riders carried back to the palace. The ways they took were almost empty, although the larger streets and alleyways were full of people crowding in for the coronation.

The palace blazed with light. Lords and servants alike labored far into the night to prepare for the great festival and holy rite. The arrival of a full quadrille of stallions and their grim-faced riders, the foremost of whom cradled the lifeless body of their empress, struck them with devastating force.

Kerrec knew how to speak to servants. It was bred into him as the Dance was bred into the stallions. He had hardly passed through the palace gate before he had a small army running to do his bidding.

By the time he reached Briana's rooms, a Healer was waiting and promising that the Master of the order would follow shortly. A bath was drawn, pungent with medicinal salts. Half a dozen mages of various orders either stood about already or came running while Kerrec surrendered his sister to the bath.

No one asked questions yet. First they had to keep Briana alive. Once she was carried out of the bath and wrapped in a light robe, the Healer set to work. The rest of the mages assisted him.

Valeria had nothing to do here. The other riders had either gone hunting whoever or whatever had done this or ridden to the temple with the news of the priests' destruction.

Kerrec was still giving orders in a brisk, dispassionate voice. The palace stirred and seethed like a hive with a wounded queen.

If Valeria had any sense she would retrieve her stallion and Kerrec's and go back to Riders' Hall. But neither Sabata nor Petra had stayed in the stable where she had left them. She could not tell exactly where they were, except it was somewhere within reach of the bay Lady.

They were being gods, damn them. And she was being useless.

Briana lay in a web of spells like a tangle of shining

threads. Valeria could see what each was meant to do, but she could also see how each had failed.

The mages did not seem to understand. They kept weaving their spells and applying their ointments and potions, treating the symptoms without comprehension of the disease.

Some wounds were best left open to heal. Bandages made them fester. These spells were bandages, and they were doing Briana no good at all.

Kerrec should have said something. He had the rank and the right. But he had found another focus for his anger and grief. As if his sister's fall had brought the late prince to life again, he summoned councils and commanded servants and sent guards to learn the causes and consequences of this devastation.

How like a man, Valeria thought, to turn away from human pain toward bloodless politics. Even while she thought it, she knew she was not being charitable. In the mood she was in, she could not make herself care.

It was not Valeria's place to argue with the Master of the Healers, or the Master of the Seers or the Mistress of the Wisewomen or the Chief Augur, either. But they were killing Briana.

The wisewoman stepped to the fore with chants and smokes and infusions of sweet-smelling herbs. As she passed her hands over Briana's body, Valeria reached across the bed and stopped them.

The spell dissipated in the smoke of sage and juniper and cedar. The wisewoman's anger rocked Valeria, but she was prepared for it.

She met that fierce, cold glare. "Stop," she said. "You're not helping."

"Child," said the wisewoman, "it is our great good fortune that your interference broke the spell and not the lot of us."

"Lady," said Valeria, "you are breaking her." She let go the wisewoman's hands and scattered the tangle of spells. It shredded like mist and spider silk.

All those master mages hissed and sputtered. Valeria ignored them. Briana lay barely breathing. Her robe was light enough that Valeria could see the burned and blistered skin beneath.

Her whole body was seared as if by strong sun, but the bolt had struck hardest in the center. Valeria folded back the robe and caught her breath.

Most of the burns would heal with little or no scarring. But not this. Flesh had melted and fused to itself or to the scaffolding of bone.

Valeria had learned from her mother to be coldly dispassionate in the face of ruin. Part of her wanted to weep and part wanted to howl in rage, but she kept her face calm and her emotions rigidly in check.

It was less difficult than it used to be. Rider's discipline had set in her bones. It helped her call forth power from the stallions who were always inside her.

She had not been absolutely certain that they would give it, but they offered no objection. They were not her enemies or Briana's—however hard that was to believe just then.

Valeria had to stop and take deep breaths, reaching far down within herself for calm. Now more than ever she could not afford to lose that inner stillness. She needed every scrap of it for what she had to do.

Through the white gods' power she traced the patterns of life and blood and breath that ran through Briana's body.

They were terribly burned and twisted, their clear flow disrupted. Still, under them she could see what had been before.

She could not bring it back. No one could, even the Master Healer. But Valeria could mend it enough to keep Briana alive until her own body and magic roused enough to do the rest.

Valeria had woven such a working before when Kerrec's spirit was as badly damaged as Briana's body. It partook somewhat of the wisewoman's art and somewhat of the horse magic. Part of it, too, so deep she hoped no one would see, was the stain of Unmaking that lived inside her. That was her greatest weakness and her most terrible secret, but it could also be turned to strength. The Unmaking could unmake evil as well as good.

Briana had smitten herself with her own power. That was what the mages had failed to see. They had shaped their workings against the enemy who they thought had done it—but that enemy was Briana.

Buried in her unconscious mind was a memory of the power that had deflected Briana's mage-bolt with such devastating force. That magic had an all-too-familiar taste, a taste of old stone and even older night.

Valeria found no surprises there. The priests of the tribes were tireless in their hatred of the empire and its rulers. But the peculiar twist she found in this was likewise familiar, and that, she had not expected.

Gothard was dead, destroyed beyond redemption. Valeria was sure of that. She had been part of the great working that broke his magic and his body together. Nothing could have survived it.

He must have had a pupil or an acolyte. The creature that

Maurus' brother had helped to bring into Aurelia had spoken in an imperial accent—provincial but unmistakable. Valeria had taken no particular note of it at the time because her own speech was rather close to it. But in the clarity of the working, she could not stop thinking about it.

Suppose then that a pupil of Gothard had led the attack. His power had repelled the bolt of magic—deliberately, Valeria was sure.

Gothard had been Briana's brother. He had known her well and hated her only a little less than he hated his father or his elder brother. He would have taught that hate to a disciple, along with the means to act on it.

Through that understanding, Valeria had a way into the heart of both spell and counterspell. Gothard's magic was stone magic and magic of Unmaking. She could meet it with fire and air and the power of the patterns that flowed through all that was. Then far beneath those, she could confront it with itself. She could unmake it.

In her heart she rode the Dance. Oda carried her, eldest and most powerful of the three stallions who had chosen her. The figures were prescribed by the nature of the working. While Oda traced them, Valeria focused on making Briana whole.

It was a long Dance, and hard. The Unmaking in Valeria wanted to bind itself to the ruin in Briana. Valeria had all she could do to keep them separate and ride the Dance and work the healing.

Long before it could possibly be done, she felt herself flagging. Oda was doing everything he could do. The rest of the stallions were willing, but she had to contain them all. She was losing strength more rapidly than she could replenish it.

A second dancer entered the Dance. No rider sat on the Lady's back. None would, unless it was Briana.

Valeria was ready to defer to that power which was greater than gods, but the Lady had fallen in behind her. She would lead, the Lady would follow.

The Lady's power flowed from deep wells in the heart of the world. Not only Aurelia drew strength from it but every tribe and nation.

That was a revelation so profound that Valeria could not let herself think about what it meant. Briana needed her first and foremost. She Danced healing for her friend who was like a sister to her—who happened to be empress of Aurelia.

Chapter Fifteen

Kerrec was running away from the truth. He was man and mage enough to recognize it, but he could not stop himself. It was simpler to give orders and set people running about than to face his sister's death or worse.

He was being of some use. Gunnar and two of the younger riders had found the source of the attack on Briana. They summoned him through Petra, so sharp and sudden that his head ached for an hour after.

He answered the call as quickly as he could. The place was not far—in fact it was in the palace, perilously and ironically near the tombs of his ancestors.

That was a deliberate mockery, but it was also a triumph of magical logic. Not only the bones of old emperors lay in the crypt. Powers were interred there that should never have seen the light of day and were meant never to see it again. Their strength must have fed the workings that were done there.

The room in which his brother riders waited was all too familiar. The dark draperies, the pale stone floor, the altar, were as Kerrec had seen them in Maurus' vision.

The shapes huddled or sprawled around the circle reminded him grimly of the priests on the headland. Most of these were dead, too. Three were lost in sleep like death, just as Briana was.

One crouched in a corner. His face was the color of cheese. His body shook in spasms.

None of the riders had touched him, though he was manifestly conscious. "He's not the leader," Gunnar said. "He seems unusually gifted with wards—which saved him. The rest are done for. The ones who survived won't last long."

Kerrec nodded. The author of the working was gone—dead, he could hope, but none of the fallen wore the face he remembered from Maurus' vision. These were acolytes, discarded when their usefulness failed.

He sank to one knee in front of the man in the corner. The hood had fallen back and the dark mantle had knotted and twisted under him as if he had scrambled away from something that struck him with lasting horror. Under it he wore the silk and gold of a courtier, a long tunic slit to the hips and loose trousers cross-gartered with golden ribbons. One leg was long and strong. The other was withered and twisted.

It was Kerrec's gift and curse never to forget a name. "Bellinus," he said.

He spoke softly, but Maurus' brother started as if struck. "Please," he said in a rasping voice—the voice of a man who had screamed his throat raw. "Please, lord. Don't take my soul from me."

"We're not in the habit of that," Kerrec said. He held out his hand. "Here, get up."

Bellinus eyed the hand warily. After a while he took it. His grip was shaky.

Kerrec pulled him to his feet. The withered leg buckled. Bellinus' breath hissed, but he caught himself before Kerrec could do it for him. Once he was upright, he limped toward the door with such speed that he took Kerrec by surprise.

Two of the riders caught him before he escaped. His resistance was fierce but brief. When it failed, he hung in their hands, breathing hard. "Kill me," he said. "Get it over with."

"Not yet," said Gunnar with gruesome good cheer. Bellinus looked up the massive golden length of him and shuddered.

Kerrec would wager that the boy had no inkling as to who his captors were. He must think they were guards of some obscure imperial regiment.

Let him think what he pleased, as long as he stayed conscious. Second Rider Cato and Third Rider Enric half carried, half marched him through the door.

Kerrec hesitated. "You go on," Gunnar said. "I'll do what needs doing here."

Kerrec nodded. As grim as that task was, he almost envied Gunnar. It was a great deal simpler than his interrogation of Bellinus promised to be.

Still, it had to be done. He straightened his shoulders and followed where the riders and Bellinus had gone.

* * *

Kerrec saw to it that Bellinus was deposited securely in one of the guardrooms near Briana's chambers. As eager as he was to discover what Bellinus and his allies had done, that would keep for a little while longer. Briana would not.

He felt the Dance begin as he passed the door of his sister's anteroom. It made itself known in the pattern of moonlight slanting on the floor. He looked up at the high latticed window through which it shone and saw the old stallion and the bay Lady weaving patterns that had not been woven before.

Even if he had not recognized Oda, he would have known whose fault that was. Valeria was not capable of standing by when there was magic afoot.

She was not capable of tact, either, or of caring for the courtesies of the magical orders. Half a dozen masters and high mages were in a fair taking, but none of them was fool enough to disrupt Valeria's working.

To the eyes of the body she knelt beside the bed with her hands on the blasted ruin of Briana's belly. The wisewoman leaned toward her, fascinated in spite of herself. The Chief Augur watched with the most dispassionate eye of any of them.

The rest, even the Master Healer, had forgotten discipline in favor of the petty dance of precedence. Kerrec drew them away with soft words and firm will. The sputtering began as soon as they passed the door into the anteroom.

He let them rant themselves into silence. While they indulged themselves, he found a chair to sit in, arranging it so that when they came out of their fit of pique, they would see him waiting with princely patience.

The Master Seer noticed first. While he was still staring, the rest exhausted their store of outrage.

The Master Healer was the last to fall silent. She was young for the office, and it seemed she was too well aware of it.

Kerrec could understand that. When he was made First Rider, the next youngest had been twenty years older than he. It was a delicate and sometimes precarious position, and it could take a toll on one's temper.

"I do not need your understanding," the Healer said with a fresh flare of indignation.

"Then I beg your pardon, Mistress," Kerrec said.

"That girl," the Healer said, "that infant, that insolent child, scattered a Great Working and overwhelmed us with her arrogance. Will you discipline her, First Rider? Or shall we?"

"I will do what needs to be done," Kerrec said quietly. "You will be needed, sirs and madam, when the working is finished. Will your courtesy extend so far? Or would it be best if I found others to take your place?"

The Healer stiffened. She did not love him for that, but it had focused her mind. "My duty is here," she said tightly. "So is theirs."

"Good," he said. "For now you may rest. Ask the servants for whatever you wish. You'll know when it's time."

They could call Kerrec arrogant—he was. Unlike Valeria, he was born to be. He remained in his seat until they bowed themselves out.

The Dance was still weaving itself behind his eyes. There were too few dancers, even with the Lady. They were not strong enough to mend what was so badly broken. Briana was fading, for all that Valeria and Sabata and the Lady could do.

Petra woke in his heart and snorted. The stallion's derision stung, but it was deserved. He was waiting in the Hall of the Dance within the palace.

So were the rest of the stallions. The riders were on their way, abandoning whatever they had been doing to answer the call. They had all felt the same urgency.

They had had no time to prepare, apart from years of training. There would be no long and leisurely gathering of forces. This was a Dance of desperation. Without it, their empress would die.

The last time Kerrec saw that Hall, the sand of its floor had been stained with blood. It was dim now and quiet, the silver-white sand pristine. The high windows were dark—the moon had set. The only light was the moonlight glow of the stallions.

There were eight of them, a proper quadrille. Petra pawed ever so gently. It was time.

Kerrec breathed deep and sought within himself for both calm and discipline. When he gathered the reins and set his foot in the stirrup, grief and anger and fear drained away. There was nothing now but the horse under him and the arena around him.

This was his art. He lived for it. It was his heart and soul.

He glanced up toward the Augurs' gallery. He had expected to find only shadow, but there were figures in white standing there, dimly lit by magelight. The summons had brought them, too. They were waiting to perform their office as the riders performed theirs.

He relaxed into the saddle. From this moment, nothing would matter but the movements he rode.

They circled the Hall in a free but cadenced walk, settling into the rhythm as they went. Once they were sure of it, they rose to trot and then to canter. The magic of each man and stallion wove into the pattern. For Kerrec it was as simple and yet as profound as balance in motion.

The Dance unfolded in long curves and interwoven figures. It traced the patterns of Briana's body, circling and circling again in the center where the worst of the ruin was. The heart of that circle, where none of the stallions happened to tread, was a point of utter nothingness.

Valeria was there. With Sabata and the Lady, she danced where nothing should have been able to dance. But they were gods, and she was something less than a god but more than a mage.

Kerrec was no simple horse mage, either. While he focused on the inner Dance, Petra had taken the lead in the outer one. That other magic which had been Kerrec's father's gift was rising like a spring from the barren earth.

It changed the Dance. What before had been a simple tracing of patterns that were already in the world or were soon to be, now was something more complex. Each footfall shifted the earth ever so slightly. Each figure shaped the course of the empire, turning it toward an end that Kerrec was too blind with mortality to see.

The stallions showed no sign of alarm. The Lady at the heart of the inner Dance seemed satisfied, as if this was going as she meant it to go.

A rider had to trust his horse, just as the horse had to trust his rider. The same was true of mortals and gods—and, Kerrec thought, mages and their magic.

He let Petra's calm flow through his body, settling deeper into the familiar movement with its thrust and surge up through the stallion's back into Kerrec's spine. Its rhythm and cadence matched the beat of his heart.

All of their hearts were pulsing together. Eight sets of hooves beat time in the sand. Eight horses and eight riders transcribed the shape of the pattern in the air.

In the heart of the Dance, Briana stirred. Pain, bloodred and jagged, threatened to disrupt the Dance, but the rhythm was too strong.

Her heart began to beat with the rest. Her pain throbbed, but with each pulse it grew slightly less. The thing inside it, the seed of Unmaking, began grudgingly to shrink.

The lesser stallions were beginning to flag. Gods though they were, the flesh they inhabited was mortal and could weaken and die. They clung to the rhythm and the Dance, but their breathing was labored, their flanks dark with sweat.

Petra was still strong. He could carry the weaker ones for a while—maybe long enough—if Kerrec could carry the riders. So could Master Nikos and his strong young Brescia, who had just come fully into his own.

Kerrec's eyes met Nikos' as they crossed at the canter, weaving a figure that was meticulous but not especially difficult. Each of them nodded and began to gather half of the patterns, spreading tendrils of magic outward through the hall.

The others clung to them. The stallions followed them, drawing strength as they went.

There was a limit to it, and that was approaching fast. Briana was healing—but too slowly. The inner Dance was struggling almost as badly as the outer.

Kerrec reached through the walls of air and darkness and found Valeria reaching for him. It was a great risk and could be deadly, but they were running out of time. As the riders faded, so did Briana. She was weakening, giving way to the pain that would not lessen fast enough.

Kerrec's mind and magic met Valeria's. His discipline and her raw strength had always balanced one another. She was more disciplined now and he was stronger. Together they were an even more potent force than he had remembered.

It was slow and it took everything they had, but it was enough—just. The Dance ended just before the dancers broke, with a last, suspended, almost defiantly brilliant passage in unison around the whole of the hall and out into the warm summer night.

They had come out not through the roofed passage that led to Riders' Hall but through the outer gate. The stars arched over them, soft with haze. The air was almost painfully sweet.

Kerrec breathed in the scent of flowers and the sea. The reek of horse sweat and human sweat and magical exhaustion nearly overpowered it—but not quite.

He looked down the line of riders. The stallions held up their heads as best they could, proud to the last. The riders clung to their example.

His heart swelled with love for them all. They had fought a battle as grueling as any between armies, and they had won it.

Briana was alive. She would heal. The patterns of the Dance were ingrained in her body.

It was the Master's place to send his riders to their rest, but Nikos inclined his head toward Kerrec. "First Rider," he said. His voice was gravelly with exhaustion.

"Master," said Kerrec. He nodded to the rest. "Go, brothers. You've done more than well."

They hesitated, bless them—offering what little of themselves they had left. Kerrec bowed in deep respect and said, "Go on. Rest. You've done a great thing tonight."

They bowed in return. More than one looked ready to topple from the saddle. But they were riders. They would hang on until they came to Riders' Hall—then, after the horses were cared for, they would let themselves fall into bed.

Kerrec would have sent Petra after them, but the stallion would not hear of it. He was tired and hungry but far from exhausted. The palace stables would provide a full manger and a stall to rest in.

Kerrec left him there, being fussed over by half a dozen grooms and stablehands. He had to wave off the servants who would have done the same for him. He could not rest until he had seen for himself that Briana was mending.

She was asleep. The pain was still sharp enough that it caught in Kerrec's own gut, but the edge was off it. The Master Healer had mastered her temper enough to begin a new working, subtler than the one that had so perturbed Valeria.

To this Valeria offered no objection. She sat by the bed, holding Briana's hand. When Kerrec came to stand beside her, she looked up.

"It didn't work," she said. Her voice was steady and her eyes were dry, but there were tears in the words. "It wasn't enough."

"She's alive," Kerrec said. "She's asleep instead of unconscious. We didn't fail."

"We didn't succeed, either."

"She'll heal," the Healer said from the other side of the bed.

"Not entirely," said Valeria.

"She'll walk, talk, rule an empire," said the Healer. "Her magic is intact. She'll recover as fully as anyone could hope after such a blow as she took."

Valeria bit her lip. Clearly there was more she could have said, but she chose not to say it.

Kerrec was glad. He was not ready to face it—not yet.

For now, he would be glad of all the things that the Healer had said. He knew they were true. The other things could wait.

He sat on the bed. Valeria offered to surrender Briana's hand, but he shook his head. His sister did not need his touch to know he was there.

It would be a long night, and he was bone-tired. He set the tiredness aside. He would rest when the time came. Tonight he needed to be here.

Chapter Sixteen

Long before she was properly awake, Briana heard the whispers. She might have ignored them, but even through a wall of healing spells the pain in her center threatened to swallow her whole. The whispers gave her a focus.

At first there were no words. She heard hissing in the rhythm of speech, but she lacked the will to make sense of it. Then slowly as she swam toward wakefulness, the whispers' meaning came clear.

"It's certain? There's no doubt of it?"

"None. The rest will recover. That, never."

"Do you think it was deliberate?"

"Perhaps not. But it serves the one who did it very well indeed."

"Pray the gods we find him soon. No death is too slow, no pain too great—"

"We'll find him."

"It won't change anything, will it? There won't be any miracle. She will still be—"

"She will still be alive. The rest we'll face when we face it."

Briana opened her eyes. Light dazzled her. She blinked until her sight cleared.

Daylight filled the room—afternoon light, slanting toward evening. The curtains were pulled back and the windows flung open. Warm sweet air poured in.

It was as fine a healing draft as any potion. Briana let her eyelids fall shut again and simply breathed.

That did not hurt as much as she had feared. The pain was dull and distant. Healers had been working their spells and brewing their medicines.

Sleep caught her again and drew her down into the dark. Part of her resisted, but not enough to win its way.

When she woke a second time, night had fallen. People were talking again—different voices, louder and less friendly. "So it's true. What are we going to do about it?"

"Wait for her to recover first. We can give her that much."

"Can we? There is nothing in the law that states—but—"

"It will have to be confronted sooner or later. If she had been crowned first, there would be no question. But since she has not yet been formally instated … it changes things."

"Are you suggesting that we—that she—"

"I am suggesting that certain consequences may be inevitable."

Briana was not ready for this. She was barely conscious, drugged and enspelled and badly wounded. But the empire did not wait on anyone's convenience.

She opened her eyes on lamplight and starlight and a circle of princely faces. Her privy council had gathered—not for a deathwatch, she hoped. She did not feel that she was dying, though when the Healers' working wore off, she might wish she were.

Her most high and noble advisors looked like children caught in mischief, guilty and trying hard to hide it. Most masked their expressions quickly behind the appearance of gladness. Some might even be honest about it.

"Lady!" cried Duke Gallio. He was one of the honest ones. Tears streamed down his scarred and weathered face. He clutched her hand in his big rough ones and looked her over carefully.

In spite of his refusal to play the game of masks and intrigue that plagued every court Briana had ever heard of, Gallio was no fool. His eyes probed her as deeply as she was minded to allow.

What he saw there seemed to reassure him, though it did not smooth away the sadness. "Lady," he said with remarkable gentleness. "It's good to see you back to yourself again."

"Not quite," Briana said, gritting her teeth as she tried to sit up.

Between effort and pain, she nearly fainted. Gallio moved smoothly to support her. Lady Nerissa, who might or might not be honestly glad that Briana had survived, fetched pillows and banked her with them.

Briana had to pause for a moment to breathe. Her council waited with courtly patience. She thought about pretending to faint, but that would only put off the inevitable.

She scanned their faces, though by now they had all had

time to put on whatever expression they wanted her to see. It was still useful to remind them that she was their empress, wounded though she might be.

"Now that I'm awake," she said, "suppose we dispense with the proprieties and get to the point. I won't be walking the processional way in—is it seven days? Will I?"

They glanced at one another. It was Nerissa who spoke for them. "Three days, lady. You had swum down deep by the time the healing found you. No, it's not likely. The Healers say you'll recover, but it will be slower than you might prefer."

Briana paused a moment to draw a breath. She must not let any of this shake her, or she would lose even more than she already had. "How slow?"

Nerissa pursed her lips. "I never got past journeyman in the Healers' order, but my betters tell me weeks at least. Possibly months."

"Weeks," said Briana. She had known before she asked, but saying it made it real. "So then. My lord Augur, you'll choose another and equally propitious day—shall we say, in the autumn?"

The Chief Augur bowed. He had never been a robust man, but it seemed to Briana that since she last saw him only two— no, five days before, he had grown terribly white and thin.

His voice was still strong and richly beautiful. "As my lady wishes," he said.

If there was any doubt in him, he was too wise a courtier to show it. Briana bent her head to him and turned back to Gallio. "I will speak to my people as soon as I can—in a day or two, I hope. Meanwhile, will you reassure them? I'm far from dead, and I have no intention of being indisposed for long."

"I can see that, lady," Gallio said.

"Good," said Briana. "Now, as little as I like it, I should rest."

They accepted the dismissal. All eight of them bowed low, turned and filed out in order of precedence.

Briana pretended not to see the glance Gallio shot her, promising another and less public meeting later. From him she would expect no less.

She was not as exhausted as she had let them think, but the presence of any human thing was more than she could bear just then. There were servants nearby, alert for any need, but they knew better than to intrude. She was as alone as an imperial lady could hope to be.

She lay back in her mound of pillows and closed her eyes. Her heart shrank from what her mind insisted on doing. She made herself do it before she lost all courage.

After any working of magic, a mage learned to take inventory. She reckoned the paths of power in her body one by one and made certain that all of them were flowing smoothly. If any was interrupted, she did her best to restore it.

It was dangerous, even deadly, not to do this. Briana had been doing it half-consciously while she slept. Now she focused her awareness on it and faced what all those voices had tried to keep her from facing.

She was badly wounded—she had known that as soon as the mage-bolt struck. Healing was well advanced in most of her body and spirit. Her magic was recovering, refreshed from the deep well of the empire's heart.

One thing was not going to come back. The bolt had destroyed it as surely and completely as if a mortal soldier had taken a spear and stabbed her in the belly.

The flesh was mending. In time even the pain would go away. But the heart's pain would never leave her.

She could not touch it—it hurt too much. She spread her hands above it. Time was when she had thought to make that gesture in joy, cherishing the child who would be born to inherit the empire after she was gone.

There would be no child now. That had been taken from her.

Her throat closed. The cry that welled up had nowhere to go. It caught in a sob that wrenched her body, then escaped in tears.

She did not weep for long. She had always been practical, and she was bred for a clear head and a cold heart.

She could well see what Gallio and Nerissa had spoken of while she was still asleep. The single most important duty of any imperial heir was to produce her own heir. If she could not, there were others willing and indeed eager to claim the position—but now of all times, she could not afford to fritter away her power in dynastic squabbles.

If she had fallen like an idiot into this ambush after she was crowned, it would have been much simpler. She would be empress without a doubt, and she could name her own heir in her own time. But she was still, in law, princess regent and heir apparent. If she could not fulfill her imperial duty, her right to claim the throne was suspect and her ability to keep it impaired.

She had done an unspeakably foolish thing, and the consequences might be equally unspeakable. Courts were like packs of wolves—they thrived on the weakness of others.

Briana was as weak as it was possible to be while she was still alive and conscious and able to claim what belonged to her.

She breathed as deep as her outraged body would allow and forced herself to be calm. A little hysteria was a healthy thing, but only if she followed it with a clear plan.

She spoke to the air, knowing her servants would hear. "Bring the rider Valeria to me, if she will come."

The response was silence, but Briana had been heard. She let herself give way to exhaustion for a while, until Valeria answered her summons.

Chapter Seventeen

Valeria was numb. The Dance had succeeded—Briana was alive. But she had paid a price that might yet destroy her.

When Briana's summons came, Valeria was in the stables, cleaning stalls with a ferocity that made the stallions keep a prudent distance. The page in imperial livery picked his way delicately down the aisle. That was hardly fair of him, since Valeria had just finished sweeping the floor until it shone, but he was a courtier. Courtiers liked to imagine that they did not breathe the same air or walk the same earth as the rest of humanity.

He delivered his message in a clear singsong. Valeria suppressed the urge to bolt toward the palace. She finished the stall she had been cleaning, deposited the barrow of sweepings in the kitchen garden then paused to wash her hands and face and rake her fingers through her hair. There was no salvaging her clothes, which were her oldest and most ragged, but Briana would not care for that.

On her way to the palace, Valeria had more than enough time for second thoughts. She never quite turned back, but her steps began to drag. She wanted to see Briana awake and well—more than anything—but she was not sure she could bear the grief that went with it.

Valeria might be a fool but she was no coward. She pressed forward as if against a strong wind.

Briana seemed unconscious, but Valeria could feel her awareness, brisk and keen like a wind off the sea. There was nothing maimed about that or the magic that filled the room. They were as strong as ever.

Valeria bent to kiss the broad clear forehead. As she drew back, she met Briana's eyes. They were dark and quiet.

For a wishful moment Valeria thought Briana did not know what had happened to her. But that was foolish. Of course she did. She lived in that body.

"I'm sorry," Valeria said. It was crashingly inadequate, but it was all she could think of to say.

"It was the Unmaking," Briana said. Her voice was very quiet. "It's in the earth, hidden deep, but it's infected the land's magic. It laid a trap and I walked straight into it."

Valeria lowered herself slowly to the chair beside the bed. "Yes," she said. "I felt it. Who woke it? The priest Maurus saw?"

Briana nodded. "He was the bait for the trap."

"This is my fault," Valeria said bleakly. "If I hadn't made

all those wrong choices, I would never have gone near the Book of Unmaking."

"We've all chosen badly," Briana said.

"You know what's inside me," said Valeria. "Now it's spread to the land I live in."

"I don't think you did that," Briana said. "Long before you were Called to the Mountain, the tribes were our enemies. They've been trying to destroy us for two hundred years. It's our misfortune that they've turned toward magic—the one thing we have that they've always refused to touch. If it's any-one's fault it's my father's, for taking a concubine who hap-pened to be a madwoman—and who bore him a son as mad as she was, who also happened to be a mage."

"Your brother is a year dead," Valeria said, "but I think this priest was one of his acolytes. This thing that was done to you reeks of him."

"It reeks of malice," Briana said. She drew a deep breath through visible pain. "Valeria. I have to ask something of you."

"I have to tell you something," Valeria said at the same time.

There was a pause. Briana tilted her head. Valeria swal-lowed hard and said it before she lost courage. "When I left here last year—when I went to the Mountain—I was pregnant. I was an idiot. I didn't know until my mother told me why I was so sick in the mornings. Grania was born in the spring."

"I knew," said Briana. "The Lady told me."

For a long moment Valeria's mind spun onward, trying to rattle off words that no longer mattered. She reined it in sharply. "We should have told you," she said.

"Why didn't you?"

Valeria could find no anger in that, and no outrage, either.

The guilt was entirely her own. It robbed her of grace but not of words. "We wanted to surprise you with her. Then my mother and I saw something that might have been this and might have been worse, and we were afraid to let anyone off the Mountain know, because she would be a target. By blood she's your heir, even if by law she can't be. And she's ours. What would all our enemies' malice do to a little child?"

"I understand," Briana said. She sounded ineffably tired.

Valeria's hands were cold. She did not want to say the words, but there was no choice. "That's what you're going to ask, aren't you? You want her. You can change the law and make us give her to the empire."

"No," said Briana.

For the second time in that all-too-difficult conversation, Valeria was brought up short. "No? But—"

"She belongs to the riders," Briana said. She drew a breath, which caught—inevitably—on pain. "I need her father."

Of course she did. The thought was dim and far away. Valeria had an answer for her, a clear and cogent one, but all that came out was babble. "You need—what? If you can't, then what use would—" She stopped and made herself start again. "He can't, either. The law says—"

"Laws can change," Briana said. Her voice must have been trying to be gentle. It only succeeded in sounding flat. "There is no one left in the direct line. The cousins are numerous but distant. Choose one of them and it's war with the rest. Whereas if I choose him—"

"You can't force him to be emperor," Valeria said. She did her best to say it calmly.

"Nor would I try," said Briana. "I intend to take what is

mine. But for the rest of it, for the part that was taken from me, I need him. I need you to understand."

"Understand what?" Valeria was being deliberately dense. If she was dense enough, all of this would stop. Briana would give up and find another way. Kerrec would not be sold off to the highest bidder as princes had been since the world was new.

Briana's gaze was compassionate but her will was unbending. "I would never ask if there were a choice."

"There *are* choices!" Valeria burst out. "You have a hundred cousins. Choose one. Quash the rest. You have the power to do it."

She could have finished what the priest had begun, and blasted Briana to ash. Briana could hardly fail to know that, but she did not even flinch. "At what cost?" she asked. "This circumvents them all. He remains outside of the line of succession, but his sons or daughters—"

"Your nobles would never allow it," Valeria said. Gods, had Briana lost her grasp on simple statecraft? Could she not see how preposterous this was? "A rider in such a position? Unconscionable."

"A rider who remains a rider, but whose blood and lineage serve the empire as only they can."

Valeria's throat hurt. It felt as if she had been screaming instead of holding back the scream.

The terrible part was that she did understand. She could see why Briana was doing this, and why so quickly. Briana had to firm her grip on the empire now or risk losing it all— and not only for herself. Whatever had wounded her could strike again, this time against the whole court or the city or even the whole of Aurelia. She had to be ready for it.

Understanding could not prevent Valeria's heart from breaking. Even the wave of pure white fury could not do that. "Who will win the bidding for him? Or does it even matter?"

"I'll have to consult my council," Briana said. "They'll present candidates. He'll be able to choose."

There, thought Valeria. There was the flaw, the great weakness in the plan. There was their escape. "Have you even asked him?" she demanded. "How do you know he'll submit to it?"

"He will," Briana said.

Pain, Kerrec had told Valeria the one and only time he would speak of what Gothard had done to him, eventually reached a point at which it was no longer pain at all. Then it became something appallingly like pleasure.

This was not pleasure. This was her heart in shards, and every fragment small and hard and cold, like the voice with which she spoke. "You really did, then. You asked me first."

Briana's eyes were steady. There was no telling what she felt—whether it was pleasure or pain or nothing at all. "Would you rather I hadn't?"

"No." That was true. Coldness was turning to clarity. In many ways Valeria wished it would not, but she had no power over the permutations of pain.

"Do you also understand," Briana asked levelly, "why we can't just order him to marry you?"

"Of course I understand," Valeria said. If her tone was somewhat sharp, she hardly thought she could be faulted for it. "He can't marry me for this. Even if I could let myself be used as a broodmare, I'm not a noblewoman. For this you need the most impeccably well-bred female you can find."

For the first time Briana's façade cracked. Valeria did not want or need to see what was beneath. Bad enough she had to feel it for herself.

"I wish we didn't have to do this," Briana said. "I wish there were a way to do it without causing anyone pain."

"There is no such way," Valeria said, "nor is there any choice. You can't show even a moment's weakness, or the one who did this to you will win the war."

Briana folded Valeria's hand in hers. Valeria stiffened and tried to pull away, but Briana would not let go. "He'll still love you," Briana said. "He'll still be yours. These state marriages are business arrangements. There's nothing in them of the heart."

"And she? Can she have her lover, too, if she has one?"

Briana did not trouble to answer that. Of course the royal lady, whoever she was, would not share the same privilege. Kerrec's heirs had to be incontestably his.

"She's the one I pity," Valeria said.

"You don't need to," said Briana. "She gets royal rank, royal heirs and great honor and privilege for her family. That's more than she might otherwise have hoped for."

"That's why I pity her," said Valeria.

Briana's grip on her hand had loosened. She slipped it free. She would have given a great deal not to say what she said next, but she had to say it. In the end, no matter what it did to her, she knew it was the right thing. "You'd better call him in now. It may take a few days to talk him into it."

"A few hours, I hope," Briana said, but she did not try to keep Valeria with her. Maybe she was as glad to see Valeria go as Valeria was to escape.

* * *

Valeria made it as far as the passage to Riders' Hall before she had to stop and press her burning forehead to the cold stone of the wall. Her hands were shaking so hard she folded her arms and pressed her fists to her sides. That only made the whole of her shake.

There should be tears somewhere, but she could not seem to find them. She had tried rage, but it was not enough. Hating Briana was a useless exercise. Better to hate the son of the One who had made this inevitable.

Hope kept trying to ambush her. Kerrec might well refuse. He had defied everything he was to answer the Mountain's Call. In the end he had made peace with his father, but Artorius had not gone as far as Briana was about to. Kerrec could decide that nothing was worth the price his sister asked of him.

Valeria shook her aching head. Kerrec could be a complete idiot, but before all else except the gods, he loved his empire. He would see as clearly as Valeria that Briana was right.

He had to do this. There was no other useful choice.

Valeria made herself stand upright and walk. She had to stop more than once to indulge a fit of shaking, but in the end she found her way to Riders' Hall.

She could not face her bare and lonely room tonight. She went to the stable instead. The stallions offered no commentary—and no objection, either.

She curled in the straw at Sabata's feet. There the dam broke and the tears came flooding. She had no choice but to cry herself out.

Chapter Eighteen

Young Bellinus was a thoroughly exasperating object. Once he had recovered from his fit of the horrors, he regained the full measure of his arrogance. Four days of cooling his heels in an empty guardroom with no one to talk to and only servants' food to eat had done nothing to soften it.

He was determined to be a martyr to his cause. Kerrec did not intend to give him that. The god he worshipped would have him in the end, but first he would live to see the full extent of what he had done.

The moment of revelation was far away yet. On this bright, hot morning that should have seen Kerrec and the rest of the riders deep in preparation for the coronation Dance, Kerrec had the boy brought to Riders' Hall. The morning exercises were over and the riders were resting. Kerrec would have liked to join them, but he could not put this off any longer.

Bellinus did not appear to know where he was. Once Gunnar and Cato had delivered him to the library with its shelves and chests of books, he sat on the bench on which they had deposited him, arms tightly folded, and demanded to know why his chains were made of magic rather than steel.

Kerrec let that go unanswered. "Tell us where the priest is."

Bellinus pressed his lips together.

"If you won't tell us willingly," Kerrec said, "there's more to the spell on you than a simple binding. We'll be careful not to kill you, though we may not be quite as careful to keep your allies from discovering who betrayed them."

"He doesn't know," Gunnar said. "He's all bluster and stupidity. While we waste time with him, the real powers are getting away."

"That may be," said Kerrec, "but this fool and his allies are what we have. One of them will crack. Then, gods willing, we'll track down their master and do to him as he deserves."

Bellinus' breath hissed. "Allies? You've got the others? But—"

Kerrec was careful not to leap on the opening and risk slamming it shut. Above all he was careful not to mention that those of Bellinus' allies who were still alive were also still unconscious.

He arched a brow at Gunnar. "What do you think? Young Mardius, perhaps? He has a delicate constitution and very little courage."

Gunnar shrugged. "We won't get anything out of this one, that's clear. Even if he knew anything, it wouldn't be enough to be useful."

"They can't all be idiots," Kerrec said.

"It takes an idiot to fall for the nonsense they've been spouting at us," Gunnar said. "Don't they understand that if they court oblivion, it won't just be the rest of the world that goes? They'll go, too—and not peacefully, either. I don't think they realize that their precious new religion is a cult of pain."

"They do seem averse to bodily discomfort," Kerrec observed. "And yet, as weak and ridiculous as they are, I doubt they're more than foot soldiers. The commanders are wise enough to stay out of sight."

"What are you thinking?" said Gunnar. "Their fathers? Elder brothers?"

"This is the eldest of his particular lot," Kerrec said. "His father is a loyal son of Aurelia. Uncle, maybe. Or—"

"Stop it!" cried Bellinus. "Just stop it! Leave my family alone. I'm the only one. The rest of them are as dull and loyal as you could ever want."

"Who, then?" Kerrec asked. "Who brought you into this?"

"My cousin," Bellinus said. "Corinius. His father has a holding near Mallia."

Kerrec frowned. Bellinus flinched. Kerrec had not meant to alarm him, but it might prove useful. He deepened the frown and fixed the boy with a cold stare. "Where is he now?"

"He's dead," Bellinus said with visible satisfaction. "He went east last summer in the middle of the war. He and his allies were going to fight for the One. They all died."

"All of them?"

Bellinus' eyes flickered. "Every one," he said. "You must know that. You were there. They say you killed them."

"I played a part in it," Kerrec conceded. "Very well, then. Who leads you now?"

"Corinius," said Bellinus.

Kerrec resisted the urge to seize him by the throat and choke the truth out of him. "A dead man? You've been practicing necromancy?"

"Everything is possible for the One," Bellinus said. "You won't find him. He passes like mist and shadow. No mortal power can touch him."

Kerrec smiled. "Not all our power is mortal," he said.

He exchanged glances with Gunnar. The big man nodded just visibly. Cato came in from the door, took Bellinus in hand and carried him off to meditate on his sins.

When he was gone, Gunnar sat on the bench the boy had vacated and stretched out his long legs. "Do you believe him?"

"I know there is a priest of the One in this city," Kerrec said, "and I know he speaks with an Aurelian accent. Do I believe he's a dead man walking? That, I'd want to see before I pass judgment."

"It's said all priests of that cult have to die in order to come into their powers," said Gunnar. He would know. His own people had come into the empire long ago, fleeing that same cult. "If this one really is an imperial noble, he may be a worse enemy than any of us needs."

"We already know he is," Kerrec said. "We'll call on the orders of mages to help us find him. The sooner he's caught and disposed of, the safer we'll all be."

"You think he's alone, then? That lot runs in packs."

"First we have to find him," Kerrec said, "and anyone who may be abetting him. Gods willing, they'll lead us to the rest."

"I'll see to it," Gunnar said. "You have more than enough to do holding it all together."

Kerrec opened his mouth to deny that, but he found he could not. The reins had fallen into his hands. He had taken them without even thinking of what it would mean.

When he was Called to the Mountain and his father declared him dead to his rank and lineage, he had thought that was the end of it. He belonged to the riders. He could not go back to what he had been before.

He had been an innocent. In spite of law and custom and ancient tradition, he had been drawn back into the web of imperial duty. He was acting like a prince, giving orders and disposing troops as if he had never left the palace.

If he was wise, he would get up now and go back to his duties as a rider and leave the rest to his sister's servants. They were perfectly capable of finishing what he had begun.

He should do that. He had seized control because he could not help himself, then kept it because no one tried to take it from him. It was time to let go.

He was about to say as much to Gunnar when Briana's messenger paused in the doorway. The imperial livery seemed unnaturally bright, its crimson and gold dazzling in the slant of sunlight through the open window. Then the boy moved, shifting into shadow.

Kerrec was no seer, but any mage of patterns could see where some of them led. He did not want to see these. There was inevitability there, and a decision that he had never expected or wanted to make.

He could still retreat to the Mountain. He had that choice. He came within a breath of doing it, but when he met Gunnar's eyes, he saw the knowledge there and the acceptance. Gunnar knew what this meant—better and sooner than Kerrec.

He answered his sister's summons. There was nothing else, in the end, that he could do.

Briana was sitting up. Her hair was combed and braided and her face was lightly painted. It took a keen eye to see the pallor beneath.

She was pushing herself too hard. Kerrec said as much.

She brushed it off. "I need something of you," she said. "You can refuse—I'll give you the right. But I hope you don't."

Kerrec's heart was still. The patterns he had seen around her messenger were even clearer here. Everything he had done since he came to the city had in some way fostered them.

He was a First Rider. He believed in destiny. He knew how to shape it through the Dance of the stallions.

There was no Dance for this. It was a human pattern made of human law. And yet the future of Aurelia depended on it.

He knew what Briana would say before she said it. He spared her the pain by saying it himself. "You're asking me to make a dynastic marriage—to give you heirs."

She went limp. Kerrec sprang to her side, but she was still conscious. She pushed him away. "Stop fussing. I'm convalescent, not dying. The only part of me that's gone is the part that makes children. I can live without it—perfectly well, it seems. Except for one thing."

"For which you need me."

"For which no one else is better suited."

"I see that," he said. Now that he was facing it, he was remarkably calm. "You've spoken to Valeria, haven't you?"

She nodded. Her eyes offered no apology. "She understands."

"I'm sure she does," Kerrec said.

"Try not to hate me too much," said Briana.

"I don't hate you," he said.

"Will you do it?"

There was the question. His stomach felt distinctly ill.

When he was a child before the Call, he had expected this. It was his duty. His father and the council would find a woman of suitable breeding, wit and fertility. He might be given a choice among several candidates, but he would have to choose one of them. Once that choice was made, he would abide by it, no matter how he came to feel about the woman he had chosen.

Even if he hated her, he would remain bound to her. That was the law. She would bear his children and administer his estates and sit beside him on the throne.

Then came the Call and it was all changed. He gave himself to the Mountain and the gods, and in time to a headstrong and startlingly beautiful young woman who happened to be a horse mage of extraordinary power. He had never meant to fall in love with her, but once it was done, he could not bring himself to regret it.

He had come through agony and loss to great joy. Now he was asked to put that joy aside, to go back to the old way and the old custom that he had left behind.

The gods were not kind. They did as they saw fit, with no care for the human heart.

He looked up from his reverie. Briana was waiting, cultivating patience. "You had to talk to Valeria first," he said. "So do I. I can't make this decision without her."

"I understand," Briana said, "but make it quickly."

"Tomorrow," he said, "in the morning."

"Tonight," said Briana.

She was as merciless as a god. He spread his hands and sighed. "Tonight," he said.

Chapter Nineteen

Kerrec found Valeria in the riding court. All three of her stallions were saddled and in motion, and mounted on each was a familiar young man. The brothers Maurus and Darius and their cousin Vincentius had come for their morning instruction.

They had been studying with Quintus the stableman since the year before and were both eager and apprehensive to show what they had learned. Kerrec could hardly pull Valeria away from them without wounding their feelings.

He could not run and hide, either, once they had seen him. He had to walk out onto the sun-warmed sand, greet them with the courtesy they deserved and survive that hour and the hour after that.

To add to the delights of the ordeal, two of them were Bellinus' brothers. They were all careful not to mention that.

They were equally careful not to speak of the message Maurus had sent, or of what had come of it.

All that care made Kerrec's head ache. That made him even less cheerful than he had been to begin with.

No one expected him to smile, at least. The last these boys had known of him, he had been as dour as a rider could be—and that was grim indeed.

Valeria could recognize the difference. But she was trapped as he was by tact and politeness. The three boys made a wall between them, and their instruction managed to consume the rest of the morning.

By noon it was too hot even in the more sheltered of the two riding courts for anyone to ride. The boys left a little hastily, and not only because of the heat. Maurus had not met Kerrec's eye once all morning, and Darius had had a tightness in him that even Marina's supple movement could not loosen.

It was a day for avoidance. Before Kerrec could confront Valeria, Master Nikos called him away. It was time, his message said, that all the riders knew what had happened and why.

It was true they had to know. There would be no coronation Dance this season, but they could still ride the Midsummer Dance before they returned to the Mountain. There was also the matter of the school that Kerrec had meant to found—whether it was still either safe or advisable to do such a thing.

Of that he had no doubt. He faced his brothers gathered together in the dining hall and said, "We have to carry on. If we pull back, we risk losing everything."

"But you are vulnerable," Gunnar said. "While you live away from the Mountain, you won't have the protections that keep the rest of us safe. Yes, you can raise your own wards and they'll be strong, but will they be strong enough? What if the empress wasn't the only target? If the pattern holds, you'll be next."

"I expect I will be," Kerrec said. "If the rest of you want to leave, I'll understand and forgive it. But I am staying."

"We'll stay," Second Rider Gavron said without hesitation. The rest nodded, even those who were supposed to return to the school after the Dance.

Kerrec had not always been proud of his fellow riders. They had treated Valeria abominably when she first came to the Mountain, and they had not been particularly perceptive when Kerrec was so badly wounded in spirit that he nearly destroyed them all.

It seemed they had learned from their mistakes. They were listening now instead of deciding what should be said according to custom and tradition. They accepted that the world was not the same as it had been, and that they had to change with it or lose everything.

The more of them there were in the city, the better their chances of defeating this new enemy. He said to them, "You have my thanks, and my sister's, too."

"This is our duty," Gavron said. "We let ourselves forget it, walled up on the Mountain and never leaving it except to Dance in front of emperors. We were never meant to shut ourselves away. Our magic is the empire's heart. We should be part of the empire, not cut off from it."

A few eyebrows rose around the circle. Gavron was a quiet man, not much given to speeches. He did most of his talking through the stallions he trained.

It seemed he spoke for all of them. Kerrec came within

an instant of telling them what Briana had commanded him to do. But Valeria deserved to hear it first.

He held his tongue and went on answering questions that never touched on the solution Briana had found. They would be expecting her to find a cousin or kinsman and name him her heir.

So would Kerrec if he had been one of them. He gave them a day's worth of blissful ignorance. They might not be glad of the gift once they knew the truth, but it gave him a few more hours of peace. However cowardly that might be, he was glad to have it.

Noon was well past before Kerrec could escape the gathering of riders. By that time Valeria was long gone. He could not find her anywhere.

The patterns that should have led him to her were blurred and confused. When he followed them, they led not to her but to her stallions.

They were not talking. Sabata snapped long yellow teeth in his face. Kerrec left him to his hay and his secrets.

Valeria was all too well aware that Kerrec was hunting her. Part of her yearned to let him find her, but the stronger part knew it was better this way. She should not tempt him out of it. Aurelia needed him too badly.

It was easy to think such noble thoughts, but if she would admit the truth, she was furious. At Briana for asking this of both of them. At the empire that demanded such a high price from its servants, and at the gods who had allowed it.

She backed the bay Lady into a corner of the mares' stable—empty now that Corcyra and her foal had gone to join the rest in their pasture outside the city. The Lady was nibbling hay and bits of grain out of a manger. Valeria stalked into the stall and bolted the door behind her.

"Where were you when all of this happened?" she demanded. "Why wasn't she riding you? If you didn't want to carry her for that little distance, why didn't you warn her? You *let* this happen. Do you hate her? Or are we all so insignificant that you don't care what becomes of us?"

The Lady went on eating through Valeria's tirade. Her ears flicked, but not toward Valeria. Her shoulder twitched to shed a fly.

That was what Valeria was to her. Briana, whom she had chosen to be her rider, was hardly more. She wore her blocky horse body and made a sometimes convincing pretense of mortality, but for once Valeria made herself face the truth. There was nothing mortal about her.

"Are you more than a god," Valeria asked her, "or are you less? At least the stallions show some sign of caring what happens to their riders. You don't care at all, do you?"

The Lady raised her head. Her dark eyes were mild. She lipped Valeria's hair and blew sweet breath in her face.

Valeria pulled back sharply. "I wish I could hate you," she said.

The Lady broke wind. As gestures of derision went, it was eloquent.

Valeria could not decide whether to laugh or cry. She should know better than to argue with the Lady. Sometimes the stallions would listen to reason, or what passed for it in the human mind, but the Lady was beyond any such thing.

Still, Valeria had said what she came to say. She felt a little better for it. "You had better know what you're doing," she said. "If you harm any more of the people I love, I don't care if I am an ant in the sun of your regard. I'll raise heaven and hell against you."

Valeria knew what happened to those who defied the gods. Histories and sacred writings were full of such stories.

It did not matter. If she was blasted from the earth, it would be all the easier for Kerrec to go to the wife his empire found for him. Then he could breed children as his duty dictated, and maybe shed a tear for the lost lover, until in time he forgot her.

They would all forget her, the first and only woman ever Called to the Mountain. She was not even a splendid failure. She had simply dribbled away into inconsequence.

The Lady bit her shoulder hard. Nothing broke, but the bruise would be a long time healing. Valeria flung herself at the Lady, pummeling her in a fit of pure blind rage.

The Lady braced herself and endured it. When Valeria could not strike one more blow, but stood breathing hard with tears streaming down her face, the bay mare bumped her gently with her head.

Valeria's knees gave way. She went down helplessly, not even caring if the Lady trampled the life out of her.

The soft whiskery nose whuffled her cheek. The big black hoof paused by her head but did not rise to crush it. Valeria looked up at a mountain she had lost the will to climb.

"I should have known," she said. "We were too happy. Fools we were, to think we'd earned our peace. We'd build our school, raise our daughter, live long and useful lives. Our troubles would never be worse than we'd had already. That was unbearable, wasn't it? Mortals can't be happy. It's not allowed."

The Lady offered no words in answer. She raised her head, ears pricked.

Someone had come into the stable. Valeria dragged herself up, not caring enough to dust off the bits of straw and hay that clung to her hair and clothes. She should pretend to be busy, she supposed. Or hide.

Hiding would have been better. Kerrec paused by the open half-door of the stall.

His eyes were more silver than grey, as they always were when he was disturbed.

"You heard," Valeria said.

He did not deny it.

"I meant every word," she said.

"I could tell." He folded his arms on the door's rim and leaned on it. He still managed to look as if he stood at attention.

"You have to do this," she said. "No matter what I think of it, your sister is right. It's necessary."

"Is it?" he asked. "She can't force me, you know. Under law, the riders are answerable to none but the gods. The ruling power may suggest and it may go so far as to recommend, but it can't command any of us."

Valeria throttled down the urge to pummel him as she had the Lady. "Stop playing the fool. You know this has to happen."

"There are alternatives," he said.

"Don't," she said. "Just don't. I've made up my mind."

"But I haven't."

"You will."

There was no way out of the stall but past him. Valeria would have given much to step between worlds as the Ladies could do, but this particular Lady offered a blandly uncomprehending stare when Valeria shot her a glance.

Past him, then, it had to be. She reached to shoot the bolt.

He caught her hand. The simple familiarity of his touch nearly broke her. When she tried to twist free, she found she could not. He had a horseman's ability to hold lightly without letting go.

"Listen to me," he said. "Even if I do this, it's duty only. It won't take any more of me than any other obligation. I belong to you. You are my heart. That will never change."

"You say that now," she said.

"I say it always." He let go her hand, slid the bolt and slipped in through the door.

What he was doing was terribly unwise. She was sure he knew it, but it was clear he did not care.

This was exactly what she had been trying to avoid. Her body had no control at all. When he drew her toward him, she went without a hint of resistance.

They fit together so well. He was only a little taller than she, but that had always been tall enough. He was strong as a steel blade, supple and light on his feet.

She let her head fall back. It was hard to see through the tears, but she never needed eyes to see his face. If she went blind in an instant, it would still be engraved in her heart.

His finger traced the curve of her cheek and lingered across her lips. She kissed it as it passed. She felt the subtle shiver in him, matching her own.

Would that other woman learn how to recognize the signs?

He seemed a cold man, with his stern expression and deep reserve, but the truth was completely the opposite. Would a stranger know how to unlock the many doors and open the windows and cast warmth and light into the heart of him?

When he leaned in for the kiss, Valeria was not there. She had slid out past him.

If he called after her, she refused to hear it. She fled the stable as if the armies of the One were driving her.

Chapter Twenty

In the ordinary run of such things, the councils alone would have taken days, then there would have been weeks of negotiations with various purveyors of fine noblewomen. After a few months, Kerrec would have been presented with a selection for his perusal. Within a year, there would be a wedding—suitably lavish, of course—followed within a second year by a healthy and indisputably royal heir, male for preference.

Briana did it in two days. She exploited her indisposition ruthlessly, leaning heavily on the precariousness of her existence. If anyone had ever doubted that she had the strength of mind to rule an empire, she proved it then.

Even Kerrec was amazed to find that his sister's will was solid steel. He went to her directly from the stable, deeply hurt and knowing it, but also knowing that Valeria was right. He had no choice. "I'll do it," he said—and unleashed the whirlwind.

* * *

He did not see Valeria at all in those two days. She was in Riders' Hall and he was in the palace. He thought often of going to find her, then forcing her to stop pushing him away, but there never was time to act on it.

There was one meeting he could not avoid indefinitely, with his Master and his brother riders, but Valeria was still a rider-candidate. She was not privy to the deliberations of her superiors.

On the second day he faced Master Nikos and the rest and told them what he had to do.

They heard him out in silence. He looked for outrage but found none. There was barely any evidence of surprise.

When he had finished, Gunnar spoke for them all. "Well, my friend. For a man whose highest ambition was to ride the Dance with some small show of competence, you certainly seem to attract the gods' attention."

"Blood will tell," Second Rider Cato said, "as much as we wish it wouldn't."

"I won't abdicate my duties," Kerrec said. "I'm a rider first and always. That will always have the best part of me."

"Of course it will," said Master Nikos. "Are you asking our permission?"

"No," Kerrec said, "sir. I'm asking for your understanding."

The Master's brow lifted.

"They're going to change the law," Kerrec said. "My sister has already drafted the decree. I won't stand in the way of her succession, but the line will carry on."

"We understand that," Nikos said. "Do you understand what the consequences may be?"

"We've ended our isolation already," said Kerrec. "This simply affirms it."

"Change," Nikos said. He sighed. "Gods, we hate change. But there's no escaping it, is there? The Dance is dancing us."

"The gods are out of patience." Gunnar rocked back in his chair. "I'll stay here, I think, at least through the autumn—with the Master's consent, of course. My belly tells me this isn't over yet. There's more to come, and it's not going to be pleasant."

Kerrec's own belly churned. He had been focused narrowly on getting through each day. Gunnar was seeing broader patterns.

Once he had spoken of them, they were visible for anyone who could see. Kerrec almost—but only almost—wished for the blindness to magic that afflicted him after his brother had him tortured and nearly killed. His sight now was brutally clear.

The attack on Briana was a nexus, a meeting of paths in the Dance. Those paths opened from it into a maze of possibilities. All led into darkness, blood and fire or oblivion.

Every path. Every one. There was worse than war ahead. Briana was at the center of it. So was Kerrec and a towering presence that at first he took for one of the gods.

Then he realized it was Valeria. When had she grown so strong? She had been able to command all the stallions since the beginning. Her skill had been growing under the elder riders' instruction. But this was far beyond what he would have expected.

Had something else entered into her—possessed her?

He shook off the thought as soon as it crawled into his mind. There was nothing wrong with Valeria but lack of experience. In the confusion of patterns, something else had, by coincidence, overshadowed her.

If she was in danger, Kerrec would see that she was protected. If danger was moving toward her, he would do what he could to turn it aside. She was the love of his heart, no matter what his duty forced him to do.

He looked from the patterns into Gunnar's fierce blue stare. Gunnar nodded slightly. Kerrec would not face this alone. His brothers in the art would dance this Dance with him.

When Kerrec returned to the palace, the guard at the gate had a message from his sister. He was to proceed to one of the anterooms.

Kerrec could feel the patterns shifting around him, coiling and uncoiling with every step he took. He was walking into another nexus.

There was still a brief while in which he could turn away. He could refuse his part in this and run back to the Mountain.

From what he had seen, it would change very little. The long night would still fall.

He could change how he fell, whether in guilt and shame or in some sense that he had done what he could. He kept on walking through each pattern that promised escape, straight to the guarded door.

Four lords of the court were waiting with four young women in painfully perfect finery. Briana was not there. Lord Gallio was, standing next to the Chief Augur by the rear wall. Someone else, a man in brown, seemed now to be there and now not.

Evidently they were trying to be unobtrusive. Kerrec stopped just inside the door. He had not felt so excruciatingly on display since the last time he attended a court function as imperial heir, half a lifetime ago.

He had lost the habit of being stared at. Riders in the Dance were barely visible in the light of the stallions. When he was with his sister, everyone stared at her.

Briana should have warned him. He came within a heartbeat of turning on his heel and walking out and never coming back. And that of course was why she had let him walk in without preparation.

Eight pairs of eyes pinned him to the wall. The fathers and one brother he knew. The daughters and sister must belong to names that clanged in his mind.

None of the four ladies either blushed or simpered. Their gazes were direct and keenly intelligent. They weighed him and took his measure, just as he took theirs.

He made himself move forward. He bent over each hand and murmured words that came to him from the depths of memory, courtly phrases so long forgotten they felt alien on his tongue.

He hoped they did not sound as strange as they felt. None of the ladies recoiled, but they would hardly do that. They were too well schooled.

Noblewomen were trained for marriage as riders were for the Dance. These had made the most of their beauty. He could be sure that they were accomplished in numerous arts, including magic. They were all mages of orders no doubt judged to be compatible with his.

None of them was Valeria. He stepped back and bowed

to them all. "Gallio," he said. "My lord Augur." He looked for the third, to name him, but the man in brown was gone, if in fact he had been there at all.

When Kerrec retreated, the two lords followed. He led them to another anteroom, smaller and less elaborately appointed than the one in which the ladies waited. There he turned. "I can't," he said. "There's no choice to make. They're all the same. I can't tell them apart."

The two high lords exchanged glances. If they had been amused, he would have blasted them with a mage-bolt. But they seemed serious enough.

"You realize," Gallio said after a moment, "that if we do the choosing, you are bound by it."

"I trust you'll choose wisely," Kerrec said.

"Are you sure?" said Gallio.

"I am sure I have to do this," Kerrec said. "I'm not taking a lover. She has to understand that. If she wants or needs more, I'm not the man for her."

"That is understood," the Augur said.

"Make your decision," said Kerrec. "Bring her to me when it's made. If she needs a duenna, send a maid. Not her father."

The Augur bowed. Gallio looked Kerrec up and down, eyes narrowing. "We can't give you your lady rider. I am sorry for that. If she were noble born—"

"Even if she were," Kerrec said, "she would never want this for our children. And I would never want it for her."

"It's not so bad," said Gallio. "You're allies in a long war. You'll learn to respect one another. Then maybe something more will come of it."

"Not for me," Kerrec said. "Go, please. Do what you will."

"We won't keep you waiting long," said Gallio.

It seemed a long while, though by the temple bells it was hardly more than an hour. Kerrec could have wandered off, but the room was not unpleasant. It had a window, and the divan across from it was surprisingly comfortable. He stretched out on it and let the sunlight soothe him into a doze.

When the door opened, he was too lazy with light to sit up. He turned his head.

It was a woman alone. Her gown was made of deep blue silk, but its cut was simple and her jewels were exquisitely restrained. Her hair was plaited and coiled with equal and subtle art, and her face was painted almost invisibly.

Her skin was ivory—that was not paint alone creating an illusion. Her eyes were enormous, dark and liquid like a doe's, but there was no timidity in them. They took in the stranger lounging like a cat in the sun. One corner of the delicately molded mouth curved upward.

Kerrec rose with what dignity he could manage. "Madam," he said. "You were not with the others."

The hint of a smile widened ever so slightly. "They were holding me in reserve," she said. Her voice was soft and pure, a purity that bespoke careful training. Her accent…

"Elladis," he said.

She inclined her head. "My father is the prince of that nation," she said. "My name is Theodosia."

"The eldest daughter," said Kerrec. "Yet I've never seen you before. Where has your father been keeping you?"

"I manage his estates," she said, "and serve as regent when he travels abroad."

"And yet you came here," Kerrec said.

"I came for the coronation and the Dance," she said.

"Will you stay to be princess consort?" he asked. "Can your father spare you for that?"

"I have three sisters," she said, "none of whom by tradition can marry until I do. They'll all be very glad when our father comes home alone."

Kerrec found himself surprisingly close to a smile. There was none of the shock of deep recognition and utter rightness that had run through his body when he first saw Valeria. But this could be a friend.

He held out his hand. Her fingers were slender and long. They were warm in his, with a tremor so faint that he could hardly feel it.

This was not easy for her, either. Outside of the Mountain, people knew next to nothing about the riders—who they were, what they did, even what they were for. They were a legend and a confusion of travelers' tales.

Kerrec was worse than that. He was dead, with his name carved on a tomb and his rank and position officially forgotten. As reassuring as it must be to find that he was human under all the stories, she must still wonder what she had agreed to.

He was not sure of that himself. He kissed her hand because that was what princes did and said, "Tell me who you are. What games you play, which dances you prefer. Do you ride? Are you sworn to an order of mages?"

"I'm an Oneiromancer of the third rank," she said, "and I can sit a horse, though not with what you would call art.

My art is the coach and pair, and my family breeds mares for it. Stallions are not so well suited to such work, you see, and geldings lack fire."

Kerrec's smile broke free. "Now I see why they chose you. Do you dance, then? Or do anything frivolous?"

"I like to play the lute and sing," she said, "and I'm a dangerous opponent at dice."

"Dice?" said Kerrec with a lift of the brow.

She laughed. "Yes, the soldiers' sport! It's all the rage in Elladis."

"Because of you?"

The lids lowered demurely over those wide and innocent eyes. "Ah well. What are princesses for but to set the fashion?"

"What fashion will you set here," he inquired, "besides raising the dead and making him your husband?"

"I suspect that will be a legend rather than a fashion," she said.

"Better that than a scandal," said Kerrec.

Chapter Twenty-One

On the day when Sophia Briana would have been crowned empress, all the pomp and ceremony turned itself instead to something unheard of. The late and occasionally lamented prince Ambrosius, who had become a First Rider of the Mountain, took to wife the princess Theodosia of Elladis.

They stood in the Temple of Sun and Moon under the canopy of gold and silver, in a bank of white roses. She was dressed in white silk and cloth of gold. He wore the simple brown of a rider, without ornament or indulgence.

He was trying to be as invisible as he still was before the law, but that simplicity made him strikingly noticeable amid the extravagance of the court. The riders ranked behind him only made him seem the more remarkable.

They would ride a Dance after this, the Midsummer

Dance. Kerrec would ride in it. He could have chosen not to, but it was important that no one forget what he was.

In this hour he stood hand in hand with Theodosia, washed in the chanting of an army of priests. Her face was veiled and her magic unreadable. The warmth of her fingers was the only human thing about her.

The tremor he had felt in their first meeting was there again, but as the rite went on, it steadied. Her courage held him in place. He had bound himself to this and did not intend to back away from it, but the tighter the chains wound around them both, the harder it was to breathe.

He needed Petra. Gods, he needed Valeria. Petra waited outside, saddled for the Dance. Valeria was nowhere that Kerrec could find her.

He breathed deep once, then twice, then a third time, holding each breath until he was dizzy. This part of the ordeal was almost over.

There were words to say and vows to speak. When he spoke them, he could not make them have meaning. They were binding even so, with the whole of the empire for witness. Theodosia's voice followed his, speaking the same words, doubling the bindings.

They did not promise to love one another. They promised respect and obedience, duty and honor. They made their families one and promised to increase them to the best of their ability.

After the words were spoken, the high priestess of the Moon wound Kerrec's hands with silver cords, then the high priest of the sun wound Theodosia's with cords of gold. "As sun to moon and moon to sun," they sang, "may you be united unto death. The gods bless and keep you. The light of Sun and Moon shine upon you. May your hearts be ever joyful."

Kerrec looked for the shadow of a face beneath the veil. Its blankness defeated him, but her hands were as warm as ever and her grip was firm. He held to that against all the rest of it.

Riders' Hall was empty. Even the servants and Quintus had gone to the wedding and then the Dance.

Valeria was gone, too, but not with the others. None of them had expected her to. They understood, or tried to understand—though being riders they made no effort to pamper her. Their way of healing her heart was to give her more to do rather than less, and to expect more of her as both student and teacher.

She supposed she was grateful. Most days she was too busy to think and too tired to lie awake brooding on her sorrows. But today was a holiday, and the riders were bound to stand at the wedding and then dance the Dance.

She should be grooming stallions and polishing saddles and making harness buckles gleam. Instead she walked through the city, anonymous in her brown coat and leather breeches. No thief reckoned her worth robbing, and no one else noticed her. Everyone was abuzz with the news that had come down from the palace.

"No coronation," a burly man said in a tavern she happened to be passing. "A wedding instead, and a rider at that. What are we all coming to?"

"The end of the world," his companion said. Valeria could not see that one—he was inside the tavern. "I heard a seer say once, if the riders come down off the Mountain, that's the end of everything we know."

"Did you really?" the burly man asked with a twist of mockery. "Or did you make it up this morning?"

"I really heard it," the other said with an air of injured honesty. "Just look. They move into Riders' Hall—which everybody knows is only for festivals every dozen years or so—and something happens to the empress that nobody's quite talking about and suddenly her brother is marrying a princess and the coronation's not till autumn. Doesn't that make you a little bit nervous?"

"It makes me happy," the other man said. "I've sold a year's worth of crockery in a week. Even the load I bought from the east that time but never could unload because nobody would pay for it—I sold it yesterday. Got my price, too."

"Maybe all this uproar is good for business," said the burly man, "and I'm not denying it's been good for us leather-workers, too, but I still don't like the smell of it. Doesn't it worry you that so many things are changing all at once?"

"If it's change for the better, I'll take it."

Valeria envied the unseen man his confidence. She passed on by, not looking for anywhere in particular, only wanting to be as far away as she could from anything that reminded her of Kerrec.

Her wanderings brought her eventually to the harbor. Every dock and quay and slip was full and bustling, but she found a quiet corner at the end of a pier. A row of empty boats rocked at their tethers, attended by a flock of gulls.

She hugged her knees and set her chin on them and stared blindly out to sea. Maybe she should get a berth on a ship and sail around the world. Kerrec would never follow her there. He was a complete landsman, a horseman and, in spite of his best efforts, a prince.

She was no sailor, either, though she could learn. Months on shipboard without a horse to ride would be agony. But she could do it if she had to.

It was shameful if she stopped to think about it. She had wanted to be a rider more than anything in the world. In her heart she still did.

But Kerrec had wound himself into the Call. When she was on the journey from her mother's house to the Mountain, he had saved her from rape and worse and dealt summary justice to the man who assaulted her. Ever since then, she had not been able to separate the magic from the man. He was her teacher, her lover, her friend. She had expected to live and die with him, riders together until death took both of them.

It was not fair or right that the first rider ever to set aside the ancient law for family duty should be Kerrec. Had he not given enough? Was he to be punished forever for being born an emperor's son?

Was *she* to be punished for loving him?

She was not even aware that the tears had begun to fall until a step and a breath behind her made her turn. Her sight was blurred and her cheeks were wet.

She scrubbed the tears away and scowled at the man who disturbed her solitude. He was a very ordinary man dressed in brown—even more nondescript than a rider's uniform.

Something about him was familiar. She was too annoyed to wonder what it was. "Are you from the palace or the hall?" she demanded. "Have you come to fetch me back?"

"Only if you want to go," the brown man said. He sat on a coil of rope beside her. "The Dance will begin soon. Aren't you going to watch?"

"No," she said.

"Don't you think you should?"

"Why? Because it's going to turn into war in heaven again? This time it won't be my fault."

"You know," said the brown man, "he doesn't love her and he never will. You're his heart. That won't change."

"Everything has changed," she said.

"Not his love for you."

"I won't share him," said Valeria. "I can't."

"Whereas he," said the brown man, "has had to share you."

Valeria's body went cold. "What do you know of that? How do you know?"

"You don't remember me?"

Her eyes seared through him. Memory flooded back. She remembered a man in brown in the late emperor's service, a mage of three magics and master of them all.

"Master Pretorius," she said.

He bowed where he sat. "At your service, my lady."

"Are you?" she asked. "Who sent you? Briana?"

"I sent myself," he said. "Your pain rings like a gong in the deep levels of the aether. It's been troubling my dreams."

"I'm sorry to disturb you," she said stiffly. "I'll strengthen my wards. You won't have to—"

"Stronger wards are seldom ill-advised," he said, "but don't do it on my account."

"You think I'm weak and foolish," she said. "It's justice, isn't it? I betrayed him with another man. Now he takes a

Caitlin Brennan

wife. How like him to take his revenge honorably and openly and for the good of the empire—whereas all I tried to do was save his life."

"Males are prone to the grand gesture," Master Pretorius said.

"You're laughing at me." Valeria pushed herself to her feet. "Please go. Tell her majesty I'll be back before dark."

"I will if you like," he said, "but I'm not her messenger. I've come with a message of my own. And," he added, "a proposal."

That made her pause before she turned to stride back down the pier. "For what? Marriage?"

His lips twitched. "Not likely, my lady. Have you given thought to what you'll do after the uproar has died down? He'll be taking his place in Riders' Hall as he had planned. I doubt he'll bring his wife there—there's no room for a princess's retinue—but he'll be in the hall every day. Can you bear that?"

That had been Valeria's exact thought. She hated him for voicing it. "It's none of your affair what I can stand or not stand. I'll ask my Master to take me back to the Mountain."

"He's not going until after the coronation," said Pretorius. "None of them is. They're staying in the city to guard it and its empress."

"Then I'll go alone," she said. "It won't be the first time."

"What if I present an alternative? Will you consider it?"

"I can't stay," she said.

"I'm not asking you to. Listen a moment and be patient. You know the empress was attacked by a priest of the One— an imperial lordling, it seems, but he gave it up to attach himself to the dark priesthood. No one has been able to find him. His allies know nothing but that he was in the city and is no longer. We suspect he's gone back over the border."

"He could be hiding in Aurelia," she said. "It wouldn't be the first time the cult of the One has escaped imperial notice. If he's not done yet—if he has more harm to do—he'll stay close to his targets."

"Indeed," said Master Pretorius. "Nonetheless, we have reason to believe he has gone back among the tribes. It also happens that imperial forces have been establishing themselves beyond the river since last autumn, building forts and securing last summer's victory. We've had word from them that there is a new high king in the royal dun. He'll need watching in case he thinks he can wage war as his predecessor did."

"That's not likely," said Valeria, "considering how thoroughly the tribes were defeated. If he has any intelligence at all, he'll know that."

"That's what our new envoys will go to determine," Master Pretorius said. "I've come to ask if you would be one of them."

Valeria scowled at him. "What in the world can I do? I'm no diplomat."

"Now that is true," Pretorius said dryly. "Nonetheless, you are a great rarity, not only the first woman to practice the horse magic but also a wisewoman of unusual power. And," he said, "you have one more gift that makes you rarer still."

He paused. Valeria refused to take the bait. He went on unperturbed. "Here we have a number of words for it, but none quite manages to contain it. In Elladis they call it *cha-*

risma. People want to follow you. More than that, they want to love you. Even the gods aren't immune to your power."

Valeria's cheeks flushed. "What are you saying? That I should be a courtesan?"

"Hardly," said Master Pretorius, "though the great ones have a glimmering of your gift. There are rough edges that might be smoothed, but both your skills and your talents are considerable. We should like to make use of them."

"I am a rider," Valeria said, though temptation tugged at her. "I've left my training often enough as it is. I won't run away again."

"Not even if your Master gives permission?"

"Why would he do that?"

"If you were in danger here," Pretorius said, "and if he were persuaded that your peculiar abilities were best put to use on this mission, he might surprise you."

"I'm not in danger here," Valeria said.

"Are you a seer or an oneiromancer? Have you studied the patterns closely? Have you looked into your heart?"

Valeria walked stiff-legged to the end of the pier and poised on the edge. Green-brown water lapped the pilings below. A pair of gulls bobbed in it, side by side.

Even the birds had one another. Her chest felt tight. Away in the city, bells began to ring, a chorus of jubilation.

The wedding must be over. It was nearly noon, nearly time for the Dance.

She knew she was being absurd. Everything Pretorius had said about Kerrec was true. He still loved Valeria, and she had no doubt he always would.

She could see the patterns easily enough. He would do his

duty with the woman who had been chosen for him, give Briana heirs then come back to Valeria. He would not be able to help himself, nor would he want to.

Valeria had had her own choice to make, too, and she had chosen Kerrec. And yet this was different.

The formality of it, the bindings that went all the way to the empire's heart, constricted her own heart until she could hardly breathe. It was not rational and it certainly was not reasonable. Even if she came to her senses—and she did expect to—she needed to go away for a while. She had to learn to live in this altered world.

She turned and fixed her stare on Pretorius. He looked like a plain and honest man, a tradesman maybe or a prosperous farmer. He would not have looked out of place in the market of Imbria, selling a cartload of radishes or downing a mug of the local ale.

Horse magic came to all ranks and stations, too, and sometimes to nations that knew little or nothing of horses— as her yearmate Batu had discovered for himself. She wondered which village Pretorius had come from, and what his people had thought of him. Had they tried to stop him from following the call of his magic, as Valeria's mother had tried to stop her?

If she went on this embassy, she might have the opportunity to ask.

If.

He endured her scrutiny without evident discomfort. If anything it seemed to amuse him.

"Master Nikos will never give permission," Valeria said.

"Can you know that until you ask?"

"Why would he? My training has been interrupted enough as it is."

"Ask him," said Pretorius.

Valeria eyed him in deep suspicion. He met it with a bland face. He was not going to give way.

She did not trust him in the slightest. Nevertheless, he offered something that she was terribly tempted to take. She wanted to be useful. She needed to be away from Kerrec. This gave her everything she needed—if her Master would consent to it.

Chapter Twenty-Two

It was dark before Valeria got up the nerve to approach Master Nikos. He had been busy with the Dance, then at the wedding feast after it. That ended at sundown when the bride and groom were carried off to bed and the rest of the guests dispersed into the night.

She more than half hoped he would be asleep when she came to his door, but there was a light shining under it and the wards were not secured. It was open to any rider or servant who needed him.

Damn the man. He knew she was there. She must be sprawled all over the patterns that he more than any had the power to see.

Even then she almost turned and ran, but Master Pretorius' voice was still ringing in her ears. The temptation was worse the harder she tried not to think about it. If she accepted the mage's offer, she would get away from the city and the empire, cross the river and enter a country she had heard of in endless tales but barely seen. Above all, she would be doing something useful—as far away from Kerrec as possible.

She knocked softly at the door. "Come," said the voice within.

She slid the latch and stepped into the warmth of lamplight. Master Nikos sat on a couch with faded crimson cushions, reading a book.

He looked up. His face was tired but his eyes were clear. "Valeria," he said.

"Master," said Valeria. She had had a speech prepared, but now she was here, it had drained out of her head.

"I spoke with Pretorius this evening," Master Nikos said. "He told me he made you an offer."

Valeria realized she was gaping. She shut her mouth with a snap. "You know Pretorius?"

"Before he was the master of three magics, he was the emperor's courier to the Mountain. In those days he could almost ride."

Valeria's lips twitched. "And now?"

"He has since acknowledged his limitations."

"I didn't think he had any."

"Neither did he," said Nikos, "when he was young." He closed his book and laid it aside. "Will you go?"

"That's not for me to say, is it?"

Nikos paused, studying her. She looked in his eyes for pity, but she did not find it. What she did find was understanding, and something else that kept eluding her. Sadness? Something remarkably like guilt?

What had Nikos done but allow Kerrec to do what they all knew he had to do? It was not his fault. It was not Kerrec's either, or even Briana's.

"You need time to knit your heart together," Nikos said. "It breaks anew every day that you stay here."

That was the pure and unflinching truth. Valeria could find no words to say.

Nikos had his fair share still. "I've given you to Pretorius for the length of the summer—until the coronation. Your lessons will continue. Pretorius has a certain facility with our magic, and he knows the books we study."

At last Valeria scraped together the wits to speak. "But my riding—the stallions—" And, she thought, her daughter—but that was no business of his.

"Have you ever honestly learned the art from a human teacher?"

Valeria bit her tongue.

Nikos nodded as if she had spoken. "I doubt you are capable of letting that go, even if the stallions would let you. You'll lose nothing and possibly gain much by doing this."

"And you? What do you gain?"

"Goodwill," he answered, "and proof that we do indeed mean to take ourselves out into the world."

"Kerrec isn't proof enough?"

Nikos fixed her with a clear, hard stare. It was strangely compassionate. "Do you want to stay?"

She hated it when he changed direction like that. "No! I want to go. But I feel as if I shouldn't. There is just so much—"

"You have my blessing," Nikos said. "Learn all you can. Pretorius has a great deal to teach you, if you will listen."

"Then I'm supposed to bring it back to you?"

"You're not a spy," said Nikos.

Valeria bit her lip. She had spoken out of turn. It was kind of him not to rebuke her.

"Go now," he said, "and rest. The caravan leaves in the morning."

"That soon?"

He bent his head.

Valeria hesitated. There was something he was not telling her. She could feel it like a shadow around the edges of everything he had said.

Was he so glad to be rid of her? She almost asked, but her courage failed.

It failed in every way—because it was easier, in the end, to follow orders than to stay and face Kerrec and, all too soon, her mother and the daughter she barely knew. She took the opening he offered and fled.

Sabata would not have stayed behind even if Valeria had meant to leave him. When she came to saddle him, she found all three stallions waiting. Sabata was saddled and bridled. The others wore their traveling halters.

"I've packed their gear and sent the chests to the caravan," Quintus said. He subjected Sabata's bridle to a last, swift inspection. "I'm sure I can trust you to keep it all in order, since there won't be anyone to help."

"It was good of you to do that," Valeria said, "but I wasn't planning to—"

"*They* are," Quintus said, tilting his head toward the stallions.

Three pairs of calm dark eyes stared back at Valeria. Three perfectly innocent faces waited for her to get over her foolishness and get them all to the caravan before it left the city.

"The school can't spare all three of you," Valeria said. "Oda at least, if you would—"

Oda was older than most horses ever lived to be. He shook his shimmering white mane and turned his back on her, trotting purposefully toward the stable door.

He was going. She could follow or not as she pleased.

There was no arguing with gods. Valeria reached to take Sabata's rein from Quintus' hand.

He held it for a moment, looking straight into her face—remarkable boldness for a man so painfully shy of women. His weathered cheeks were several shades darker than usual, but he held his gaze steady as he said, "Take care of yourself, rider."

"I'll do my best," Valeria said.

"Do better than that if you can," said Quintus.

Valeria frowned, but as with Nikos, she shied away from pressing too hard. She did not want to be maneuvered out of doing this. Whatever the outcome, she had to do it. It might be the only way through the darkness that shadowed every path.

The Unmaking was close. It hid in every shadow. Even the morning light seemed dimmer than she remembered.

It had been coming on since a priest of the One stepped out of air into a hidden chamber, but for the first time Valeria was consciously aware of it. The priest's coming had opened a gate. His attack on Briana had flung it wide. Now something was in the world that should not be—not if the sun was to keep on shining.

Was the Master sending Valeria away to protect her? If he was, he had a strange way of doing it. She was going to the heart of the One's country, among that nameless, shapeless power's own people.

There must be something Nikos expected her to do. If he had wanted her to know what it was, he would have told her. Riders never told anyone anything if they could teach through example.

She had lessons to learn, then, and those lessons were in the east. If she healed a little in the learning, she reckoned Nikos would be satisfied.

She paused in the light of early morning, with the first birdsong lilting in her ears. The bit jingled as Sabata champed it. She set her foot in the stirrup and sprang astride.

Even as she hung in the air above his back, he surged into motion, rocking her into the saddle. The other two stallions were already pulling ahead.

It was a fine morning and would be hot when the sun was up. There was hardly anyone in the streets between Riders' Hall and the east gate where the caravan waited. Those few who were abroad were too fuddled or too preoccupied to notice the passage of a rider with three white horses.

The stallions were doing what they often did away from their own places, dimming the light and making themselves look common. They did that very well. Oda appeared as an old, swaybacked nag and Marina plodded dully, his big round hooves echoing on the cobbles. Sabata never had played the game well—he was too vain—but he managed to keep his head down and his gait as lackluster as it could bear to be.

Even as slowly as they seemed to move, they passed through the city remarkably quickly. The sun was still not up when they reached the court in front of the gate where the caravan was taking shape.

The embassy was only a part of it. There was a long train of mules and carts, a small army of guards and near the middle, a company of men on horseback. They did not look like guards, but they had a certain air of quiet about them that told Valeria they knew what fighting was and were not afraid of it.

In the middle of those was Master Pretorius on a horse as carefully unremarkable as he was. Valeria looked for the rest of the lords who must be riding with him, but he was the only one.

He caught her eye and grinned. "Ah! There you are. Come here."

Valeria thought briefly of pretending she had not heard, then insinuating herself into another part of the caravan. But three white horses, even in their mortal disguises, were difficult to hide. With a mental sigh, she made her way toward the mage.

Midway, she met an obstacle. Two of the mules had taken exception to their places in the line. They registered those objections loudly and at length. The rest of the line milled and scrambled to escape the flying heels.

After some moments, Oda slipped his halter, stepped onto the battleground and snaked out his neck. The nearer mule was the larger—a great dray mule a solid foot taller than Oda. The stallion clamped teeth in the mule's nape, bunched his body and heaved.

The mule flew end over end, bowling over its erstwhile adversary and tumbling in a heap against the city wall. It lay stunned, but Valeria could feel the life in it still. There was no harm done except to its dignity.

Oda trod delicately out of the circle and back to Sabata's side. The astonished silence broke as the caravan came back to itself. After a moment, no one seemed to remember what he had seen.

Oda's nonchalance was palpable. He had gone back to looking like a farmer's nag, with lower lip slack and back sagging.

Master Pretorius' amusement washed over Valeria. "See? You've made yourself useful already."

"Any Beastmaster could have done that," Valeria said.

"Not with such an able assistant," said Pretorius. "I foresee we'll be blessed to have you with us. Now come, the caravan master has asked to make your acquaintance."

Valeria knew the courtesy of caravans. She made no objection when Pretorius led her away from the guards—two of whom fell quietly in behind—and along the line of the caravan toward the man who oversaw it all.

As she drew closer, she started slightly. He was a smallish man, slight and wiry, with a luxuriant black beard and an intricate pattern of lines and curves tattooed on his cheeks and forehead. Her start was not for the strangeness but for the familiarity. Her yearmate Iliya bore such patterns, the marks of a prince from the desert tribes.

If Iliya was a prince, this must be a king. His patterns were dizzyingly complex. They reminded Valeria of the map of a Dance that the Augurs drew as they interpreted its turns and pauses.

Apparently this lord of the desert was accustomed to being read like a book. Pretorius' introduction had ended some moments since, but he waited politely for Valeria to come back from wherever her mind had gone.

"Please," she said, "pardon me. I think one of your kinsmen is my friend."

A wide white smile parted the black beard. "My cousin! Yes. He went to the Mountain and never came back. He passed the testing, then?"

"He passed it well and honorably," Valeria said.

The caravan master clapped his hands. "Ah! Splendid! Once we're on the road, you'll have to tell me everything."

"I'll be glad to," said Valeria.

His smile flashed once again. He bowed with graceful extravagance. "Later, then," he said.

"That was well done," said Pretorius as they returned to the middle of the caravan. "Rashad would do his duty in any case, but if he's well disposed toward us, our way will be easier."

That should have been obvious, Valeria thought. Aloud she said, "Has anyone ever read the patterns on his face?"

Pretorius' brow twitched upward. "His kinsmen have, I'm sure. They're marks of royalty—but you knew that, yes?"

"I know what they're supposed to signify," she said. "Has no one seen what they really mean?"

"Why? What do you see?"

Valeria shivered in the rising heat. "I'm not an Augur. I ride patterns. I don't interpret them."

"Don't you?"

Her teeth clicked together. "Tell me you see them, too."

"I'm not a horse mage," Pretorius said.

"You are an Augur," she said, "and a Dreamweaver and

an Astrologer. All of your arts and skills are focused on reading patterns and foretelling the future. What do you read in that man's face?"

"Royalty," said Pretorius, but he paused. After a while he added, "I see uncertainty. A shadow fallen across our path. A Dance of death."

He seemed to be seeing it for the first time as he spoke. When he stopped, he looked narrowly at Valeria. "How in the gods' name did a death Dance weave itself into the clan marks on a tribesman's face?"

"I was hoping you knew," said Valeria.

He spread his hands, lifting his shoulders in a shrug. "His clan bred a horse mage. Maybe lesser talents were born in it, too, not strong enough to answer the Call but strong enough to see the patterns of a Dance."

"But to carve them on a kinsman's face? Why would he do that?"

"To be read, I would suppose," Pretorius said.

Valeria had to admit the logic of that. She found herself almost pitying the man who had been so beset with visions that he had had to record them in living flesh. The living flesh did not appear troubled—which meant that it was likely the caravan master did not know what he carried.

She was not about to enlighten him. He could rest in his innocence, content with the knowledge that he was blessed with clan marks of exceptional beauty and intricacy.

While her mind wandered, time had been passing. The gate was open and the sun was up. She took up the reins with a sense of almost shameful relief.

The caravan began to move, slowly at first as caravans always did. Once it was through the gate and on the open road, it would find its pace.

She deliberately did not look back. This was Kerrec's city. It would never be hers. She had been foolish to think it could be.

Chapter Twenty-Three

"It's done," Gothard said, straightening from the black stone with which he had been scrying. His head came just short of the summit of the stone hut he had claimed for his own. He yawned and stretched and twisted his neck until it cracked.

Euan Rohe winced at the sound. Not only was he cramped and squeezed into this tiny box of a hut, he had had no sleep the night before. A warband from one of the eastern clans had come in to the hunting camp, requiring a proper welcome from the new high king. They had brought with them a vat of what they called ice wine, which tasted innocuous but had a kick like an imperial mule.

As far as Euan knew, Gothard never drank. He never ate, either. Maybe he really was a ghost walking among the living and feeding on their souls.

Euan shook off the horror of the thought. "You've done it? She's dead?"

Gothard frowned slightly. "Better than dead. While she lives, she'll never bear a child."

"She's still alive," said Euan. "The stroke failed, then."

"It went somewhat awry," Gothard admitted, "but it's not a failure. There's still the law of the empire. She hasn't been crowned and she can't produce an heir. Her right to rule is open to challenge."

"You think they'll choose you, after all you've done?"

"They're slaves to the law," said Gothard. "In law, if the heir is incapable of producing an heir, a scion of the direct line may claim his place."

"You have a brother," Euan pointed out.

He had done it in part to watch Gothard's eyes go flat—not a laudable thing, but one took one's pleasures where one could. "In law," Gothard said in a voice as flat as his eyes, "a rider cannot claim any place outside of the Mountain."

"I wonder," said Euan. But he had to concede that if ever a man lacked imperial ambition, it was the First Rider Kerrec. He could have been emperor, but he had thrown it away for the white stallions.

"Aurelia is mine," Gothard said, "and I will do whatever I have to do in order to take it."

"So you always have," Euan said with careful lack of expression.

He left Gothard's hut in an odd mood. Mention of the Aurelian Empire could do that to a man of the people.

The war that had failed so devastatingly last summer would

leave scars for generations. Euan saw it in the dearth of young men among so many of the clans, and the women and children left alone for any man to take—if a man was left to take them. A terrible number of them had died in the winter.

Now in summer the tribes found themselves blessed with plenty because there were so few to consume it. But the legions were taking care of that. All along the river and for a week's march into the hunting runs of every clan and tribe, they were building forts and marking out towns and taxing the tribes to pay for them.

Taxes were not only paid in hides and furs and fruit of the land. They wanted human bodies, young men and women to till the fields and join the legions, and older folk to labor in the towns and build the forts. If those were not given willingly, the soldiers took them.

They had not come as far as Dun Mor. Rumor had it that an embassy was coming to greet the new high king, but there was as yet no sign of it.

Euan had gone on this hunt in part to elude the embassy if it came. He had set up his hunting camp in a valley that had held many a war camp in the days when the people could afford to indulge in such things.

Strictly by coincidence, of course, various of the more distant clans had happened by for a night or a handful of days or a fortnight. They were not plotting a new war, not so soon after the last one, but they were making themselves known to the Ard Ri and coming to know him in turn.

They all told the same story of famine and death, loss and sorrow. Some clans were gone. Others were so broken that they had joined with others to survive. They were even talking of going to the legions and giving themselves up, becoming citizens in return for houses to live in and bread to eat.

That was the empire's way. First it conquered with steel and magic, then it corrupted the hearts and minds of the people it had defeated. It took away their spirits and transformed them into imperial citizens, slaves to their multitude of gods and their armies of mages.

This was his predecessor's doing. Euan had the dregs and remnants and a legacy of bitterness that he could use to his advantage. He could turn the empire against itself. Gothard was part of that legacy, with his imperial blood and his potent magic.

The sorcerer had not been trying hard enough. His instrument had left Briana alive, though it was like him to prefer suffering to a clean death. In that he was a better son of the One than Euan, who would rather get rid of the obstacle and move on. Gothard liked to toy with his prey, even if it cost him the victory.

This time he would not do that. The tribes had lost enough. The empire would pay—and Gothard might dream of ruling it, but that would not last long. Gothard had never been meant to be emperor.

Euan stood straight under the tumbled sky. A storm was brewing, appropriately enough. The wind tugged at the long plait of his hair and tried to unwrap the plaid from around his body. He tucked it in tightly and strode away from the huddle of priests' huts.

The camp proper filled the valley of a narrow river, down below the hilltop on which the huts were perched. Euan let the slope of the hill carry him down into it. He was almost running as he reached the bottom, loping long-legged through the outlying tents. Most of the men who lived in them were still sleeping off the night's excesses, but those who had drawn sentry duty were at their posts, awake and sober.

That was a change Euan had made, and he had enforced it. After a laggard or two endured a long and exquisitely painful night with the priests, the rest had seen the virtue in keeping close watch on all the ways in and out of the camp.

All was quiet, this morning's guards said. A young boar had blundered in among the Imbri, but he had killed no one and wounded only a few. Euan found him turning on a spit over a clan chieftain's fire.

His flesh had a sweet taste. The creature must have been feeding on the succulent roots that grew along the river. A dozen of those had been roasting in the same fire. They made a fine accompaniment to the boar's meat.

Euan's hosts were honored to have the high king at their fire. Euan was careful to eat not so much that anyone in the clan went hungry but not so little that he seemed to spurn their hospitality. He downed a cup of their mead, too, and listened to the inevitable ode to the beauty of the chieftain's daughters—any three of whom, their father declared, would be worthy mothers of royal heirs.

When at last they would let him go, Euan went on his way, replete but not content. He had been studying patience. It might be years until Aurelia was in his hands, this latest game of Gothard's notwithstanding. Today he could not seem to be still.

He should take the high seat and set about being king. But as he turned rather desultorily toward the council circle, he was waylaid by a small whirlwind. He laughed and caught it and spun it completely around.

His son whooped with delight. But when Euan stopped and set him on his feet, he looked up with an unexpectedly somber expression.

Euan's grin died. "What is it?" he asked.

Conor's frown mirrored his father's. "They're coming," he said.

Euan suppressed a sigh. The child was given to such utterances. He should get a thrashing for them, because they were not fitting for a warrior and a king's son, but Euan was too soft-hearted. "Who is coming?"

Conor's eyes narrowed. He was not looking at Euan, not by then. He could see through things—very far, sometimes.

That too should not be permitted. Children who showed such signs were given to the priests to be killed or made one of them.

Euan could not endure the thought of either. This was his heir, the son whom he had lifted up in front of the people. He would be king when Euan had had enough of it.

"Listen to me," Euan said. "Whatever you see, don't tell anyone but me."

"I know," said Conor. "I remember. *They* can see, you know. They don't need to hide it."

"What, priests?"

Conor shook his head sharply. "Priests are full of emptiness. These are full of everything. They're coming here. They'll be with us after you run down the spotted stag."

"You're not making sense, boy," Euan said.

"I will when you see them," said Conor.

Sometimes Euan wondered if his offspring was touched in the head. But Conor's eyes were clear and full of intelligence. He was in all respects a proper son of the tribes, and would be a strong fighting man when he was old enough.

Euan cuffed the boy lightly, more love-pat than blow, and said, "Don't tell anyone else what you've told me. Let them be surprised."

Conor nodded. He grinned when Euan swung him up onto a broad shoulder, and whooped like any other child. Please the One, there would be no more cryptic utterances today or for a good many days to come.

As for what this one meant, Euan refused to wonder. It would happen when it happened.

His only prayer was that Conor would remember his father's warnings and keep his visions to himself. He always had. Pray the One he always would.

Chapter Twenty-Four

Valeria had been on the road four days before she realized that part of the caravan was not exactly like the rest. The armed men who she thought had been Master Pretorius' escorts were in fact escorting a handful of prisoners.

They were not visibly manacled. The chains of magic on them were masterfully subtle—Master Pretorius' doing, which she could not mistake once she woke to its existence. They were dressed plainly and mounted on undistinguished horses. When they ate, they ate together, sharing the same bread and cheese and occasional scrap of meat or fruit as the rest of the caravan. No one in this riding traveled in state, least of all Master Pretorius.

She might not have noticed the prisoners even as quickly as she did if one of them had not tried to escape. It was late in the day and a storm had caught the caravan, lashing it with wind and sudden torrents of rain. They were on the open road with no shelter within reach, and nothing around them but fields of ripening barley.

They stopped to wait out the storm, sheltering as best they could under cloaks or beneath the carts or even the horses' bellies. One enterprising soul thought to retrieve his tent and pitch it in a lull between squalls, but before anyone else could follow his example, a blast of wind ripped the canvas out of his hands. Hard upon it, lightning struck the pole he had raised, blasting it to shards and hurling him headlong into the side of a cart.

In the tumult that followed, the prisoner made a run for it. He almost succeeded—but he had reckoned without the pair of grey cobs that ran loose with the remounts. Oda and Marina between them ran him down and herded him within reach of Sabata's teeth.

He was mad or desperate if he had thought he could succeed in this open country, with a withered leg. Valeria knew him by that and by the resemblance to his brother Maurus. Maurus' features were finer, but they had the same shape to the face and the same angle to the shoulders.

The rain passed as suddenly as it had come. The man who had been struck by lightning would live, though not with the caravan. They left him in the Healers' temple in the town beyond the fields.

Bellinus went back to his fellow prisoners with even stronger bonds on him and actual, physical chains to make sure he stayed where he belonged. It seemed he understood now what the three stallions were—he watched them constantly with an expression that made Valeria's shoulders tighten.

It was two days and another storm before Valeria could catch Pretorius alone. She was sure that was deliberate. But she was wise to mages' ways.

She let the patterns fall together toward evening. Tonight they lodged in a caravanserai that had been built when this part of the empire was still the frontier.

Its walls were three man-lengths thick. A moat had surrounded it once. The deep trench was a garden now, growing beans and corn for the kitchens, and apples and pears and plums in orchards around the edge.

Master Pretorius took the air in the evening on top of the wall, looking down on rows of carefully pruned trees. Valeria could tell that he had been waiting for her.

Her temper flared and then died. She neither liked nor trusted this man, but she had agreed to throw in her lot with him. The least she could do was treat him civilly. "Tell me," she said, "what milord Bellinus and his associates are doing in this caravan."

Pretorius spared her the annoyance of pretending not to know what she meant. "We're taking them where they think they want to go," he said.

"To the tribes? Have you lost your mind?"

"Possibly," Pretorius said. "Can you think of a more appropriate penalty?"

"I can think of several," she said, "none of which takes the risk of their turning the tribes against us once they've been handed over."

"The tribes have always been against us," Pretorius said.

Valeria bared her teeth at him.

He smiled back. "Yonder fools think they want to worship the god of the tribes. We'll give them their wish."

"You'll give them over to pain," Valeria said. "Who consented to this? Not Briana, surely. This isn't like her."

"Her majesty has more pressing matters to occupy her," Pretorius said. "This was her brother's doing."

Valeria stiffened. "Kerrec? He'd no more do it than she would."

Pretorius shrugged, an eloquent lift of one shoulder. "Nevertheless, the order comes from him."

"I don't believe it," Valeria said, but even while she spoke, she felt her certainty wavering.

Kerrec was a quiet man, a tender lover, gentle with those he loved, but he had a core of edged steel. Once she had seen it bare, when a young nobleman would have raped her on her way to the Mountain. Kerrec had appeared out of nowhere and struck the man down—then gelded him and flung the remnants to the crows.

That cold ferocity, that merciless justice, could all too easily sentence a pack of traitors to the torments of the One God. Kerrec would know no guilt, either. When he was sure that he was right, nothing could shake him. In that he was altogether an emperor's son.

She missed him suddenly, terribly, even as she recognized the darkness in him. There was worse in her, much worse, and it was trying ever more persistently to wake.

She could turn back. Nothing would stop her, even the stallions. She could make herself share him. Other women had done it. Surely she could, too.

His face was as clear behind her eyes as if he stood in front of her. The smell of him, the taste of his lips, the feel of his skin, struck so sharp and so close to the heart that she caught her breath.

She met Pretorius' calm dark eyes. Deep within them she saw a room. It was dim and lamplit, rich with silken draperies. Its chief furnishing, dominating all the rest, was an enormous and sumptuously carved bed.

There was room enough on that gold-and-crimson coverlet for half a regiment. Two figures lay twined in the center. One was wrapped in a white robe so finely woven as to be transparent. The other was unabashedly naked.

His brown hand traced the shape of her ivory face. She was exquisite, of course. Princesses in Elladis were bred like fine horses, and this was a triumph of that breeding.

He was no less well bred and no less beautiful. He bathed her body in kisses until she purred like a cat.

He smiled with tenderness that was bitterly, painfully familiar. He murmured in her ear—words of love, it seemed. In this vision Valeria could only see, not hear.

Her heart went cold. Deep within it, the Unmaking raised its formless head. She spun away.

If it had been simple courtesy, a dance of duty, she could have made herself bear it. This was more than duty. Maybe it was not the love she had shared with him, but it was close enough. He was not suffering for this sacrifice that he had made.

She clenched her fists on the parapet. By the gods, she would not suffer, either. She would do what she had to do—just as he did. If she happened to enjoy it, so much the better.

Pretorius' satisfaction was distinct behind her. Of course this served his purpose, whatever that truly was.

She let Pretorius think he had won the game. She trusted him even less now than she had when she first met him, but the stallions would protect her. They had their purpose, too, even more incalculable than his. The time would come when Valeria knew all of it—and then she would do as she thought best.

That was probably blasphemous. She was hard put to care.

Chapter Twenty-Five

It was a full ten days before Kerrec understood not only that Valeria was gone but where. He had brought that ignorance on himself, first because he could not escape the festive duties of a royal wedding, and then because his injured pride would not let him go looking for her.

When he came to Riders' Hall after the wedding and saw that she and her stallions were no longer in the city, he thought she had gone back to the Mountain. That hurt, but he could hardly quarrel with it. Gods knew she would be safer there from whatever was coming.

Something most certainly was coming. Kerrec felt it in the earth. Patterns were changing, and not for the better. The empire braced as if for a monstrous storm.

Theodosia dreamed of it. Every night she woke pale and shaking.

The first night, the wedding night, began in exquisite discomfort. The day had been endless, with wedding and Dance and feast thereafter. Nothing disrupted the Dance, but the patterns it revealed were dark and confused.

The Augurs could not read them. It was as if, they said, there was no future. The world went on for a little while in no particular order, then simply stopped.

They would not admit to fear, but the recording Augur's hand shook as he wrote in the scroll of the Dance. There had never been a foretelling like this before, although the omens had been leading to it since the broken Dance.

Kerrec was already unsettled in his mind. The Dance and its auguries only made it worse. The feast struck him as a garish spectacle, an excruciating ordeal of stares and whispers and none-too-subtle intrigue.

He could not eat and dared not drink. He feigned to do both. Theodosia at least was in some comfort—the noble bride attended her own feast with her ladies and the ladies of the court.

With the coming of evening, both feasts ended with the bride and the bridegroom carried off to be ceremonially bathed and robed and conducted to the wedding chamber. Kerrec felt his face go stiff at the ribald jests and bawdy songs. He was a frightful stick as the younger riders would say, but there was nothing he could do about it.

The bath was not as bad as he had feared. The servants were respectful if inclined toward significant glances and slantwise smiles. The robe he was given was both simple and modest, without bawdry or extravagance.

For the wedding and for as long after that as it suited both of them, Briana had given them the old queen's wing of the palace. Theodosia had settled into it with the retinue and estate of a princess.

This was Kerrec's first sight of it under its new ruler. The rooms were clean and freshly appointed, and the furnishings were clearly to Theodosia's taste.

He found them more or less pleasing, as luxury went. Theodosia preferred elegance to opulence. The colors were subtle and rich, the furnishings often understated as such things went.

The bedchamber was a notable exception. It seemed half as wide as a riding court, and the bed in it could have held a quadrille. Theodosia sat upright in that broad expanse of silk and linen, wrapped in layers of shimmering silk. Her veils were gone, her face bare and set as if she waited for a war and not her wedding night.

One mercy they were granted. The wedding crowd did not follow Kerrec in and set up camp around the bed, roaring and singing while the groom did his poor best to deflower the bride. Some of them roistered without, but the room was large and the door thick. Kerrec could hardly hear the clamor.

He bolted the door behind him, then made sure every other door was also bolted and the windows locked, with wards laid upon them all. That took very little time by the turning of the stars. When he finished, Theodosia was still sitting where he had found her, watching him with grave attention.

Even here she was exquisitely coifed and gowned, with a shimmer of paint on her cheeks and eyelids. Kerrec would be a fool to compare her to Valeria, who had never worn paint in her life and whose hair was left to fend for itself.

Sometimes she took it into her head to visit the barber and get it cut boy-short, but mostly she let it be.

She was more beautiful than this lady, though to be fair, not by much. She always smelled of horses. Theodosia's perfume was subtle and exquisite, like all the rest of her.

Kerrec had to stop thinking of Valeria or he would not be able to do this. He focused his mind deliberately on the patterns that surrounded Valeria, wrapped them tight and secured the edges and tucked them away. Then he looked at Theodosia for herself.

She waited patiently. That more than anything was an art of princes. Kerrec had it when he trained horses or riders, but he had lost it in the rest of his life. He would have to get it back.

He moved toward the bed, carrying himself light and alert, as if he approached a mare of whose temper he was uncertain. Theodosia did not shy away, nor did she lash out. Her eyes on him were grave, studying him.

He hoped she found him acceptable. It was too late to change her mind—the rite bound them until one of them died. He might not have chosen that, but she had asked for it. Maybe she had hoped to bind him, but she had also bound herself.

He eyed the bed and considered strategies. She was not going to come to him, that much he could see. He risked shocking her by discarding his robe.

She neither flinched nor looked away. He could not tell if she knew what a man looked like. He made his way across the expanse of bed, trying not to make too much of a fool of himself.

She did not laugh at him. Neither, when he reached her, did she make any move toward him.

He sat on his heels, at a loss. None of the few women he had loved in his life had sat so still or shown so little evidence of desire. They had all wanted him at least as much as he wanted them.

If Theodosia had been a horse, he would have known what to do.

Well, he thought, why not? He shifted carefully until he sat cross-legged just within reach. From there he could see that her stillness concealed a deep tension. She held the coverlet like a shield, pressed tight above her breasts.

Wise noblemen made sure their daughters were taught to do their duty in the bedchamber. It seemed the Prince of Elladis was not wise. This lady was terrified, and doing everything she could to hide it.

Once Kerrec realized that, rather to his surprise he relaxed. Terrified creatures, human or animal, were nothing strange to him at all. He stayed where he was, deliberately unthreatening, and let her accustom herself to having him so close.

It did not take long. He ventured the beginning of a smile. She smiled shakily back.

He held out his hand. After a moment she took it. He sat still until she steadied. Then, slowly, he asked with a closing of the fingers.

If she had refused, he would not have pressed her. But she took a deep breath and closed her eyes. When she opened them, she moved, letting the coverlet fall.

Her breasts were full and firm. The gown that covered them was all but transparent. It aroused him in subtle ways—more than if she had been naked.

Her eyes widened. She never had seen a man, then, or been warned of what happened when his body warmed to a woman.

She was brave, or else she remembered stallions—for surely she had seen those. She neither screamed nor fled. He let her examine him, which she did with a remarkable lack of embarrassment.

Another man might have seized her and done what was necessary, but if Kerrec had done that, he would have lost her. He steadied his breathing and held the moment, though that meant holding it a little short of pain.

Just as he decided that tonight was going to come to nothing, she rose to her knees. Her cheeks had flushed. She touched him diffidently, then with more confidence, tracing the shape of his shoulder and the length of his arm.

She had good hands, light but clear in their intent, as a horseman's should be. He shivered slightly, pleasurably, as they explored his body. Again he resisted temptation. If he touched her in return, she would lose her courage.

Rather than deadening his desire, this enforced restraint made it all the stronger. He set his teeth to keep from groaning aloud.

She leaned forward suddenly and brushed his lips with hers. It was like a kiss of subtle fire. He dared to offer something more, something deeper. With a sound half of fear and half of surrender, she opened to him.

His body tried to surge toward her. With all his strength he held it back. She took him instead as suddenly as she had kissed him, driving him back and down with strength that caught him by surprise.

Either she had had a little teaching after all or her body

knew more than her mind could have learned in her father's palace. She bestrode him as if he had been a stallion.

A soft cry escaped her. There was pain, but beyond it was pleasure. Kerrec knew better than any how that could be.

This was no torture, and he was no Brother of Pain. As she stiffened, he moved swiftly, piercing the barrier and then holding still while she woke to understanding of what he had done.

At the first sign of softening in her, he began to move in the old dance, slow at first and gentle, then faster as she warmed to him. She was unskilled and they were not so closely matched that they fell naturally into one another's rhythm, but Kerrec was a rider and this was his art.

His mind was oddly cool and distant. His body took pleasure where it found it, but the rest of him kept to itself. When the climax came, he held it for as long as he could, until her breathing quickened and her body pulsed and he could let go.

She fell back, still breathing hard. The gown clung to her sweat-dampened body. Her scent was sweet and strong, poised on the edge between alluring and cloying.

He kissed her softly. She stared without recognition, then a smile bloomed. "Beautiful man," she said.

Women always said that. He had learned to suffer it. He laced his fingers with hers and brought them to his lips. "Beautiful lady," he replied.

Her smile deepened. "I'm very fortunate," she said. "I could have been given to an old man or a cruel one, or a man who simply took what was his and never asked if I was willing."

"No rider would do that," Kerrec said.

"Riders are a rarity and a wonder," she said. "If more of us knew what you are, we'd be importuning our fathers and brothers to make marriages with you, and never mind the princes we were meant for."

"It's best kept a secret, then," he said.

She nodded with a tinge of regret. "Probably so. I'll enjoy my good fortune in solitude, and thank the gods for granting it to me."

"The gods have blessed us," he said honestly enough.

She smiled again. Her eyelids were drooping, her body loosed with the aftermath of pleasure.

Long after she fell asleep, he lay watching her. What he felt was not love but a fierce protectiveness, a sense that this was his and nothing must harm it. A stallion felt the same toward the mares of his herd.

Kerrec must have slept. The lamp's light had dimmed and the air had the first faint scent of morning. He lay beside Theodosia, not knowing at first what had roused him. Then she stirred again and cried out, a low wail that raised the small hairs on the nape of his neck.

He drew her to him, holding her tightly. She shuddered in his arms. The scent of magic overwhelmed the sweetness of her perfume, filling his nostrils with the sharpness of heated metal.

She was caught in a magical dream. He dared not force her to wake, though her trembling had grown so strong he feared for her. All he could do was hold her and pray, and muster what power he had to keep her safe.

After what seemed a long while, her tremors stilled. Her breathing quieted. The reek of magic faded. She lay limp, drawing shallow breaths.

The rhythm of her breathing changed. He looked into wide dark eyes full of sleep and something else that made his skin prickle.

"Darkness," she said in a voice he barely recognized. "Oblivion. I see…nothing. Nothing at all."

The Augurs had said the same after the Dance. Kerrec thrust down the surge of panic. Now of all times, his mind had to be clear.

"The One is coming," she said. "The bonds of earth are loosed. When they break, so will all that is."

"Who—" Kerrec began—unwisely, maybe.

"You know," she said.

"But—"

"Where you hate most," she said, "the One is there."

Kerrec did not hate anyone living, even the tribes who worshipped the Unmaking. He decided not to say so. In this half-trance on the edge of dream, she was not seeing as mortals saw.

"Where you love most," she said, "there also is the One. Between hate and love is the world's ending. So close—so terribly, terribly close."

"What can we do?" he demanded. "How can we stop it?"

"There is no stopping it," she said. "The maw of Unmaking is open. No power of earth can close it."

"That can't be true," Kerrec said. "There must be a way."

She had no answer for that. She could only say, "Look to the east. It's stronger there—but when the One comes, it will be strongest here."

"There is a way," he said. "There has to be."

She was silent. After a while he realized that her breathing had settled into the rhythm of sleep.

He would not sleep again that night. What she saw, what he felt in the patterns that shaped the world, woke such dread that he could barely move or think.

That was the end of his wedding night, with a brass-bright dawn and a day of suffocating heat thereafter. He had four days of feasting to survive, and four nights of loving that at least were pleasurable, though she was not a passionate woman and he had not fallen in love with her. But after every night's loving she slept, and in sleep she dreamed—and every dream led to the Unmaking.

On the fifth day he found Valeria and her stallions gone. On the tenth, criminally late, it dawned on him that she had not gone to the Mountain. As he traced patterns in the wake of Theodosia's dreams, he could not find Valeria where he thought to find her.

He did find the skein of her presence interwoven with all of the stallions—but three had moved away from the rest. They had gone eastward toward the wall of shadow that was the frontier.

They had gone to the tribes—to the One. If it had been Valeria alone, it would have been bad enough, but all her stallions were with her. She was riding straight into the jaws of oblivion, and they were carrying her as if it were eminently and blessedly safe.

When the truth struck, he wasted no time with mortals—though both Briana and Nikos would feel the sharp edge of his anger. He went straight to the stallions in their stable and confronted the lot of them.

They regarded him with bland curiosity, as if they had been mortal horses and he had been a crazed invader of their nightly peace. He refused to be drawn into the game. He stood in the center of the aisle and lashed them all with a hot fire of rage. "You did this. You let her go. Why? Why do you keep trying to destroy her?"

Even Petra had no response to that. He buried his face in his manger, hunting for stray bits of hay from his dinner.

Kerrec caught him by the forelock and pulled his head around. His eye was large and dark and completely opaque. "First Briana and now Valeria," Kerrec said. "What do you have against our women?"

The lid lowered over the unreadable eye. Petra nipped at Kerrec's hand, an unexpected flash of temper.

"Of course I don't understand," Kerrec snapped. "You won't explain. At least let me warn her. She doesn't know, does she? None of you told her. She's going straight to the barbarians' hell, and she thinks she's doing—what? Playing ambassador? Bringing your light to the heathen?"

In that eye he saw three stallions like a living spell of ward and protection. All around them was swirling chaos. Within their circle was quiet, and Valeria.

Kerrec shook his head. "I don't believe you. Are you our enemies after all? Do you want to see us gone? Is that what this is for?"

Petra's teeth closed on Kerrec's wrist. Kerrec stood very still. Those jaws could snap off his hand with terrible ease, or crush the bones without breaking the skin.

"Do it," he said, though his breath came somewhat fast. "Be honest for once. Do what you yearn to do."

Petra shook him, but lightly—then let him go.

That surprised him. He stood a moment, rubbing his

bruised wrist, not knowing what to say, before the words came flooding. "At least warn her. Tell her what she's walking into. Give her a chance to defend herself when the darkness falls."

She has always had that.

The gods never resorted willingly to words. Kerrec refused to let them sway him. "Warn her. Or let me. Take my words to her. Tell her to be watchful and defend herself with all the power she has. The Unmaking is waiting. It will swallow her if it can."

Petra stood motionless. Kerrec drove the words at him with voice and magic. *"Warn her!"*

The proud head bowed. In the stalls around them, the stallions were perfectly silent.

Valeria could speak to them all. No other rider could or ever had. If they deigned to send Kerrec's warning, she would hear it. Please the gods, whether these or any others, she would listen.

Chapter Twenty-Six

Valeria had crossed the river during the war, but she had gone only half a day's journey into the lands that belonged to the tribes. At that time the empire's magic had reached no farther than the water. Everything past it was wild, untamed, with magic running free in earth and water and air. No orders contained it and no ranks of mages kept it tightly bound.

Now that the war was won, she had expected to find the wild magic at least partly tamed. Imperial legions had been building camps and fortresses, with roads and the beginnings of towns, three and four and five days' ride from the river. Tribute parties had ranged farther than that, though what they could have been collecting after the tribes' great defeat, she could not imagine.

And yet even along the river, the air was different. The veneer of imperial order was as thin as a sheet of parchment and hardly more substantial. Dark things, wild things, surged beneath.

For any mage of the empire it was not the most comfortable country to travel in. For Valeria, even with the stallions to ground and center her, it was almost physically painful.

Here the Unmaking had been worshipped for time out of mind. It was close to the surface of things, urging the nothingness inside her to wake and grow and swallow her whole.

She should not have come here. She knew that within a day. By the fifth day she decided to turn back. Whether that was cowardice or foolishness or simple good sense, it was the only safe course.

That night the caravan camped outside the easternmost outpost of the legion, which had been named Artoria in honor of the late emperor. The rest of the caravan could eat and rest in peace, but Pretorius and Valeria, in their office of imperial envoys, were obliged to dine with the commander.

He was an older man, hard-bitten and devoid of illusions about this country he had been sent to tame. From his age and accent Valeria concluded that he had come up through the ranks—a rarity in this age, and testimony to the quality of the man who had done it. Pretorius the commoner-mage and Valeria the centurion's daughter received as warm a welcome as Gerontius was capable of.

The dinner he served was plain but well cooked, roast venison and summer greens and fresh-baked bread. Valeria had not expected to have an appetite, but the emptiness in her craved to be filled.

Gerontius was a taciturn man, but with a little wine in him

and the evening light to soften his mood, he unbent enough
to ask, "You really mean to go on into the wild country?"

"It's not as wild as that," Pretorius said. "The tribes are
civilized after their fashion. They spend the winter in duns,
which are built rather like this fort, and in the warm season
they farm and hunt."

"And wage war," said Gerontius.

"Not this year," Valeria heard herself say.

"You don't think so?" Gerontius said. "War is their life's
blood. They'd no sooner give it up than one of us would give
up breathing."

Valeria bit her lip before she said something unfortunate.
This was the empire's choice to stand point, this man who
knew nothing of the tribes and did not care to learn. Any
move they made, he would interpret as hostile. Then, no
doubt, he would take what he considered appropriate action.

She wondered if Briana knew anything of this. If she did,
maybe she did not know what it meant. She had never been
east of the river.

Pretorius caught Valeria's eye. She could not read his expression. "We are going eastward," he said. "We bring gifts
to the new high king."

"The high king should be bringing gifts to you," Gerontius said. "His people belong to the empire now."

"They may not agree with you," Pretorius said. His tone
was light, pleasant. "We have our orders, Commander, as
you have yours. Is there anything you can tell us of the man
who rules the tribes?"

"There's not much to tell," Gerontius said. "He's a fighting man, they say, and well bred as they reckon it—he comes

from a long line of their kings. Some say he speaks our language, others that he refuses to learn. He's a better enemy of the empire than the old king, that much is certain, and they say he's a better general. It's not a matter of whether he'll try to start another war but when."

"That is one of the things we've been sent to determine," said Pretorius. "I've been given authority to enlist a cohort of your men. Can you spare them?"

"I don't think he should," Valeria said.

Both men stared at her. She would not have said they were affronted, but she had spoken out of turn. She watched them remember what she was.

"If we go to the king's dun with a troop of legionaries," she said, "we go as conquerors. That will invite their hatred and possibly get us killed. We'll be safer if we go as envoys from one royal personage to another. Aren't embassies sacred to them? We have our guards, who aren't obviously imperial troops, and our magic, which they aren't trained to recognize. Those will protect us."

Pretorius regarded her in what she could only interpret as pride. "So we shall," he said, "and if three of our royal envoys walk on four feet instead of two, the high king may even be impressed."

Valeria opened her mouth to say that she did not intend to take herself or the stallions any farther than this fort, but the words did not come. *We*, she had said, and while she said it she meant it. She had been thinking of the empire then and not herself.

How safe was it for the empire if her magic lost control and loosed the Unmaking?

It would not. She had three white gods to guard her, and a mage of three magics.

Three was a number of the tribes. Aurelia ran in fours and eights. She hoped it was not a bad omen.

They left the last of the caravan at the fort. The guards and the five prisoners rode on with them, a company of two dozen in all, with mules to carry provisions and gifts for the high king and the lesser kings who might come across their path.

It was not a long journey to Dun Mor—half a month, maybe, at a steady pace, or a month if they stopped along the way. The tribes were quiet, engrossed in the summer hunt. The women and children stayed behind in the duns while their men ranged the hunting runs, sending back whatever they found to be preserved for the winter—meat dried or salted, hides tanned, hooves and bone and sinew turned to every use imaginable, from flutes and harpstrings to drumheads and quivers and the framework of shields.

Valeria had thought she would be riding into the maw of the Unmaking. To her astonishment, the magic of the land grew calmer the farther she rode from the fort. It was still nothing like imperial magic, but it had found its own order. It ran in the streams and grew in the groves and copses.

As forest opened into moor, its wildness took on shape and form. It embodied itself in stands of stones, shrines rank with old blood and the dregs of pain. More than once the riders passed pallid hills that as they came closer resolved into heaps of skulls and interwoven bones.

And yet the duns and camps were warm and pulsing with life. The people might make a cult of anguish and worship oblivion, but in the daylight they had a bright strength that even war and loss and bitterness could not destroy.

Valeria remembered the names of the tribes and clans that she passed. None of them was the Caletanni. They were not in this part of the world. She would have to go farther south and somewhat west to find their hunting runs.

She could not say if she was disappointed. One man of the Caletanni might remember her, though it was hardly likely that memory would be fond. She had spared his life twice in the face of death and defeat. She knew better than to expect gratitude for that.

In any case it did not matter. The people were all strangers here. Aurelia to them was a land of war and conquest. They knew no more of it than Gerontius knew of them.

It was true that envoys were considered blessed, but travelers of any kind were sacred. Everywhere the embassy stopped, the clans offered them warm and open-handed hospitality.

When they had been traveling through this stark and often surprising land for close on a month, they stopped in a hunting camp among a clan the name of which in Aurelian was the Dun Cow. Its chieftain's banner was the hide of just such a beast, and he wore the skull and horns as a crown when he sat down to dinner.

He was a big man, redheaded as so many of his people were, with thick copper-colored plaits to the waist and exuberant mustaches of which he was clearly proud. He did not look terribly much like another redheaded tribesman Valeria had known—he was heavier, less graceful, less pleasing in the face—but still he struck her with familiarity. She caught herself missing Euan Rohe rather than hating him.

People in this country could drink and feast all night long, but she was not so hardy. She went to her own camp as soon as she politely could, but once she was there, she found that she could not sleep.

She tossed on her blanket. These high northern moors had nothing like the heat of lowland Aurelia, but the night was close and still, the sky heavy with cloud. Lightning flashed along the horizon. Occasionally she heard a rumble of thunder.

As she lay on the ground in the sweet scent of heather and summer grass, the thunder seemed to come from below rather than above. Her skin prickled. The slow heat that rose in her did not feel like anything of hers. It was part of the spell inside her, born of this land and its people.

Something was trying to pierce the walls that protected her mind. It was strong but blessedly distant. Even through her defenses she could feel the sense it brought of fierce urgency and deep foreboding.

It could be—must be—a trap. It could not be what it seemed. Kerrec was not calling to her through the massed voices of the stallions, trying to warn her against—what? Doing what she was already doing?

She owed him nothing. He had done his duty, as he must. So had she. His sudden attack of desperation did not help—it was too little and too late.

She raised her walls even higher and made them even stronger. The call muted enough to be almost bearable.

She pushed herself to her feet. The rest of the embassy slept in a circle. Beyond them she heard the sounds of late carousing growing slowly fainter as the night grew later.

Her stallions had been tethered with the rest of the horses, but as she stood upright, Sabata loomed in front of her. She ran her hands down his face and along his heavy arched neck. His mane was rough under her fingers.

She grasped it and swung onto his back. That deep sense she always had when she rode him, of coming home, was so sharp she almost let out a cry.

Without her urging, he moved forward. His long swinging stride calmed her somewhat. She did not know or care where he was carrying her.

As long as she was on him, the call from Aurelia did not trouble her. It was still there, but far away and all but silent.

She closed her mind completely to it. Sabata waded through tall grass, ascending the long hill that rose above the camp. For a while she heard the burble of a stream and smelled the coolness of water until he turned away from it toward the summit.

The lightning was moving closer. A small wind had begun to blow. The scent of rain was in it, distinct from the smell of the stream—thicker, darker, wilder.

Beneath the roll of thunder she heard another sound. Drums were beating in the rhythm of a slow heartbeat. Voices chanted in a language she did not know, the same word or words over and over.

As with the spell of Unmaking, it did not matter whether she understood. The words themselves were the spell. Once heard, they became a part of her.

They were words of bleak and empty places, barren earth and cold stone and the breath of graves. Even their paean to pain was dulled and crusted over.

Valeria buried her face in Sabata's mane. The familiar pungent smell and the warmth of his body gave her something to cling to. Without them she would have spun down into nothingness, lacking even the strength to care.

He shook his head and pawed lightly. She made herself look up, though her arms were still wrapped around his neck.

He had come to the summit of the hill and descended a little distance. Down below was a stony valley such as priests of the One favored. No grass grew there and no water ran. The earth was blasted bare as if with lightning or a mage-bolt.

A deep shudder ran through Valeria. Neither magic nor lightning had done this. The valley was half Unmade. What substance it had left was as thin as a layer of dust, held together by the magic that bound this country. Even a breath gone astray could destroy it—and once it was gone, the world would follow.

That valley was like Valeria's own heart. Its existence was just as precarious. The priests who stood inside it were feeding on the delicate balance of being and unbeing. It made their own powers stronger, even as it threatened to unmake them.

Sabata stood on the boundary between mortal earth and immortal nothingness. That boundary was shifting—growing. It could unmake a god as easily as any human thing, but he was not afraid of it.

In that much, the white gods were like the horses they resembled. They lived in the present. There was no past or future. There was only the eternal now.

That now would be unmade—and then there would be nothing at all. All that was would be swallowed in oblivion.

Valeria had only to let go and she would be gone. No pain and no sorrow and no shame of jealousy, ever again.

She wrenched herself from the seduction of that thought. The priests' chant had faded. She looked for the victim who was the crown of such rites, but there was none.

The Unmaking was the sacrifice. They were both sustaining and restraining it. They moved in slow patterns, subtly bent and twisted, sweeping their long robes along the bare and dusty ground.

One by one the robes fell. Valeria was prepared for it, but it was still a shock to see those naked bodies like corpses walking. Some bore mutilations of elaborate complexity. Others were clothed in scars. Some were blind, some faceless, others missing limbs.

None was whole—that was the requirement of their order. Every one was in some way touched by their god.

The chief of them was the last to discard his mantle. He stood in the center, straight and steady as few others were. There was no mark on his body and no visible scar.

His scars were of the spirit. That was a gnarled and stunted thing.

When he raised his face to the starless sky, Valeria hissed between her teeth. She had not wanted to recognize him—she had not believed what her eyes told her.

It was Gothard. He was alive. There could be no mistake.

She knew that face as well as she knew Kerrec's, and hated it as much as she had loved his brother's. Those blunter, plainer features were close enough to Kerrec's that one could not mistake their kinship. That heavier body still had a ghost of the elder brother's grace.

As if her shock had triggered a spell, he turned until he stared straight at her. His shock was as strong as hers. Then it changed.

Hate—she had expected that. Outrage and desire for revenge, twisted together and bound with old rancor—that was no surprise. But above and beyond them all was triumph. As he recognized Valeria, his whole soul was a cry of victory.

Chapter Twenty-Seven

Valeria woke to the drumming of rain on the roof of her tent. She had no memory of pitching the tent or going to sleep in it.

Had it been a dream, then? Had she imagined Gothard in the field of Unmaking? It had felt so real. The shock of it was still with her, knotting her belly.

Her hand felt strange. She was clutching something so hard her muscles were knotted and the edges had dug into her skin. With an effort she unfolded her fingers.

It was a stone, round and glossy black and sharp enough to cut. One of the cuts had bled.

The stone was like the pupil of an eye, staring at her. Magic nested in it. Deep inside, she saw Gothard's face.

She flung it as far away from her as she could. It was true—it was real, whether she had gone there in the flesh or in dream. Gothard was alive. He was in this country, working his magic against the empire and his own kin.

And now he knew she was coming. Sabata had betrayed her.

That could not be true. There must be another meaning in this. The stallions were Aurelia's heart. They would not hand her over to Aurelia's enemy.

And yet...

The Lady had allowed Briana to be all but destroyed. Now Sabata had brought Valeria to this. The gods had turned against Aurelia.

Valeria shook her head hard. No matter what she had said to the Lady, she refused to believe that. The empire had shown a distressing tendency to forget that the white gods existed, but that was the riders' fault. They were making amends. They were doing what the gods wanted them to do.

Sabata must have brought her to this country to bring Gothard down. With all three stallions here and the rest within her, she could do it.

Maybe it was not only Gothard who would fall but the One itself. Her heart thudded at the thought. Could she destroy Unmaking with Unmaking? Could she unmake the nothingness inside herself?

If she had been alone, that would have been grand hubris. With three white gods and a master of three magics, it might be possible.

The patterns were no clearer after she swore to herself that she would do this. They were still like a tangle of leaves and vines growing toward the edge of a cliff. One moment they were dense with life, the next there was nothing. They were all gone.

She scraped herself together as best she could. The rain

had stopped. She peered out of the tent into a suddenly bright morning.

Everything was washed clean. Tribesmen who had fallen asleep under the sky were rising, blinking, sopping wet but grinning broadly.

When they caught Valeria's eye, some stiffened, but many kept on grinning. They did not know what she was—either female or a rider. To them she was simply one of several small dark imperials trespassing on their lands. Their grins dared her to make something of it.

She declined to be provoked. It was a wonder that any of the embassy was still alive, considering how the tribes hated them. But there was courtesy here, and inviolable custom. They were safe unless they said or did something that could not be forgiven.

The guards were up and saddling horses. The prisoners, who had spoken hardly a word since they passed the river, huddled together as far from the clansmen as their bonds would let them go. It seemed their worship of the One did not extend to the One's chosen people.

As Valeria broke her fast with a loaf of last night's bread and a cup of heavily watered wine, Master Pretorius emerged from his tent and calmly dismantled it with a gesture. It collapsed its poles, folded its canvas, and put itself away in a mule's pack.

Valeria gaped as foolishly as any tribesman. She had heard of such magic but never seen it. It was not an art any of Pretorius' three orders was known for.

She shut her mouth with care. Pretorius went on his way so casually that she knew he was feigning it.

In Valeria's mind he had done a deeply stupid thing, but she kept her thoughts to herself. She found her stallions on the lines, wet and gloriously muddy, and applied herself to making them fit to be seen.

Gothard looked like a cat who had got into the cream. His usually sullen face was almost cheerful as he hung about the camp.

Euan Rohe did not try overly hard to find out what had brought an almost-smile to replace the perpetual frown. If he was honest with himself, he was afraid to ask. It could be nothing good.

The hunting from this camp had been waning for a few days, enough that he had begun to think of moving on. Then suddenly the woods were full of game and the moors alive with birds and coneys and herds of deer.

"Fire in the east," his kinsman Conory said as they got ready for the morning's hunt. Conory had been out on his own and had come back just this morning. "Lightning's been walking all along the moors. The grass is burning from Caermor to Dun Gralloch."

That was not good news for the duns and camps in the path of the flames. Euan sent messengers to prepare the duns near them for the fire, but also to order that they take in any clansman who happened to be fleeing from it.

He should go there himself, and he would—but this morning he had promised his people a hunt. Some of them were mounted but most were on foot. A horse was waiting for Euan, but he chose to run like a proper tribesman, leading the pack of them out to the braying of horns and the baying of hounds and the laughter and song of men hungry for a good run and a clean kill.

The cares of a king fell away. Euan whooped with the best of them, sounded his horn and set the game to running. Birds flew up in a thunder of wings. Coneys darted out from underfoot. Off to his right, someone started a wild pig—a young one, squealing in terror.

Darts and arrows were flying, but Euan had different prey in mind today. He craved a fine haunch of venison, rubbed with herbs and roasted on a spit.

Deer liked the river that ran into the camp. He followed it upstream with a handful of his warband and a few odd clansmen at his back. The rest of the hunt veered off southward after the pig's kin. From the racket the hounds were making, there was at least one big boar in the lot.

He paused a moment, torn. He did love a good boar hunt. But he would look weak-minded if he turned back now.

While he paused, his eye caught fresh deer sign. A herd had made its way up the track not long before, does and fawns and one large, heavy track that would be the stag.

He was a big one, with hooves as wide as Euan's palm. Euan forgot the boar in contemplation of a stag as tall as a horse. Now there was quarry worth hunting.

He grinned at Conory who was directly behind him, tireless in spite of having been on the road all night. Grins flashed beyond. No one appeared to regret their choice of prey.

The track led them through a thicket—the trees much torn with the stag's antlers—and back out onto the heath. It was steep in places and sometimes seemed to disappear altogether as the herd leaped falls of brush or sudden out-croppings of stone.

The hunters meandered along the side of a long ridge. The sign was fresher now. Euan reckoned the deer must have rounded the ridge and settled to graze in the valley on the other side. The grass there was greener than elsewhere, watered by a bubbling cauldron of springs.

The footing was treacherous, but it was rich pasture and a good hunting ground. Euan thanked the One for sending the herd there.

He glanced from side to side. His companions had slowed as he had, sensing that their prey was close. They paused to string bows and ready throwing spears, then rounded the ridge with care, crouching low against the background of rock and brush.

The valley stretched below, a long oval between two arms of the ridge. On the far side it opened onto the moor.

The deer were moving slowly along the far end of the valley. There were half a dozen does, stepping delicately. All but one had twin fawns.

At first Euan did not see the stag. Then he emerged from behind a moss-covered heap of stone.

Euan's heart stopped. The rest of the deer were red or dappled as they should be. The stag was marked like one of the people's cattle. His coat was as dark a red as Euan had seen in a deer, seeming almost black at that distance, but all through it were spots and splashes of white.

The spotted stag, Conor had said. And there he was, as big as Euan had imagined, with antlers spreading wider than

Euan's arms could stretch. He had seen them first above the stone like the branches of a leafless tree.

One by one, with all the stealth that hunters of the people could manage, the Caletanni made their way down into the valley. There was precious little cover there, but dun leather trews and bodies smeared with mud and ocher made them invisible to passing glances. The wind favored them, blowing in their faces, bringing them the heavy green scent of the valley and, strong beneath it, the musk of the stag.

The men nocked arrows to the strings of their hunting bows. Euan left his bow slung behind him and firmed his grip on his spear. It was a less reliable weapon than a bow, but heavier. He felt in his belly that with this stag, he would need it.

They crept in file down off the ridge and through the valley, picking their way around the springs and the marshy hollows. The deer were calm enough, engrossed in the deep green grass.

Euan kept his eye on the stag. The great beast had moved toward the end of the valley, where the grass was thinner and the springs had stopped coming up through the earth. He cropped the lesser forage warily, lifting his great crowned head often and drinking deep of the air.

The hunters had come within bowshot of the herd. They advanced a little closer, then bows came up and arrows aimed. The first one flew from Cieran's bow, straight to the heart of a fat doe.

She fell so quietly the rest of the herd barely noticed. Then another fell, and a third.

The stag loosed an explosive snort. Those of the herd who survived leaped into motion, springing high and wide and away from the hunters.

Euan left his men to deal with the three they had shot, rising to his feet but crouching low. The stag alone was still, guarding the herd's escape.

Euan aimed along the shaft of his spear. There was a winding stream of white on the shoulder like a river on a map, marking the path to the heart.

He cast the spear. The stag leaped in the air. The spearhead clipped its shoulder, opening a long bloody track, and dropped away.

Euan abandoned stealth. He strung his bow at the run, nocked an arrow and aimed and shot. The bolt flew wide.

A wise man would have given up. They had three fat does to bring back to camp. He could find the stag again, this time with horses and better strategy.

That was imperial thinking. Euan was not—refused to be—an imperial.

The stag was wounded. It was not a deep wound but it was bleeding freely. Loss of blood would weaken him, then Euan would take him.

Euan paused to drink from the last of the springs. The cold clear water made him dizzy with its purity. Behind him the rest of his men were butchering deer.

Conory looked up and met Euan's eye, and nodded as if words had passed between them. He spoke briefly to Cyllan who was nearest, won a nod from him in return, washed the blood off his hands and picked up his weapons and trotted toward Euan.

They went on together, still without a word spoken. The stag's blood trail was clear, first in grass and then in heather. The pied splendor of him bounded strongly still, leading them away from the remains of the herd.

They settled into the wolf's pace, the long loping stride that could cover long leagues without tiring. It would take as long as it took—that was tribesmen's thinking. Euan would still be Ard Ri when he came back. When he brought the spotted hide with him, he would prove yet again that he was fit for the office.

Part of him was aware of the distance he traversed, marking the lie of the land and taking note of where he was in this country that he knew better than the inside of his new and royal tent. The stag had turned from north to west, then south toward the hunting runs of the Dun Cow. It was slowing a little, though its strength was still remarkable.

It never quite let him get within bowshot. That was a clever coincidence. He would not allow himself to wonder if it was more.

By the One, he hated magic. This was a perfectly ordinary if large and oddly marked stag. The fact Conor had spoken of it…his mind would not go there. Nor would it go where Conor had gone, foretelling what would happen after he had chased this particular stag.

If Euan was not careful, he would see a rider on the stag, a tall and slim child with fiery hair. Of course Conor was not riding the beast. That was absurd. Conor was in camp with the other menchildren, learning to hunt and fight.

Euan shook the vision out of his eyes and quickened his

pace. Conory matched his stride as easily as ever. They were closing in—at last, if slowly. It would only be a little longer before they could bring the stag down.

Chapter Twenty-Eight

By noon of the day they left the Dun Cow, the embassy was deep in country so barren and deserted that one might think it was the edge of the world. Mile after mile of stony heath and purple heather stretched away into the blue distance. Every now and then, as if to mock the travelers with memory of gentler places, a copse grew in the wasteland.

Those marked water, Pretorius said, though it might be far beneath the ground. The trees were low and stunted, and most were evergreens, dark and fragrant. Beasts and birds lived there in surprising abundance.

"This is rich country," Pretorius said, "though it looks so bleak. There's more than enough forage for deer and boar and the wolves and cats that prey on them, and there are more shapes and races of birds than anywhere else we know of. The land feeds the tribes' cattle well enough, and their sheep and goats and pigs, too."

"Where are they?" Valeria asked.

"Camped in hidden valleys," he answered, "or secure in duns on hills and ridges. They need a great deal of space, do the tribes. As empty as this land looks, in their minds it's growing unbearably crowded."

"So they keep trying to cross the river and conquer us," Valeria said. "But if this is crowded, our empire must be impossible even to contemplate."

"Ah," he said, "but we're not human people. We're quarry—not nearly as noble as deer. We're rabbits, rather, infesting the grass. We'll feed and serve them, and they'll live off our lands."

"Do you think we can ever learn to live together?"

Pretorius's eyes narrowed as he pondered that. After a while he said, "Not as we are now. Either or both of us would need to change profoundly."

"Artorius tried to do that," she said. "He took hostages and made them learn our ways. Some he even sent to the School of War."

She stopped abruptly. Some indeed he had, and she had known them. She had more than known one—and done her best ever since to forget him.

Pretorius seemed unaware that she had meant to say more. He nodded slowly. "Most say he failed, since those princes took the opportunity to turn our own powers against us. Still, I wonder. They learned our language, our customs, and some of our ways of peace as well as war. That has to have left a mark. Maybe they hate us—but our words are inside their heads. They don't think purely as tribesmen. Not any longer."

"You think so?" Valeria asked.

"How can it be otherwise? Words are power, lady."

"The white gods think words are beneath them."

"Ah," he said, "but they are gods."

Valeria smoothed Marina's mane on his neck. He was taking his turn carrying her while the others ranged where they pleased. At the moment that was just behind her, matching Marina's pace as if they had been in a quadrille.

It kept them amused. Marina was the softest-gaited of the three, which made for a pleasant day's ride. The land for all its bleakness had its own beauty, which she could learn to grow fond of.

The magic was less jarringly wild here, or else she was growing accustomed to the randomness of its patterns. It was beginning to make sense to her.

Was this what it had been like in Aurelia before the orders of mages imposed their own patterns on it? That was how it felt—raw and unformed. Here and there she could sense the beginnings of order, places where magic had begun to take coherent shape.

There were more than she might have expected. Some were close to this place, and one or two were like beacons in the dark.

The embassy had been following what might be a sheep track, but Pretorius insisted it was a road. Mostly it kept below the summits of ridges, and it seemed to cross every brook and rill in this country. A number of those came together at the foot of a crag, where swans swam in a dark and bottomless lake.

The unexpected beauty of the place brought her up short. Marina halted obligingly and dropped his head to crop the grass that grew on the shore.

Oda did the same—wise beast. Sabata waded knee-deep into the lake and drank in long luxurious gulps. Valeria smiled as with each gulp his ears ratcheted back and then forward. It was one of the small and silly things that made horses so endlessly fascinating.

The lake from which he drank was so still that it reflected each swan and every crack and fold of the cliff. A second Sabata glimmered in it.

On the far side around the foot of the crag, a pied shape appeared, running swiftly. At first she took it for a long-legged horse, but then she saw the crown of antlers. It was a stag, and he was wounded. Blood ran from a long slash in his shoulder.

There was magic in him, drawn up from the earth itself and bleeding out again as he ran. The stallions raised their heads to watch him. They were more than magical—they were magic. They recognized the kinship.

Someone was riding the stag, a child with long red hair and wild golden eyes. He flickered in and out of sight, as if he were only half there. The magic in him was even stronger than that in the stag.

She heard Pretorius breathing beside her. He was watching, too, though she could not tell what he saw.

Two men ran in pursuit of the stag. They were redheaded like the child, dressed in breeches the color of the heath. Their faces and bodies were painted all over with dun and ocher. Both carried bows in their hands, and the straps of quivers crossed their broad bare chests.

Valeria blinked. Surely there was only one of them—not two who looked exactly alike.

Her eyes persisted in showing her a pair of tribesmen. There were differences after all, she saw as they drew nearer. One was slightly taller and the other was slightly narrower. The one in front, the taller one, wore a golden torque as thick as a child's wrist. The other's torque was silver and set with dark red stones.

The smaller man's eyes were green. His companion's were as yellow as a wolf's.

She would know those eyes anywhere. The face under the paint was older, broader, stronger, but it was still the face she knew. Her eye looked for and found the scar on his shoulder where a boar had tusked him when he was a boy.

The stag plunged into the lake and began to swim, trailing a ribbon of blood. Without knowing what she did or why, Valeria reached from inside herself and laid healing on the wound. She felt the strength pouring out of her, but she was not alarmed. Marina's own strength poured in, restoring everything she had lost.

Euan Rohe stopped a short bowshot from Valeria. His eyes were wide with shock. She supposed hers were the same.

The stag was halfway across the lake. The man with Euan—it was Conory, Euan's kinsman who could have been his twin—raised his bow and aimed.

The arrow flew, but it dissolved into air. Conory let the bow fall and spread his hands. His expression was wry.

Euan wore no expression at all. The last Valeria had seen of him, he was escaping from the slaughter at Oxos Ford. He must hate her beyond measure for being the cause of that bitter defeat.

She did not want him to hate her. She wanted…what?

Not love. That was not possible. He was Aurelia's enemy and therefore hers. She had made her choice.

Had she not?

Pretorius spoke from beside her. "A good day to you, clansmen," he said civilly in the language of the tribes.

She understood it better than she wanted to. Euan Rohe had taught her.

Euan did not speak—probably words were beyond him. It was Conory who said, "A good day to you, man of the empire. Where would you be traveling?"

It was a proper question, politely expressed, but there was no mistaking the edge with which he asked it.

Pretorius' response was perfectly smooth. "We're riding to Dun Mor, unless the Ard Ri happens to be elsewhere."

Conory glanced at Euan. Euan had stiffened almost invisibly. Again it was Conory who said, "He's hunting around Glen Mor."

"I thank you for that, clansman," Pretorius said.

Conory saluted him with a touch of hand to forehead. "You'll find the road takes you there, man of the empire, if you follow it north and east."

That happened to be back the way he had come. He did not offer to guide them there.

Valeria was glad of that. When the embassy rode on, she refused to look back, still less to look at Euan. She could feel him refusing to look at her.

That hurt, though she had wished for it. She almost stopped, turned back, spoke—though what she could say, she did not know.

She left him by the lake with his kinsman. The stag was

long gone, for which she was glad. They could find something else to hunt, something less alive with magic.

Euan stood long after Valeria was gone, eyes fixed on the place where she had been.

Finally Conory took it on himself to speak. "Well? Are you going to try to get back to camp before they get there?"

Euan shook himself out of his trance of shock. "Three gods from the Mountain. Three. Here. In our country."

"So I noticed," Conory said. "You think they've come to enslave us to their religion?"

Euan had not even thought of that. "I think they've been lured here. Have you seen Gothard lately? He's been smiling."

"*He* brought them?"

Euan could understand Conory's incredulity. Gothard had failed twice because of those fat white horses. And yet the sorcerer had come back stronger each time. This time maybe he was strong enough to bring them down.

Now there was a dream befitting a high king. So was the woman who rode them.

Euan had had women flung at him by the dozen since he won the high kingship. A few he had taken out of courtesy or because they had belonged to the Ard Ri before him. Most he had managed to elude. None had caught his fancy enough to hold him for more than a night.

He had to take a queen soon. Every Ard Ri had that duty. The Ard Ri's chief wife ruled the women of the tribes as he ruled the men. For that reason he had to find a woman who could stand beside him in everything he did, who was a match for his heart and spirit.

There must be such a woman among the tribes. But now Euan had seen that face again and looked into those green-gold eyes, he could not get them out of his head.

He should hate her with all his heart. She was the reason for his defeat in Aurelia and again at Oxos. She had loved and then abandoned him, running into the arms of her stiff-necked rider-prince.

She was still Valeria. Every blessed inch of her was burned in his memory. He could still taste the honey and spice of her lips and smell the perfume of her body, musk and clean herbs and the pungency of horses.

Only on her could he bear that smell. It was as much a part of her as her slim strong hands and her high round breasts.

He was growing hot, here by Craig-y-Danu, where the waters swelled up from the earth's cold heart. He turned abruptly. With Conory silent at his back, he set off by another way than the imperials had gone—the short way rather than the long.

He would be in camp hours before them. Then let them see who was the Ard Ri. He hoped Valeria would be suitably impressed.

Chapter Twenty-Nine

The high king's hunting camp was smaller than Valeria had expected. It was large enough, she granted that, but if all the tribes were there, they must be taking turns pitching tents along the little river. Dun Cow's camp had been no less than a third the size, and that was only one clan.

This was a new king in the aftermath of a strong defeat. Probably he had a great deal to do before the tribes would follow him wholeheartedly.

Unlike the camps and duns she had seen in the past month and more, this one had guards clearly in evidence, barring the way into the camp. They were polite, but their spears were long and their shields substantial, and they made a wall across the track.

One of them spoke Aurelian rather well. He must have

been a hostage like Euan, although she did not recognize him. "Sirs," he said politely. "Your names, please."

"My name is Pretorius," the mage said, "and I come with gifts for the high king from the Empress of Aurelia."

The tribesman took them all in with a sweep of the glance that managed to suggest the small size, negligible estate and generally unimpressive character of their so-called embassy. "Indeed," he said. "She weighs our high king light."

"On the contrary," Pretorius said, "she shows her trust and respect for his office. If she had lacked either of those, she would have sent a legion with a general to lead it. Now mind," he added sweetly, "if that is what your high king feels is due his rank and station, we would be happy to oblige."

Valeria held her breath. The high king's guards were looking distinctly unfriendly. Pretorius sat at ease on his plain brown horse, smiling as if he had no care in the world.

She did not try to imitate him. Sabata, who had taken Marina's place an hour or two ago, was a coiled spring under her. She knew better than to tighten rein or leg, but if he exploded, she would be ready.

The tribesman hawked and spat. "We're not imperials here. We don't play courtiers' games. You and the one on the white horse—you come with us. The rest stay here."

"But, sir," Pretorius said as sweetly as ever, "the rest are the gift, along with certain trinkets in yonder mules' packs that might sit ill with your king if he discovers them missing."

The tribesman peered at the prisoners. They were not a prepossessing lot. His sniff said as much. "These aren't our people. What would we do with them?"

"That's for the high king to determine," Pretorius said.

"Do by all means come with us or send an escort—that's only proper. But we will see him as we are. Those are our orders, sir. We'll be pleased to swear on our lives and souls that we will do no harm to the king or his people."

The tribesman's eyes had narrowed. Valeria waited for him to refuse. Instead he said, "Very well then. One guard for each of these mongrels. The rest stay with us to keep us company and share a jar of not excessively bad wine."

And serve as hostages for the others' good behavior. That went unspoken, but they were all aware of it.

Pretorius spread his hands in surrender. The captain of the guard made his choices quickly. Those who rode onward took charge of two of the dozen mules. The rest, men and beasts alike, stayed with the camp guards, quiet and watchful but not visibly dismayed.

Pretorius' guardsmen were better armed and better trained than they looked, and they were mages. If anyone could be safe here, they would be.

All of Valeria's stallions went with her into the camp. The high king's guards made no effort to stop them, though she saw how their eyes rolled.

None of the citizens of Aurelia that she had met had recognized the three grey cobs for what they were. But among the tribes, everyone seemed to know them.

She was not afraid or even particularly uncomfortable. She was the only woman and almost the only Aurelian in that valley, and yet the eyes that followed her had no hostility in them. They were curious, intent, sometimes grim, but they did not hate her.

That was astonishing. Her own people would have

loathed the very sight of the conquerors, but these tall fair people seemed prepared to take them as they came.

She had no doubt whatever that if a battle began in the next instant, these sons of the One would do every possible thing to destroy her and all her kind. But as guests in the camp, Valeria and her companions were made as welcome as if they had been kin.

Pretorius and Valeria left the horses in one of the outer circles with a pair of guards to look after them, assisted by a handful of tribesmen. When they continued on foot, the three stallions followed.

Valeria had neither power nor desire to stop them. Nor, it seemed, did anyone else. With that more than royal escort, they made their way to the high king's tent.

The camp was pitched in circles of tents around a central fire. That fire burned high in spite of the heat and the daylight. A whole fat deer turned on a spit, with a handful of young tribesmen in attendance.

Beyond the fire rose a tall tent, very large as such things went, with the front of it rolled up. There were rooms beyond that Valeria could see, marked off by curtains of woven plaid and deep-dyed wool. The room that opened on the fire's circle was spread with carpets from the east, a touch of surprising richness. Over them lay the pelt of a vast grizzled bear, the claws intact and polished until they gleamed.

The bear's head hung from the tent pole, its fangs as long as Valeria's smallest finger and inlaid with colored stones. Its eyes were carbuncles, ember-red and glowing as the sun caught them.

The high king sat on the bearskin. He was a big man but still rather rangy with youth, broad-shouldered and lean in the flanks. His plaid was the color of heather on the moors, shot through with the gold of the broom. His hair and his long moustaches were as bright as the flames of the fire. Around his neck was a golden torque as thick as a child's wrist.

Euan Rohe's yellow wolf-eyes met Valeria's. He dared her to be shocked or surprised—or for that matter angry.

Anger she could easily manage, but not at him. It took all the self-control she had to keep from whirling on Pretorius and railing at him in front of everyone.

He had known. He had brought her here because this of all possible men among the tribes had managed to make himself Ard Ri.

Never mind how Pretorius knew the rest of it. He was a dream-mage and a reader of omens. He could have seen every moment she spent with Euan, damn him—and now he used it and them for his own purposes.

Her fists clenched. Not if she could help it. She looked Euan in the face and smiled.

It must have been a terrifying sight. He blinked, but then he went still again.

"My lord high king," Pretorius said, "it's a great pleasure to meet you at last."

Euan turned a heavy-lidded gaze on him, a look of calculated insolence. "We've met," he said. "We sent you the long away around."

"So you did, my lord," Pretorius said affably. "It was somewhat easier on the horses than the tracks you chose."

"That it was," said Euan. He drew up his knee and

rested his arm on it. "So. What brings you to the far edge of the world?"

"Courtesy," Pretorius replied, "and gifts."

Euan's brows rose. "Not anything lethal, I hope."

"I do hope not, my lord," Pretorius said.

He flicked a glance. The guards brought the prisoners forward. They were so tightly bound with magic that they could barely walk, but their eyes were open as wide as they would go.

Euan looked them up and down as his camp guards had. "I don't believe these are mine," he said.

"And yet they are, my lord," said Pretorius. "We offer them to you with our empress's compliments. It seems they have a great passion for your god and your people."

The only passion they were showing at the moment was a desperate desire to run away. All but Bellinus—he seemed fascinated by the high king, as a mouse might be by a snake.

Valeria hardly took pity on them, but she was tired of the dance. "You're supposed to give them to the priests," she said. "That absolves both you and us of the need to dispose of them, and the priests get a more or less useful set of sacrifices."

Pretorius winced slightly. Euan threw back his head and laughed.

So did the tribesmen who had gathered to stare and listen. They were not laughing because their king did—they honestly seemed to find her words hilarious.

That was interesting, because she had spoken in Aurelian. She had not known her language was so widely known among the barbarians.

There were a great many things she did not know. One of

them was the whereabouts of Gothard. He was somewhere near here—she could feel him. But he was not letting himself be seen.

The roar of laughter died down at last. "You should have been one of us, rider," Euan said. "You tell the truth as you see it."

"So do we all," said Pretorius. "There will be other gifts as well, as we come to know you better. In the meantime, along with these young devotees of your god, we offer you our goodwill and a token or two thereof—gold and silver, such jewels as you might be presumed to take pleasure in, and a few small things for your amusement."

As he spoke, two of the guards unloaded the mules and spread the contents of their packs in front of the king. They made a glittering display. There were torques and necklaces and rings, earrings and armlets, a belt made for a giant and wrought of plates of solid silver inset with bright blue stones, a full banquet service of silver and gold with goblets of sea-blue glass and bolts of silk in a dozen shimmering colors.

Valeria had never known wealth to tempt Euan, except insofar as it gave him power. She watched him count it up and reckon its worth. Then he nodded slowly. "My people will be glad of this," he said. "I thank you for it."

Pretorius bowed. "The pleasure is ours, my lord."

"You'll dine with us tonight," said Euan. "Both of you. My people will show you where to bathe and rest beforehand. We eat at sunset."

Pretorius bowed again, lower than before. "We'll be honored, my lord."

Valeria did not say anything, though Euan's eyes were on

her again. He had trapped her and he knew it. It seemed to amuse him.

This was revenge of a sort, she supposed—though whether it was for saving his life or helping to destroy his army, she could not tell. Probably both.

She would survive this. Who knew? She might even enjoy it.

Chapter Thirty

The envoys bathed in the river, which was icy cold, and rested in tents pitched in one of the circles that orbited the king's tent. Valeria thought of feigning exhaustion or illness, but when Pretorius set out for the feast, she went with him.

This time the stallions stayed behind. She felt oddly naked, though she was thoroughly clothed. She had deliberately and somewhat defiantly put on her rider-candidate's uniform, the grey coat and close-cut breeches and high boots in which Euan had seen her many times before.

Pretorius wore his usual brown robe like a scholar's, without ornament or badge of any order. That was an affectation, too. It made her feel slightly better about her own silliness.

The sky was ragged with blood-tinged clouds. Around a dozen fires, the clans feasted and danced and sang. The king's fire leaped high as the darkness fell, catching the gold of Euan's torque and the bright stream of his hair. He had taken it out of its plait and let it fall loose to his waist.

There were a hundred men around him, but she hardly saw them. The sheer male beauty of him had captivated her since she first saw him riding as a hostage to the Mountain. He had been a dreadful rider then and probably still was, but it had never mattered. On foot where he belonged, he had a wild grace that made her heart flutter.

The place beside him was open, waiting for her. Pretorius had to settle for one well down the circle, in between a pair of gold-decked chieftains.

They were wearing some of the gifts Pretorius had brought. So were most of the others at the feast—all but Euan. He had kept none of it for himself.

The prisoners were nowhere to be seen. The priests must have taken them. Valeria did not want to know what was happening to them.

Euan lolled at ease on his bearskin, dressed as she had seen him before. Except for the loosening of his hair, he had done nothing to adorn himself for the occasion.

He needed no more than his youth and strength and the beauty that had grown stronger as he grew into himself. Valeria sat stiffly beside him. The heat that came off him was strong enough to burn. Her belly kept trying to melt.

It did no good to think of Kerrec. That only made her angry, and anger made Euan seem all the more irresistible.

He insisted that she have the first taste of everything. She could refuse none of it without giving offense. The best she could do was eat small bites and take tiny sips and try not to get dizzy with having him so close.

He seemed content to torment her with his presence but not his conversation. He indulged in an interestingly small quantity of that with the tribesmen around him—most of it having to do with hunting.

Some of them seemed to think Valeria was a boy. She heard two debating it, down past Pretorius. In the way of large and boisterous gatherings, once in a while there was a lull, and one's ears could catch snippets. This one was brief but telling.

"Yes, that's one of the riders—a horse mage. Or priest. I'm not sure which."

"I thought they were all men."

"They are."

"That one's not."

"You don't say? Are the horses female, too?"

"Not hers. I looked. One of them tried to drop a load of manure on my head. If those are gods, they're gods with leaky guts."

Valeria swallowed a startled burst of laughter. That made her choke, and then cough.

A cup appeared under her nose. There was water in it, cold and clean. She gulped it down.

Euan had already turned away from her and back to the rest of his guests. But he was aware of her in his skin, as she was of him.

She took the only escape she could, which was to mutter about the jakes and then run for it.

She did not need it as badly as that, but it seemed wise to be seen to tell the truth. None of the tribesmen squatting or standing along the redolent trench seemed to notice her in her twilight-colored clothes. When she was finished, she slipped away toward the horselines.

Oda and Sabata and Marina were in comfort. They had grass enough to graze—since this camp had so few horses, it was not all gnawed down—and water from the river. They stood together in the fitful starlight, nose to tail, flicking night insects from each other's faces.

Someone or something was lying on Oda's back. The stallion showed no sign of minding it.

Valeria caught herself before she leaped forward to strike it off. When she advanced, she moved slowly, peering in the dimness.

The shape was human, if small. A child-sized hand trailed down the heavy white neck, working fingers into the stallion's mane. Oda stretched out his neck and wiggled his lip in bliss.

Valeria halted. The other two stallions stood between her and the small rider. She rubbed Sabata's shoulder, which happened to be closest, frowning as she decided how to feel about the interloper on her stallion's back.

Oda was not hers or anyone's. That thought came from all three stallions. He was here because he chose to be. He had chosen her, not she him. As long as he pleased, he would stay. If his mind changed, he would go.

He was a god. That was his right.

Valeria flushed faintly at the rebuke. It was hard to set aside human ways of thinking and remember that these were not horses. No matter how thoroughly horselike they might seem, they were something different—and that something was divine.

Softly and by his leave, she swung up onto Sabata's back

and lay as the child was lying, watching as he gradually became aware of her.

He did not stiffen or show alarm. His head turned. His face was a pale blur in the starlight. "Rider," he said in barely accented Aurelian.

His voice was grave and courteous. It was also very young. He was large enough to claim eight or nine summers in Aurelia, but among his tall people he might only have five or six.

"Do you all speak our language?" she asked him.

"My father made me learn," he answered.

"That was foresighted of him," Valeria said.

"Oh, no," the child said in quiet horror. "We don't do magic."

Valeria's brows rose. "That's not magic," she said. "It's only prudence."

The child shook his head firmly. "We are not supposed to see ahead. Or tell people about it."

"Not in my country," she said.

He sat up on Oda's back. His eyes were perfectly round. "You're not safe here. Not if you have magic—and say you have it."

"Everyone knows," Valeria said. "These white horses and this coat I wear tell everyone what I am."

"You aren't safe," the child repeated. "Nobody with magic is safe with us. Except…"

He stopped. Valeria opened her mouth to prompt him, but something about his expression warned her not to.

She could guess what he had not said. Only priests could practice magic among the tribes. He was not a priest—he was too bright and clean-spirited a creature. She would wager that his father was taking great care that the priests did not notice him.

All that care might prove useless if priests of the tribes could sense the power in this child. It was damped down with impressive skill for one so young, but one look at him and any mage would know.

Because she could not help herself, and because it would thwart the worst of her enemies, Valeria wrought a small working on the child. When it was done, his wards were so secure as to be invisible. To any mage's eye he would seem the most ordinary of unmagical children.

He shivered so hard he nearly fell off, but then he took a deep breath and closed his eyes. "Thank you," he said.

Valeria's teeth clicked together. Gods, he was strong, if he had felt that.

Oda turned his wise old head and blew gently on the child's foot. The child laughed, tumbled down and somersaulted and scampered off like the simple mortal youngling he pretended to be.

He had distracted Valeria wonderfully. The heat of Euan's presence had left her. She could go to her tent and undress and lie down without wanting to jump out of her skin.

She lay on her blankets with their familiar smell of horses and camp smoke, listening to the sounds of revelry without.

The pressure of foreboding was back. It had come and gone even after she banished it, but tonight it was stronger than it had ever been. Her defenses were barely enough to keep it out.

"Too late," she said aloud. "I'm already here."

Her words made no difference to that far distant outcry.

It was a beacon and not a living voice, blaring forth the alarm until she either heeded it or went mad.

She intended to do neither. She stuffed the blanket in her ears and shut her mind more tightly than ever. In the almost-silence, she willed herself to sleep.

A light hand followed the curve of Valeria's spine. She shivered in pleasure and turned her head to smile at Kerrec. "Such a dream," she meant to say. "Gods forbid any of it should come true."

The words died before she spoke them. Euan Rohe sat on his heels beside her, looming large in the small space of the tent.

"Get out," she said.

He made no move to obey. She had not expected him to.

"If you refuse to leave," she said with studied calm, "I will flay you alive and dance on your bones."

He grinned. "You could do that," he granted her, "but you won't."

Valeria weighed the living fire in her hand. His yellow wolf-eyes followed it, but they were obdurate in their refusal to be afraid. She hissed at him. "Are you challenging me?"

"I know you," he said.

"Not anymore."

"Always." He stretched out beside her. The tent was just long enough for him.

She pushed herself as far away as she could. That was not very far at all.

She should not have stripped naked. It was a warm night, to be sure, but any person with wits would have known enough to keep her clothes on in an enemy camp.

She had not been using her wits. Euan had scattered them beyond recall.

She pressed up against the tent wall. No more than she could blast him would he rape or harm her—that was not why she had to get away. The danger was in herself.

She had made her choice. She had gone with Kerrec and borne his child and given herself completely to the riders and the Mountain. And yet, one clear sight of this avowed enemy of all she was and she was lost all over again.

If Briana had not been so badly hurt, if Kerrec had not had to do that thing which Valeria had encouraged even while her gut twisted with the pain of it, maybe she would have had some resistance. Even now, knowing Euan most likely had had something to do with it, she had all she could do to keep her hands off him.

"Sometimes," he said in that warm deep purr of a voice, "two people are made for each other. They may come from opposite ends of the earth. Their nations may be sworn to destroy one another. They may be avowed enemies from the very beginning. And it doesn't matter. They belong together."

"I belong with Kerrec," Valeria said through clenched teeth.

"I don't see him here," Euan observed. "Somehow I can't imagine he sent you, either, seeing that you're here to seduce me."

"I am not—"

He cut her off with a flick of the hand. "Don't lie to me, rider. Don't lie to yourself, either. The only reason one of your kind would be allowed out of Aurelia is if no one else would do for the task—and while I have the utmost respect for your talents, if all they needed was a rider, they would have sent one with more training and less—shall we say controversy?"

Valeria had had that exact thought. Hearing him say it made it real.

He leaned back on his elbow, lounging with an attitude she well remembered. "Now I grant you, you probably had no inkling until you saw me on the bearskin. You always were more interested in your horses and your magic than in human intrigue. That brown ferret who brought you suffers from no such deficiency. He knew exactly what he was doing."

That, too, Valeria had been thinking. "What is he doing?" she demanded.

"Using us," he answered.

"Aren't you using him? You're not the hopeless innocent I am. You can't tell me you didn't have anything to do with what happened to Briana."

He showed no sign of surprise. That disappointed her a little. She had hoped he might not know—but that had been foolish.

Of course he knew. Another man might let himself be a puppet king, but not Euan Rohe.

"I wanted her killed," he said. "I was overruled. This will serve us better, I was told. I don't suppose you're here to soften me up for her? I'd make a fine prince consort, don't you think?"

Valeria's blow laid him out flat. She stood with stinging hand, even more startled than he was.

He lay where he had fallen. His eyes were full of wolf-laughter.

She locked her hands behind her to keep from hitting him

again. "That would have been too simple," she said. "They changed the law. A rider still can't take back any rank or office he left behind—but his offspring can."

"Ah," said Euan as understanding dawned. "Ah, so. You wouldn't be the royal broodmare."

"I couldn't," she said. "I'm not noble born."

"Yes, that would matter to them, wouldn't it?" He sat up, keeping a wary eye on Valeria, and clasped his knees. The bruise was already coming up on his cheekbone. On that milk-fair skin, it was strikingly obvious. "So they're looking to put a horse mage on the throne. That can't be popular."

"Oddly enough," she said almost dispassionately, "it does seem to be. It's the mystery, you see. And the tragedy. The people love tragedy."

"You don't."

"I am the tragedy."

Valeria bit her tongue, too late. She should never have said that. It was that damnable sense she had always had with him, that they understood one another. Maybe they did—but that did not mean she could trust him. At all.

"So," he said after a small but significant pause. "You chose him. So did the empire. He did the proper thing, of course. And that left you in the cold."

"I hope I'm not as pathetic as that," she snapped.

"Never," he said. His tone was light, but he was not mocking her.

She chose not to notice that particular nuance. "Laugh all you like. He would have refused if I had made him. I didn't. I told him to do it. I chose the empire, too."

"Of course you did. Hurt like merry hell, didn't it?"

This time when she lunged, he was ready for her. His arms were even stronger than she remembered.

She had grown up with a yard full of brothers. She did not fight fair.

Neither did he. He gripped her wrists and held her at arm's length and let her flail herself into immobility.

She hung above the floor, breathing hard, with the sweat drying on her and nothing else between her and his bright golden stare. After a considered interval he lowered her onto her feet, but he kept his hold on her wrists.

"Let me go," she said.

It took him a moment's thought, but he obeyed. She stood where he had set her. "I don't know what anyone thinks I can do. You're not corruptible. They're idiots if they think you are."

"Every man has his price," Euan said. "You are very close to being mine."

She went still inside. "For what?"

"For anything," he said.

"You'd stop being high king? Give up all your plots? Stop making war on us?"

"I said 'close,'" he said.

A faint sigh escaped her. "Not close at all, then."

He shrugged. "As these things go, you're a serious temptation. I'd certainly listen to you where I'd throw any other ambassador out on his ear."

"But I have nothing to say," she said. "I'm here because of Pretorius, and because I couldn't stand to be in Aurelia. He has all the words and gifts and negotiations. I'm one of the gifts, I suppose."

"And your white horses."

She shook her head. "They're not here for you. They won't Dance your future."

"Are you sure of that?"

"They're not for you," she repeated. "Nor am I—whatever you might be thinking."

"I am thinking nothing but that whoever tries to use you for his own purposes will live to regret it."

"Including you."

"Including me," he agreed. He bowed to her as if he had been an imperial noble, brushed her forehead with a fugitive and altogether impertinent kiss and ducked through the tent's flap into the night.

Chapter Thirty-One

Euan made it all the way to his own tent before his knees failed him. Safe inside, with the usual hangers-on either asleep or elsewhere, he let himself sag to the floor.

He lay for a long while and simply breathed. He would wager his kingdom that she did not know what she could do just by living and breathing and being Valeria.

Horse mages had power over men as well as horses—he had learned that in the School of War. What no one admitted was that these were not simply Beastmasters with a predilection for horses. They were riders and horsetamers only because their gods chose to take that form.

They could work their will on gods. They could manipulate time and fate and sway the course of nations. They were mages the way their gods were horses.

Valeria was all of that and a woman besides—a beautiful woman whose body he knew all too well. Lying on the floor of his tent with the weight of the night pressing down on him, Euan faced the truth.

He'd been slow to take a wife not because it was too soon or he was too preoccupied with securing his place but because none of the women he had been offered was Valeria. She had gone so deep under his skin that he could not even want to be free of her.

And here she was, all noble and heartbroken. She was usually in that state, he had noticed, where Kerrec was concerned.

"I never did like that man," he said to the roof of the tent.

"Why? Is he a bad man?"

Euan jumped half out of his skin. Conor curled in a corner, watching him with big owl-eyes.

"By the One!" Euan burst out. "Have you been here all along?"

Conor nodded, but his mind was not on the question. "I saw her," he said. "She came and we sat on the white horses. She doesn't think magic is bad. In her country, she says—"

"I know what she says," Euan said, cutting him off. "That's her country. This is ours." He paused as the rest sank in. "You *sat* on the white horses?"

"The old one," said Conor. "He's older than anything. His fur is soft. His back is wider than I am."

"You sat on a white god." Euan was often amazed by this child of his, but this went beyond anything he had seen yet. He was not about to call it frightening—he would not take it that far. He would be damned if he would give this boy up to the priests, no matter how many times Conor proved that they would lust after him if they knew.

Conor came and nestled in the curve of his side, clasping warm small arms around his middle. Euan tugged at the thick red hair, so like his own, and tilted the boy's face up. "You won't tell anyone about this, either."

"Just you," Conor said. "And her. I can tell her anything. She has it, doesn't she? She has magic."

"You can see that?"

Conor nodded sleepily. "Our cousin is all black and empty. She's full of light. I saw her coming from a long way away. She makes the stars shine brighter."

That was how Euan felt, almost exactly. "You like her, then?"

Conor nodded again. "Almost as much as you."

Aiee, Euan thought as his son dropped into sleep. He could not blame the boy's gifts on contagion from Aurelia's mages. He had sired Conor when he was hardly more than a boy himself, before he went off to his first full-fledged war.

The people had lost that war, too, to the marching ranks of Aurelia. Someday they would win. If the One was so disposed, Euan would bring about that victory.

Euan was high king of the people. Conor would be more than that. There would be other sons—that went without saying—but this was the firstborn, the child of his youth. In the way of the tribes, all the highest honors went to him.

Conor would be worthy of them. He would grow out of his strangeness and learn to curb his tongue.

As for Valeria…

Euan smiled in the last of the lamplight. The One had given him a gift. He would be ungrateful if he refused it.

Euan made sure Conor was safely and soundly asleep. Then he went looking for Gothard.

As far as Euan knew, the sorcerer never slept. When Euan found him, Gothard was sitting in front of his stone hut, head back, scanning the stars.

Euan did not want to know what Gothard expected to find there. "Tell me what you've done with our gift from Aurelia," he said.

Gothard lowered his gaze from the sky to Euan's face. Euan watched his mind come back from wherever it had gone. He showed no annoyance at the interruption—which proved to Euan yet again that he was either dead or resurrected. The Gothard he used to know had had a vicious and barely controlled temper.

This Gothard saved his passion for destroying the remnants of his imperial kin. He tilted his head slightly. "Why? Do you want it back?"

"Is any of them still alive or able to speak?"

"See for yourself," Gothard said, flicking his hand toward the hut.

Euan eyed him in deep suspicion. He stared back coolly. With sudden decision, Euan peered into the hut.

A shielded lamp hung from a rafter. By its dim light Euan saw five huddled shapes lying close together.

As he looked close, nostrils flared to catch the smell of blood or death, one of them stirred and muttered. Neither the movement nor the sleep-heavy voice showed any sign of injury.

Euan turned back to Gothard. "Bring me the one most likely to make sense."

Gothard seemed to find that amusing. "As your majesty commands," he said.

He did not move or speak, but inside the hut, one of the sleepers rose and came stumbling out.

Euan scowled. Gothard knew how he hated sorcery. The more it served his purpose, the worse he hated it.

He shifted his scowl to the imperial princeling who stood blinking and gaping in front of him. With time and practice he had learned to tell them apart, but they did all look alike— smooth brown skin that turned greenish when the sun was off it, curling blue-black hair, delicate aquiline features.

This one was prettier than some, but he had a deformity, a withered leg that he tried unsuccessfully to hide. "The priests will want that one," Euan said to Gothard in his own language.

"I want to be priest," the boy said in a horrible accent and worse grammar. "I worship One."

Euan ignored him for the moment to return to the hut. The rest of the prisoners were still asleep—drugged or en-sorcelled, it little mattered which. They did not wake when he plucked away blankets and examined each one.

They were all whole, young and strong. The magic in them made his teeth ache.

The priests would want them as sacrifices, but Euan had already seen what use Gothard made of young imperial mages. The last lot had all been destroyed, all but one. This lot might not last much longer than that one had, whether Gothard won or lost his latest war against Aurelia.

The imperials had to know this. For a fact the brown

man did. Which raised the question of why he had allowed this gift to be given.

There must be a sting in the tail. Something to do with magic. With imperials, that was always the way.

Had they known about Gothard?

Now there was the question.

Euan left the four young nobles to their ensorcelled sleep. The lame one was still standing in front of the hut, eyes wide and vacant. Gothard had gone back to his contemplation of the stars.

Euan shook the young nobleman out of his fog. The boy blinked and peered. "Priest?" he asked.

"The One forbid," Euan said in Aurelian. "Tell me something."

The boy's lip began to curl. Then transparently he remembered where he was. "Whatever you wish, sire."

"Why were you sent here?" Euan demanded. "The truth now—not what we've been told."

"It is the truth, sire," the boy said. "We struck a blow to the empire's heart, or should we say its womb? We would have died gladly for the One, but they reckoned it a worse punishment to keep us alive and send us here."

Euan shook his head. "It's not that simple. There's a trap in you somewhere. You would do well to find it before it springs on us all."

The boy stiffened. "Sire, if any such thing had been done to us, we would know."

"Would you?"

"Most likely not," Gothard said, joining in at last. "I have examined them, cousin. So far I've found nothing."

"Look deeper," Euan said. "It may be set to spring if one of them dies."

"What if there is no trap?"

"Then it's something else," Euan said. "Find it. Then get rid of it."

"As his majesty wishes," Gothard said.

Euan grinned, showing all his teeth. The boy flinched. Even Gothard's eyes flickered.

That made Euan grin the wider. "His majesty does wish."

There was a large and scowling tribesman outside Valeria's tent in the morning. "The Ard Ri invites you to ride with him," he said.

Valeria was only half awake and desperate for the privy. She scowled even more blackly than the high king's messenger, tucked her head down and thrust past him.

His astonishment enveloped her, then dissipated as he stalked in her wake. When he could not have mistaken where she was going, he slowed somewhat but stayed close.

She hoped he enjoyed the view. Relieved at last and somewhat more awake, she turned to face him. "The Ard Ri hates to ride. Where is he going that is so far he has to subject himself to the back of a horse?"

"Dun Gralloch," the man answered. He was Caletanni from the color of his plaid—royal clan, Euan's clan.

"And what is in Dun Gralloch?"

"Need," said the Caletanni.

He did not elaborate. Valeria was intrigued, as surely she was meant to be. "I'll ride with your king," she said. The decision might seem sudden, but it felt inevitable.

* * *

Pretorius was not to go. When he went to find his horse, a wall of tribesmen stood between. The messenger who had come to Valeria said, "You and the rest stay here. She comes with us."

"Not alone," Pretorius said.

"Certainly not alone," said the messenger. "We'll all be with her."

"I must insist—" Pretorius began.

"Don't," said Valeria before the Caletanni could speak.

"Lady," said Pretorius, "this is dangerous. If he takes you prisoner, holds you hostage—"

She leaned toward him and lowered her voice. "Sir," she said, "this is what you brought me for. Will you turn coward just as the battle begins?"

"You need my protection," Pretorius said.

"I have the stallions," said Valeria. "Stay. Learn what you can. Find our most particular enemy and weaken him—the more the better—before I come back."

"If you come back."

"I will come back," she said.

Even then Valeria thought he might try a working to force the king to change his mind, but it seemed he reconsidered. When she rode Sabata toward the king's tent with Oda and Marina following, Pretorius stood where she had left him, watching her with flat dark eyes.

He did not look affable then. She wondered who would bear the brunt of his ill temper. The guards who were forced to stay with him would earn their pay.

So would she, riding without human escort in the midst

of the barbarians. Part of her agreed with Pretorius that she was doing a deeply foolish thing. She clung to the part that had spoken before she paused to think. That part was often wiser than the rest of her.

Chapter Thirty-Two

Euan's men were still struggling with their horses when Valeria joined them. The beasts were either shaggy moor ponies—absurdly small for such long-legged riders—or liberated imperial remounts. The red gelding Euan was riding was branded on the left hip with the mark of the legion Valeria was named for.

That was deliberate, she was sure. Euan was no more graceful a rider than she remembered, but the School of War had taught him at least to stay off the horse's mouth and stay balanced in the middle.

That was more than she could say of the rest. The worst of them rocked and swayed on their staggering horses, while the poor beasts spun and yawed in protest.

A properly diplomatic envoy would have averted her eyes. Valeria was capable of no such thing. She gritted her teeth for as long as she could, which was not very long, then waded in.

Within the hour, a much improved company rode out, with girths tightened and bits properly fitted and men riding, if not well, then somewhat less abominably. None of them seemed unduly put out. Euan's amusement persisted in making her own lips twitch, though she did her best to stop it.

She fixed her eyes firmly on the road ahead. It was a broad highway by the standards of this country, a whole foot wider than a sheep track, winding up the hill from the camp.

Down below, the clans had gathered to see their high king off. She would have expected a chorus of whoops and shouting, but instead they stood in a long curving line and sang.

Her command of the language was not strong enough to make sense of the words, but the melody made her shiver. It began low and ended high, a long wailing sound like the cry of the wind through empty places.

Euan saw the shiver. His brow arched. "You were expecting a paean to my glory?"

"What is it?" Valeria asked. "It sounds like a dirge."

"It says, 'Remember you are mortal. Life is fleeting, death is eternal. Be wise, be brave, come back to us.'"

Valeria shivered again. "I'm not in Aurelia, am I?"

"Some of your countrymen might beg to differ," Euan said.

"Not I," she said.

The song was fading, carried away on what wind there was. The day had dawned warm and was growing hot as the sun rose. It was a heavy heat, thick and oppressive, under an all but colorless sky.

The horses were sweating already though the day had

barely begun. Their riders had stripped to breeks and stowed their plaids to ride half-naked.

Valeria wished she had the courage to do the same. Her shirt was light and let the air in while keeping the sun out, but it weighed on her. Even her skin would have seemed heavy on such a day as this.

Marina under her was in little distress. The black skin showed through the white coat behind his ears where the bridle lay, and he had the slightly pungent, slightly salty smell of warm horse, but he breathed easily. He had not broken out in a sweat as the mortal horses had.

Euan's escort had fallen into a rough and frequently mutable order, some behind and some in front of her. Euan seemed content to leave her to herself. Sometimes he forged ahead and occasionally he brought up the rear.

The camp was already out of sight beyond the hill, invisible as if the earth had swallowed it. The moors stretched ahead as far as the eye could see. Neither mountain nor forest rose to break that long, rolling expanse.

Its beauty was subtle but strong. The grey of rock and the gold and green of grass and the purple of the heather, with here and there the bright yellow of gorse, told her where the clan plaids had come from. They were woven images of the land.

The magic here was less jarring than it had been nearer the border. Either Valeria was growing used to it or the proximity of the empire had disrupted its patterns. Here they flowed almost uninterrupted.

They were not familiar patterns, but they were not chaos, either. They made sense in their way, like the tangle of brush in a thicket. Each strand had grown for a reason, and the whole had meaning, though she lacked the knowledge to interpret it.

She had not expected to find something to love in this country. What had been a land of exile could become a face of home, if she let it. Its wild beauty could work its way into her heart, as its wild people already had.

She glanced sidelong at Euan, who had fallen in beside her. His profile was clean cut, the nose long and straight, the jaw firm. He denied any knowledge or possession of magic, and yet here in his own country he was shimmering with it.

He was bound to this land as Briana and Kerrec were to Aurelia. She doubted he knew it or would want to know. Euan was willfully ignorant of anything that had to do with magic.

His was a darker binding than Kerrec's. Blood and pain secured it. Strong warriors had been sacrificed so that he could win it.

Valeria was riding deeper into his land—putting herself in his power, Pretorius would say. All the men around her were Caletanni. Euan had brought his own warband on this riding, leaving the rest of the clans and tribes behind.

As the sun rose toward noon, she began to understand that the distance was blue for another reason than the heavy heat. There was a pall of smoke over it. When she shaded her eyes and looked close, she glimpsed a red line of flame.

The moors were burning. Euan's face was grim as he took in the extent of it.

"It's not gone as far as Dun Gralloch yet," he said to Conory who had ridden up to join him.

"Cullen Moor is gone," said Conory. "There can't be much hope for Duncillian."

"Dun Gralloch stands on its rock," Euan said. "Whatever's up there will be safe until the fire passes."

"Can't you stop it?" Valeria asked.

"Nothing stops the wildfire," Conory said.

Euan's eyes narrowed. "Rain stops it."

"That comes when it wills," said Conory.

"Not always," Euan said. His gaze was on Valeria. "Not where she comes from."

This much Valeria could say for Euan—he never wasted an opportunity. *Need,* his messenger had said. This was the need.

"You'd have done better to bring Pretorius," she said.

"He's not that kind of mage," said Euan.

"How do you know?"

He shrugged.

"He told you."

She did not mean Pretorius. From the flicker of Euan's eyes, he knew it.

"Where is he?" Valeria demanded. "Where is he hiding?"

"Nowhere near here," Euan said. "He's in the priests' huts back in camp."

"Hiding," she said.

"Not from you. He told me you can bring the rain."

"That art is beyond me," Valeria said.

"He said not. He said your power is so great and your bond to the gods so strong that you can call the wind and it will obey you."

Valeria laughed. It was that or hit him, and she had already done that. "You should know better than to trust that one."

"In this I do," Euan said. "I can read, you know. I read a book a two when I was on the Mountain. There isn't

anything a rider can't master, is there? Even the lightning."

"I am not a Weathermaster," Valeria said.

"Have you ever tried?"

"A vital part of every mage's art," she said, "is knowing
when to stop. I don't have the training."

"But it's in you."

She brought Marina to a halt. Euan's chestnut stopped so
abruptly he tipped out of the saddle and fell ignominiously
into the heather.

He lay winded but grinning. She had no smile to offer
in return. "Gothard wants me dead," she said. "Did that
never occur to you when he was telling you what I can and
cannot do?"

"Of course it did," Euan said, still wheezing a bit. "It's dangerous, but you're sitting here with three gods around you.
They'll help if you ask."

"You don't know that."

"I asked your brown mage," he said. "No one knows what
you are capable of, because no one has ever been like you.
Look ahead and tell me you'll let people die because you
wouldn't try."

"That," she said quietly, "was badly judged. Do you know
what happens if a mage exceeds her skill but not her power?
Did either of your so-wise counselors tell you that?"

"Ask your gods," he said.

She did not mean to look up and see how much closer the
flames were and how much higher they burned than just a
moment ago. Her nose caught the faint acrid smell of smoke.

As barren as this country seemed, it was home to a dozen

clans with duns and camps and scattered farmsteads. All of those were burning or would burn if nothing stopped the fire.

Kerrec could have brought the rain. He was a First Rider. He had arts and skills that she could only dream of.

He was in Aurelia siring heirs for the empire. She was the only rider in this part of the world—still a rider-candidate, not even tested for Fourth Rider.

Marina cropped grass idly. Sabata seemed asleep. Oda was watching her.

He had an unusually large and liquid eye. Sometimes he allowed her to read the expression in it. Just now it was like deep water.

He had come off the Mountain a year ago, long after he was thought to have died in the body, to carry her in the Midsummer Dance. He had stayed for reasons no one professed to understand.

"Was it for this?" she asked him. "Were you behind all of it? Is the fire yours?"

He did not dignify that with so much as a flick of the ear.

"I can't do it without you," she said. "Any of you. If I can't trust you, if you turn against me, I'm done for—and so is everyone else, between the fire and the magic."

The men were listening. She meant them to be. They should understand what they were asking.

Rider's discipline was many things. One of those was to know one's limits, and what would happen if one transgressed them. She had hardly even arrived on the Mountain when two of the Called died because one could not rein in his magic. Briana had been tricked into the same deadly mistake.

Valeria was not that much of a fool. She watched the fire

burn and reckoned the lives and possessions it would take before it reached the edge of the moor.

That was a long way. She sensed the lives in spite of herself, hundreds and thousands of them. They lay like a web of jewels across the grey-green land, gathered in duns and hunting camps. Here and there were sparks of magic, but most were simple mortals, as human as any of her own people.

Her hands were shaking. She pressed them to Marina's neck. She knew what one did to call the lightning. It was like calling any other power.

Controlling it was not so easy. Neither was summoning the clouds and commanding the wind, then making the rain. It was all patterns, seeing and then shaping them. The Dance was a similar magic, stronger by far and more dangerous—but weather-working could undo the patterns that made the wind blow and the sun shine. It might not unmake the world, but it could starve a city or drown a nation.

If she saved these lives, other lives in other parts of the world might suffer. The patterns were unimaginably complex—even more so than the tangled thicket that was the magic beneath this earth.

A god could understand them. She laid them before the stallions, both those in front of her and those who were always in her heart. "Help me," she said simply.

She would never demand. She would only ask. She spread her hands and offered them humility. "Not for me," she said. "Not for any glory."

The white heads bowed. The dark eyes bade her open her spirit.

It would not be easy or comfortable or safe. It might break

her—because they were gods and she was fragile mortal flesh. But if she would do this, they would work through her.

It was different from a Dance. There was no movement of the body here. The magic did it all, drawing up strength from the earth and calling down power from the sky.

The patterns of wind and water, earth and fire, ran through her hands. One slightest slip and they would run through her instead of the air and blast her to ash.

The world turned in its orbit around her. To the Caletanni she did nothing but sit on her fat white horse.

Only Euan watched her as if he could see. She had taken him for a man completely without magic. She had been blind.

It was a different magic, one that eyes in Aurelia did not know how to see. She had had to leave her own country and learn to see the beauty beyond it, to understand what this man was.

No wonder she was so drawn to him. He would destroy Aurelia if he could, and use her to do it, and yet he was her match. His power was different and altogether unacknowledged, but it was tremendously strong.

There was the key, in that thought which crept through the glory of the working. The stallions gave her the art and the strength, but Euan Rohe gave her the powers of earth and water and air.

She called the clouds from the far cold mountains. They met the heavy heat of the moors and clashed like armies. Thunder cracked. Lightning ran in fiery rivers.

Fire on the earth cried out to be fed. Lightning had begotten it. Lightning would nourish it until it overwhelmed the world.

The skies opened. The rain came down.

The fire hissed in fury. Smoke billowed. Valeria turned her face to the torrent and laughed.

Chapter Thirty-Three

Right in the middle of that joyous shout of laughter, Valeria dropped as if shot. Euan had just enough warning to lurch up out of the heather and catch her.

She was lightly built and for one of his people she was small, but she was a surprising weight. She was all muscle, whipcord and steel. With the sense gone out of her, she was a dead weight.

Her body was cold. That was the rain—it had to be the rain. She had not killed herself for this.

He roared at his warband until they brought a plaid to raise over her. The tightly woven wool kept off the rain. Another plaid wrapped her body while Euan rubbed warmth into it.

He would not let her be dead. The magic had taken her wits away for a while. That was all.

She had warned him. But he was too caught up in being king to listen.

She was motionless in his arms. Her head lolled when he shook her. There was no breath in her. Her pale brown skin had gone green and then faintly blue.

Euan sprang away from her through the lessening downpour, caught the bridle of the nearest fat white horse and put all his rage and fear and despair into the glare with which he met that blank dark eye.

It was the old horse—he was snow-white and his head was more emphatically ram-nosed than the others. Euan raised his fist where the beast could see it. "You bring her back," he said low in his throat. "You don't get to keep her. She's not ready to go. *I'm* not ready to lose her. Bring her back!"

The old stallion blinked stupidly. If Euan had not known better, he would have felt like a fool for imagining a dumb beast could understand human speech.

These beasts understood it perfectly well. One of the others, the young one who was still more grey than white, picked his way over the rocks to the place where Valeria lay. He thrust his long nose under the improvised canopy and breathed in her face.

Euan held himself back forcibly from driving the horse away. The air was notably cooler than it had been before the storm began, but still not cold enough for a horse's breath to turn to steam. And yet there it was, puffing from the flared nostrils and drifting in tendrils around her.

More damned magic. If it brought her back to life, Euan would make himself be glad of it.

The stallion nuzzled her, nibbling her hair and the sleeve

of her shirt. Her breast heaved. She rolled her head away from that insistent nose.

Relief was as sharp as pain. Euan looked the old stallion in the eye once more and said, "Thank you."

The beast lowered his head, then raised it, nodding like a human king. Then he wandered off in search of grass.

Euan sucked in a breath and let it go. When he was as steady as he could be, he walked back toward Valeria.

The young stallion was still there. Though Euan kept a wary eye on him, he did not move as Euan ducked in under the plaid. Valeria was unconscious, but she was breathing.

"She needs help," Conory said behind Euan.

Euan nodded. "As soon as the rain lets up, we'll ride."

"Back to camp?"

"Dun Mor is closer."

"But if she needs the other mage—"

"Send a man to fetch him," Euan said.

Conory went promptly to do that. Euan stayed beside Valeria, hoping futilely that she would wake.

She kept on breathing at least. Euan was reassured—until it dawned on him that the rhythm of the wind was the same as that of her breathing.

That terrified him out of all sense. Although it was still raining, it was no longer a cloudburst but a steady, soaking downpour that would extinguish every last ember. He called the warband together and gave the order to ride.

None of them argued with it. Even the horses seemed glad to be moving again.

The only difficulty was Valeria. Euan did not intend to fling her over a saddle like a sack of meal. When he tried to mount his gelding so that Conory could hand her up to him, the youngest of her stallions drove the gelding off and menaced Euan with hooves and teeth.

The beast had not gone near Conory. Euan took note of that with the ringing clarity that possessed him when he was in battle. Nor had the horse touched Euan, though the gelding's rump would bear the scars for a good while.

The stallion was standing exactly where the gelding had been. Euan shook his head vehemently. "No. Oh, no. You don't want to carry me."

The stallion tossed his head and stamped. It was not Euan he wanted to carry—it was Valeria. If Euan happened to be a part of that, so be it.

This was not a thing Euan had ever wanted to do, even in his boyish dreams. But it seemed there was no choice. His heart beat foolishly hard as he grasped rein and mane and pushed his foot into the stirrup.

The stallion stood like a rock. He grunted when Euan's ungraceful weight landed on his back, but he neither staggered nor collapsed. He was wide enough to strain Euan's thighs apart.

Euan gritted his teeth. It was going to be a long, long ride to Dun Mor.

Conory passed Valeria up to him, wrapped securely in Euan's plaid. There was no way Euan could control the horse while he held her, but he doubted he could control one of these horses in any case. He was a glorified pack saddle, and that was all there was to it.

As soon as Valeria was safe in Euan's arms, the stallion flowed into motion.

Euan had never felt movement like that in a horse before. It was like riding a boat in a long swell. Smooth fluid power surged up from behind and through the saddle and up in front of him.

It did strange things to his own back, not painful but disconcerting. He had to will himself not to lock up, because when he started to, the blasted beast snaked its head around and snapped at his leg.

Stop that, said a voice in his head. *Be still. Breathe. Be.*

Euan almost lost his seat with the shock of it. Unlike any other horse he had ever heard of, this stallion had no intention of losing him or the burden he carried. That improbably supple back shifted to stay under him, and that clear inhuman voice spoke once again. *Forget who you are. Be wind and rain.*

It should not have made sense, but it did. When Euan was running or dancing or fighting, he let his awareness go and became pure movement.

It was most like dancing and a little like fighting. The edge of panic was almost pleasurable once he gave in to it. Even the discomfort rising to pain, because he was never made to sit on a barrel, seemed an inevitable part of it.

The rain blew away and the sun came back. It was hot, but not nearly as hot as it had been. The wind was in his face, carrying away the reek of the drowned fire. The moor ahead of him was washed clean.

This was not his own country—that was the fierce and tumbled landscape around Dun Eidyn in the Caletanni lands—but he was learning its ways. He rode into Dun Mor in the bloodstained light of sunset, mounted on a white god from Aurelia and carrying the still unconscious rider.

The women and children of the high king's clan had seen him coming. They had an ox roasting and the hall ready and a song of welcome prepared, shrilling across the moor.

His mother met him at the door to the hall. The stallion carried him straight up to her and then stopped, hunching his back in a way that warned Euan not to linger.

Hands were waiting to take Valeria. Euan tried to dismount at least decently, but the best he could do was a lurch and a drunken stagger.

The stallion spared him the lash of scorn. Pity was not much better, but it was fleeting. The beast submitted to a somewhat shaky hand on his rein—one of the boys from the royal clan, so wide-eyed he looked like a startled owl—and went off placidly to be unsaddled and rubbed down and fed.

And here was Euan, thinking of a horse with a hall full of curious people to deal with and Valeria vanishing into the women's quarters with his mother in close attendance. He pulled himself together before any of them saw his preoccupation as a weakness. The Ard Ri must never seem weak.

The ride had been long but the night was longer. He had to laugh, feast, and be king to his people, when all he wanted to do was hover over Valeria.

He did it because he had to. He put Valeria out of his mind and sat in the hall under the heavy carved beams, wreathed in smoke from the firepit in the center, and drank mead and ate roast ox until the last of his warband rolled snoring under the table.

Then he could escape. The mead had barely taken the edge off. He was wide awake and cold sober.

It was work to get up. His legs had had enough many

leagues ago. Walking hurt like fury, but the pain brought him into focus.

He had to stop and think before he went looking for his mother. In Dun Eidyn the queen's rooms were well away from the hall, whereas in Dun Mor they were almost directly behind it. Here she could put her ear to a certain wall and hear everything that was said—a useful thing sometimes for the king as well as the queen.

As long as Euan had no queen, his mother was entitled to the queen's place. Murna would not sleep in the queen's bed, but she had no objection to the rest of the rooms, which were large, convenient and well appointed.

Murna's women were asleep when Euan came looking for her, but she was awake. She had ordered Valeria to be laid in the bed that she herself would not claim. It was the largest and most comfortable bed in the dun, and the room had windows to let in the light and air.

Tonight a soft rain was falling. The scent of it filled the room, damp and clean.

Valeria was dressed in a linen shift, lying perfectly still under a light sheet. She looked like the dead laid out for burial.

Euan leaped toward her. She was still alive—her breast rose and fell. Relief almost felled him.

"Don't fret," his mother said from the other side of the bed. "There's nothing wrong with her that a good night's sleep won't heal. She'll wake in the morning with the mother of all headaches, ravenous as a bear in the spring."

"How do you know that?" Euan demanded. "Do you know what she did?"

"I know," Murna said. Her voice was soft, but it reduced Euan to wide-eyed silence.

"You did well," she said. "You kept her warm, let her sleep and brought her where she can be looked after. She's a strong young thing. She'll be none the worse for it."

"Pray the One you're right," Euan said. He pulled a stool up beside the bed and perched on it. "I could have sworn she was dead."

"It would look that way," Murna agreed. She bent over Valeria, smoothing the black curls on the ivory forehead. "This one may be worth keeping."

"In spite of everything she is?"

"Because of everything she is." Murna stooped to kiss her son. "If she gives her heart to you, you'll have a more powerful ally than any high king before you."

"I had thought of that," he said.

"I know you have," said Murna. "Good night, my heart. Sleep if you can. She'll not be dying tonight."

Euan stared for a long while at the place where his mother had been. She had vanished as if she were a mage herself, but it was only a dark mantle and a slant of shadow and an inner door.

He wanted with all his heart to believe what she had said. Valeria did look more alive than dead. Her hand was warm when he folded it in his.

He breathed in the clean smell of her. The herbs were familiar—his mother used them on herself. The smell of horse was much reduced, but it would never quite go away. It had soaked into her skin until it was a part of her.

The bed was big enough to hold them both without

crowding. He only meant to lie down for a moment, to rest his eyes and let go the tension that had ridden in him since she fell from her stallion's back. Of course that was foolish, but he was too tired to care.

Chapter Thirty-Four

Valeria opened her eyes and wished she had not. A spear of light pierced her skull.

She squeezed her eyes shut until the pain died to a dull throb. Then with utmost care she cracked one eyelid. The light was still dazzling, but after a while she could almost bear it.

She had never been royally drunk in her life, but this was what everyone said it was like. She chased down scattered fragments of memory. The last she knew, she had been sitting on Marina's back on a moor, calling the rain.

It must have come—she could smell it. But she was not on the moor. Whatever she was lying on was much softer than heather and bracken.

Someone was lying beside her. She reached in sudden hope and found a body much larger than Kerrec's but almost as familiar.

It was Euan Rohe, and this was a bed, and she was in a room that she did not recognize at all. The stallions were quiescent behind her eyes. If there had been any danger, they would have known.

She considered being angry, but there did not seem to be anything to be angry about. She would have been angrier if it had been Kerrec—either because the rest of it had been a dreadful dream or because she was not ready to take him back.

She might never be ready for that. Whereas Euan...

He was deep asleep and snoring softly. He still wore the heavy torque that marked the high king. His breeks were on and securely belted.

She would have known if he had done anything to her. Not that he would have done it in any case, not without her consent. Euan was capable of many things, but rape had never been one of them.

She lay nursing her pounding head and watched him sleep. Very soon she was going to be ravenously hungry, but at the moment food was not what her body wanted.

It had been a long while since she felt this way. It was an ache in her, a fierce and pleasurable pain, tightening her breasts and melting between her legs. Her breath came quickly. Her skin felt strangely tender, as if a glance could burn.

She laid her hand ever so lightly on his cheek. Stubble pricked her palm. His moustaches were smooth and silky. His lips beneath were surprisingly soft. They tasted of mead, which was honey kissed with fire.

His eyes were open, clear and unclouded with sleep. She brushed the lids with a kiss.

His arms closed around her. She caught her breath, but not in protest.

His belt was little enough obstacle, his breeks even less. The shift she had been dressed in was long gone. She rose above him, hands locked with his, and took him inside her.

His back arched. He brought their joined hands together to cup her breasts. She found a rhythm that she well remembered.

It was like the language he spoke, deep and rolling. Its high notes made her cry out.

At that he laughed, a rumble of mirth. She swooped down and stopped it with a kiss, and then another, and a third.

She trapped their hands between them, pressed body to body. His delight sang in her. His pleasure fed hers as hers fed his, until she could not tell which was which.

Gods, he loved her. She—yes, she loved him. She always had. Not in the same way that she loved Kerrec, but with equal intensity.

Her body spasmed. Her mind emptied of thought. There was nothing left but pure sensation.

Euan Rohe purred when he was happy. He was not aware that he was doing it and would have sputtered denial if Valeria had told him. The soft rumble reminded her of a cat on a village hearth.

She lay with her head on his chest and listened to it. Her body was more deeply relaxed than it had been in a long time. Her mind was avoiding certain difficult thoughts.

She would have to let them in sooner or later, but for now she chose later. She deserved a little contentment.

No one troubled the high king when he was in bed. The

dun was awake and humming, but the door remained shut and his people stayed on the other side of it. Valeria watched a spot of sun work its way along the wall.

When it was halfway to noon, Euan's purring stopped. Valeria raised her head. He looked down at her, eyes narrowed slightly, deep in thought, though he smiled when her gaze met his.

"My heart," he said in his own language.

It was more than an endearment. It was truth.

Valeria's fingers brushed his lips. He kissed them as they passed. "Do you know where we are?" he asked.

"Dun Gralloch?"

"Dun Mor," he said.

Her brows rose.

"It was closer," he answered, though she had not asked the question aloud. "This is the queen's chamber. Do you like it?"

"I like the bed," she said, "and what is in it."

He grinned. "Do you now?"

"I hope its usual occupant doesn't mind," she said—the first difficult thought, and probably the easiest.

Strange that she could bear the thought of him having duns full of wives. He was barbarian and a king. That was what they did.

Then he said, "There is no usual occupant."

That surprised her, though there could be a sensible reason for it. "It's too soon, I suppose. You can't have been Ard Ri for long."

"Since spring," he said. "Kings and chiefs have been throwing their daughters at me. Sometimes I've caught one, kissed her and praised her and sent her home again."

"You didn't inherit the old king's harem?"

He snorted. "That's the east you're thinking of—where is it, Parthai? When a king dies here, the women who don't accompany him to his barrow are free to go back to their clans. They might decide to stay, but mostly they go."

"That's a merciful thing," she said.

"It's practical. They go on living to bear sons, and the new king makes alliances with other clans."

"Wise," she said. "I'm glad there's no queen yet. It might have been uncomfortable."

"It's worse than that with him. Isn't it?"

And that was another difficult thought. Valeria faced it more steadily than she had expected. Aurelia seemed unreachably far away, and Kerrec's face though burned in her heart could not quite overcome the sight of Euan Rohe naked in the high queen's bed.

"It's not as bad as it was," she said.

He smiled. If he had been smug she would have recoiled, but he was simply happy. The purr was back, very soft, hardly to be heard. "I'm glad," he said.

She let the silence go on for as long as it wanted to. When Euan broke it, she was half in a dream, though she could never have said what that dream was. "This could be your bed. If you choose."

"Oh, no," she started to say. "I don't need the best bed in the dun."

Then she realized what he had said.

"I'm from Aurelia," she said. "I'm a mage—a rider, no less. What will your people say?"

"That you brought the rain and saved the people."

"That doesn't overcome the rest."

"Oh, but it does. We're practical, remember."

"You'd use me."

"Of course. And you'd use us—to cherish you, serve you, be your people."

"My people?" She contemplated the long leanness of him, the bright hair and the wolf-eyes and the tracery of battle scars that marked his milk-white skin. She was fair-skinned and tall for an Aurelian, but her hand was a small brown mouse of a thing next to his big white one.

There were imperial citizens who looked like him—First Rider Gunnar for one. It was not the body that made the difference. His mind, the way he thought of magic, the god he worshipped and the things he believed in were alien.

He would happily destroy everything her father and grandfather had fought for, bring down the empire and enslave her people. His god was the Unmaking, his devotion given to death and pain. He had tried three times to kill or maim the rulers of Aurelia and would try again without a qualm.

And yet...

She laced her fingers with his. "Let me think about it," she said.

He nodded. He did not seem too disappointed.

He knew her well enough to understand how enormous this decision was. If she chose him, everything would change for her. She would live in a new world.

From this there would be no going back. She kissed his fingertips and rose, hunting for her clothes.

They were folded on a stool, clean and brushed. She

310 Caitlin Brennan

would have liked a bath, but there was none to be seen. There was a chamberpot—its use was obvious, and she did use it—and that was all.

She dressed and combed her hair with her fingers. Euan was asleep again, or pretending to be. She took a deep breath and braved the door.

The only lock was on the inside. She opened it on a short passageway with closed doors on either side of it. At the far end of it was a narrow stone stair.

The hum and buzz of a royal hall in the daytime grew louder as she went down. On this bright day she could suppose that most of those who lived in the dun were out and about, but there were still a good two or three dozen idling in the long stone chamber.

Some were sleeping or communing with cups of mead or ale. A good few listened to a singer with a harp. He had established himself in a corner and was chanting in a strong musical voice.

It was Master Pretorius, dressed in brown leather and looking very much at ease. His command of the language was notably better than Valeria's.

He took no notice of her until his song was done. Then he passed the harp to the man next to him, smiling and shaking his head when his audience begged him to give them another song. He stood and bowed and left them.

"Did the whole camp come here overnight?" Valeria asked him when he came up beside her.

He smiled. "Only a few of us. A frantic messenger came to drag me off. He seemed to think you were dead or worse."

"They don't know mages here," she said.

"So I told him," said Pretorius, "but he was insistent and I have an aversion to violence. I let myself be persuaded."

"I'm sure it suited your purpose," she said.

He shrugged, still smiling. He began to walk toward the door of the hall. Valeria followed.

Even as crowded as the dun was, the wall that surrounded it was deserted except for the men on watch—one at each corner, alert and diligent. They had little interest in a pair of imperials jabbering in their own language.

Halfway down the eastward wall was a stone bench, so ancient its edges were worn smooth. Pretorius sat on it. Valeria preferred to lean against the parapet.

"Now I need the truth," she said. "What exactly am I supposed to be doing here?"

"What do you want to be doing?"

"No," she said. "Not that game. Not now. You knew what I was riding to. You foresaw what I would do. You know what has come of it. What do you expect of me?"

"I expect you to follow your heart," he said.

She clenched her fists and drew deep breaths, fighting for calm. As satisfying as it would be to pound that smiling face to a pulp, it would not get her anywhere. "I told you, no games. I want the truth now. You brought me here as bait. For what? What is the trap?"

"Love," he answered.

It was so direct and so succinct that it caught Valeria flat-footed. Her mind spun on for a while before she could reel it back. "What—"

"Love is a god more powerful than any on the Mountain," Pretorius said. "It can destroy nations, but it can also save them. If a rider is high queen of the tribes, what might she not do to gentle them to her hand?"

Valeria had already seen that. She needed more. "What if I fail? They keep their women in the duns here—which might as well be cages. I can't see him suffering me to ride with him on his hunts or his wars. Especially his wars."

"I think," said Pretorius, "that he would give you whatever you asked. He's besotted with you, or hadn't you noticed?"

Valeria caught herself blushing. Nevertheless she shook her head. "He's not a simple man or a stupid one. He's high king at his age, which is not common. Even allowing for the losses of the last war, he had to fight hard and win hearts to take that office. He may dote on me, but he loves his people more."

"Surely," Pretorius said. "Even so, a lover can do things an ambassador can't. How often have you persuaded an unwilling stallion, a god no less, to do your will? It's the same art for much the same purpose."

"He knows that," said Valeria. "He's thinking the same thing."

"So you use one another," said Pretorius. "It's to both your benefits—and it serves Aurelia."

"Does it serve me? How can I be a rider if I'm mewed up here?"

"You have three white gods to be your teachers," said Pretorius, "and you have me."

Valeria could not deny that he was a fair teacher. The stallions were much more, and always had been. "Nikos knew, didn't he?" she said.

Pretorius's head tilted. It was barely a nod.

"He must have been glad to get rid of me. I've been a thorn in his side."

"It grieved him," said Pretorius. "He argued strongly against it. Still, in the end he admitted that this was your fate and your task. You were Called not to the Mountain but to the empire—and the empire needs you here." His eyes were bright, dancing on her, seeing things no one else could see. "It's not so onerous, is it? He's a match for you. The children you will make together…it's a wonder to see."

Valeria's breath came short. She had not thought that far. Of course children came of what she had been doing all morning. She had a daughter in Imbria to prove it.

And what of her daughter? If Valeria chose this, she might never see Grania again. Could she bear that?

Grania would not suffer. She had her nurses and her grandmother, and her father would never forget her. She did not need her mother.

With utmost care Valeria buried that thought before Pretorius or any other mage could find it. She did not know why she was still so careful—if Euan had her, he was unlikely to go hunting for her firstborn—but some deep instinct drove her to keep the secret as safe as she always had. Euan was not the only or by any means the worst threat to a child of that particular breeding.

"I'm not ready to think of children," she said. "It's hard enough to see myself as anyone's queen. I don't know if I can do it."

"You of all people can," said Pretorius. "Believe that, lady. No one else is better suited."

Valeria bit her lip. There was one more question she had to ask. "Why you? What do you get out of this?"

"I?" He spread his hands. "I get a decent night's sleep. The dreams go away when their prophecy is fulfilled."

That might be the truth, but it was not all or even a significant part of it. Valeria had had enough of pulling facts out of him. She let him think he had won the bout.

Maybe he had. She had to think. If she could have run away she would, but that was not possible here.

She settled for staying on the wall after Pretorius left. Her belly was knotted with hunger, the effect of a great working on a sorely taxed body.

She ignored it. Even more than a breakfast big enough to feed a troop of starving soldiers, she needed to be alone. She had to face the truth apart from pleading eyes and calls to duty—and above all, the simple physical presence that was Euan Rohe.

Chapter Thirty-Five

"Enough," Kerrec said. "I'm going to find her."

"You will not." Briana had been waylaid between one council and another, and her mood was no better than her brother's. "She has three white gods and a master mage to look after her. She does not need you. Whereas we do."

That was almost word for word what Master Nikos had said when similarly confronted. Kerrec stiffened in frustration, but before he could speak, Briana continued, "If that doesn't sway you, think of this. Valeria left because of you. If you go galloping after her, you'll only make it worse."

"You don't know that," Kerrec said sharply.

"Of course I do. I know you both. Besides," she said, "if you really meant to go, you wouldn't have bothered to get our permission. You'd simply leave."

"I would not—"

"You have before," she said.

"That's why." His fists were aching. He unclenched them. "Call her back, then. She's in danger where she is, and it's getting worse with every day that passes. Get her back here before she loses everything."

"Everything? Or just you?" Briana met his glare. "We don't see it, Kerrec. As soon as she crossed the river, the patterns shifted. A few aren't quite so dark. Here and there is even a ray of light."

"Whereas I don't see that," he said. "I see false hope and deceptive brightness—and beyond them a worse darkness than we've seen before."

"That's the quarrel between you," said Briana. "If you pursue her or we pull her back, she may never forgive you. At least let her finish what she's started before you go chasing after her like a jealous lover."

"I am not—"

This time Kerrec stopped himself before Briana could do it. As much as he hated to admit it, there might be some truth in that. He had been dreaming of her every night and thinking of her through the days, seeing patterns of ill fortune locked tight and choking the life out of her.

It had been a month and a fortnight since Valeria left and a good half of that since he lay with Theodosia. He dined with her each night, for courtesy and because she was pleasant company, but after dinner and conversation he went back to his bare ascetic room in Riders' Hall.

Theodosia did not seem to mind. She spent her days in the empress' council, where she spoke for Elladis, or else in her hall entertaining guests and petitioners of her own.

At dinner she undertook to show interest in Kerrec's riding and the school that, even through all that had happened, was taking shape. She was becoming a friend, but she was not, duty aside, a lover.

All of that ran through his mind in an eyeblink. Briana's voice cut through it. "Be wise for once in your life, brother, and let be. You've both made your choices. If she's meant to come back to you, she will."

Kerrec shook his head. His sense of foreboding had not abated. Maybe he was not healed after all. Maybe old scars and never-forgotten torture had left him twisted inside.

He stood back to let his sister go on with her duties. She was walking well, he noticed. She too would never be the same, but she would do well enough.

So would he, if he could bear to. He had duties of his own, for which he was already late. He disciplined himself to face them.

There were a dozen young men waiting to be instructed. Each day one or two more came sidling into Riders' Hall, saying he had heard from a friend or kinsman that the riders were teaching their art. They were not all nobles, either, though most were sons of wealthy houses. One or two were tradesmen, sent by fathers driven to distraction by their sons' importuning.

It was a call of sorts, though far from the Call. One did not need to be a mage to be a horseman. As one of them said when he presented himself, "I could hire my own riding master, but he wouldn't be a master from the Mountain."

The stable was full. Briana had sent geldings this time instead of mares. They were handsome animals, not too badly trained, well suited for instructing these boys in the art of horsemanship.

Gunnar and Quintus oversaw the saddling and bridling that was part—often to these lordlings' disgust—of their instruction. They greeted Kerrec with a nod and a glance. Kerrec nodded back.

Outside in the riding court, Cato had one of the geldings on a line, instructing a boy whom Kerrec had not seen before. The boy had the stiff posture and increasingly dismayed expression of an aristocrat who thought he could ride.

Even in the mood Kerrec was in, he bit back a smile. A rider should not indulge in pettiness, but young nobles were terribly predictable. Although some never did learn, most learned to try. A few even became competent riders.

This one had a long way to go. Kerrec turned to acknowledge the slightly pale, slightly shaking young thing who held the rein of a placid bay. As kindly as he could, Kerrec said, "Here, up. We'll begin with simple exercises."

The child nodded, tongue-tied. Kerrec sighed inwardly. He never meant to be terrifying, but somehow he always was.

He softened his expression even further, softened his voice to match and set about unlocking all that tension and turning it into properly toned art. It would be slow with this one, but Kerrec had time.

The boy who followed that one was cocky, which needed a dose of the terrifying glare. The one after that was Maurus.

He had come in late, slipped around the edge of the court and gone quietly to fetch a horse. Gunnar, who usually caught the tardy ones, was preoccupied with a pupil. Kerrec might not have noticed, either, if he had not happened to look up just as the boy ghosted past.

That was not a casual choice of word. Maurus looked haunted, pale and shadow-eyed. Kerrec did not recall having seen him for some days. Not as much as a month, surely—but it had been a while since he came to ride.

It was understandable. Maurus' brother had been sent to exile and probable, painful death. That was a blow, no doubt worse because Maurus had helped to cause it.

Yet here he was, presenting himself to be instructed. Kerrec nodded without comment, waited for him to mount then began to lesson as if there had been no interruption since the last one.

It went well enough, all things considered. By the time it ended, Maurus was the only rider left in the courtyard. The rest were long since done and gone.

That was intentional, Kerrec was sure. At the lesson's end, when he would have taken the rider's flying dismount and crisp bow of thanks, he stopped Maurus with a hand on his knee. "Tell me now," he said.

Maurus blinked. "I—what—how did you—"

He was better at hiding it, but he was at least as terrified of Kerrec as young Harinus. Kerrec shook him lightly. "Easy, lad. I don't bite."

"Yes, you do."

Maurus clapped his hand over his mouth.

Kerrec laughed—painfully, but the mirth was real. "Truth, sir. I'm as human as you. I'm just better at pretending I'm not. Now get down and let's cool this gentleman out, and you tell me why you braved the terrible First

Rider after avoiding him for more days than either of us wants to count."

"Twenty," Maurus said in a strangled voice. "Twenty days." He lifted himself in the saddle, balanced and sprang down with unconscious skill that could in time be transformed into art.

Once he was on his feet, he drew himself up with visible effort. "Sir, it's not what you're probably thinking. It's not—it's not her, either. Though she did leave because of you."

Kerrec's shoulders tightened. "Valeria? What do you know of her?"

Maurus paled but stood his ground. "Just that she's gone east with my brother, sir, because you did what you had to do, and she couldn't stay and watch. I understand it, all of us do, though we miss her terribly."

"So do I," said Kerrec.

He should not have said it, but there was no taking it back. Maurus' face twisted in sympathy. "I'm sorry," he said. "We know you did it for the empire—the same as we all do, sooner or later, whether it's marriage or war or an embassy to the edge of the world. That's what I came to say, sir. My brother got what he deserved. My mother has not been taking it well, but even she agrees that for what he did, it was a fair sentence."

Kerrec began to walk around the edge of the court. The gelding and the boy followed.

As he had expected, his silence drew the rest of it out of Maurus, though it came in fits and starts. "I haven't been running away, really, sir. I've been hunting. It took a long time because now my brother is gone, the rest of us are watched constantly. Nobody wants to lose another one of us to bad company."

Kerrec nodded. Maurus jittered a bit, dancing in place like a restless horse. "The only time I could get out without at least two guards was when they delivered me here. I'd talk them into not coming in—then I'd slip out the back."

"Clever," Kerrec said.

Maurus shied, nearly colliding with the horse he was leading. The horse took it with good grace. "I wasn't trying to be clever, sir. I was trying to find the priest who hurt the empress. Yesterday I think I found him."

Kerrec stopped. "You think?"

"I couldn't stay to be sure," Maurus said. "I was already late getting back to the guards, and they were about to storm the gate. Today I was going back to see, but then I thought I'd be safer with help. I don't expect you to help me, sir, but if one of the other riders will come, maybe you can find a way to keep the guards off the scent?"

"Is there a particular reason why they can't come with us?" Kerrec asked.

"No, sir," Maurus said. "Not really. It's just, sir—*us?*"

"It's barely noon," Kerrec observed. "Do you need to rest or eat before you go? Think before you answer. If there's a long hunt or a fight, you'll wish you'd taken the time."

"I could eat," Maurus said faintly.

"Come, then," said Kerrec. "Horse first, then kitchen."

Maurus trailed after him. Kerrec saw to it that the horse was unsaddled, rubbed down, fed and stabled, then that the cooks filled the boy full of bread and cheese, meat, fruit and a cold tisane of mint and lemon.

Maurus had a noble hunger once he acknowledged it. Kerrec was somewhat empty himself. He did not remember eating breakfast. He had been too distraught over Valeria.

That was still there and still strong. This hunt of Maurus' might be utter foolishness, but it gave him something to do that might in some small way avert the future he kept seeing.

Just as everyone else insisted that Valeria was in no danger, so did they declare that the priest had gone back over the border. Kerrec could not see that, either. Whatever power had attacked Briana, its pattern was still in the city. There were numerous other patterns superimposed on it, a web of glamour and deception, but Kerrec kept sight of it easily enough.

Once Maurus had eaten his fill, he led Kerrec out of Riders' Hall by a door Kerrec had not known was there. The guards were on the other side of the hall, waiting with amazing patience. Kerrec opened his mouth to point this out, but changed his mind. He was inclined to give the boy his head, at least for the moment.

Walking was never a rider's favorite mode of transportation. It did allow a closer view of one's city and a more circuitous route through alleyways too narrow or too thoroughly closed in with low balconies to allow a horseman passage.

Maurus seemed remarkably familiar with the twists and turns of Aurelia's less savory quarters. He trotted through them like a hound on a scent. Kerrec was careful to follow closely behind, with every sense alert and all his defenses at the ready.

Even so, when Maurus halted, Kerrec was taken by surprise.

There had been no change in the patterns and no indication that the hunters were drawing near to what they hunted. As far as Kerrec could tell, the wall in front of him was exactly like every other wall on that narrow and fetid street.

The street was deserted, which was not usual. Not even a rat disturbed the stillness. Streets on either side were full of the sounds of voices calling, cartwheels rattling, feet passing swiftly or slowly.

Here the only movement was a scrap of torn linen hanging from a nail. Kerrec felt no wind on his face, but the bit of cloth was fluttering.

His eyes sharpened. Maurus tugged at his sleeve. The boy's face was white and scared, but his jaw was set and he radiated determination.

"There?" Kerrec asked almost soundlessly.

The boy nodded.

Kerrec frowned. At the very least he should fetch the nearest detachment of the city guard. It was rank folly to go into this unknown place unarmed, unprepared, not knowing what he would find.

He was a master mage. He had weapons that few outside the school even knew of. The land of Aurelia was in him with all its power.

He shrank from breathing too deeply in that alley with its reek of dung and urine and ancient middens, but he drew himself up and gathered his courage. He nodded briskly to Maurus.

Chapter Thirty-Six

The boy's hand trembled as he opened the door that hid behind the fluttering cloth. Chill air wafted out. Kerrec had expected black darkness, but there was light at the end of the passage.

The outer wall was brick but the inner walls were stone. They were very, very old. The floor underfoot was so heavily worn that it must once have been part of the street.

Something about that place made Kerrec think of the tombs of emperors beneath the imperial throne. It also reminded him of the ancient and now destroyed temple in which Briana had been attacked.

All three fit together within the pattern that had been tormenting him. He regarded Maurus in newborn respect. This was no simple magic, but the boy had found his way to it alone and unaided.

The end of the passage was a circle of wan daylight at what looked like the bottom of a well. It was a tower without a roof, strange and seeming purposeless.

And yet there was something…

Kerrec raised the strongest wards he knew. Maurus was halfway across the circle already, moving quickly and beckoning Kerrec to follow.

There was another hidden door across the circle. Crossing the empty space was strange and not at all pleasant, as if the paving underfoot were ice and the depths below were full of dark and hungry things.

Kerrec was almost glad to reach the second door, though his heart shrank from what he might find behind it. He slipped through into the corner of a courtyard—proving that the circular space was indeed a tower.

The court was square and bordered by a crumbling cloister. It might have been a garden once, but whatever had grown there was long gone. It was a barren and unlovely place, dusty and somehow dim, as if the bright summer sunlight could not reach inside those walls.

Maurus led Kerrec down the cloister, through a broken door and along a passage lit by narrow windows. This might have been an inn once, or a caravanserai built before the emperors rose in Aurelia. The rooms were small and identical, all the way down along that side and up around the corner.

The one Maurus was looking for was on the far end, where tiny cubicles gave way to suites of rooms. Noble guests would have lodged there with their servants nearby and their horses in the stables below.

Kerrec did not have to see the stables in order to know

they were there. Anything could have been underneath the passage he trod softly through, but he was a horse mage. He knew where horses were or had been.

Maurus stopped abruptly. He was shaking so hard he could barely walk.

Kerrec's senses sharpened even more than they already had been. He heard nothing to alarm him, not even the scuttle of a rat. There was no living thing in this house. Even the flies shunned it.

That was alarming in its own right. He moved past Maurus, who made no effort to stop him, and set his hand to the door.

It opened to his touch. He listened with every resource of mind and body, but nothing stirred within.

Someone had been living here. There was a cot in a corner of the dusty, dingy room. A wooden table and a battered stool stood near the cot.

The dust on the floor was full of footprints. The windows were latched open. But there was no sign of anyone still living there.

Maurus' shoulders sagged. "He left," he said. "He must have known I found him. Yesterday his things were there—clothes and bread and a blanket for the bed. Now they're gone."

"How did you know it was the one you were looking for?" Kerrec asked.

"I saw him," Maurus said. "He came out of this house when I was hunting a rumor and a feeling, and I went in when he was safely gone and found this room. Then I went back outside and waited hours until he came back."

"You were lucky," said Kerrec. "He could have laid a trap for you."

"Maybe he did," Maurus said.

Kerrec tensed reflexively, but there was no threat in this room. The priest was gone and would not come back.

Something down below caught his attention, a sensation in the earth that had been there since he began but now was growing stronger. It felt like a beacon such as mages left for one another, a message visible only to those with magic.

He knew better than to go running after it. He searched it with every art and sleight he had, and found nothing. If it was an ambush, it was marvelous well hidden.

This suite of rooms had a door in the rear, leading down to the old stable. A musty smell came up from below, a memory of long-dead horses and hay long gone to dust.

The steps were swept clean. Kerrec still could not find any sign of danger, but he descended with great care.

There were wards below, lightly enforced. His skin crackled as he passed them. Maurus, behind him, jumped and cursed.

A heavy silence lay on the stable. Its stalls were empty and its outer door hung askew. Motes of dust danced in the light that shone through the cracks.

A soft sound at the far end dropped Kerrec into a fighter's crouch. A better instinct, since he did not even carry a knife for cutting meat, was the swift canvass yet again of the patterns that ran through this place.

None of them was aimed at him. They clotted around the last stall, which was larger than the others—meant for foaling, maybe, or for some animal other than a horse.

Even before he reached the stall's door, his stomach tightened with dread of what he would find. "Stay back," he said to Maurus. "You don't want to see this."

"Why?" Maurus asked like the innocent he was. He had not seen or suffered what Kerrec had. Nor did he know what priests of the tribes were truly capable of.

Kerrec knew. He braced to open that door and breathe air that was worse than fetid. A magelight burned within, hovering over the message that the priest had left.

There were three of them. One had been flayed, all but the face, and raised like a trophy in a wooden cross. One had had the bowels ripped from him and wound about his body like a horrible shroud. The third lay in pieces, carefully arranged, with each severed arm pointing to the others and the severed legs bent in the shape of a broken wheel.

Maurus' retching told Kerrec of his disobedience. Kerrec made no attempt to reprimand him. The nightmares he would live with were punishment enough.

Kerrec swallowed bile. His natural coldness was a little help—it kept him from running off as Maurus had done, still gagging and choking—but it did not inure him to what he saw. Nothing could do that.

The limbless torso stirred. The others, thank the gods, were dead, but the maimed man was still alive. Worse, he was conscious.

His eyes were far beyond pain. They had also left sanity some distance behind. "You're late," he said. "You should have been here hours ago."

From somewhere Kerrec found the strength to say, as politely as one nobleman should speak to another, "I beg your pardon. It seems we were delayed."

"Ah well," the man said. "You were kind enough to come. My lord bids you accept this offering in the spirit in which it was given, and asks your indulgence in the matter of his absence. You will understand, he is certain, that for his safety he must take himself elsewhere."

That was no more or less than Kerrec had expected. He set aside the rising rage and knelt beside the maimed man. The wounds had been cauterized skillfully and very painfully.

If the man was lucky, he had gone mad before that, watching the others die in exquisite and carefully calculated agony. He looked up at Kerrec with something close to amusement. "It's a rare man who engenders such hatred as you have in my lord. He wishes you the very worst in all respects, and assures you that whatever he can do to cause you misery, he will do it gladly."

"Gothard," Kerrec said in loathing so pure it was almost tender.

"Oh, no," the maimed man said. "My lord is no kin to you, my lord. He wagered that you would not remember him—my hand for his mercy. But he remembers you. He will never in his life or undeath forget."

That took Kerrec aback. Enemies of the Mountain and the empire he could understand. His brother was—had been—the most personal of adversaries. But Kerrec had never to his knowledge run afoul of a priest of the One.

"He was not always a priest," the maimed man said—which told Kerrec nothing at all.

"His name," Kerrec said. "Tell me his name."

The maimed man smiled with devastating sweetness. His eyes were glazing. The spell that had kept him alive was fraying, his little scrap of sanity melting along with his consciousness.

Kerrec could not force the man back to full awareness—not because he lacked the skill but because he lacked the cruelty. It was swift once it began, a long fall into night.

He closed the staring eyes and entrusted the tormented soul to the gods' hands. As he knelt there, caught between outrage and bafflement, he heard the scrape of Maurus' boot at the door. The boy had come back, however brave or foolish that might be.

"Go," Kerrec said to him. "Fetch the city guard."

"But—" Maurus began.

"Go," Kerrec said, setting in it the crack of command.

The boy fled. Kerrec would dearly have loved to do the same. He stayed because he had to.

The souls of all three men had left their bodies. He traced the path of their departing and made certain that they had not been unmade. His unknown and hitherto unsuspected enemy had not gone that far.

That eased his grief a little but did nothing to soothe his anger. He left the dead where they were so that the guard could see for themselves what horrors had been done here, and went as far as the door.

The air was hardly cleaner without, but at least it was brighter. Petra stepped out of that brightness.

His white calm washed over Kerrec. His neck was solid and familiar, his smell blessedly sweet after the stench of death in torment. Kerrec buried his face in the stallion's mane and simply stood, too deeply shocked for tears.

As much as he would have loved to stand so until the world went away and all grief was forgotten, Kerrec had to draw himself upright and face the detachment of the city guard that came at the run. Maurus ran ahead of them, skidding to a halt at the sight of Petra. His whole body sagged then, so that Kerrec more than half expected him to collapse. But he kept his feet.

The guards were a little wide-eyed themselves, although they had to have been warned that the one who waited for them was a rider from the Mountain. Their captain, older and stronger-minded than the rest, saluted crisply. "Sir! The boy says there's been murder done?"

Kerrec nodded and turned back to the stable, though he would have given much never to pass that door again. Petra followed, bolstering him with familiar strength.

The captain set half his men on guard outside and ordered half to follow him in. They had been warned, but even to a hardened soldier, this was a difficult thing to confront. None of them emptied his stomach, but their faces went stiff.

"Our thanks, my lord," the captain said in a voice drained of all emotion.

It was a dismissal, as subtle as any courtier's. Kerrec should have resented it—he far outranked this lowly guardsman. But he was glad.

The man knew it, too. He was being merciful. Kerrec bent his head, which was as low a bow as a rider should offer, and fled back into the light.

Chapter Thirty-Seven

Kerrec brought Maurus back to Riders' Hall and put him to bed there, with the stallions on guard over him and a strong dose in him to make him sleep. He protested, but feebly. That stopped when Kerrec assured him that his guards had been sent to his mother with news of Maurus' whereabouts.

Kerrec would have liked to fall into bed with a bottle of strong spirits himself, but he had to settle for cold spiced wine and the bracing company of Nikos and Gunnar and, as evening closed in, Briana. She arrived in a fair fury, ready to take his head off for risking everything on one boy's word.

"I trust him," Kerrec said before she could launch into the full tirade. "That trust proved well founded."

"What if the priest had been there?" she demanded. "He could have destroyed you."

"I was prepared," said Kerrec. "You were not."

She hissed at him. "Nor were you! Do you know what I was told just before I came here? The city guard have found two more such scenes of slaughter—one in an inn near the jewelers' market and another in the temple of holy wisdom."

That, Kerrec had not known. "Three noblemen each time?"

"Yes. Always noblemen and always known for a predilection toward the barbarians' cult."

"He's culling the herd," Gunnar said. "Getting rid of the weak and untrustworthy and showing the rest what happens if they fall away from the cult."

"Or," said Kerrec, "they're willing sacrifices."

"Maybe both," Briana said. Her temper had cooled though she was still glaring at him. "Do you even care how close you came to being an unwilling sacrifice?"

"He doesn't want me dead," said Kerrec, "yet. He hates me too sincerely. So much so that I thought it was Gothard back from the dead. But the dying man said no to that. It's another enemy I never knew I had."

"So he told you."

"He was telling the truth," Kerrec said.

"We'll find the priest," Nikos said grimly. "This senseless killing will stop."

"It's a diversion," said Kerrec. "Better to find what else he's doing that this is meant to hide."

"I have mages on the hunt," Briana said. "Seers and Thaumaturges and Oneiromancers. The Augurs are alert for omens. And you, Master, with your riders, will search the patterns."

"It is being done," Nikos said.

"Good," she said.

* * *

Briana could not stay long. Kerrec welcomed the reprieve. The wine made him a little dizzy, but his head was clear.

The priest was still in Aurelia and still mocking those who hunted him. His web of bindings and alliances stretched over the city. Kerrec would wager that every noble house had at least one would-be traitor.

Those who were dying were but a fraction of the whole. That was frightening. Aurelia had a worm in its heart, and it was eating its way outward.

Maybe Valeria was safer among the barbarians after all. The attack on Briana had been the barest beginning. More and worse was yet to come.

Dear gods, what if his fears were misplaced? What if it was Grania who was in danger? What if—

Kerrec reined himself in sharply. Grania was the safest of all of them, hidden and unknown and with Morag to protect her. If the Unmaking itself came, Morag would do her best to face it down.

He prayed for the day when Valeria came back and Grania could be with them, acknowledged and loved as she deserved to be. He would suffer much to win that outcome.

It was late to visit Theodosia tonight. Too late perhaps. He could all too easily let it go. She would understand.

And yet he bathed quickly for the second time since he had come back to Riders' Hall. Even then he did not feel entirely clean, but it would have to do. He put on a clean shirt and fresh breeches, found his second-best coat in the chest with the rest of his clothes and ventured out.

Summer was passing already. The long midsummer twilight had given way to a swifter late-summer dusk. The air was still warm and the earth rich with ripening fruit, but autumn was coming—and with autumn, at last, the coronation.

This time it would happen. Every loyal mage in Aurelia had undertaken to make it so. Whatever trap their enemies laid, whatever magic was raised against them, they would stop it.

Why then could they not stop one vicious animal of a priest?

They would do it. Whatever power gave the priest his strength, they would find and destroy it.

Kerrec was almost himself as he acknowledged the guards at Theodosia's door. They bowed and let him in.

She was sitting under an arbor of roses, lit by a tracery of lamps. A net of pearls confined her hair. Her mantle was of dark and shimmering silk, her gown of pale linen glimmering in the soft light.

She had been playing on a lute, but it lay on the bench beside her. Her head was bent, her face pensive.

When she looked up and saw Kerrec, she brightened enormously. Her gladness stung him with guilt. He had not thought of her through the whole of that day, although Valeria was never far from his mind.

He sat beside her and kissed her hand. She embraced him with unusual fervor, not seeming to notice how he stiffened. He did manage to catch himself quickly and return the embrace.

After they separated, she sat smiling, though there was a hint of darkness beneath. "I heard," she said, "about the men who were killed."

Of course she had. Her web of spies was the envy of the court.

He had no doubt she knew about Valeria. Did she know about Grania, too?

No matter now if she did. Kerrec said, "It's been a grim day."

"Then maybe I can make it a little less grim," she said. The darkness had sunk deep in her eyes, overwhelmed by a luminous brightness. She took his hand and laid it on her belly.

His throat closed.

She nodded as if he had spoken.

That did indeed lift his heart, though it half blinded him with fear. Grania was hidden and might be safe, but the world knew that Theodosia would bear the empress' heir.

"We should not speak of this," he said. "Not until the coronation at least."

"Of course," she said, "though your sister should know."

"You haven't told her?"

"Not without you."

"I don't deserve you," he said.

She smiled. "I'm content with the bargain I've made."

"Do you really know what you've sworn yourself to?"

"I know your heart is not mine to give," she said. "It doesn't matter. Not all of us live for love. I have all that I need, and my freedom with it. Do you know how rare that is for any woman?"

"This is freedom?" Kerrec asked.

"For me it is," she said. "I have my own property, my own household and servants and my own mark to make on the world. In time—a very long time, one hopes—I'll be empress mother. Meanwhile I can ride the patterns of this court and secure my place and the place of my children. I'm more than pleased."

"I don't think I understand you," he said.

She laughed, but gently. "You turned your back on it to embrace your magic. I do understand that, but it's not my pattern. This is. Just be glad that it makes me happy, and visit me now and then. That's all I need of you."

"I should hope to give you more than that," said Kerrec.

She gave him back his hand. "You have been the very soul of consideration," she said. "You don't need to try so hard. Be the friend you want to be and not the husband you're not truly suited for."

Kerrec stiffened, but he smiled. "I feel properly rebuked," he said.

She patted his shoulder as a friend would. "You have a kind heart," she said. "Go now, you look exhausted. Come back when you're rested and your mind is at ease. Until then, if I can help you, call on me. Whatever I can do, I will."

Kerrec drew breath to say that there was one thing—that she could delve into her dreams and find the priest.

But she was carrying his child. It was no more than the tiniest spark as yet, so fragile that a breath could blow it out. There were Oneiromancers of great power and skill, masters of their art, dreaming dreams at the empress' command. Theodosia's task was subtler and much more important.

He leaned forward and kissed her brow. "I know that," he said, "and I will. Rest well, my lady."

Her smile stayed with him as he left the palace and returned to Riders' Hall. There might have been a hint of sadness in it.

He told himself he was imagining things. She had been telling the truth. She was happier than she had ever expected to be. She thanked the gods for giving her such a marriage to such a husband.

Now she was with child. He was glad, but not as glad as she was. She shimmered with joy.

No happiness was perfect. He of all people should know that.

He would sleep tonight, he thought. The nightmares would not be so very bad.

Chapter Thirty-Eight

The world was spinning faster than Valeria could run. After she spoke with Pretorius on the wall of Dun Mor, she went down to the kitchens and ate as much as she knew was advisable. She drank rather more than that.

Then she found Euan Rohe among the hunting dogs, judging the worth of a pack of half-grown puppies. His glance when he saw her made her skin shiver. "Yes," she said. "Yes, I will do it."

He waded through dogs and clansmen—none of whom she had noticed until that moment—and swept her up and spun her completely around, baying like one of the hounds. By the time he set her down, her ears were ringing.

He was dizzy with gladness. She did not know what she felt. Dizziness, yes, but it could be shock—or desperation.

This must be what Kerrec had felt when he agreed to

marry for the empire's sake. Except that he did not love the woman and barely knew her.

The sickness in Valeria's belly and the coldness in her heart came near to breaking her. No matter what choices she made or what happiness she found for herself, she would always mourn what could not be.

She had to put it aside, bury it deep and teach herself to forget. That was a dream. This was the life she had to live. It was a good life, a useful life, with a man she knew and loved.

Valeria had no illusions that Euan Rohe would soften toward Aurelia for her sake. Yet he might change how he waged the war—and for certain they could make a marriage.

It would be a wild ride, more like war sometimes than love. With Euan clasping her so tight she could barely move and with his jubilation blazing around her, she caught the fire of it herself.

This could be glorious. It could also be a disaster.

She shut her ears to that small voice. When Euan bent his head to kiss her, she reached up, hungry for the taste of him.

Then the headlong gallop began. There were clans to summon, feasts to prepare, celebrations to be part of.

That Valeria was a foreigner seemed to matter little. Men took wives outside their clans—far outside them sometimes. Their rites were aimed at welcoming a stranger to the tribe.

When that stranger was the high king's chosen, the whole nation gathered to greet her. But because women of rank did not speak in public or show their faces outside of their own quarters except for the ritual itself, when for the first and last time all the people looked on their queen, Valeria was not asked to prepare her own wedding. That was left to the high king's mother, who presided over a world of which Valeria had hardly been aware.

A good half of the dun belonged to her and the rest of the women and the children—girls of all ages and boys up to five or six summers. Boys older than that went to the men's side. Girls and women lived on the women's side from birth until they died. They only left it to be sent to other clans in marriage.

Within an hour of making her choice, Valeria stood in a hall as large and high as the men's hall but much more interesting to her eyes. Its beams were carved and gilded and its stone walls were softened with embroidered hangings. Instead of rushes strewn on the floor for the dogs to piddle in, woven mats kept the paving warm and clean.

The hall was full of tall fair women in gowns of grey-green and saffron and gold, misty blue and violet and the browns of peat or walnuts or the pale nut of the beech. Even the children were as tall as Valeria or nearly so. She saw a brown head here and there, and one or two were not quite as tall as the rest, but she was the only little dark person in that assemblage.

One of the tallest came toward her with the grace of a queen. Her hair was more red than gold, and her eyes were amber. She looked strikingly like Euan Rohe.

Valeria wondered if she should bow. A rider did not, and that she still was. She settled for the tilt of the head that signified high respect.

The queen responded in kind. Her gaze was level, measuring Valeria minutely. Valeria could not tell if she approved.

What Valeria could tell was that Euan's son came by his

magic honestly. The queen was a mage. Her power was a banked fire, but it was strong. Even more than Euan, she was a part of this earth, bound to the land.

Euan lived on it. His mother lived in it. She was the earth's child.

In Aurelia she would have been a wisewoman. Here she was a queen.

At length she nodded as if she had asked a question and received an answer. "Rider," she said in barely accented Aurelian. "My name is Murna."

"Valeria," said Valeria.

"For the legion, yes," said Murna. "I'm to make you welcome and teach you what you need to know. The rest will help. I understand you speak our language?"

"A little," Valeria said in that language.

"Good," said Murna, still in Aurelian. "You will learn more. But first there is a ritual. Please indulge it, and trust us. We mean you no harm."

That roused a spark of apprehension, but Valeria did not let it show on her face. "Of course, lady," she said. But as women came forward to take her in hand, she dug in her heels. "One thing we must all understand. I remain a rider. My horses, my freedom—I keep those. Is that clear?"

"Perfectly so," said Murna as the women surrounded Valeria.

They carried her off with much chattering and laughter, remarking freely on the cut and color of her clothes and hair and cooing over her skin. "Like cream," one said.

Her own was milk, which was hardly to be sneered at, either. Valeria resisted the urge to fight her way out of the crowd, even as they started to undress her.

When she was naked, too shocked to be ashamed, the crowd opened to reveal a silver cauldron steaming on a hearth. Before she could ask if they meant to cook and eat her, they lifted her into water perfectly balanced between warm and hot. A dozen hands bathed her with sponges and handfuls of herbs that foamed over her skin and hair and filled her nose with fragrance. Then they coaxed her down into the cauldron.

The water came to her chin. In spite of herself, her whole body let go its tension, pouring it out in the scent of herbs and sweet blossoms. She hardly needed urging to duck beneath the surface and wash the foam out of her hair.

They raised her up with her skin all rosy, tingling with cleanness. A linen shift was waiting, with a gown to go over that, woven of green and brown and gold, almost the same color as her eyes. She wondered how they had known.

Then her glance found Murna, who was watching in silence. Euan had told them, of course.

The women had begun to sing. It was no one song but a mingling of many—cauldron songs and weaving songs and sweeping songs. For Valeria there was a greeting song, which turned into a song of joy that the high king was taking a bride.

The high king's mother did not seem as delighted as the rest. She was reserving judgment, studying Valeria with a cold clear eye. She reminded Valeria of her own mother, with the same iron backbone and indomitable expression.

Valeria knew better than to smile. A smile was a confession of weakness. She nodded instead, briskly, as her mother would have done.

Murna nodded in return. It was a détente of sorts. In time it might turn into an alliance.

Today Valeria was to learn the ways of the women's side. She had no duties as yet, but she was expected to know what each duty was and how and by whom it was performed.

It was at least as complicated as her lessons on the Mountain. She would be expected to know every name and face, because not only were these the friends and servants her choice had given her, they would be her companions for the rest of her life.

If she thought too much on that, she would lose all her courage. She focused on the moment, on the faces in front of her and the names that went with them.

The day whirled away into night. She was not to sleep again in the queen's bed until the title was formally hers—and that would be when next the moon was dark. Now it was full, which gave her half a month to learn all she was expected to know.

The bed she was given all but filled one of many tiny rooms around the edge of the hall. Besides the bed, it just managed to contain a stool and a box for belongings. A curtain divided it from the larger space.

The bed was wide enough for two—just. That was a good thing, because Euan Rohe was in it, waiting for her.

She should not have been surprised. "Don't you have carousing to do?" she asked.

He grinned. "Yes," he answered.

"They'll be missing you."

"I don't care."

Nor did she, but if she was to do this, she had to do it properly. "Is this allowed?"

"It's encouraged," he said. "They all know where I must be. If I know them, they'll be wishing me luck."

Valeria could believe that. Young men were the same everywhere.

This young man was splendidly eager for her. For an instant she hesitated—caught between the dream she had to leave behind and the reality she had chosen. What she felt was grief—and yet, with it, a kind of dizzy joy. She dropped her gown and shift and sprang into Euan's arms.

The day after Valeria made her choice, her life fell into the rhythm that it would keep. She was up at dawn, slipping out of Euan's warm embrace and pulling on her riding clothes. Her stallions were pastured outside the dun in an enclosure of their own, separate from the rest of the horses.

That enclosure was roughly the size of a riding court. It was level and not too stony, and the grass was cropped short by sheep and cattle before horses ever came there.

She had found her saddle and bridles in the stable of the dun and brought them down with her. She groomed and saddled and rode each horse, practicing the exercises that she had been studying before she left Aurelia. The stallions had their own opinions as to her proficiency, which she took to heart.

It was hard instruction but fair, and it took her through dawn to sunrise. As she cooled down Sabata whom she had ridden last, she saw Pretorius sitting on the stone wall that rimmed the pasture. He had a satchel of books and a purpose in mind.

He was choosing to forget what she had said to him on the wall. She never would—but she needed the instruction he was willing to give. Even if she never used it, it was part of a rider's training. She would cling to that for as long as she could.

By full morning she was back in the dun, studying the many things that a queen of the tribes should know. Evening found her again with Euan Rohe, whose appetite for her grew stronger the more he had of her.

On the second day she rode Sabata out of the pasture. She did not go out of sight of the dun, but they both needed to breathe freer air. Valeria brought the stallion back without too much reluctance, expecting Master Pretorius to be waiting for her, but he was not there yet.

Someone else was, a familiar small redheaded figure with a clear and penetrating stare. "You were in the hunting camp," Valeria said.

"I came back," the child said. "Will you teach me to ride?"

That startled laughter out of Valeria. The boy blinked, not understanding.

"I'm sorry," she said. "I'm not laughing at you. Once when I was in Aurelia, a boy came and asked the same question."

"Did you teach him?"

She nodded.

"Will you teach me?"

"I can try," she said.

"Now?"

It was late already. Brigid would be waiting to teach Valeria to thread the loom for the simplest of the many complicated patterns that made up a clan plaid.

Valeria had hated weaving when she was learning it in her mother's house. She would far rather teach a child to ride.

Oda was willing. He had carried this child before and was disposed to like him.

"Tell me your name," Valeria said.

"Conor," the child replied. "Conor mac Euan."

Valeria stopped short. "Euan? Euan is your father?"

Conor nodded. "Don't I look like him?"

"You're his very image," Valeria said. Now that she knew, it was obvious. He looked like Murna, too, with his long, strong bones and slanting eyes.

He must have been conceived when Euan was hardly more than a child himself, before he left to become a hostage in Aurelia. It was an odd sensation, not surprising exactly, but unexpected.

Would Euan feel the same when he found out about Grania?

That would not happen soon. Even if Valeria had trusted Euan, she trusted no one else here, including Master Pretorius and his Aurelian guards. She would keep that secret, whatever it cost her.

This boy was no secret, though no one had seen fit to tell Valeria about him. He must have been on the men's side. He was young for that but not overly so.

He had a rider's instincts and inborn balance. Unlike his father, who had no grace in the saddle, Conor rode as if he had been born there.

This first day's instruction was brief. Pretorius arrived as it was ending. Apart from a raised brow, he said nothing. He simply opened his book and began where he had left off the day before.

Valeria was monstrously late to the women's hall, but a queen-to-be could not be whipped like a serving girl. Her lessons there would take place when she chose to appear.

That was a great pleasure to discover. Valeria was not accustomed to privilege. She had always been under someone's command, bound to obligations she could not shirk without punishment. There were such obligations here, but they were grander things than threading a loom or wrapping her tongue around new and alien words.

Even so, once she came round to those particular tasks, she applied herself diligently. They had their own significance, as did the people who taught her and those who saw her doing them.

A queen should be either loved or feared. Valeria was not a devotee of fear. She did her best to be loved by the people she had chosen and the king who, when the moon had finished waning, would be her husband.

Chapter Thirty-Nine

Euan Rohe stretched and smiled. Valeria was out riding her horses, and he should be up now that the sun was. The sooner he began the day, the sooner he could end it with her in his arms again.

It was irresistibly pleasant to lie in this bed that smelled of her and remember the warmth of her body and the softness of her skin. In memory he traced the shape of her face that had become as familiar as his own, looking into those eyes that were neither brown nor green, with flecks of gold like dapples of sunlight on a forest floor.

Entirely different eyes stared down at him, raising a brow at his visible arousal. That withered under his mother's stare, but his smile barely faded. "Good morning, Mother," he said.

"Very good for you, it seems," said Murna.

His smile widened to a grin. "Isn't she splendid?"

"She is rather remarkable," Murna said.

The words were pleasing, but her tone wiped the grin from his face. "You think I made a bad choice."

"She has the capacity to be a very good queen," his mother said.

"But you don't like her."

"I don't trust her." Murna sat on the stool beside the bed. "She works hard, she means well, but she's Aurelian to the bone."

"She came here of her own will. She chose us."

"She chose you," Murna said. "She does love you—that's clear in everything she does. And yes, I do like her. If it were only a matter of your happiness and her ability to please you, I would be glad you've made so good a match."

"But?" he asked when she did not go on.

Her answer came slantwise. "Did you know she's had a child?"

Euan frowned. "What? Of course she hasn't."

"The signs are clear if you know what to look for. Somewhere in Aurelia, she's left a part of herself."

Euan sat up. He could not seem to keep his mind focused on what Murna was saying. "You think it's mine, then? Maybe she lost it. Maybe—"

"It's more recent than that. The marks are still new. This past winter or spring, I would guess."

"Well, good!" Euan said with forced heartiness. "She's fertile, then. She'll bear strong sons for the clan."

"Ask yourself why she hasn't told you," said Murna. "Why is she hiding it?"

"Because it's his," Euan answered promptly. "He's keeping

it hidden, I suppose. With as many enemies as he has, everyone would be after it. If he knows his brother is still alive—"

"All true," said Murna, "but if she trusted you, she would have told you."

"She'll tell me when she's ready," Euan said. "Of course she doesn't trust me completely yet. We're born enemies."

"Exactly," Murna said.

Euan glowered at her. "If I didn't know better I'd think you were jealous. Are you afraid she'll take your position away from you? That won't happen. The queen mother outranks the queen."

"I'm not afraid of that," Murna said with a touch of heat. "I am afraid of what she will do when she remembers what she left behind."

"I won't let that happen," Euan said. "Nor I think will she. She's wiser than you give her credit for. She knows what she's doing."

"Does she? She came here in a fit of pique because her lover had to take a noble wife. When that pique passes, she'll go back to him. No matter how much she loves you, you're as different as doe and bear. The stag will call and she'll answer. She won't be able to stop herself."

"I don't believe it," Euan said. `

"There are ways to bind her," said Murna, "if we must."

"No," he said. "No, we will not. She'll stay of her own free will."

"But if she changes her mind—"

"Enough," he said with hard-fought restraint. "No more. You are my mother and I owe you respect, but keep on with this and I will know that you are my wife's enemy and therefore mine. At the very least, let her prove herself. If she turns against us, I'll be as harsh as you could ask."

"I'll hold you to that promise," his mother said.

Murna had dampened Euan's spirits thoroughly. He fought his way out of the black mood by reminding himself that Valeria was not what his mother insisted she was. She was wiser, saner, kinder—and more trustworthy. Once she had given her word, she would not break it.

There was a way to make sure of that. The priests would object, but in such things they were bound to the Ard Ri. His will would prevail over theirs.

He pulled on his breeks and scraped his hair into a plait. People were yelling for him in the hall. He waved them off.

Some of them followed him out of the dun. He let them do it. They would be witnesses.

After days of heavy heat, a storm had rolled through in the night. The morning was grey and cool, with a mist lying on the heather. Everything past a furlong's distance was lost in the fog.

Valeria was not in the pasture where she rode every morning. All three of her stallions were gone.

Euan shut out the voice in his mind that sounded exactly like this mother's. *What did I tell you? She's run for it.*

She had not. She rode out in the mornings, explored the country around the dun and came back when the sun was fully up. If he waited, she would come.

The brown mage was sitting on the wall. Euan had not seen him in the mist until he moved. "My lord," the mage said.

Euan nodded curtly. The man made his skin creep. If any imperial was not to be trusted, it was this one. The man had made no secret of his intentions. He had brought Valeria to seduce the high king—and she had.

Euan owed him either thanks or an axe in the skull. He settled for suffering the man's company.

For once there was no oily stream of chatter. They sat on the wall at a discreet distance from each other as the mist thickened and the air took on the heavy smell of rain.

Valeria had had a restless night. Her courses were trying to begin, which did not trouble her, but they brought with them a strange, painful sensation. She felt as if the skin had been stripped from her body.

Euan's delight in her helped a little, but he fell asleep all too soon and left her alone to listen to the wind and thunder and the pounding of rain. Although the storm passed soon enough, its tumult lingered in her heart. The sense of foreboding was on her again, the awareness of desperation beating on her shields from without.

She should have been free of that. The choice she had made brought a glimmer of light for them all. She was glad of that choice. She could live with it and the man she had chosen.

And yet as the night went on, she grew more agitated instead of less. Finally she gave up trying to sleep, dressed in her riding clothes and scavenged bread and cheese and a bottle of barley beer from the kitchen.

Not even the cooks were awake. The dogs blinked sleepily at her as she slipped past the men's hall. She lulled them back to sleep with a touch of magic like the brush of a hand over each shaggy grey head.

It was dark and thick with fog beyond the gate. She made

her way with other senses than eyes. Her saddle and bridles were safe in their box—no one here would steal them, between awe and misunderstanding of what they were. She had heard one burly warrior tell another that without them she could not control the stallions.

Those wild and incomprehensible creatures were grazing together peacefully in a corner. Whatever was troubling her seemed not to touch them.

Sabata's awareness brushed past her first with a flash of sudden gladness. His hooves were almost soundless on the grass, except when now and then they struck a stone. She traced his advance in that intermittent clatter, then in the soft moonlight glow that brightened the fog.

The shimmering shape loomed in front of her. She ran her hands over his damp body. He was clean, for a miracle—horses and especially white horses had a heartfelt attraction to the vilest and blackest mud they could find.

She brushed him quickly, picked out his hooves and did the same for the others as they came crowding near. As she slipped the brushes and pick back into her saddlebags, Sabata pawed impatiently.

He never did like to stand about when he could be dancing. As she spread the saddlecloth over his back, she realized that the glimmer on it was more than the stallion's own light. Dawn was coming.

It was a grey, dank morning, with a new storm closing in. This one was as soft as the one before it had been violent. Slow rain would dampen the earth, quenching its thirst far more thoroughly than torrents that ran headlong into the streams and rivers.

She would be done and gone before the rain began in earnest. She strapped the saddlebags in place and mounted.

When she opened the gate, Oda and Marina were waiting to follow. Usually they stayed with the grass, but this morning they were in the mood for a run on the moor. Oda was unusually lively, rearing up on his hind legs and regaling them all with a triple leap.

Valeria laughed. The darkness was still in her heart, but he had lightened her spirits.

Sabata coiled under her and sprang into a gallop. The others fell in just behind. They ran surefooted on the narrow stony track, rounding the steep hillside on which the dun was built, then winding away across the moor.

They were long out of sight of the dun before they consented to walk. Sabata was dancing and blowing still. The older stallions strode out strongly, aiming for the stream that was the usual limit of their morning run.

The stream flowed around the feet of a ruined tower. It must once have been part of a stronghold, but not even the outline of it was left in the heather, only the broken stump of the round tower.

It was light enough now to see the wall looming in the fog. Valeria was minded to pull off the saddle and let the stallions graze while she ate her breakfast under the last remaining bit of roof.

There was someone sitting where she had meant to sit. A handsome bay horse plucked grass within the circle of the wall, ignoring the stallions outside.

It was a gelding from one of the legions, she could not mistake that, but she kept imagining that he shimmered and changed, shrinking somewhat in height and broadening considerably in girth. Then he was a mare, a bay Lady with eyes that dared her to say a word.

That was impossible. Valeria was conjuring images out of fog. Never in this world would a Lady ally herself with the man who sat on the broken bit of wall.

Gothard's wards were up, strengthened by the stone that surrounded him. He was armed, too, with a short sword. Clearly he was taking no chances.

It was like him to waylay Valeria far away from any other human creature. But the stallions were with her, unmoved by his attempts at defenses. If he was hoping to trap her within his wards, he would fail.

Valeria refused to speak first. If he wanted an opening, he could make one for himself.

He never had had much patience. The silence had hardly grown unbearable before he said, "Good morning, lady."

Her lips tightened. "What do you want?"

"Ever the soul of courtesy," Kerrec's brother said. He did not look much like Kerrec—he was taller, broader, and fairer of skin and hair. His mother had been Caletanni, and stark mad.

He had not inherited her beauty, but he did share her tenuous grip on sanity. His eyes were a little too wide and a little too intent. Wherever he had been and whatever he had done there, he had not come back whole.

He had been dangerous before, with his desperate hunger to be emperor and his visceral hatred of his full-blood kin. Now Valeria could not tell what he would do, except that it boded ill for Aurelia.

She had seen the Unmaking in him when he raised it to

destroy his father. It was stronger now. The strength of stones held him together, but his heart was absolute emptiness.

The Unmaking stirred in her, like calling to like. She caught herself before she backed away. She had to stand fast. He must not know how weak she was.

Sabata clambered up from the stream and dropped his head over her shoulder, holding her to his chest. She wrapped her arms around his nose to keep from falling over.

He could not have sent a clearer message. Gothard acknowledged it with a stiff bow.

Sabata let Valeria go but stayed beside her, watching Gothard with ears pricked and nostrils slightly flared. "I think," she said, "that you had better speak fast and forget whatever game you had in mind. Sabata is not patient."

"They know," Gothard said, "about the child."

Chapter Forty

Valeria's knees went weak. When she had ordered Gothard to be direct, she had not expected him to obey. This struck like a blow to the gut. "What—who—"

Gothard smiled. It looked like the grin of a skull. "Your husband-to-be and his mother," he said, "have deduced that you have a child in Aurelia. It appears not to matter to him, but she sees it as a tie that may bind you when the game plays itself to the end."

"I've made my choice," Valeria said, tight-lipped. "His mother may not approve of me, but he does—and he is the one who matters."

"You think so?" Gothard said. His tone was dispassionate, as if he lectured in a schoolroom, but his eyes were a little too wide and a little too fixed. "The queen mother rules the dun and through it the tribe. The high king may vaunt himself in war and in front of the men, but his mother tells him what to do and what to think. She doesn't love you, and she isn't pleased that he's chosen an imperial woman for his queen."

"I don't believe you," Valeria said.

"Believe this, then. The Ard Ri is coming to claim you. He thinks that if he binds you with the marriage vows, you can't turn against him when he mounts the next assault on the empire—and that is coming fast. My sister's downfall has begun. The One's servant in Aurelia is leaving a trail of blood and slaughter. Each ritual and each sacrifice brings your lover closer to the throne he's lusted for since he first knew it existed."

Valeria swallowed bile. "That's all your doing. Isn't it?"

Gothard laughed like a cry of pain. "Do give your lover credit, lady. Whatever I did to help him on his way, his foot was on it first. He wanted your empress dead, not merely damaged. Behind that charming smile, your dearly beloved barbarian is no better a man than I am."

"You are not fit to fasten his shoe."

Gothard shrugged off her scorn. "He uses me. I use him. How am I different from you? You'll be empress if he wins the game. Then you'll have what he promised you years ago, the Mountain for yourself and the palace to play in. Does that make you happy?"

"It will never happen," Valeria said. "His armies are broken. It will be years before they can think of invasion—and in all that time, the empress will be strengthening the empire against him."

"This invasion has nothing to do with armies," Gothard said. "He believes that once you're bound to him, he can use your magic and the power of the stallions to finish what he's already begun."

"That goes both ways," Valeria said. "I can use him, too. Have you thought of that?"

"Often," said Gothard. His head tilted as if a new thought had occurred to him—or as if he had seen something new and utterly fascinating in Valeria's face. "So has he—and he's taken steps to stop you. As soon as he has you secure, he'll call in the priests to bind your magic. Your white gods are strong, but the One is stronger. But you know that, don't you? The One is inside you. The heart of your magic is the Unmaking."

Gods damn him for seeing what no one else but Briana had ever seen. In those eyes Valeria saw herself as in a dark glass.

However strong she was, however skilled her magic, its center was primordial nothingness. She was the worm in the empire's heart—more than anyone else, more even than the spies and priests who crept through the shadows of Aurelia.

Now she was in the One's country, betrothed to the One's chosen. Away from Euan's warmth and inescapable humanity, she could see clearly what she was doing and what would come of it.

Her dreams of peace had been merest fancies. These laughing people with their strong music and their visible joy in life were altogether different when they stood in front of their god. Like the twofold god of the empire, who looked both before and behind and ruled over both darkness and light, they presented one face to the daylight and another to the moon's dark.

"There will be nine sacrifices in the dark of the moon," Gothard said in a tone of dreamlike contentment, "and nine vows made to eternal Night. What will happen to you, lady, when those vows open the doors of Unmaking? You may hope to destroy the people who would use you so—but once those doors are fully open, all that is made will be unmade."

"They won't allow that," Valeria said. "*He* won't. He wants to live and rule, not vanish into nothingness."

"Ah," said Gothard, "but he doesn't know what you really are. He thinks he has a horse mage in his power, a strong one who will tax his priests' best efforts to control her, but simple enough in the end. He doesn't know what else is inside you."

"Then I'll tell him," she said.

"If you do," said Gothard, "no matter how much he loves you, he will hand you over to the priests. His people would rise in revolt otherwise. They know what they worship—and how to keep it from destroying them."

Valeria pressed her hands over her ears to keep from hearing any more. This was the worst enemy Aurelia had, worse than any barbarian king, because he knew the empire so well and hated it so profoundly. Every word he spoke was calculated, shaped and honed to snare her heart and soul.

And yet, as terrible as they were, those words made sense. She wished to the gods that they did not.

Sabata tossed his head. Droplets of mist flew from his mane. She pulled his nose around and pressed her forehead to his.

She found calm in him, but she also found the same truth Gothard saw.

And she saw another thing. She saw Euan Rohe waiting for her, alight with purpose. He meant to bind her now, tonight. He would carry her off and speak the words and make her his before she could muster the wits to resist.

The choice she had made with such lofty intentions was crumbling under the onslaught of doubt. She had not thought it through. She had taken one look at Euan Rohe's fine white body and all good sense had flown out of her head.

She straightened and turned to face Gothard, fixing him with her hardest stare. "Tell me what you get out of this. Why aren't you letting it happen? I would think you'd prefer to see me caught in the trap."

"It would be a pleasant prospect," Gothard granted her, "but there's too much risk. I want the throne after he's taken it for me. That won't happen if you have any say in it."

That too was true. "What, then? Is this an ambush? Will I be dead within the hour?"

"You'll be gone," Gothard said, "but you'll live as long as you can keep running. I'll give you a spell that will keep the priests and the warbands off your trail until you cross the river."

Valeria's nape prickled. "I have spells of my own," she said.

"None like this one," said Gothard. "The One's priests can find the Unmaking in you and draw it back to them. The wards you know won't help you. The priests call like to like. My spell blinds them. And," he said, "it will blind the mage who inveigled you into this."

Mention of Pretorius swayed Valeria more than she liked to admit. She stiffened her spine. "Why should I trust you? Why don't you just kill me and have done with it?"

"Because if I did," he said, "your stallions would rend me limb from limb. I want you away from this place and these people. I don't care if you survive to reach Aurelia. It will fall no matter what you do."

"I will do my best to prevent that."

"I'm sure you will."

Valeria stood motionless. All the careful structure of her world was crumbling around her.

It should not be doing that. She had chosen already. She would take Sabata and ride back to Dun Mor and finish what she had begun. What difference did it make whether she said the words now or five days from now?

She could not be entertaining for a moment the thought of sealing a bargain with this of all creatures in the world. And yet if she did that, she could go home.

Home. Aurelia. The Mountain and the school.

Kerrec with all of his faults and his sharp edges and his princess wife. Kerrec who had never stopped loving Valeria, even while he did what he had to do.

In Euan Rohe's arms, she had taught herself to forget that other half of herself. She loved Euan—she did, truly, as much as she could love any man who was not Kerrec.

Anger flared up anew. Damn Kerrec, and damn her foolish heart. The harder she tried to drive him out of it, the deeper he wormed himself in. She could not even tell where she ended and he began.

Once more she turned to Sabata. Oda and Marina stood behind him, ears pricked, waiting. For them this had already happened and would always happen. If the world ended because of the choices she made, then so it did.

There was no choice. Under Pretorius' influence, in the fog of her own anger and confusion, she had thought there was. She had imagined that she could do this thing, marry this man whose whole life was focused on destroying Aurelia.

She was never meant to be a queen. The only throne she had ever needed or wanted was a horse's back. She was a rider first, foremost, and always—just as Kerrec was.

Cold sickness had lodged under her breastbone since she turned her back on him and sent him to his bride. It twisted suddenly into pain so fierce she gasped. In that pain was a bitter clarity.

The patterns around her were shifting and changing, transforming themselves with dizzying speed. When she looked toward Aurelia and Kerrec, the tides of fate and time were incomprehensible. If she turned back toward Dun Mor, the fortress and its people sank into night.

If she removed herself from the patterns around the dun, the Unmaking faded. She searched through them over and over, to be sure, but there was no doubt about it. She was a curse on that place and its people, and above all its king.

She had been blinded with delusion. Now in the misty morning her sight came brutally clear.

If she wanted to destroy Euan's people, she had only to stay in Dun Mor and let him make her his queen. It would serve Aurelia splendidly. But it would devour her soul.

Gothard nodded, seeing that clarity in her. He drew a fistful of silk from the purse at his belt. Magic thrummed in it.

Valeria made no move to take it. She wanted nothing from this man, now or ever.

"Come, lady," he said. "Be sensible. It's a long way to the border, and this is his country. He knows every hill and crag of it. He'll hunt you without rest or mercy, and he will catch you. He can't let you go. Even if his heart would allow it, his honor won't."

No matter how much Valeria hated him, he was right.

"I can protect myself," she said.

"As you protect yourself against the Unmaking?"

She hissed at him. He stood holding out his bit of silk, letting the silence stretch and the truth of his words gnaw away at her resistance.

This billowing fog of words must conceal some deep and deadly lie. But she could not tell what or where it was.

She needed any help she could get if she was to win through to Aurelia—and Gothard's spell would make her magic stronger. She would have to trust that whatever harm was in it, her own protections were strong enough to turn it aside.

She gritted her teeth and let him drop the thing into her palm. The silk slipped back from an ordinary black pebble. Part of it was smooth and rounded, and part was sharp-edged like shattered glass.

She remembered that stone. It had been in her hand when she woke after Sabata showed her the place of Unmaking. She had cast it away, but it had followed her.

When it touched her skin, she gasped as if a dart of ice had pierced her hand. Her fist clenched convulsively.

The stone both froze and burned. Icy fire ran through her body and burst from the top of her skull. The Unmaking screamed.

White calm surrounded her. Sabata held her up. Oda and Marina breathed on her, driving away the cold.

She thrust the stone into her purse. It tried to cling to her hand. She scraped it off. At last, thank the gods, it dropped away.

There were wards around her, as strong as stone and as

transparent as glass. Anything that tried to find her would slip over and past it without touching her.

She gulped air into burning lungs. Her whole body shook. It took all the strength of will she had to stop the trembling.

Gothard watched her in cold amusement. "You'll never make a stone mage," he said.

"Gods forbid I ever wish to." She pulled herself into the saddle. She did not thank him and she did not particularly care what would happen to him when Euan discovered what he had done, but she had to ask. "You'll be safe?"

"No one touches a dead man walking," he said.

She nodded once. Sabata turned before she could ask. The rain was setting in at last.

She pulled a woolen cloak from her saddlebag. It was Caletanni weaving, a gift from Euan on the morning after she agreed to marry him.

She should have cast it away, but it was closely woven and warm, and she would need it. She wrapped it around her, trying not to let the smell of it wake memories.

She could still go back. She could dare to hope that these new visions were as false as the rest.

Sabata's head faced westward. He did not stop or turn at the tensing of her thigh in the saddle. He was going home.

She sagged on his neck. Hot tears mingled with cold rain on her cheeks. There was nothing to see if she had looked back. Rain concealed the world behind a thick grey curtain.

Sabata was warm and strong. The rhythm of his paces soothed her body's tension.

Her mind had gone numb. She stayed in the saddle by force of habit, letting him carry her where he would.

Chapter Forty-One

By the time the rain closed in for good, Euan Rohe knew Valeria had made a run for it. There was no reason to think that except Murna's words and his own unease. He told himself he would find her in Dun Mor, dry and warm and doing women's things.

The brown mage said nothing when Euan left the wall. The last Euan saw of him, he was perched in the same place. The rain barely dampened him.

More damned magic. His expression was so grim that Euan looked away in self-defense, pulling his plaid over his head and running toward the shelter of the dun.

Conor perched on the empty pedestal that stood beside the door to the men's hall. He was as still as if he had been made of stone, but his eyes glittered in the torchlight.

"She's gone," he said as Euan paused in front of him.

There were marks of tears on his cheeks. "She's gone away, and all the bright ones went with her."

Even though Euan had known it, his belly clenched. What rose in him was enormous and blinding and completely without reason. The heart of it was Valeria's face all soft with pleasure, and her eyes smiling while her voice promised that she would be his queen now and always.

He flung open the doors of the hall. They crashed back. "Up!" he roared at the men who sat up blinking and yawning. "*Up!* Every man who can sit a horse—get that horse and ride!"

Half a hundred men sprang up, wide awake and ready to fight. Euan grinned ferociously at them all. When he spun on his heel and bolted toward the stable, they were behind him, snatching clothes and weapons as they ran.

There was a hard, driving rain coming down as they thundered out of the dun, but none of them cared. Euan glanced back once. Dun Mor was a grey shadow in the downpour, with Conor's small pale face peering out of its gate. Then a pair of arms pulled the boy inside.

Euan pulled the hood down lower and bent over his horse's neck. The road was slippery but the heath alongside offered good enough footing. He led his warband out across country, aiming for the place where Valeria was most often known to go.

The broken tower had an occupant, but the horse was bay and the rider was Euan's least beloved cousin. Gothard was dry and apparently warm though there was hardly any shelter in the wind, and he was smiling.

Euan pulled up in front of him. "What have you done to her?"

Gothard's smile widened. "The arrow has flown," he said.

Euan leaned down and clamped his hand around the madman's throat. *"What did you do?"*

Gothard laughed. It did not seem to trouble him at all that Euan was trying to choke the life out of him. "I told her you know about her child," he said. "It's a daughter, I think. Shall I find her for you?"

Euan's fingers tightened until Gothard's face darkened from crimson to blue. "If you harm a hair of either head, I will gut you with a blunt knife." He let go abruptly, flinging the sorcerer to the rain-wet stones.

Gothard grinned up at him. "She believed me—every word. Because I told her only the truth."

Euan knew Gothard's kind of truth. Each word might be true, but the whole was twisted into an elaborate lie. "Where has she gone? What have you made her do?"

"She's going home," said Gothard. "It was wonderfully easy to convince her. She'll serve us there as only she can. With her, we'll win it all."

"This is her home," Euan said through clenched teeth.

"Not to her. I hardly had to mention it before I had her in my hand. She is fond of you—no one can deny that—but she's Aurelian to the bone. Which," said Gothard, "is our great good fortune. She'll give us the empire, its gods, everything. We'll win back all we lost."

Euan's heart clenched. He had dreamed of such a weapon and such a stroke. He had done everything he could to make it happen.

He had never meant that weapon to be Valeria.

It was not going to be Valeria. He whirled his horse around, tumbling Gothard underfoot. His warband was more than ready to follow.

In Dun Mor Valeria had forgotten the strange things this country's magic could do to her. As she rode away from it, the strangeness came back tenfold. Her head was light and she was dizzy, and she could not seem to focus properly.

Part of that was her body's betrayal. Her courses had come on fast and hard, doubling her up with pain.

She was glad. Grania did not need a half-barbarian brother or sister. No one did. Gothard was proof of that.

She paused to do the necessary, got the cramping under control, mounted again and went on. She had to get to the border, and then she had to make her way to the imperial city. She had to find Kerrec.

Above all, she had to see Briana. Briana more than any must know what was brewing among the tribes.

The rain lightened to a drizzle and then to a mist. It was well past noon, but the stallions showed no sign of tiring.

They would stop when it pleased them. Valeria was neither hungry nor thirsty, though she had her bit of breakfast if she was minded to eat it. She closed her eyes, but that only made the dizziness worse.

At first she thought she heard thunder. Then she recognized the thudding of hooves—a herd of horses, dozens strong.

It could not be pursuit. Gothard's spell protected her against it. It must be a hunting party from one of the clans.

The mist blew away in a sudden swirl of wind. She looked directly into a pair of yellow wolf-eyes.

Gothard had lied. She dug heels into Sabata's sides, so hard he squealed in protest and leaped forward.

"Valeria!" Euan roared behind her.

She urged Sabata from hand gallop to headlong run.

Euan's voice boomed over the moor. "Valeria! *Valeriaaaaa!*"

She felt nothing. It could have been the baying of hounds or the cry of a horn. All it meant was that she was hunted— and her erstwhile ally had betrayed her. Fool that she was, to trust him even for an instant.

Euan Rohe had his whole warband with him, his closest friends and companions. They were all mounted and riding breakneck behind their king.

An arrow flew past her. She crouched as low as she could. Sabata's mane whipped her cheek.

Euan shouted again, not her name this time. It sounded as if he was cursing the man who had shot at her.

That could not be so. He wanted her dead. They all did. She had broken her word. No high king could suffer such dishonor.

Euan would have to kill her. He had no choice.

First he had to catch her.

Damn the woman, she would not stop. Euan howled at her, promising her anything if she would leave off running. She only rode the faster.

It must be true. All her promises had been false. The moment she had the chance to go back to her own country, she had taken it.

Euan refused to believe that. Gothard lied. When he did not lie, he twisted the truth out of all recognition.

If Euan could only catch her, he would find a way to explain. She did love him—he was as sure of that as he was of his own love for her. He would break whatever spell Gothard had laid on her, take her home and finish making her his queen.

She could win the world for us.

That was Gothard's voice, winding like a snake through Euan's mind. Euan shut it out. They did not need her. All their forces were moving into place, preparing to strike before the empress tried again to take the throne.

Valeria would sit on that throne. She would fight it, and for a while she would hate Euan, but she would come round to it in the end. She would see the advantage in her position—the ability to speak for her people before the high king, and the capacity to make him understand them.

But first she had to stop and listen. Her white horses were not as fast as Euan had been led to expect. They ran like the thick little cobs they were—doughtily and with great endurance, but speed was not their best virtue.

His fingers twitched toward his bow. The idiot who had shot at her would get a flogging with the flat of a sword, but he had reminded Euan that a wise cavalryman shot at the enemy's horses.

These were not horses. If one of them was wounded or killed—if they could be killed—the One alone knew what the consequence would be.

Euan was not that desperate. Yet.

In all this mist and fog, no one could properly tell where

they were. There was no road or track to guide them. They must be going westward, but how far they had come, Euan could not have said. All of his distances were calculated at the speed of a man on foot.

He only had to outlast her. His horse was a strong beast as well as fast—they bred for it in the imperial studs. Euan's rump was not nearly as well accustomed to a saddle as hers, but it was only pain. Pain was his gift to the One.

Euan had stopped roaring at her, which was a relief. He had not stopped following. The moor went on forever and so did the chase, silent now and as relentless as a nightmare.

She was not going to wake from this one. Sabata's neck was slick with sweat as well as rain. He had to slow soon, to breathe and drink. She was not a barbarian who could ride his horse into the ground and not care.

The moor had been mostly level, but now it began to slope downward. The fog that seemed to have been lifting was thicker here. It had a cold smell, almost like the sea.

There must be a river nearby, but there was no sign of it in the mist. Valeria could not have heard it running through the pounding of hooves and the hammering of her heart.

When it seemed the chase would truly be endless, like the hunt of the gods-cursed in old stories, the long slope leveled. A shape appeared in the mist, a shadowy man on horseback, beckoning urgently.

Valeria caught the hot-metal smell of magic even as she recognized Master Pretorius. It truly was the mage and not the traitor Gothard—his magic was unmistakable even to her fuddled senses.

He was calling to her to turn aside from the direct way and cross the slope slantwise. Her belly knotted. Did she dare to trust him?

If it ended this chase, even an ambush would be welcome. Sabata was flagging. Marina and Oda, though unburdened by a rider, were not as fresh as they had been.

Oda's breath came hard. God he might be, but his body was old.

One of the pursuers' horses went down, rolling end over end. The others did not even check their stride. Another arrow flew, this time toward the riderless stallions.

Marina ducked and veered. Sabata stumbled, rolling stones underfoot, but just as fear opened wide in Valeria, he recovered and went on as strongly as ever. Thank the gods, the arrow had not touched him.

Pretorius glimmered ahead of them. He seemed to float in the mist, hovering above the tumbled ground.

Sabata plunged through him and swerved—and the earth gave way.

Valeria looked down into empty space and, far below, a swirl of foaming water. Sabata scrambled frantically as the cliff's edge crumbled. His hooves slipped and flailed.

Valeria acted by pure instinct, lying back as far as she could go. The sky whirled overhead. It was raining men and horses.

Sabata hurtled downward. By some miracle he kept his haunches under him and his shoulders up. At least one horse somersaulted over him, saddle empty and stirrups flying.

Sabata's fall ended abruptly, nearly launching Valeria over his head. She held on with every scrap of balance she had.

A thicket of brambles had caught him, stabbing her with innumerable thorns.

She welcomed the pain with all her heart. The river roared just beyond the thicket, tumbling the bodies of Euan's warband among the carcasses of their mounts. Of Oda and Marina she saw no sign.

A narrow track ran along the riverbank. Sabata needed badly to rest, but she dared not stop, not there. Once they had extricated themselves from the brambles, she had just enough room to slip off his back and spare him the effort of carrying her.

She tried to go upstream away from the tumble of drowned men and horses, but the brambles there were impenetrable. The only way to go was downstream.

It was a wet, slippery, grueling road. She was scratched and bleeding, but the multitude of small pains kept her in her body. Sabata plodded behind her, head low in exhaustion.

Road and river bent around the base of the cliff. Valeria knew better than to look back, but she could not help herself.

Most of the warband had been carried away downstream, dead or dying. A handful of twisted bodies lay on the bank. Even if any of them had survived, he would not be following her.

One big red horse lay dying by the water. His back was broken.

He would not last long, nor could he be in pain. And yet Valeria could not leave him to die in fear and confusion. She left Sabata where he stood, with some relief that he immediately began to search for bits of forage among the brambles.

The red gelding's eye was already glazing. Valeria stroked peace into him. He sighed as he let go, and his body went still.

She bowed over him, murmuring a blessing in his ear.

A stone clattered. She whipped about.

A tall figure swayed on the bank. His body was a tapestry of bruises. He did not seem aware of her at all. He was pulling another out of the water, battling the strong current.

Valeria was beyond insane. She got a grip on one wet and slippery arm and helped to heave the drowned man onto the shore.

She looked down into Euan Rohe's face. A nearly identical face bent above him—Conory his cousin, too numb for grief.

Euan's lips were blue. He was not breathing. He was as battered as Conory, and at least one leg appeared to be broken—ribs, too, from the look of them. But that did not matter to a drowned man.

"No," Valeria said.

She should be rejoicing. A great enemy of Aurelia was dead. He would have killed her or worse if he had caught her, and then he would have gone on with his long fight against the empire.

Twice now she had helped him to escape imperial justice. Against divine justice she had no defense.

Maybe not—but she could try. She sat astride him, ignoring Conory's gasp of outrage, and set her lips to his. She breathed for him—forcing air into the waterlogged lungs even as she pressed water out of them. Broken ribs ground under her hands.

He remained cold and still. Conory reached to fling her aside, babbling of insult and dishonor.

Euan coughed, convulsed then heaved up a great quantity of water. Almost too late, Valeria tipped him onto his side and held him until there was nothing left inside.

He was broken—rather badly. But he was alive. She set a kiss on his lips that were no longer blue or cold, weaving into it as much healing as she knew how to give. If the gods were kind, it would take root and grow. If not...

As she straightened, she met Conory's stare. "Take care of him," she said.

Conory said nothing. She had not expected him to love her, but the absence of hate took her somewhat aback. If anything, he regarded her in pity.

She did not try to understand. Sabata was waiting. He had recovered enough strength to carry her, but she spared him for yet a while.

Conory made no move to follow them. Just before she rounded the cliff, she looked back. He bent over Euan, rubbing warmth into cold limbs.

More likely than not, Euan would die. He was a long way from home, at the bottom of a cliff, with no one to help him but one exhausted clan brother.

The healing she had given him would be enough. It had to be. Valeria had made the last choice she could make between Euan Rohe and the world she was born to. This time it was irrevocable.

Chapter Forty-Two

Past the bend of the river, Marina and Oda stood together, waiting. Water still streamed from them. Marina's nostrils fluttered as Valeria approached. Oda raised his head but made no sound.

Valeria sagged and nearly collapsed. Thank every god and power, they were safe.

She ran her hands over Marina who was nearer, down his legs and under his belly, lifting his hooves to peer at the soles. Apart from a scratch and a bruise or two, he was unharmed.

She wrapped her arms around his neck and pressed her face to his mane, not ready to let the tears run yet, but too overcome to stop herself. With an effort she made herself let go.

Oda was shivering. As she left Marina, his knees buckled. By the time she had run to his side, he was down.

His eyes were calm. There was no fear in him. He was not mortal. He knew what he faced.

Her hands, seeking frantically, found the broken shaft behind his elbow. The arrow that had missed Marina and Sabata had struck him in the heart. Somehow he had gone on, surviving the fall and the river, until she found him and he could let go.

"No," she said. "Oh, no, no. Not you, too. I can't lose you."

Not lose. He gave her the rare gift of words. With them came a deep, singing joy and a sense of profound peace.

She tried to fight it, but he had gone beyond the obedience a white god chose to offer his rider. As she knelt in the mud and stones with his head in her lap, he let go the flesh in which he had lived for so long.

All the world was light. In that single, blinding instant, she saw the whole vast expanse of fate and time, the patterns woven when the world began and unraveling at the world's ending. It lay like a shining net over the face of nothingness, a web of creation in the midst of endless unbeing.

She fell back into her body with a gasp of shock at its countless small pains and dragging exhaustion. Already her memory of that moment of godhood was fading. She tried to hold it, to fix it in her mind, but it slipped away.

Oda was gone—in body as well as spirit. She looked for grief, but in its place she found supernal calm.

He had not left her. He was still there in the circle of stallions, watching over her. She reached for him, wishing with mortal persistence for the solidity of a living body. But he had left that behind.

One last time he gave her words. *When all hope is gone and all that is is unmade, call to me. For that I came to you. For that I stay.*

He did not answer the questions that came flooding. When she pressed him, the rest of the white gods closed in, easing her gently but firmly away from him.

She knelt in the mud, wrapped in a cold mantle of fog. There was nothing left of Oda but the mark of his body on the bank and the brightness in her heart.

Marina's breath ruffled her hair. Sabata closed his teeth on her sleeve and tugged.

It was time to go. She rose slowly, weighed down with grief for everything that she had lost. The sense of distance had come back, the dullness inside her that had afflicted her since she let Gothard bind her with a spell.

She fumbled in the purse for the stone. Ugly, useless thing—it had failed to do what it was meant to. Instead it had betrayed her.

She would cast it in the river and be rid of it. Maybe then her head would clear.

Her fingers were stiff and unwieldy. The stone eluded them, rolling away amid the coins and oddments. When she thought she had it, she drew out a bit of barley sweet that she had stolen from the riders' dining hall months ago and forgotten to feed to the horses.

Sabata was glad to relieve her of it. He was also insistent that she stop dallying about and get on his back. He was refreshed. He could carry her. They must go.

She gave up hunting for the stone. Night was coming and it was a long way yet to the border.

Her heart was near to breaking. She was going home, but she left behind a whole world. She had had such hopes for it, and now they were all gone.

She blamed Gothard, which was just, but she blamed Pretorius even more. He had wielded magic to save her, and he had succeeded. For that she supposed she should be grateful.

Oda was gone and Euan Rohe might be dead. She hoped Pretorius paid for that in the currency of the tribes, with ample pain and a slow death.

Kerrec had been suffering through an odd, fretful day. Chill rain had been rolling in off the sea since yesterday, and the horses were restless and irritable. During the morning exercises, one of the most placid of Briana's geldings objected unreasonably to a shadow in the corner of the school, flung off his young rider and bolted.

The boy would recover from his cracked collarbone. The rest of the exercises proceeded less explosively but were only a little more satisfying. Kerrec ended them early and sent everyone home.

He had more than enough to do in his study, but his mind refused to focus. The rest of the riders were out and about, some pursuing their training in the library or the riding court, others taking a holiday. He contemplated joining one or the other.

Both were tempting, but he could not decide between them. He leaned back in his chair, rubbing his eyes. The world around him felt oddly fragile, as if a hard blow would crack it.

The patterns were as dark and confused as ever. The Augurs had not had a sensible reading of the omens since Briana was wounded. Each day the signs grew less comprehensible.

Today they were impossible. When he tried to follow the line of each major and minor pattern, it disappeared into fog and murk.

Either the world was ending or the patterns were being undone. The thought was preposterous, but it would not let him be. Something at the core of things was causing it to unravel.

No one else seemed aware of it. The orders of mages were chasing priests and sacrifices and courtly conspiracies. The Augurs were peering into their books of omens and finding no answers there.

They were looking in the wrong places. This thing was not coming for them. It was already in them, laired in their hearts.

When Kerrec had the time, he was going to be very much afraid. He stared at the books and written pages scattered over the worktable. They were suddenly strange, as if he had never seen their like before.

The lines of letters shaped a pattern. It looked like a map, a landscape of mountain and moor cut through with rivers. A wild hunt rode there, pursuing a shadowy quarry.

The hunt ended on a cliff above a river gorge. The quarry fell, and the hunters fell with it, tumbling down into the wild white water.

Kerrec felt the dizziness of the fall and the shock of icy water. He recoiled before he followed the rest of the way, torn out of the body and cast into nothingness.

The pages were simply pages again, and the words only words. His head ached dully.

He rose, staggering and then steadying himself. He needed Petra's back and the calm of the riding court. In those patterns he would find his center.

Gunnar and Nikos were there ahead of him, intent on their own exercises. Kerrec watched while he led Petra out and warmed the stallion's muscles, letting their patterns inform his. It was a peaceful pursuit and long familiar, and today it was blessed.

As he rode the familiar exercises, it seemed there was a fourth white stallion in the court with them, a shining shape that flickered in and out of his vision. Its patterns wove through the rest, completing some and binding others.

Sometimes a Great One who had passed out of the body would come into the school and join in the exercises—for the pleasure of the dance, it was said. Kerrec had not seen it since he was a Fourth Rider, ten years and more ago. Then it had been a bit of brightness on a dark winter day, a rarity to remember but never quite understand.

As he recalled it, the Great One had seemed solid in the light and transparent in shadow. This one was a pattern of light and darkness, only intermittently wearing the shape of a horse.

They all ended together as if on the same note of music. The Great One melted into the light, just as Kerrec recognized the strong arch of the nose and the deep eye.

Kerrec called after him, but he was gone. Truly gone—departed from the body.

Rider's discipline was second nature, but Kerrec had to fight for the patience to cool Petra out, then unsaddle and groom him and feed him his ration of hay. Nikos and Gunnar were still tending their stallions when Kerrec was done.

He stood in the aisle and tried not to shake. Nikos looked out over the stall door. "Steady, lad," he said.

"That was Oda," Kerrec said. "He's left the body."

"Yes," the Master said.

"It doesn't matter to you?"

"It matters a great deal. But the consequence will happen in its own time. The patterns he danced with us were patterns of stability. They bade us hold fast and wait."

"I can't do that," Kerrec said. "If Oda is dead, Valeria has lost her strongest guardian. She may be dead or dying herself."

"Do you feel that?"

Kerrec stopped short. "I feel nothing. The place where she was is empty."

He had not known that until he said it. The bottom dropped out of his stomach. "Dear gods. Valeria is dead."

"No."

He stared at Nikos.

"If she were dead," Nikos said, "we would all know."

"Would we? Do we know anything at all? Everything we knew has turned on itself."

"We would know," said Nikos.

"I have to find her," Kerrec said. "Do you understand? I can't be patient any longer. I have no discipline left."

"You must be patient," Nikos said. "You will be patient. If she is safe—and she still has two stallions and a master mage to defend her—anything you do may harm more than help. If she is in danger, I believe devoutly that she will do her utmost to find you.

"Think, too," he said, "that from the beginning this has been a game of feints and indirection. If you gallop off alone to play knight rescuer, you lay yourself open to attack. Stay here where your power is strongest and wait. If she can come to you, she will."

"And if she cannot?"

"Are you a mage, sir?"

Kerrec opened his mouth to snap that of course he was. But that was not what Nikos was asking. He wanted Kerrec to stop thrashing and think.

Yes, Kerrec was a mage. He carried the full weight of two magics, the pattern magic of the Mountain and the earth magic of the emperor. But again, that was not what Nikos meant.

He had not had so thorough a dressing-down since he was new to the Mountain. It stung, as it was meant to. First Rider he might be, but he was carrying on like a love-struck boy.

He bent his head stiffly to his Master. Nikos inclined his glance in return. "I'll not do anything to endanger myself or any of us," Kerrec said. "You have my word."

"I trust you," Nikos said.

That was both simple and devastating. Once Kerrec was away from the stable, he had to sag against a wall and think carefully about breathing.

Nikos was a quiet man. He could deceive even the First Riders into thinking that he was little more than a glorified headmaster. He kept his school in order, made sure it ran smoothly and rode herd on the riders.

He was also a master of masters, a mage of great and subtle power. As a trainer of men as well as horses, he had few equals.

Kerrec felt as if he had been ridden to a standstill. He pushed himself erect. There would be no wild ride into the east, but he had been all but ordered to do whatever else he could to get Valeria home.

* * *

The Master Seer covered the silver scrying mirror. His broad ruddy face had gone sunken and sallow. "I can't. There's nothing to see."

"Try harder," Kerrec said, relentless.

Master Omeros started as if stung, but he shook his head. "Four times I've tried with all my art and power. She is nowhere to be found."

"She is in this world," Kerrec said. "She is not dead."

The Seer spread his hands. "Rider, I am sorry. If I could find her, I would."

"Look for a spell," Kerrec said. "Look for nothingness."

"Rider," the Seer said, "the world is full of it and growing fuller. I can't know what is hers and what is not."

Kerrec bit back the words that came flooding. Master Omeros had done his best. It was hardly fair of Kerrec to afflict him with his own anxiety and frustration.

He thanked the Seer as honestly as he knew how. Master Omeros nodded wearily. "I wish you well," he said, "and pray we all find a way through what is coming."

"Gods grant it," Kerrec said.

Chapter Forty-Three

Valeria had no clear memory of the road between the river gorge where Euan Rohe's warband died and the walls of Aurelia. There must have been garrisons, towns, caravanserais. She must have eaten and slept and made sure that her remaining stallions had forage and places to rest. The whole of that journey was a long, dim dream.

She woke from it twice. The first time, she was about to cross the river that marked the border of Aurelia. As she paused on the edge of the ford, she saw Pretorius in front of her.

She thought he might be barring the way as he had before, but when she rode through him, nothing happened. She turned on him. "Why?" she demanded.

There were more meanings to that word than even she could keep track of, but she suspected that Pretorius could. Even so, she was surprised when he answered. "Fate," he said.

She reared back slightly. "What, you're the gods' instrument?"

"Aren't you?"

"I hope," she said, "that you suffer every torment you've ever inflicted on your victims. All but death. I don't want you to die. I want you to live and know pain."

"The Ard Ri is alive," he said. "He'll walk with a limp for the rest of his life, but he's mending."

Valeria could not breathe, let alone speak.

Pretorius' eyes were bright and preternaturally clear. "When all this is done, you above all will understand. Go on now. Finish what you've begun."

She was not a child or a servant, to be ordered about as if she had no will of her own. She opened her mouth to say so, but he was gone, vanished into the mist.

She was melting herself, falling back into the long dream. Whatever thoughts or questions she had were gone as thoroughly as Pretorius.

The second time she woke, she found herself outside the north gate of the royal city, under a grey and tumbled sky. Sun was another thing she did not remember. All through her dream, she had traveled in clouds and fog.

A storm was brewing over Aurelia. The sea roared against the harbor walls. Wind shrilled around the towers. Even the gulls had sought shelter rather than battle the gale.

She was the only person to pass through what was usually a busy and crowded gate. The streets beyond were all but empty.

It was not only the storm. The city lay under a pall of fear. When she looked for the source of it, she recoiled.

The Unmaking was closer to the surface than it had ever been. Only long practice and great effort kept the spell inside her from opening wide and swallowing itself.

This horror was bought with blood and pain. It made her think of the priests' circles among the clans, but swollen and twisted out of all measure.

The tribes knew how to worship the One. Whoever was doing it here neither knew nor cared.

The Lady could have withstood that assault, but Valeria could not find her anywhere. The orders of mages were defenseless against it. Their magic could not touch it without being unmade.

Gods knew, Valeria was living proof of that. She shielded herself as best she could and rode through the silent streets. Doors were locked and windows shuttered, markets empty and taverns dark.

Where there was life at all, it was furtive and fearful, slipping through the shadows from doorway to doorway. The sight of a rider with two white horses only deepened their fear.

The wrongness of that wrenched at her heart. She urged Sabata to quicken his pace. The sooner she was in Riders' Hall, the sooner she could rest.

She refused to think of what would happen if Riders' Hall was deserted—if the Riders had followed the Lady back to the Mountain. They would not do that. Now more than ever, this city and this empire needed them.

As little good as it will do them, a voice whispered in her mind. It sounded horribly like Gothard's.

She refused to think of him. He did not deserve to be thought of. He had helped her escape, but that meant no more than that he saw better advantage in her absence than her presence.

She was pathetically glad to see the wall of Riders' Hall on the far side of the temple square. It was low, nondescript and not particularly forbidding. Its gate was shut but not barred.

She dismounted just inside and led Sabata and Marina into the stallions' stable. They were all still here—Petra, Alta, Flora, Alea, Benedicta and the rest. They greeted her with muffled snorts and the odd whicker, calling to her stallions as the brothers they were.

What she felt in them most of all was relief and a sense of imminence. Now, they seemed to say, whatever they had been waiting for could begin.

Matters in Aurelia had gone from bad to worse in the fortnight since Oda appeared in the school. Every mage in the city labored day and night to hold the world together, but it persisted in unraveling. The riders had gone so far as to ride small Dances in their schooling exercises in hopes that the patterns would hold and the world's fabric mend itself.

So far they had only briefly succeeded. As soon as a Dance was over, the rot in the heart came back.

Gunnar had proposed just this morning that they Dance day and night, hour by hour, in shifts like a roster of guards. He was not dismissed out of hand as he would have been only days before. It was action, even if it would drain them dry. Kerrec was no longer alone in yearning to do something, anything, against the forces that were eating the city alive.

That was the worst of it. No one knew what to do. The

slaughter of nobles had stopped after three nines had died—twenty-seven scions of wealthy and powerful families, thoroughly and excruciatingly dead. Not long after that, the city's heart had begun to crumble.

The long Dance would begin in the morning, unless someone could find another solution before then. They had already tried to find the Lady. Her stall had been empty for days. She was not in the palace. As far as anyone knew, just when Aurelia needed her most, she had gone back to the divine seclusion of the Mountain.

It was hopeless for any mortal to comprehend the Ladies. The white gods were bad enough.

Kerrec could not help but think that she had something to do with the malaise in the city. She had not, gods forbid, either caused or condoned the blood or the terror, but she must know how to end it.

There was no spell to summon a Lady. No one had ever dared. Kerrec was halfway tempted to stand in the middle of a riding court and howl until she listened.

That could be a very long time. He paced his study, where a fire was lit against the chill.

A tottering pile of books nearly overwhelmed the worktable. He had found nothing useful in them. All any of them said of the Unmaking was that a mage must never under any circumstances either read or perform its spells. There were nine of them, and each brought a greater degree of dissolution. The ninth was the last, the end of all things.

Kerrec wanted to ask who knew this, how he had discovered it and what had become of him. But there was no one to ask. The orders had banned all such study. Even the locked room of the palace library, where the blackest of black books were kept under heavy guard, had no books of Unmaking.

Kerrec had authority to scour the empire for whatever he needed. But there was no time. The mages thought that the attack would come at or just before the coronation Dance, which was a fortnight and more away.

Kerrec would have liked to believe it, but his bones knew they did not have a fortnight. If they were lucky, they had a handful of days.

Briana would be crowned—for certain this time—at the first full moon of autumn, which happened to fall on the day when sun and moon shared the sky equally. That was a high and holy day in the empire.

But their enemies were not imperial mages. They worshipped another power. That power was strongest not at the moon's full but in its dark.

Tomorrow was the dark of the moon.

Kerrec shook himself. He was dreaming or deluded. The enemy had always attacked during or shortly before a great rite. He needed the rite to draw power. Then from that power he wrought destruction.

What if he had found another source of strength?

Great gods, had the Lady gone over to the enemy?

Impossible. Even the priests of the One could not corrupt a being who stood above gods.

Kerrec could not allow himself to doubt that. Whatever was coming, it was something or someone else.

He paused by the fire. The flames wove patterns that he did not try to read. He had had enough of them for the moment. He only wanted to rest his eyes and bask in the warmth.

The door opened behind him. He spoke without turning. "What, time for dinner already?"

"I don't think so," said a voice he had prayed every morning and every night to hear again.

He whipped about. Valeria stood in the doorway, ragged and mud-spattered and worn thin. She looked as if she had ridden hard and far on light rations, but her voice was clear and her eyes were steady.

He had no memory of crossing the room. He gripped her shoulders, shaking her until her teeth rattled. "You! Damn you! Where in all the gods' name have you been? I've been out of my mind with worry."

"I know," she said. "I'm sorry. I thought it would be better if I went away."

"It was not."

She shook her head. Her eyes were shadowed. "I wish…" She did not finish the thought.

He paid it no mind. His hands had stopped wanting to shake her. They passed over her body instead. "Gods, you're skin and bone. Have you been remembering to eat at all? Come to the kitchen. We'll get you fed."

She blinked at him. "You're fussing like an old grandmother," she said.

"Can you blame me?"

She shrugged. She must be dizzy with hunger and exhaustion, but she insisted on walking down to the kitchen and seating herself in a corner by the hearth.

The cooks fed her newly baked bread and a bowl of stewed mutton. They clucked and fussed even more than Kerrec had.

She bent her head over the bowl and inhaled the fragrant steam. "Gods, I've missed these spices," she said.

"Eat," said Kerrec. He stood over her while she did it, sharpening his glare whenever she threatened to slacken.

Only after she had eaten every bite and cleaned the bowl with the last of the bread and eaten that, too, would he relax his vigilance. The master cook himself brought her a tisane of herbs and honey, for her to sip slowly while it was hot. She wrapped her hands around the cup as if she welcomed the warmth.

Her eyelids were drooping. Kerrec caught the cup before it slid from her fingers and lifted her all too easily.

She had always been slender, but what weight she had had been solid, supple and strong. Too much of that was gone.

"Send for a Healer," he said to the cooks, not caring which one obeyed. In the event, half a dozen of them sprang for the door, where they settled quickly who would go and who would stay and fret.

The most surprising people loved Valeria. Kerrec's throat wanted to close.

Foolish thing—the Healer was a precaution, that was all. She was not dying. Nothing was eating her from the inside. He was being a silly old woman, just as she had said.

He carried her back up to his study. The couch there was wider and softer than the bed where he slept, and the room was warm.

As he settled her on the cushions, one of the servants peered around the door. "First Rider?" he asked diffidently. "May we…?"

Kerrec stood back. He was unexpectedly reluctant to let

anyone else touch her, but with the clairvoyance of servants, the man had brought four of his subordinates to carry her off to the bath, scrub her, dress her in fresh clothes and wrap her in blankets in front of the fire.

Kerrec stayed with them. He need not have done that, but he never wanted to take his eyes off her again.

She was sound asleep before they finished bathing her. When they laid her on the couch, she sighed and murmured and burrowed into the cushions.

Kerrec glanced at the door. He saw without surprise that Nikos was there, with Gunnar looming behind. The rest of the riders were hovering in the hallway, trying to be inconspicuous.

They moved aside for a Healer whom Kerrec had not met before, a brisk, unsentimental woman who reminded him of Valeria's mother. "Out!" she said to them all with such authority that they retreated in haste. Her eye caught Kerrec and then Nikos. "You two stay. The rest of you, find something else to do."

The air seemed less heavy after the riders dispersed. They did not go very far—Kerrec could feel them in the rooms nearby, watching and listening along the threads of the patterns.

The Healer shook her head but let them be. She took her time examining Valeria. Her expression was calm, intent, giving nothing away.

Kerrec kept a tight rein on his temper. If he had been a horse he would have been wild-eyed and shying at shadows.

Nikos, whose discipline was legendary, sat in the chair by the fire with one of the books from Kerrec's worktable. Kerrec could find something to do on that table, too, but he could not stand to be that far away from Valeria. He pulled the stool as close as he dared, then perched on it and waited.

At long last the Healer raised her head and drew a breath. "There's nothing wrong with her," she said, "but too much riding and not enough food or sleep. Let her sleep, feed her when she wakes, and she'll be back to herself in a day or two."

Kerrec could not let go the tension in his middle. "With all respect, madam, does it truly take so long to find nothing?"

She seemed unoffended. "If you're thorough, rider, it does."

"Tell me what made you pause."

Her brows drew together. No mage liked to be challenged, and Healers were especially prickly when it came to their art. But Kerrec had faced more terrible powers than this without flinching.

"It's nothing," she said. "Her defenses are unusually strong, and she has a spell of obscurity on her—to make it easier to escape the enemy, I'm sure. Some of what I might have done, the spell prevented. Still, I managed to do enough. Her recovery may be slower, but she will recover."

The Healer seemed content. Kerrec wished he could be.

Valeria could be a deeply secret and reticent person, but her magic had always had a clarity to it, a brightness that was missing from it now. It was dull and blunted, like a fine blade gone to rust.

He was not cruel enough to wake her and ask who or what had done this to her. She was exhausted, that was all. When she woke, the brightness would come back.

Chapter Forty-Four

Valeria's dreams were all of endless night. And yet she was not afraid. That part of her was lost somewhere between Dun Mor and Aurelia, between Euan Rohe and Kerrec.

She opened her eyes on a familiar ceiling. When she turned her head, she saw an even more familiar face.

Kerrec had fallen asleep in the chair by the fire. The sight of him made her want to burst into tears.

Part of her wept for Euan Rohe. That part was mad and foolish, but he did deserve that much of her. He had loved her and meant to use her well.

Kerrec had never used her. When he could or even should have, he had done everything possible to keep from doing it.

He could be difficult. His reserve clashed with hers at times and flung them both apart. But they always came back to one another. They always would.

She would have to tell him what she had done. All of it—
and he would not be happy to hear it. It might drive them
apart again.

She hoped not, considering what he had been doing while
she shared Euan Rohe's bed. Kerrec was prickly and proud
and incurably arrogant, but he was seldom unfair.

Gods, she loved him. A surge of wildness rushed into her,
a crazy delight. It came out of nowhere, filling her until she
was like to burst.

She was perfectly rational. She was aware that the city was
in terrible straits—worse than it knew—and that she tee-
tered on the edge of the abyss. The Unmaking was closer
than it had ever been. Even in the battle at Oxos Ford when
the emperor died, it had not been so near or so strong.

That had been a great working of the tribes, aimed and
focused with skill and careful intent. This was a far less
coherent thing. Whoever had wrought it did not care what
it destroyed.

As if in response to that barely controlled working, the
storm had broken. Wind howled outside the walls. Rain
lashed the windows so hard the shutters rattled.

It was still warm in the room though the fire was nearly
dead. Valeria got up, wrapping the blanket around her, and
stirred the embers back to life.

As she laid a log on the newborn flames, she felt Kerrec
behind her. He was awake, watching.

She finished what she was doing and turned. He scowled
at her. She laughed and sprang into his lap.

His arms closed around her before he could have thought

about it. She flung hers around his neck. Her head was spinning, which only made her laugh the harder.

His scowl deepened. "What have you been into? The wine?"

"Not a thing," she said. She leaned back, the better to see his face. "I'm here. I'm alive. You're beautiful."

"You're drunk on something."

"Joy." She kissed him. At first he would not respond, but she persevered until the swift heat rose in him.

His lady wife and her royal lover faded from memory. There were only the two of them as there had always been.

She pulled him down by the fire. He was more than ready—to his own visible surprise. That only made her laugh the more.

He stopped fighting, though he still would not smile. Poor troubled thing. She made love to him in every way she knew and some she had just discovered.

He caught a little of her joy. He was glad to have her back—a deep gladness that sang inside her. It even, somewhat, drove out the fear.

Everyone was so very afraid. They should learn to laugh as she did. There was nothing to fear. The night was beautiful. Oblivion was sweet.

Kerrec would not understand. She gave him what she had to give and made him as happy as he could be.

They dozed for a while, lulled by the crackle of the flames. Valeria hated to get up, but although the sky was still dark, the sun had risen. The day had begun.

She kissed Kerrec awake. "I have to see Briana," she said. "Will you go with me?"

"Now?" he asked drowsily. "Can it wait? It's high court

today. She won't be free until evening. You should rest in any case. Later in the day, we'll send a message. I'm sure she'll—"

"I would like to go now," she said. "Is it a great spectacle, this high court?"

"I suppose," he said. "The ladies wage a war of dressmakers. The lords aren't much better. There are speeches, which are interminable, and dancing, which is terribly stiff and old-fashioned. And then there is a state dinner, where everyone practices excruciating manners."

"When I was growing up in Imbria, we told stories about such things. I'd like to see it, to know whether the stories were true."

He shook his head, but the first hint of a smile touched the corner of his mouth. It vanished quickly. "What do you have to say to my sister? Is it a warning? Is there a new war coming?"

"There are things she needs to know," Valeria said. "I think she should know them as soon as possible."

He sat up. His face had gone somber. "Gods, yes. I'd forgotten—it's the dark of the moon. All the patterns—the omens— Are you sure you're fit to go out? The Healer said—"

"Grandmother," she said, laughing to take the sting out of it, "I've never felt better. Come with me and hover if you must, but I will go. Only tell me first. Dress uniform? Or—"

"It doesn't matter," he said.

"Dress uniform," she said. "I don't suppose you remember where mine is."

"The servants will," Kerrec said. She heard the hint of a sigh in his voice.

That sigh was a surrender. She kissed him and danced away, aiming toward the bath.

Kerrec had never seen Valeria so lively. His first thought, that she had drunk a little too much wine, came back to nibble at the edge of his mind. But there was no sign of either wine or drug in her, and no spell that had not been there before.

It seemed there was a giddy girl inside her after all. He let her play servant in the bath—with a little more teasing than strictly necessary—and helped her dress in the uniform that one of the servants had brought. It was stiff with newness and, in spite of how thin she had become, rather tight. She had gained curves since she was measured for it.

She looked wonderfully elegant in the grey coat with its silver piping, and the soft grey breeches and the polished black boots. No one could mistake her for a man, but Kerrec had never seen a woman to match her.

He stopped short. Theodosia would be at court. Was that why Valeria insisted on doing this?

If it was, it did not seem to dampen her mood. She was smiling, tugging at him. "Come! We'll be late."

A last vestige of wariness slowed Kerrec's response. He made himself see her clearly.

She did look well, if thin. There was no sickness in her. The Healer had wrought well.

He gave in abruptly, letting Valeria tug him toward the passage to the palace. Perhaps what she had to say to Briana would hold the answer to his forebodings. She might not know that she had it, but if it was there, he would find it.

* * *

High court was a dazzle of color and light, voices and laughter and strains of music from every corner of the great hall. The speeches were mercifully over and the dancing had begun. It would go on for hours yet, until the doors were opened to the inner hall and the banquet that concluded the long and regal day.

This year's fashion seemed to veer between elaborate gowns of blue and silver and green like the face of the sea, and a palette of night and stars—black and deep blue flecked with diamond or opal or pearl. One or two brave souls had tried to combine the two. For the most part, to Valeria's uncharitable eye, the result looked like a spectacular bruise.

It all made her terribly dizzy. As she struggled to steady herself, a cup appeared in her hand. It was full of spiced wine. She had drunk half of it before Kerrec plucked it from her fingers.

"That," he said, "you don't need. Come, there should be fruit ices—though maybe not in this weather—and tisanes and bits to eat that won't unsettle your stomach."

"I'm not hungry," she tried to tell him, but he was not listening.

He drew her with him around the edge of the hall. It was set much higher than the rest, a ring of stairs that turned the upper reaches into a gallery. She stopped midway to look down at the dance.

Humans unaided did not Dance as the white gods did. They had no such power. And yet the patterns below had the same intricacy as a Great Dance.

Kerrec tugged, but she held her ground. She had to see

the patterns. They meant something. If an Augur could stand here and look at them, he would know.

She felt as if she stood above the sky. Its clear blues and ethereal greens had cracked like a bowl flung on the floor. Black nothingness yawned beneath.

A flame darted through the vision. Briana had defied the dictates of fashion with a sweeping gown of crimson and gold. Her hair was piled high on her head, plaited with strings of rubies and golden topazes.

She swooped and spun from hand to hand, knitting together the shards of the world. Her voice rose above the rest, bright with mirth.

Where she was, there was no fear. Grim faces softened. Her people remembered how to smile and even to laugh.

It was a great working, a wonder of its kind. Valeria clapped her hands in admiration.

Briana looked up. Her eyes widened, then lit with joy. She altered the dance with a deft turn here and a dip and twirl there, aiming across the hall to the foot of the stair on which Valeria stood.

The wildness brimmed over in Valeria. It cast a golden haze over the patterns below her, the storm above and Briana's face amid the crowd of the court.

There was something in Valeria's hand. She did not remember searching in her purse, but Gothard's stone clung to her fingers. She looked down into Unmaking.

When she looked up, it was all around her, inside and out. The world was as thin as a film of water, a shimmer over oblivion. In that moment of cold revelation, she knew the mad glee that had possessed her for just that—possession.

Someone else was seeing through her eyes and ruling what she felt and saw. That alien power set hooks in the Unmaking and tore.

She flung the stone away in a spasm of revulsion. For a wonder, it let itself go. Even while it flew across the gallery, her fingers stung and burned.

The stone struck the wall and shattered. Each shard was a piece of uncreation. Out of it rose a shape of mist and smoke that gained solidity as it grew.

Gothard smiled his broad, mad smile. His eye glanced past her to the far side of the gallery, where another figure in black was standing as if it too had distilled out of air. The priest whom they had all been hunting stood brazenly above them, with his bleached eyes and his long colorless hair.

The dance spun on below. The music was shrill, its rhythms frantic. The dancers were bound, caught in the spell, dancing their own dissolution.

That same spell wound like chains around Valeria. The Unmaking was wide awake in her. She had no defenses left.

She was the key. The dance was the door. Through them Gothard and the priest undertook to rouse the things that slept beneath the palace—old powers and ancient evil, bound to the Unmaking.

Briana broke free of the dance. Her heavy skirts hampered her as she ran toward the stair, tangling her legs and slowing her pace to a rapid walk.

Valeria's power worked itself free of her will and lashed out with all its force. Briana was full in its path.

Another sprang between. In flesh he was as drab as his sister was vivid. In spirit he was at least as fierce a fire.

That fire seared Valeria to the center, the core of nothingness that opened to swallow the world. In her agony she willed them both to be gone, to stop, to be unmade.

Chapter Forty-Five

Kerrec had been watching Valeria with increasing unease. He had never seen her so light or so wild. When it all began to unravel, he was almost ready for it.

In his wariness he had raised defenses that were not enough—nothing would ever truly be enough—but they were a beginning. As Gothard and the priest took shape out of air, Kerrec gathered every scrap of power that he had.

Even as he grasped it, it tried to shrivel and fray. The Unmaking was laired in Valeria, infecting everything around her. While Kerrec fought to keep the patterns from melting away, she turned against Briana.

Briana drew herself together to fight back. Kerrec leaped between them. He had no coherent thought except that he could not let either one destroy the other.

Unmaking tore at him. He clung desperately to shape,

form, pattern. Words grew out of it, a high, fierce cry to the gods of earth and air, land and sea, and above all the white powers of the Mountain.

That cry rang over the wild music and the ensorcelled dance, strong and clear as the trumpeting of a stallion.

The earth was opening, its substance dissolving. Dancers shriveled like leaves in a black wind.

Kerrec called again, even higher and fiercer than before. "Come! By all that is holy, by everything you ever wrought or were, come to us! Lords of the Mountain, Ladies, Powers—come. Help us. If we ever served you, if you ever loved us, defend us now. Save us from Unmaking."

He had no hope that he would be heard. The gods had allowed this to happen. They were weary of their creation—even that part of it which was their own selves. They were letting it be undone.

Even as the thought took shape, Kerrec refused it. One last time he called up his power, spending it without care for the cost. He summoned the gods. He commanded them to save not only this world that they had made but the being they had created in order to destroy it.

Valeria fought against that terrible destiny. Far down in the heart of her, even through the Unmaking, she struggled to resist the forces that bound her.

"If you love her," Kerrec said to the gods, whether they chose to listen or no, "help me save her."

White shapes appeared as Gothard had, spread in a wide circle through the hall. Each of them straddled a stretch of nothingness. In the center of the circle the Lady stood, dark beside their whiteness.

They would stand sentinel at the world's ending. It was coming swifter now. Gothard danced on the face of it, dipping and whirling, black robes flying.

His laughter was sweet and utterly mad. He had little power of his own—he had always relied on stones to heighten it. Now he relied on Valeria. There seemed to be no end to her strength, as if the Unmaking itself were feeding it.

Despair gnawed at Kerrec's spirit. As he faltered, losing hope, Briana's hand slipped into his. Her fingers were warm, her grip firm.

Riders appeared on the backs of the stallions. Kerrec recognized their faces, but their humanity was stripped away. There was nothing left of them but the raw power.

Fear gripped him. He could not let go as they had. He dared not. What if he could not find his humanity again?

What if they were all unmade?

Petra's back was solid under him. Briana was still on the stair, and yet he could feel her hand in his.

Up above them, Valeria was a shape of living darkness. Below their feet, that same darkness roiled. Only the most fragile shell of existence stood between them and oblivion.

They had to Dance. They could not ask how—they simply had to do it. Kerrec urged Petra into motion.

The stallion obeyed as he always had. His brothers followed his lead. Only the Lady was still, the center of the turning wheel.

Kerrec did not know or care what the others Danced for. He Danced to save Valeria's soul. Every pattern he wove and every shape he transcribed in shimmering and unstable space was for her, to unmake the Unmaking and make her whole again.

It was a hopeless thing, but he did it regardless. He loved her. He could not bear to live without her. If they were all going to be unmade, at least she could go whole and unbound into the night.

A blast of Unmaking smote the Dance. Kerrec spun away from Valeria toward the sorcerer who had enspelled her.

The patterns wavered like images in water. The hall's edges were fading. He could not bear to think of what was happening to the world without.

The only stability was in this wheel of white dancers and the bay Lady. They forsook the intricacy of the Dance of Time for the profound simplicity of the world's own order. They walked and trotted and cantered through circles within circles within circles—rim and center, sun and planets, great wheel of creation that turned in everything that was, from the greatest to the infinitely small.

Gothard's dance spun onward, unmaking whatever the Dance sought to make. With each turn of his hand and each stamp of his foot, whole fields of stars died. And all the while, he fed on Valeria, consuming her magic and her substance.

Valeria had been living in a dream. As it turned to nightmare, a tiny and essential part of her came awake. Gothard's spell had crushed it far down and nearly unmade it—but not quite.

She had been fighting the Unmaking for so long that the core of her will had actually grown stronger. It opened its eyes and saw what she had been made to do—all of it, every failure, every deception, every betrayal. Her reticence and secrecy had fed it, and her fits of pique had played directly into Gothard's hands.

Her magic was his now. He no longer cared for the petty

revenge of seeing his brother and sister die in agony. He had found a better game. He would end it all, until only he remained, dancing over the abyss.

It was because of Valeria that he could do it. He had no magic left. He had spent it all in his escape from death. What he had, and what he had brought back from that foray into ancient night, was the gift of taking other powers as his own.

The priests of the One had been feeding him since he came back to life. His disciple, the priest who even now poured out his magic in the hall, had given him the last essential edge of imperial magic. With that he had lured and then captured Valeria.

There was nothing left of her but a thought. That thought was deeply, abidingly angry—at him for destroying them all and at herself for being such a monstrous idiot.

Anger burned like fire. Like mortal flame, when it found fuel, it grew.

There was much for it to feed on. Gothard's working and the Dance of desperation made the flames leap high. The courtiers dead or dying and the servants swallowed in Unmaking gave it an edge of potent grief. Even as her body dissolved into air and darkness, she looked on Gothard's dance and knew the perfect whiteness of rage.

In that perfection she found the white gods. They had always been there, forever a part of her, since before she wore this fading body. They Danced in their circle and so, for a little while, preserved the solidity of things. But the Unmaking was stronger than they.

If it was so strong, how had anything ever been created? How could any creation endure?

The Lady knew the answer to that. Maybe, with her sisters, she was the answer. She was the hub of the wheel, the heart of the Dance. Around her the earth turned in its orbit.

Moon and stars were fading. Light was draining from the world. There was a strong seduction in it, a terrible sweetness in that utter absence of thought or struggle.

Gothard's mother had killed herself rather than live in madness. Gothard preferred to kill everything that was.

He had his fair share of imperial hubris. Valeria the soldier's daughter, the unregenerate commoner, had no use for that. With the last spark of self that she had, she understood perfectly her mother's exasperation with foolishness of any kind—mortal or divine.

She seized the Lady by the shoulders as if she had worn human form and shook her hard. "Enough," she said. "Enough of this. We've learned our lesson. We'll keep on learning it as long as we're alive. Now give me what I need."

The Lady slipped free of her with boneless ease and stood as the bay mare she most loved to be. Stallions and riders had winked out of existence. There was only the dancer in his madness and the Unmaking in its immensity, and the sturdy, foursquare, insistently mortal form of the Lady.

She stamped her foot. The dancer faltered.

Her head tossed. Black mane flew. Oblivion streamed over her and wrapped around her.

She strained against it. Its bonds tightened. Her eyes bulged. She was strangling—dying.

Valeria did not know what to do. All she could offer was the honed edge of her temper.

It slit the worst of the bonds, filling their nothingness with the essence of humanity. With a scream that rang in Valeria's nonexistent skull, the Lady broke free. Stars sprayed like sparks across the emptiness.

Valeria felt them as pinpricks of burning pain, as if they had been living embers and her body had been the Unmaking. That was the price she paid for her defiance—and she welcomed it. It proved that she was alive.

She clasped it tight, deep in the heart of nothingness. It took root and grew, until all of her that still was, was part of it.

The barbarians had the right of it. Pain was life. Its existence was blessed and its power divine. It burned away the darkness and brought back the light.

Chapter Forty-Six

Kerrec looked around the circle of the Dance. The floor was no longer transparent underfoot. The walls were rising again and the roof taking shape overhead.

The Lady was still in the center of the circle. Briana stood halfway up the stair that rimmed the edge of the hall, burning bright in her panoply of crimson and gold.

A shadow hovered above her. It looked vaguely like Valeria, but its face was indistinct and its eyes were full of stars.

Gothard had stopped his dance. He stood lightly, poised like a spearman about to cast, with Valeria's magic gathered in his hand.

There was no mistaking what he had. Kerrec would recognize it if he lost every vestige of either wits or power.

This was the last throw, the final gamble. The shadow-

Valeria was a shell around Unmaking. If that shell broke, whatever was bringing back the world would fail.

Again and yet again, Gothard had waged this war through diversion. He was perilously close to winning it. Kerrec wrenched his mind away from Valeria—though it cost him bitter anguish—and focused the full power of it on Gothard.

Valeria's voice cried out in pain and fear. Kerrec fixed his eyes grimly on his brother's face. Hate was easy—and it was a diversion of its own.

He set hate aside and anger and even fear. The world's patterns hung on the brink, half made and half unmade.

Gothard had no magic. That was Kerrec's focus. Valeria's magic belonged to the pattern that was Valeria. Gothard's pattern was empty.

Kerrec wove the patterns as they should be. Valeria's magic was in Valeria. Gothard was nothing. No heart, no soul, no self. Gothard did not exist.

Gothard howled in agony and rage. The white ball of magic had escaped him. He scrabbled after it.

It wavered as if part of it were still bound to him. His fingers closed around it.

It blasted him with fire. As he reeled, Kerrec struck—not with magic but the devastating simplicity of his clenched fist.

Gothard dropped, sprawling on the floor that was nearly as solid now as it should be. He was breathing, but consciousness had fled.

Kerrec had a brief thought of sparing him. It was not mercy. Gothard would die at the hands of a Brother of Pain, if Kerrec was given the right to decide his sentence.

Gothard had cheated death once. This was the result of it. As long as he lived, nothing in this world was safe.

One sharp snap would break his neck. Kerrec knelt and reached for Gothard's throat.

His heart was cold as a judge's should be. His dreams of revenge had all been unmade. This was justice, no more and no less.

Fiery pain stabbed his back, piercing a shoulder blade and glancing off it. Kerrec dropped and rolled. A knife flashed past his eye.

Gothard's priest lunged at him. He scrambled to his feet. One thing he owed Gothard's torturer—he knew how to shut off pain.

He balanced himself on the balls of his feet. The priest grinned. His face was like a skull, his eyes pale blue and clouded like a drowned man's. He darted in, aiming low.

Kerrec twisted aside. A second line of fire traced the edge of his hip.

There was no time for this. Gothard would come to himself and escape.

It was all a game of lies and diversions. Kerrec sprang toward the priest. The creature recoiled, startled, and stared at his empty hand.

The blade slid smoothly up between Gothard's ribs. The membrane of his heart resisted, but Kerrec was prepared for that. He drove the knife home.

The priest's weight fell on him. The knife's hilt dug into his belly. He twisted, but those arms were like steel, grinding his ribs together and squeezing the life out of him.

* * *

Valeria could not remember what it was to be whole. Was that what this was, this sense of fullness where she had been utterly empty?

She was in the gallery again or still, swaying on knees that had gone weak. The Dance had slowed but still continued. The floor was solid and the walls were up. Riders and stallions were, in a manner of speaking, thatching the roof.

Petra Danced with the rest, but his saddle was empty. Movement caught Valeria's eye. Two figures, one in black and one in brown, grappled across the gallery.

Bright blood stained the brown coat. The anger that had brought the world back to itself was still there, burning under her breastbone. Maybe she ran or maybe she flew, but however she had come there, she fell on the man in black. He whirled away from Kerrec to turn on her.

Lank fair hair trailed across her face. Muscles coiled, whipcord and steel. The two of them rolled and tumbled down the stair.

Valeria lay winded on the floor of the hall, throbbing with bruises. The priest's face hovered over her.

Memory gripped her and would not let her go. She lay in a field outside of a town called Mallia. A pack of nobles on the hunt had brought her to bay. Their leader fell on her, tearing at her coat and breeches, ripping them from her.

This was his face. It was thinned to the bone and bleached of color, but she would never forget the shape of it. Nor would she forget how it had dropped away and Kerrec's had replaced it, black curling hair and hawk's profile and strange light eyes. She thought he meant to rape her, too, until she saw what he did to the man who had tried it.

He had taken summary justice on that field. Valeria could still see the two swift cuts and the offal cast away, and the raven that caught them and carried them off.

In those clouded eyes she saw the same memory, twisted into bitterness and unending hate. That one unflinching act had led to this.

For every act there is a consequence. Valeria had learned that from her mother. She drove up her knee—with not nearly as much effect as if he had still been entire, but it caught him by surprise.

She heaved him off her. He rolled away. She went after him.

A white shape reared up over her. She flung herself flat.

The stallion screamed in rage. Strong black hooves clattered on the pavement. The priest knotted himself into a ball.

Valeria lay beneath the broad white belly. It was not Sabata's—he was still dappled with youth. Marina was never so low or so wide.

Oda's head snaked down, plucked up the priest by the nape and shook him quite literally out of his skin.

Valeria had no dinner to lose. Her stomach tried to vomit itself up instead.

Oda dropped the raw and bleeding thing that had been a man and methodically, dispassionately trampled it to a pulp. When there was nothing left of human life or shape, he turned back toward Valeria and blew gently in her face.

His breath was sweet. She reached for the warmth of him,

but he was already fading. A moment more and he had melted into light.

He had come as he had promised. His justice had been even more summary than Kerrec's. It had been no more necessary, either.

Men and stallions—there was no reasoning with them. She stood up stiffly, averting her eyes from what was left of the priest.

The Dance was almost done. The riders were beginning to look human again. The void was still there beneath all that was, as it always would be, but the earth no longer faced dissolution.

Sunlight slanted through the high windows, casting clear golden light on the floor. Figures of lords and ladies, priests and mages and servants, took shape in it. The court came to life again in the midst of its mortal dance.

Their patterns caught and tangled around the stallions. To them the white gods must have appeared out of air, standing statue-still around the edges of the hall.

As the babble of curiosity and speculation swelled to a roar, Briana descended the stair and approached the Lady. The dancers had drawn away from her, so that she stood in a circle of silence.

Briana sank down in a deep curtsey until her forehead touched the crimson billows of her skirt. She rose smoothly, with exquisite grace. "Thank you," she said.

The Lady shook her ears—as close to a shrug as made no difference. She turned, imperious.

Briana eyed the multitude of her skirts and the height of the Lady's back. The Lady knelt.

That was clear enough. Briana gathered her skirts as best she could and sat astride.

The Lady stood upright and pawed once.

Valeria felt that stroke in her own body. Doors of the spirit slammed shut. Powers receded, sinking deep into the earth. The stars fell into their accustomed orbits, and the sun shone with all of its remembered warmth.

The world was real again. Inside Valeria was a memory and a deep scar, but she could not find the Unmaking.

It was gone. She could not believe it, but the more she hunted for it, the clearer it was that it was not there to be found. When the Lady remade the world, she had also remade Valeria.

Strong arms held her up. She clung as fiercely to Kerrec as he clung to her.

He was alive, breathing, standing upright. His ribs creaked when he breathed, and the wound of the knife in his back still seeped blood, but the rest of him was sound enough.

There was a new, deep quiet in him. The others would have no memory of the oblivion that had taken them all, but it was sunk in him as it was in Valeria. Some fraction of it would never leave them.

That was little enough price to pay for all that they had won. As they looked down into Briana's gaze, they saw the same memory there, and the same lesson learned.

Briana drew herself up on the Lady's back. Her chin lifted. She raised her hands to the sun and loosed a clear, high call—the first note of the hymn to the newborn god. Its light poured down over her, crowning her with living gold.

The stallions stirred. Petra stamped. Sabata whinnied shrilly.

Once more they were to Dance. The weariness that had weighed them down had melted in the sunlight. The hall cleared, courtiers jostling and crowding to fill the edges and overflow up the stairs into the galleries.

Valeria was untrained and unprepared, but that had never mattered to the stallions. Sabata was as young in the body as she was. This was his Dance as much as it was Petra's or the Lady's.

When the moon was full, older stallions and trained riders would dance the Midsummer Dance. On this day of the moon's dark, Valeria and Briana shared a different Dance altogether. It was a Dance of joy and victory, of life and light and renewed creation. It was, in the purest sense, a coronation Dance.

Augurs would ponder its omens for years to come. Seers and dreamers of dreams would remember the patterns as they unfolded. Scholars and courtiers would debate its meaning, and the pious would declare it incalculable, like the gods.

For Valeria it was a Dance—as much art as craft, a mingling of magic and skill that came as naturally to her as the air she breathed. The patterns it laid were as solid as the rest of this new-made world. It established order and gave shape to the randomness of things.

She followed the lines of it as they appeared in front of her, matching Sabata's paces to the shape and substance of the Dance. The others were doing the same, each on his own path, but all of those paths combined into a luminous whole.

Inside Valeria where the Unmaking had been, the gods' satisfaction was a swelling warmth. Even they had been afraid that their great stroke would fail and their gamble prove false. They had trusted in mortal strength and human stubbornness, and that trust had proved well founded.

When the Dance was over, Valeria was going to crawl into a corner and shake until her teeth rattled out of her head. For the moment she let the great working carry her, even as the doors of time opened and the movements of the Dance shaped the reign that was to come.

Never in a thousand years had the empress herself danced that Dance. This reign more than any before it would belong to the ruler whose name it bore. For good or ill, she determined its course. She made the choices that would inform the reigns that followed.

She bore up well—better than Valeria could have hoped to do. Whatever fear she felt, she was trained not to show it. She was steady before her people, clear and focused in her movements, directing the Lady along the paths that seemed most clear to her.

Valeria did not agree with all of them. The time would come when she could say so, but in this Dance she followed where her empress led. So was the world's order maintained and its foundations made strong, secure against the Unmaking.

Chapter Forty-Seven

The battle was over. The long war was won. Gothard was dead—truly, permanently dead—and his most vicious disciple had suffered the white gods' justice.

The Unmaking was gone. Valeria's heart should have been whole.

But she took no pleasure in praise and public adulation. She only wanted to go back to the life she had had before, when no one beyond the Mountain knew who she was. Being recognized on the street and in the palace, being followed and worshipped and exclaimed over, made her intensely uncomfortable.

By the fourth day after the high court, Valeria did not want to leave Riders' Hall at all. The day before, she had lost her temper at the baker from whom she was trying to buy a seed-cake in the market. "Aren't you the girl from the Mountain?" he asked. "I hear you saved us all."

He meant well. She knew that even as she lashed out at him. "I didn't save anyone. I'm the one you all had to be saved from!"

She left him blinking, holding her penny and the cake she had meant to buy. She was shaking and fighting back tears—stupid, senseless thing, but she seemed to have lost any discipline she once had.

Then in the night, dreams beset her. She had been sleeping like the dead each night until then, safe and warm with Kerrec in her arms. Tonight she paid for that.

She floated in the sea of Unmaking, adrift in absolute darkness. It was no longer inside her—even in the dream she had that blessing—but nothing that she had done or would do could diminish it.

Out of nothingness, form began to emerge. Creation, she had learned at great cost, was as inevitable as destruction. She looked down into light, the flicker of lamps in a stone room, glimmering on the bright head of the child who sat cross-legged on a narrow bed.

Conor mac Euan had been doing something aimlessly magical, but when he sensed her presence, he looked up and smiled. "Good evening," he said politely. "I'm glad to see you well."

He must have been practicing. His Aurelian was almost without accent.

"I'm glad to see you," she said, and she meant it. "Everything's well, then?"

He nodded. "He's got his leg in a splint and he's walking

with a stick, and he's as cross as a bear in the spring. Grand-mother says that means he'll live."

Curse the boy for knowing her too well. Bless him, too. "Does he hate me too badly?" she asked.

"He doesn't hate you at all," said Conor. "Mostly he's sad. I would be, but the other one is teaching me to ride."

The other mage, he meant. That could only be Pretorius. "Is he really? Nobody's gutted him for what he did?"

"He's an envoy," Conor said. "And a guest. That's why he stays here. Nobody will touch him."

Valeria could see that. If she ever got her hands on Pre-torius, she would not answer for the outcome.

Conor's clear eyes stared right through her. She could not tell what he thought. "He doesn't ride as well as you," he said.

"Not much of anybody does, off the Mountain," said Va-leria.

"Someday I will," Conor said. His head tilted. "Will you talk to me sometimes?"

"If I can."

"You can."

The dream whirled Valeria away, but not before she caught a glimpse into another room in the dun. Conor's much older and more battered image lay on a familiar bed.

Euan's arm was flung over his eyes. His mouth under the red moustaches was turned down. He looked sulky, cross-grained—and alive. Her magic curled around him like faint glimmering tendrils, mending what was broken and strengthening what was whole.

Valeria stooped in her dream and brushed a kiss across his

lips. He started as if he could feel the touch. His arm came down. His eyes were wide, darting around the room. "Valeria?"

She was already receding, drawn inexorably back into the dark. Just before the dream winked out, she saw how his face fell. It was only a small thing, no grand rage or paroxysm of grief, but it wrenched her heart.

She made herself wake to the room that belonged to her and the lover who was meant for her. But the dream stayed with her. She could never be free of Euan Rohe, any more than she could expunge the guilt for what she had done—falling into Gothard's trap and letting him use her magic to destroy them all.

That morning she both taught and was taught in the riding court, but when she should have gone to court for a reception in the riders' honor, she barricaded herself in the library instead. She expected Kerrec to come and reprimand her for rank discourtesy, but no one troubled her solitude.

Probably no one noticed she was missing. Kerrec, who was most likely to, had more on his mind than ever. Most of it was good, now that the court had seen what use the white gods were. Kerrec was doing his best to make sure everyone remembered.

He was good at it. It made her proud. But unlike the late prince Ambrosius, she had no talent for politics.

It was as well that she had let herself be lured away from Dun Mor. She would have made a wretched queen.

She opened the first book that came to hand and stared at it. Master Nikos had promised to test her for Fourth Rider by Midwinter Dance, if she applied herself diligently until then.

She had a great deal to do. Pretorius had taught her reasonably well and the stallions were the best of teachers, but she had been rather distracted. She had to stop being distracted and start remembering how to focus.

That was not happening today. She pushed the book away.

There was one thing gnawing at her, one difficult thought that would not let her be. Kerrec had not asked her—yet— what she had done on the other side of the river, and she had not told him.

She would, and soon. But that was not the difficult thing. Before she had that conversation, there was something she had to do.

She pushed herself to her feet. She still had fits of dizziness— remnants of the spell and the toll it had taken on her body. This one passed as the rest had, and she promptly forgot it.

She had grown terribly familiar with the passage between Riders' Hall and the palace. It had been getting a great deal of use lately, and would get even more as Kerrec's school grew. Half a dozen new pupils had appeared this morning, with more promised.

At the moment Valeria was the only rider in that corridor. The lamps brightened ahead and dimmed behind as they should, with no fear of attack or ambush. That war really was over, though it was a divine surety that others would come.

She passed by the usual door, which led to Briana's rooms, and the increasingly usual one that opened on a servants' passage not far from the great hall. The passage beyond was much less well trodden. She tried not to recognize the shape and spacing of the tracks in the dust, but she knew Kerrec's distinctive narrow foot and long light stride too well for that.

The most recent tracks, she could not help but notice, were old enough that a thin film of dust had fallen over them. That pleased her too much. She should be dispassionate and practice rider's discipline.

She had her face under control, at least, when she reached the door and opened it. This part of the palace she had never seen. It had been closed off when she was here before.

Now that she was in it, it surprised her. She had expected a great deal of overwrought ornament, flocks of chattering maids and clouds of perfume. Instead she found well-lit, airy rooms, the occasional discreet servant and, here and there, a subtle hint of scent.

It was still not her taste, but she could have lived here. The colors were clear and not too soft, the furnishings understated. The servants noticed she was there but did not interfere.

They recognized her, of course. Everyone did now. Strange because when she had mended the broken Dance, no one had remembered the rider on the white stallion. But Valeria in the high court, grappling ignominiously with a renegade priest, had impressed herself on every mind.

In these cool and peaceful rooms, she found an unexpected degree of serenity. There must be a healing spell here, woven into the substance of each exquisite space.

Maybe there was no need for magic. It could be simply the quiet and the soft notes of music playing at a distance, and the ripple of falling water as she passed by the door to a garden.

She was tempted to linger, but she had to do this thing now, before her courage failed. She gritted her teeth and turned toward the jangle of human presence.

* * *

The princess from Elladis held court as she did every morning, seated in a tall chair set four steps above a shimmering hall. Its pillars were of alabaster and its floor was a mosaic of silver and ebony and translucent white. The hangings on the walls behind the pillars were older than she could possibly be, but they had been newly cleaned. Their colors shone softly around the edges of the hall.

Theodosia was as beautiful as Valeria had expected. Her skin was flawless and her features were exquisitely molded. When she moved, her grace bespoke centuries of breeding and a lifetime of training. Even the curve of eyelash on her cheek must be calculated to the last degree.

Valeria refused to suffer the comparison. She was what she was. But she could not help feeling tall and awkward and grossly underschooled as she stood in the shadow of a pillar and watched Kerrec's wife conduct the business of her office.

This palace was a fair reflection of the self that Valeria saw—and like those rooms and gardens, the princess was a surprisingly comfortable presence. Valeria had not been looking for comfort. She wanted to hate everything about this woman.

That would have been too easy. Briana's counselors were nothing if not perceptive. Most of them were mages and most had known Kerrec before he was Called to the Mountain. They would hardly have forced him to mate with a woman he could not stand.

It would not be at all difficult to like this bride they had chosen for him. She was soft-spoken and gentle but her will was steel.

Valeria saw it in the justice she dealt a petitioner who had stolen a sheep. The man swore on holy images that the sheep was his. Theodosia nodded gravely and spoke a word over the likenesses of Sun and Moon on which his hand rested. Then she asked, "This is true?"

"As true as the sunrise, highness," the man declared as he began to draw his hand away.

The image of the Sun clasped that hand in stony arms. He shrieked like a girl and pulled back with all his strength, but the image gripped him fast.

"Do you swear?" Theodosia asked as coolly as ever.

He stood shaking and sweating, with all the color gone from his face. When he opened his mouth, he screamed again. The image's grip must have tightened.

"Indeed," said Theodosia. She flicked her hand.

The image let him go. He fled without waiting to hear her judgment.

A little showy, Valeria thought, but effective. No one else dared test the princess's patience. One or two of those who were waiting, in fact, ducked their heads and slipped away.

After the last petitioner had spoken his part and received his judgment, Theodosia turned her calm gaze toward the shadow where Valeria still stood. "A fair day to you, rider," she said.

Valeria had not been trying very hard to hide—if she had been, no one would have known she was there. She came out from behind the pillar, debated modes of respect and settled on a short nod. "And to you, princess."

Theodosia smoothed her skirts—the first gesture Valeria had seen that was not perfectly measured. Her eyes were better disciplined. They maintained their impenetrable calm.

Valeria could not hope to equal that seamless self-control. She stood at ease and let the silence stretch. That, she was good at.

Theodosia smiled faintly. "So, rider. Have you come to challenge me?"

"No," said Valeria, "nor to order you away from him, either. I wanted to see what you were."

The perfectly plucked brow arched. "And?"

"I understand why they chose you."

"I'm flattered."

Valeria frowned. "I don't think we can be friends," she said.

"That would not be proper," Theodosia agreed.

"But," said Valeria, "we had better be allies. Is that possible?"

"Always," said Theodosia. "Even the worst enemies may work together for a common cause."

"Are we enemies?"

"I think not," Theodosia said. And then, deliberately, "No more than you and the Ard Ri of the clans."

Valeria went still. "So. You had something to do with that."

"Not I," said Theodosia. "We do however have a friend in common."

"Not Euan?" Even as she said it, Valeria knew that was impossible. Her voice went flat. "Pretorius."

Theodosia's eyelids lowered in the subtlest of nods.

"That man is no friend of mine," Valeria said with banked heat.

"Ally, then," said Theodosia with unshakable composure.

"I wonder," Valeria said.

"He is impeccably loyal to the empire," Theodosia said.

"Are you sure of that?"

"I am," said Theodosia. "He handled you badly, I see. I'm

sorry for that. He's a strong ally and a great mage, and a good friend in tight places."

Valeria set her lips together. She supposed he had been a friend when he pulled the earth out from under Euan Rohe's warband so that Valeria could escape. But that needed more forgiveness than she had in her. She would never be sure of him, of what he wanted or whom or what he served—apart, of course, from himself.

It was enough for now that she spoke civilly to Kerrec's wife and received civility in return. Theodosia she did trust.

It was instinct rather than reason, and in some things she might trust Theodosia to act powerfully against her. But those things would be clear and Theodosia would warn her. At heart, for all her artifice, Theodosia was an honest woman.

Valeria was almost at peace with herself as she walked slowly to Riders' Hall. The riders had come back and were scattered through the hall, riding or resting or practicing their magic.

She found Kerrec in his workroom, scowling at columns of numbers. Valeria leaned over his shoulder and tapped one of them with her finger. "There's your problem. It's been entered twice."

He aimed the scowl at her. "How did you do that?"

"Fresh eyes." His shoulders were one long knot. She worked her fingers into it. "I've been to see Theodosia."

The knot turned to iron. She dug in. He gasped. "Gods! Are you trying to kill me?"

"Not you," said Valeria, "and not Theodosia, either. I like her."

"You do?"

"Did you know you're having twins?"

He surged up and around and out of her grip. His eyes were almost white.

"You didn't know," she said. "Don't tell me you've been avoiding her."

"Not intentionally," he said through clenched teeth. "There was the little matter of the world being unmade."

"And remade." She drew a breath. "There is something you should know."

"That you agreed to be the barbarians' queen?"

She sagged against the wall. "You knew?"

"Not until this morning," he said. "Briana told me. She said it probably wasn't her place to say it, but someone should tell me before you did, in case I said something unfortunate."

"Did you?"

"I don't think I said anything at all."

She searched his face. He was not angry. He did not seem flattened by the betrayal, either.

"I agreed willingly," she said.

"But you didn't stay."

"It doesn't matter? What I did?"

"Of course it matters," he said. "I also remember where I was and why you left. We can have a rankling quarrel or we can remember that the world has been remade."

"Even for us?"

"Especially for us," he said.

He had thought about this—more carefully than she had, if not nearly as long. She reached to touch his face. His finger traced the line of her cheek.

She bit her lips. His twitched upward. There was no hope for them ever to be apart. They even thought alike.

"Can you bear it?" she asked him.

"If you can."

She pulled him the rest of the way and bound him with a kiss.

Chapter Forty-Eight

Morag rode into Aurelia with her husband beside her in the wagon and Portia behind, stretched out in comfort with Grania asleep in her arms. The baby had howled most of the way down from Imbria, but as they came out of the hills onto the plain, her wailing had stopped.

Grania was well and thriving—Morag assured herself of that every hour at least. She ate and slept as she should. She crawled around the wagon bed and babbled at people and animals who passed—more likely the animals than the people—but she never cried. It seemed she had cried herself out.

Three days of blessed quiet were more than anyone with a baby deserved. Morag swept the child into her lap as Titus maneuvered mule and wagon into the crowd of people looking to squeeze itself through the gate.

"Last time I was here," Titus muttered, "there weren't half as many people."

"That was twenty years ago," Morag said tartly, "and you weren't trying to get in the week before a coronation."

"Yes, and whose idea was that?" he shot back. "If anyone had listened to me, we'd have waited till after it was over, then we wouldn't be fighting for road space. Not to mention inn space. What if—"

"We don't need an inn," she said. "We have a place to stay."

"What if we don't? Where else will we go? I'll wager every crack and cranny is packed full of people come to see the empress get her crown."

"Stop fretting, old man," Morag said. "I know what I'm doing."

He rolled an eye at her, but he stopped fussing. He was a wise husband, all things considered.

The wagon crawled toward the gate and on through it. The streets were as crowded as Titus had feared, but Morag had the way clear in her head, as the riders' Master had told her. Straight down the processional way, left through the cattle market, up and around and down into a broad square lined with blank walls.

There were not so many people there. Most of them clotted around the temples and the palace or overflowed the markets. Most of the traffic on this street was highborn or connected to it—nobles and servants going about their business.

A farm wagon from the provinces attracted its share of supercilious glances, but Morag stared them down until they flinched and scurried past. Grania bounced and laughed in Morag's lap, shouting after them in her own peculiar language.

Riders' Hall was as unprepossessing as Nikos had said. Morag found that reassuring. She always had hated pretension.

The wagon just scraped through the widest of its gates. Luckily for Titus' nerves, the courtyard inside was more than big enough, and there was a man in it, squat and stocky and smelling of horses.

He did not have riders' magic but he had something close to it. "Sir and madam," he said with commendable courtesy. "We've been expecting you."

Morag nodded. The stableman took charge of the mule and wagon and handed its passengers over to a flock of servants.

That was its own ordeal, but Morag brought them to order. She dismissed all but three, one of whom would escort them to a suitable room while the second arranged baths. The third brought word to the Master that his guests had arrived.

They were well trained, as one would expect of servants in the horsemasters' house. In very short order, all four guests were bathed, fed and installed in a room of reasonable size and minimal pretensions.

Morag's messenger to the Master came back with a message of his own.

"Yes, of course," she said.

She beckoned to Portia. The nurse had the baby dressed and ready. Morag took her granddaughter in hand and nodded to Portia, who was not at all displeased to enjoy an hour's peace.

The school was thriving, from the look of it. The riding courts were full of horses and young riders. Morag, with Titus behind, followed the Master's servant to the second of the two courts.

Both Kerrec and Valeria had students on the long line. Their instruction was completely separate and yet they moved together like partners in a dance. Their voices intertwined and their corrections had the same intonation and often the same words.

Morag's brow rose. Her dreams and the pattern of omens since she left the Mountain had troubled her deeply. When she heard that the First Rider had married a princess and Valeria had gone across the border, she had been beside herself.

All that had kept her from galloping after either or both of them had been those same omens. Grania was safe as long as Morag protected her. If Morag left her, gods alone knew what would come hunting.

Morag had stayed in Imbria until the gods' own storm lashed the world from end to end. In the middle of it, the earth had shrugged and then straightened itself like a carpet shaken out over a floor.

The quiet that followed was enormous. All the omens had changed. The flow of the world's magic was clean again.

Then she told Titus to get out the wagon. They were going to Aurelia.

He only asked one question. "Any particular thing we're going to see?"

"The coronation," she answered.

He grunted. He knew better than to argue with her when she was in that mood. From the speed with which he went to do as she told him, she could tell he had been fretting, too. Titus had his own magic, though he never made much of it.

Now, after eight days on the road, they both saw what they had really come to see. Valeria was here, and so was Valeria's man, in harmony that told Morag all she needed to know. The tension that had been riding with her drained away.

Grania had been wide-eyed and quiet as they passed through Riders' Hall, except when she saw the horses. She whickered at them as if she had been a horse herself. But when her eyes fell on her father, she all but leaped out of Morag's arms. "Da!" she roared. *"Da!"*

She had a noble pair of lungs. Every horse in the court stopped short, sometimes to the young riders' distress. The horse mages grinned at one another, all but Valeria, whose face was perfectly blank—and Kerrec, who dropped the line and ran.

It was worth a long week on the road to see that rigorously disciplined master mage sweep his daughter out of Morag's arms and cover her with kisses. She bubbled with laughter, pummeling him joyously. "Da, Da, Da!"

Valeria came more slowly. Morag peered narrowly at her, but she did not seem hurt that Grania so transparently preferred her father.

Morag released the breath she had been holding, just in time for Valeria's embrace. Titus wrapped his arms around them both and lifted them off their feet, laughing like the boy he had not been in some fifty years.

Valeria laughed with him. Morag did not. She would have plenty to say to him—later. Kerrec had passed the baby to her mother. For a mercy, Grania did not protest.

Valeria did not have Kerrec's ease with the child. She knew how to hold a baby—she had held her share of them when she was in training to be a wisewoman in Imbria. But for her it was a learned skill. Kerrec simply knew.

She kissed the round soft cheek and drew in the scent of the black curls, but she did not linger over it. She handed the baby back into Kerrec's willing arms.

Riders were attending to the horses, with many pauses to burble over the baby. They were all as besotted as Kerrec. He stopped once, remembering belatedly that he had duties, but a golden bear of a rider rumbled at him to let be.

"We'll finish for you," the big man said. "You go."

Kerrec did not even pretend to object. He left the riders to it and carried his daughter off into the hall. As far as Morag could tell, they were conversing at a rapid rate, he in Aurelian and Grania in her own language.

"That child will be spoiled rotten," Valeria said.

She sat with Morag by the hearth in Kerrec's workroom, which seemed to be the most comfortable room in Rider's Hall. The moon was riding high, shining through the window. The fire was welcome—though the days were still warm, the nights were growing cool.

They were both replete with the feast the Master had laid on for his guests. There was wine to finish if they were minded. Morag had set her cup aside, but Valeria turned hers in her hands, resting her eyes on the dance of the flames.

The men had gone to bed. Kerrec had Grania with him, rocked to sleep in the cradle that Morag and Titus had brought.

Morag wondered how long it would be before he let the child out of his sight again. If she had to wager, she would say years—a dozen at least.

Valeria took a more dispassionate view. "With him for a

father plus a hundred uncles, she'll never want for a thing. They'll indulge her slightest whim."

"Probably," said Morag. "But they are horse trainers. They'll give in to their instincts sooner or later."

"What, they'll break her to saddle?" Valeria sipped from her cup, grimaced and set it on the table beside her. "I look at her and see twenty years of training exercises. He looks at her and sees the love of his life."

"You are the love of his life," Morag said. "That is his first-born, which is another kind of bliss altogether."

Valeria snorted softly. "Tell me again I'm not a bad mother. I thought I might feel differently when I saw her after so long, but it's still the same. I'm not in love with her."

"You're not a bad mother," Morag said, "any more than I am. I'm not in love with my children, either. I love them with all my heart, but I don't drift in a pink fog around any of them."

Valeria fell back in her chair, arms flung wide in mock despair. "Oh, gods. I've become my mother."

"It happens to the best of us."

"I never wanted it to happen to me."

"None of us does," Morag said.

She leaned toward Valeria and took her hand. The gesture was rare, and Valeria's glance took note of it even as her fingers closed around her mother's.

"Child," Morag said, "I'm proud of you."

Valeria's brows rose. "Even though I'm nothing you ever expected me to be?"

"You're everything I hoped for," said Morag, "just not in the ways I expected. That's always the way with children.

Yours, too, as she grows older. She'll go her own way, which is seldom the one you might want for her—but in the end, if you raise her as I know you will, it will all come right."

"I hope so," Valeria said. "It scares me—knowing how easy it would be to ruin her. Knowing…what I can do when I'm at my worst."

She was working magic, whether she knew it or not—drawing in the shadows and making the fire burn hotter, so hot the flames burned blue. The memories in it did not need to haunt either of them tonight.

Morag broke the spell with a sharp gust of breath. "Ah," she said, slapping Valeria's hand hard enough to startle a yelp out of her. "Babies are tougher than they look. Bring her up right, teach her to ride and dance and tell the truth, and the rest will take care of itself."

Valeria cradled her stinging hand, transparently torn between gratitude and resentment. That had always been the way between them. Morag did not expect it to change now they could talk to one another like mother and grown daughter instead of captor and hostage.

Then Valeria surprised her. She said, "You're a wise woman. Did you know that?"

"I would think so," Morag said dryly, "considering that that's my title."

"You know what I mean," Valeria said with a flash of impatience—quickly and laudably suppressed. "Will you stay with us for a while?"

Morag's throat was tight. Ridiculous—getting choked up because her most rebellious offspring had stopped wanting to see the last of her. But there it was. She got herself under control and said, "We can stay for a few days. We thought we'd see the coronation and the Dance."

"I'm not riding in the Dance," Valeria said.

"I didn't think you were. You're not a full rider yet, after all. I still want to see. That's a rare sight for the likes of us—not just a Dance of Time but a coronation Dance."

"Rare for all of us," Valeria said. "Blessed, too. We've seen the last of all the disruptions. The gods have promised us."

"I know," Morag said.

Valeria shot her a glance but did not ask what she meant. She drew Morag's hand to her lips and kissed it and held it to her heart.

Damn the girl, she would have her mother in tears next. Morag should reclaim her hand and go to bed like a sensible woman, but she could not bring herself to do it.

She sat where she was, trapped more willingly than she would ever admit, and watched her daughter watch the fire. Valeria's heart beat under her hand as it had once under her own heart, strong and clear. Even from the beginning it had set its own rhythm.

Morag closed her eyes. She would remember this. When they fought again, as they inevitably would, the memory would bring them back into harmony.

For a while. But then, thought Morag, everything changed—and everything remained the same. That was the way of the world.

She was a wisewoman. She knew. Valeria herself had said so, and Valeria was as wise as any young thing could be.

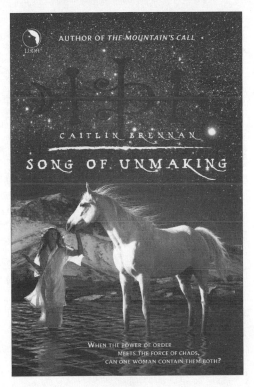